CHURNING WATERS

MEREDITH T. TAYLOR

Grey Circle

Grey Circle Publishing
www.GreyCirclePublishing.com

The characters and events portrayed in this book are fictitious. Any similarity to real persons, living or dead, is coincidental and not intended by the author.

Printed in the United States of America

Second Printing, 2014
10 9 8 7 6 5 4 3 2

ISBN-13: 978-0-9960637-1-5
ISBN-10: 0-9960-6371-5

For Mom who had the strength
to hold me when the waves
were too high …

And for **Dad** who had the courage
to teach me to swim in the
first place.

For Scott who provides
the kind of love
people write stories about …

And for **Madeline, Merissa,
Michaela and Mia,** who have
shown me a love worth
dying for.

PREFACE

M organ's long copper curls were carried high into the warm salt air before falling to her slender shoulders. The day was perfect. Her husband, Robert, had coerced her to bring the family out for an afternoon of sailing. Robert always insisted on testing every boat that left his shipyard, but this one was entirely unique, as he had designed and built it especially for his family. Morgan initially protested. Bringing the children to sea always carried a risk, but the beauty of the day seemed to override any concern. The midday sun sent shimmers across the smooth South Carolina water. Smiling to herself, she was glad that she had relented.

Robert emerged from below with two cold drinks in hand. After so many years, he still looked at his wife with a fire in his eyes that any woman would desire. The love they shared was rare indeed. Morgan had the life most of "her kind" could only dream about. A family such as this was uncommon in the world in which they were born. She smiled as she watched their two children holding onto the rail of the bow. Her son, who had the appearance of an eight-year-old, but the demeanor of a child much older, barely seemed to fit into the life she had chosen for him.

Morgan wondered how long William could pass for a normal human boy. He towered over his little sister who had just turned two. They were so beautiful—too beautiful. Morgan scowled. How long could she keep them hidden away? She had thought it would be easy to blend into this life, and yet, recent events only proved how impossible that challenge would be.

"Why don't you pose with the children for a picture?" Robert said to his wife as he pulled out a small camera from his pocket. "They are growing so quickly, and we hardly have any pictures of Madeline." Morgan smiled faintly at the young beauty whose light copper curls hung almost as long as her own. He was right; there were few pictures of the children and none whatsoever of the pair together.

"Alright. I suppose there isn't any harm in a few pictures." She took their hands lovingly and turned along the bow's railing to pose.

Robert raised the camera snapping several shots, when the look on his wife's face caused the camera to slip from his fingers, banging off the deck and into the water below. The look of terror could only mean one thing: somehow they had been discovered. As he turned, he saw the malice-filled eyes of the dark-haired beauty behind them. It was the face he had always feared would come. It was the same creature whose eyes would often keep him from his slumber. He was instantly overpowered by the pungent smell of gasoline. It was too late.

"Morgan!" He screamed, but she was already a blur of motion. In one powerful move, she cast both children far from the vessel and into the churning waters below.

Their almost perfect world enveloped in flames.

1

"If I find in myself a desire which no experience in this world can satisfy, the most probable explanation is that I was made for another world."

C.S. Lewis

I wasn't sure if I was dreaming or awake. I knew logically it had to be a dream, as I was swimming and I don't swim...ever. The ocean waves spilled over me as I was drawn farther and farther away from the shoreline. I closed my eyes and leaned back into the flowing current. My body felt strong, alive. Smiling, I went to kick my legs, but something stopped me. Frantically, I realized something had a hold of me. I wanted to scream, but the panic trapped my voice deep in my throat. Long, thin, white fingers had wrapped themselves around my ankles, pulling me farther out to sea. I struggled and turned to get a better look at my captor. Long flowing brown hair framed what appeared to be the enchanting face of a woman. But as she turned to me from under the depths, I could see her eyes—green glowing, bright and evil. My panic became unbearable as I struggled to scream for help, but no sound would escape my lips.

The creature began to pull me under, her fingers tearing into the skin just above my ankle. I started to scream in pain, but the salt water rushed into my lungs. I began to panic as my lungs burned for air. And then, a small strong hand not much larger than my own stretched out to me from beneath the water. It grabbed hold of my hand, and with powerful strokes began to pull me toward the shore. I opened my eyes trying to see the face of the one rescuing me, but it was impossible to see through the swiftly-moving surf. Unable to stop the powerful strokes of my protector, the creature still trailing from my ankle, released me with a malicious bloodcurdling screech.

I awoke in a sweat, still shaking and trying to catch my breath. I didn't usually dream, and rarely about this. But when this nightmare managed to slip into my sleeping thoughts, it was always the same, down to each vivid detail. I brushed the tears from my cheeks, my heart still pounding in my chest. "It was a dream," I reminded myself, but a dream that once had been all too much a reality. I was eight at the time of the incident. And just like in my dream, the one who saved me remained as much a mystery to me as the creature who tried to take me, leaving only the horrifying memory and the scars on my ankle to prove that it had actually happened. I was safe, I reminded myself, but not unscarred. Water was now my constant fascination, obsession even, and yet I had not ventured out into it since that ill-fated day.

My family had been supportive but dismissed the whole ordeal as my imagination running wild. They, of course, could not discount the deep scratches to my ankle, which they assumed could have been caused by some type of large fish or fisherman's net that had been broken free entangling me as it drifted through the surf. I knew the truth. Something was out there—something not quite human, something evil.

I also couldn't help but remember the hand that had intertwined tightly into mine, pulling me to safety. Though it wasn't much larger than mine, it was stronger—possibly a boy's hand. When I was younger, I would allow my childlike mind to imagine it could have been a mermaid, and I spent many hours doodling pictures of what my rescuer could have looked like. The entire incident, however, only seemed to upset my parents—especially my mother, so I learned to keep my drawings and my thoughts to myself. It was easier that way, and so I tried to forget. Over the years I even tried to convince myself that I had been mistaken. The world is a far easier place to live in if you pretend that such things don't really exist, but deep down, I knew. I was usually able to suppress the memory from my daily consciousness, but certain things are impossible to erase from your mind, no matter how many years pass, and this was decidedly one of them.

I pulled out the grey leather-bound book that I often carried with me and began to jot down some details of my dream. The book wasn't a journal exactly, more of a miscellany of poetry, quotations, and thoughts. Most of the journal writings were my own, but it also included writings of other authors—all things that I didn't want to forget. As disturbing as it was to relive the details in the dream, I didn't want to lose even the smallest detail of it. Any kind of evidence that could help explain what had happened to me so long ago would be worth remembering.

I pulled my white Jeep into one of the only remaining spaces in the back of the West Florence High School parking lot—late again. Great! I could see Caleb's jaw harden as he flashed an angry look in my direction. Luckily, my younger brother held his temper as he pulled his overstuffed book bag out of the Jeep. I tucked the strand of blondish-brown hair that had fallen loose back behind my ear and bit my lower lip.

"Sorry Caleb, I'll try to do better." I tightened the belt of my long grey sweater coat, and braced for the worst. Caleb hated to be late, and this was the third time I had made him late this week.

His expression softened a little. "Three more months and I'll be trading in this permit for a real license! And believe me, I'm counting the days!" I could see he was still heated, but he kept his anger in check as he hurriedly gathered his belongings.

"Am I really so bad?" I stepped out of the Jeep and cocked my head to the side, my lips curled in an over exaggerated pout. Any remaining anger vanished as he tossed my book bag in my direction and loosely draped his arm around me. I wasn't sure if the gesture was to move me more quickly toward the school building or if it was his attempt at an apology.

"Nah, just hate that you have to tote me around and wait for me after school, that's all." Caleb had a thoughtful side that made him quite charming.

"I don't mind waiting for you. It gives me some extra time to read," I shrugged as he pulled me closer to the school building.

"Um yeah, speaking of which, if you would go to bed earlier and not spend half the night with your face in a book, we actually might be able to make it to class on time." He was right. It was impossible to pull myself out of bed in the mornings when I had spent almost the entire night immersed in the unprincipled adventures of Becky Sharp. *Vanity Fair* was to blame this time. The book had recently been added to my list of favorites. It was easy to relate to the plight of a heroine who struggled to find her place in the world. I never seemed to fit in anywhere.

"Sorry. I promise to get up earlier tomorrow." It was a promise I'd made many times before.

He shook his head in disbelief and gave me a reluctant smile as we walked into the large outdated building that apparently would be our school for the next few years. As he walked away, I notice he looked back over his shoulder with an expression that was new to me. Was it pity? Had I become so socially reclusive that even my little brother felt sorry for me?

This was our sixth new school together since kindergarten, equating to six new towns and countless displaced friendships. The few friends we'd made over the course of our childhood were always left behind. As a result, we learned early to mostly depend on each other, but recently things had changed. Caleb had become quite involved in sports, so I was left on my own a lot. Being alone had never bothered me. In fact, on most days solitude was my preference. I had little need for the constant companionship and relentless affirmation that so many other silly teenage girls sought. I was different. It wasn't that I was unattractive. I knew that some people even thought me pretty, but a certain awkwardness kept me at a distance from others. Eventually most of my classmates seemed to accept this, and no longer bothered trying to form a close friendship with me. I had tried on occasion, and sometimes successfully, to form female friendships, but, none lasted more than a year or so. They would eventually grow bored with my lack of interest in the friendship, and we would fall into mere acquaintances.

As a child I had longed for a "Diana" like one of my favorite book characters, Anne Shirley, had found in *Anne of Green Gables*. But as the years had passed, I realized that such a person didn't exist—not for me anyway. It became easier to stop trying to "fit in" than to deal with the constant feelings of insecurity and inadequacy associated with being a teenaged girl. It didn't seem to bother me.

My first few weeks at West Florence High had been much the same, with one exception. Caleb, who was naturally shy, really seemed to have come out of his shell. He now held a starting position on the soccer team and had made some real friends. His dark hair and features, combined with a small but fit frame, made him quite attractive. I was genuinely thrilled that he'd finally found a place that made him happy. I was surprised that some girl hadn't seen what was so plainly obvious to me, as I couldn't recall him ever having a serious girlfriend.

When we first arrived, I had immediately gained some unsolicited attention from some of the boys, as any remotely attractive new girl would do. The most persistent of the group was Blake Lakely, all-around jock, handsome, and for all intents and purposes a pretty nice guy. After breaking most of the school's football records, he'd added track to his list of accomplishments by breaking the county's 400 meter dash record of 49.68 seconds. He was kind, funny, and very likeable. I accepted his friendship with caution, as by no means did I want to encourage him, especially with his ex-girlfriend Jennifer Mason shooting daggers at me anytime he was close by. Jen was unbelievably beautiful. To call me plain beside such a great beauty would be an understatement. She could easily grace the cover of any magazine. I knew the type well: platinum blonde, head cheerleader, prom queen—the works. She fell into every cliché imaginable and promptly put me on her hit list as soon as she discovered Blake's attentions toward me. But despite her glares, Blake's attention toward me only increased.

All of West Florence's sports congregated on a large field after school for practice. Funding for sports in smaller schools such as this one was scarce, so the field was home to most after-school athletics. The soccer team was set up on the northeast end. The football team was on the southeast end. Track and field took up most of the west side of the field, and the band took over the back parking lot. The cheerleaders practiced off to the side of the football area. Several small sets of bleachers set up between the soccer field and track arena. No bleachers were needed near the football practice field, as all of our football games were played off campus at a local college's stadium. I waited patiently, and quite content, on one of the sets of bleachers after school each day for Caleb during soccer practice, always immersed in my latest book. Blake was practicing with the track team since football season had ended and was in rare form as he kept desperately trying to draw my attention from my book.

"MARGO!" He waved in my direction as he passed by the bleachers. I tentatively returned the wave but continued reading. "MARGO WESTLEY!" His words grew louder as he passed again.

I looked up from my book briefly to see Blake successfully jump over a hurdle. He looked back in my direction for some type of affirmation. Not to be rude, I flashed a quick smile at him and returned once again to my book, trying to hide my growing aggravation. On his third lap around he seemed to grow more determined.

"HEY MARGO!" He was loud enough this time to draw attention from the other students on the field. My face flushed as I noticed too many pairs of eyes now looking in my direction. I looked up to find that Blake had now left the track lane with the other runners for a lane with more hurdles. I watched as he leapt over three hurdles in a row before his foot got caught on the fourth, causing him to stumble hard to the ground. I instinctively wanted to jump up to check to see if he was alright, but thought it would be less of an embarrassment for him if I pretended not to have seen his fall. But Jen *had* seen it and rushed over to the track protectively. He brushed her off completely and continued running. Jen, unaccustomed to being given "the cold shoulder," glared over at me in the bleachers. I took a deep breath and braced myself as she glided across the field toward me. Her eyes glared with anger. I couldn't help but be reminded of one of those horror flicks where the cheerleader becomes possessed by a zombie. She looked as if her head might spin around at any second, and I am pretty sure actual smoke was coming from her ears.

"You know, Blake and I've been *together* for like, *forever*. We're just on a 'break' right now." Her angry beautiful smile loomed over me. I looked up at her blankly not really knowing how to respond. That was the best she could come up with?

"Um, ok. Good. He seems to be a nice guy. I'm happy for you both." My response seemed to just anger her more. She flipped her silky strands back and continued her mini-tirade.

"What I mean is…everyone knows he's off limits." She didn't smile this time but held her eyes firmly on mine. I noticed that Caleb seemed to be finishing up on the soccer field, and I needed any excuse for an escape.

"Yeah well, that's not a problem as far as I'm concerned. I'm really not interested." I stood without meeting her glare and started to leave, but absentmindedly tripped on my book bag at my feet. *Great! Could I get any more awkward!*

She took on a sweet exaggerated tone. "You know, cheerleading tryouts for next season start tomorrow. Are you planning to come?" Surely she didn't really think that I was coming to tryouts.

"Um, no—not really my kind of thing." Actually, trying out for cheerleading was about the last thing that would ever cross my mind. I put my book in my book bag and began to walk away.

"Yeah, I really didn't think so." She looked me up and down again. I wanted to hide under the bleachers. "You don't look much like the athletic type." I looked back up at her to find her crystal blue eyes staring at me. It was true. I had been born with "two left feet," but the way that she looked me over infuriated me. The full effect of her intentionally spiteful comment took me by surprise. I felt a surge of anger travel through me, something unexpectedly fierce inside of me began to boil. Other girls like Jen had been at my past schools, but none had set a target on me quite like she did. I looked down at my knuckles. They were white, as my hands were now coiled tightly into fists. I continued down off of the bleachers, trying hard to ignore her.

I thought I was successful until I heard her mutter, "Like *she* could ever play a sport. Someone needs to go back where they came from." She was spitefully laughing at me. I snapped. Surprising even myself, I swiftly turned back to where she stood still looking at me smugly.

"Huh, I didn't know that shaking pompoms even qualified for a sport." I shot back at her as I turned and briskly walked across the field toward the parking lot without giving her a chance to reply. It was the best that *I* could come up with. I was new to this kind of banter. I would have time to regret the comment later. So much for flying under the radar; I was sure to be moved now from the hit-list to the firing squad. The truth was that I really did appreciate the amount of work and athleticism that some of the really talented girls possessed. I thought many of them were quite amazing, but I went with the only retaliation that I could come up with on the spot.

Caleb ran up beside me as I moved briskly toward the Jeep. Sensing my anxiousness, he looked back over his shoulder at Jen and the rest of the cheerleading squad who were now all looking angrily in my direction. "Uh oh—what did you do now?" His words were both lighthearted and genuinely concerned.

"Just managed to piss off the *entire* cheerleading squad," I said as I hoisted my book bag into the Jeep.

"Nice!" He jumped in the passenger side. "Guess I will never get a date for the prom!" he laughed.

"Not a chance," I replied less cheerfully, but I couldn't help the smile that escaped as we pulled out of the parking lot.

****

Six months earlier, our family had moved into the moderately sized four-bedroom ranch-style house. The house was comfortable, and I no longer had to share a room with my little sister Lucy, who had surprised

9

our entire family six years earlier with her unexpected arrival. God's surprise had been our blessing; Lucy was perfect in every way!

My parents married during their second year of college, and I had joined them just three years later. They had been childhood sweethearts and seemed pretty happy for the most part. My father was hard working and reserved, which was in perfect contrast to my mother's vivacious spirit. We were close and constantly depended on each other, as would be expected of a family who relocated often. It had always just been Caleb and me, so when we learned that my mother was expecting again, we were shocked. Lucy's beautiful chestnut curls and flawless olive skin were just like Mom's. I looked like my father, so Lucy and I didn't favor each other at all. Her spunky personality kept the entire family rolling with laughter and seemed to occupy a lot of my mother's free time—a fact that I very much appreciated. It wasn't that my mother's attentions were unwelcomed. It was more that with Lucy's arrival, her attentions were more balanced, and I was free to pursue my own interests without feeling like I had disappointed her.

I dropped the last dinner plate into the sink full of soap bubbles sending a wave of dirty dishwater onto the counter. Lucy sent out a trill of laughter as bubbles drifted through the kitchen. My mother shot a stern look of disapproval in my direction, as I scurried to find a dishtowel to clean it up.

"Sorry." I replied with an exaggerated look of apology. I hated washing dishes and couldn't fathom why we were the only family in town who didn't use their dishwasher.

"Oh, I almost forgot!" She said retrieving a letter and a small box off of the counter. "There is another letter from James, and a package arrived for you today. I think it is from your grandmother. We were talking about how much worse your eczema had gotten in the last few months, and she said she was going to send you something to try." I was pleased to receive another letter from my best friend James, the third this week, but cringed and what could possibly be in the box. *Here we go again.*

"You know it is usually worse in the colder months. I am sure as soon as it starts warming up…"

"Marguerite! Stop being so stubborn! You've been fighting with that skin of yours for your whole life. Must be from your father's side, because my family always had flawless skin. Anyway, anything is worth a shot."

"Great." I replied trying not to roll my eyes. *Another useless product to disappoint my mother.*

I had developed an unknown skin condition as a child that had gotten progressively worse with each year that passed. The doctors, not quite sure what to call it, had label it as eczema, but no traditional eczema creams or medication seemed to make any difference. The light red patches now covered the inside of my arms, my back, stomach, and my upper thighs. It was not drastically uncomfortable, just slightly tender to the touch. My mother purchased every item and medication on the market in multiple failed attempts at a cure. I had grown so accustomed to it that I hardly even noticed now.

I opened the small box to find a corked glass bottle. The contents appeared to be some type of finely ground sea salt. Small flakes of a green substance, which looked to be some type of kelp or seaweed, were mixed throughout the bottle. I uncorked it, expecting an added fragrance, but there was none, only the slightly unpleasant smell of the concoction. I would have thrown the contents away immediately, but my grandmother had sent it. I admired her immensely.

From the box, I pulled out a note that immediately put a smile on my face. Unlike the bottle, the note unmistakably smelled of her perfume; White Shoulders.

Marguerite,
~Add a tablespoon of this in with your bath water each day. Be sure not to use too much. I think this may help. Come see me soon. I love you,

Grandmother

I folded the note and stuck it in my pocket before heading to my room to begin my homework. "Margo, promise me you will try that!" My mother called out to me as I headed down the hallway.

"Promise, Mom," I called back before reaching my room. I tossed the bottle onto my bed and retrieved the note from my pocket to put it in my shoebox of keepsakes.

I knew that tonight another bad dream was inevitable and postponed sleep as long as physically possible. With my homework done and *Vanity Fair* once again complete, I looked over at the small bottle beside my bed. *It couldn't hurt, right?* I went into the bathroom and began to fill the tub. I sprinkled a small amount from the bottle into the running water before getting in. I winced as the hot water touched my tender skin, but the discomfort was brief. I instantly felt wonderful—somehow *more* than wonderful. My body began to tingle in the warm water.

I leaned back to reread the letter from James, haphazardly knocking the remainder of the uncorked bottle into the water. I clumsily tried to spare the remainder of the contents, but the concoction had emptied. A momentary twinge of guilt spread through me for being so careless, but all thoughts were erased once I leaned back to allow the water to overcome me. I'd never felt anything like it before; it was as if instantly my body felt alive. Time slipped quickly away as I soaked in the heavenly mixture of salty bubbles. At last the pounding on the door brought me back into reality.

"Margo! You alive in there?" I leapt up out of the bubbles at the sound of Caleb's voice stumbling out of the tub as I quickly grabbed my robe and wrapped it around me. "You've been in here for almost an hour!" he grumbled.

"Sorry…I will be out in a minute!" I grabbed a towel from off of the rack and quickly wrapped my wet hair in it. My legs were still dripping with bubbles as I opened the door to let Caleb have his shower.

"Uh! What is that smell?" He said holding his nose.

"Something Grandmother sent for my skin."

"You should send it back. It smells awful—like the salt marsh!"

"I like the smell of salt marsh."

"You would! I seriously hope you don't smell like that for school tomorrow."

"I think I sealed your fate today anyway. It's all downhill for you at this point—welcome to social Siberia, little brother."

I tossed and turned for several hours before succumbing to the nightmare that I knew would come as soon as I surrendered to sleep. It finally came.

The creature was more vivid, more vicious, more beautiful than the night before, but in this dream there was no outstretched hand waiting to rescue me. I felt her long, icy fingers burning into my skin as they wrapped tighter and tighter around my ankle. Pain. I screamed, looking back at the shoreline where my family waited innocently unaware. I began to panic looking for the outstretched hand to rescue me. No hand…no hand! I felt myself slipping, being pulled farther and farther out to sea. "No!" I thought, and suddenly all panic and fear was gone. Anger began to boil inside of me. I trembled with rage. Determination took control, and I became something else. I was strong. Tearing through the water, I ripped the creature's arm from my body. The creature hissed, and its eyes flared with an intense bright light. It sprang at me again, this time with both hands. I coiled and with little effort landed the heel of my foot against its chest, projecting the creature deep into the dark water. All was still. It did not return.

I awoke this time with a much different feeling from prior dreams; there were no tears, no fear, I was just…still. I felt like I was waking up for the very first time. Everything about me felt different somehow. I felt stronger—fearless. I rolled over to look at the clock: 4:20 a.m. The house was still, but my mind was racing in all directions at once. I knew that returning to sleep was completely out of the question. Something indescribable was stirring inside of me.

Jen's words rang out again and again in my head. "Yeah, you don't look much…." Uh! I became more and more agitated at myself for allowing her words to bother me. It was completely out of character for me to ever allow a few spiteful words to have any effect. What was it exactly about those words that had made such an impact? I instantly knew the answer; it was the challenge.

After some contemplation, I shrugged. Jen's comments were justified; I truly was not athletic. I lay there for the next half hour with my head spinning. The truth was that I had spent my life avoiding anything that posed a challenge. I had chosen quite early to take myself out of the game. I had struggled through a year of ballet at age five, a few months of gymnastics at seven, and a few school plays here and there. I had no real interest or talent at any of it and would always beg until my mother let me quit. However, I was passionate about reading, often wrote, and when I really inspired, I would paint. I had shown a talent with a brush even at an early age. My room was layered with canvas artwork that I had created since early childhood, but I rarely showed them to anyone. I kept most of them private, my own secret way of expressing myself, but I had gone almost a year without picking up a brush.

But tonight, something *had* changed. I felt it.

I slipped on my navy Converse low tops, not bothering to change out of my crumpled sleepwear of sweats and t-shirt. I quietly grabbed my keys off of the counter and made my way into the garage quietly, as to not wake anyone. Caleb's soccer bag was lying on the steps, and I slipped my hand into the side pocket for his stopwatch. I slid into the driver's side of the Jeep still unsure of where I was going or what had come over me.

The school was dark and empty, as I pulled into the lot. Instead of pulling around to the student parking, I drove up into the grassy lot adjacent to the track. Without planning, without thinking, I made my way for the very first time ever, onto the smooth, black asphalt and headed towards the starting line. The air was cool and the sky still black except for the stars above. I closed my eyes and clutched the stopwatch firmly in my hand. Then, like a racehorse coming out of the gate, I sprang into full motion. I had never tried to run before, not like this. I took off faster than I ever dreamed possible, with no learned form, no training, and no previous desire to attempt anything of the sort. My heart raced faster and faster as my shoes hit the track. My legs were now moving so fast that I felt as if I were flying. The second I passed the finish line, I slowed to check the stopwatch. It read 43.8 seconds. Impossible! I knew nothing about track or run times, but I knew that I had made it around the track several seconds faster than Blake's record, which was 49.68 seconds. I reset the stopwatch again. This time, more carefully, I took my mark. As I took off, I let go of everything inside of me—I was at a place that I never dreamed was possible. My heart, my legs, my feet soared beneath me. Faster! Faster! Nothing held me back as my feet glided all too quickly over the finish line. I looked at the stopwatch again—43.8 seconds. It had to be broken; I was sure of it. Either that or I had somehow miscalculated something. Surely it was impossible for someone with no formal training, no proper shoes, no known athleticism whatsoever, to accomplish such a time. Impossible!

I looked back over at the dark track in amazement. What was I even doing out here? I looked again at the time on the stopwatch. Broken. It had to be. I threw the stopwatch into the trashcan outside of the field and climbed into my Jeep to head back home. The sun had not yet peaked over the horizon, but it wouldn't be long. I wanted to be sure to return before I was missed.

When I arrived back at the house, I hurried to my room to slip on some clothes. Caleb would awaken soon, but I didn't want to disturb Lucy. She needed her sleep. I had planned to shower, but despite the early morning's events, I still felt clean. Huh—no sweat. Clean but thirsty. The thirst felt unquenchable. I tossed back glass after glass of water, but my throat still felt dry, too dry. I wondered if I was becoming ill.

I pulled out a brown skirt and a light green, long-sleeved shirt to hide my rash. As I began to pull the shirt over my body, I stopped frozen. Tears welled up in my eyes. I saw *my* skin—just my skin: no rashes or red spots, no whelps or sores. I looked over my entire body. It was clear, smooth, and soft. In awe, I ran my fingers across my smooth skin as if I were feeling it for the very first time.

I tried to calm myself long enough to think. Whatever my grandmother sent must be responsible, and I had clumsily wasted the remainder of the bottle! *Would the symptoms reappear now that the treatment was gone?* I would refrained from telling my family, especially my mother. I couldn't bear to give her false hope if it were to reappear. This would give me time to ask my grandmother what was in the bottle and how I could get some more. I would call her right after school.

I slipped on my tennis shoes despite the skirt. I pulled my hair up in a messy bun, as it was still slightly damp from the shower, grabbed my lip gloss, books, and was ready. In the kitchen awaited the breakfast that my father ritually prepared each day. I took a bite of eggs. Caleb found me at the breakfast table. He was impressed.

"Wow! We may actually be on time today—just look at you…a skirt too!"

"Yeah, didn't want you to pout again like yesterday!" I rolled my eyes.

"Takes one to know one, you've been pouting ever since we moved here."

"I'm still holding out for Grandmother." I didn't look up at him, as I knew well what his response would be.

My grandmother lived alone along the South Carolina coast in a small house fittingly called Inlet Joy. It was nestled just south of Myrtle Beach in a small community called Garden City. Her property was on a small peninsula across the road from the ocean on a small waterway called Murrells Inlet. I had spent the entirety of my summers there with her since I was a small child, as she lived alone and much appreciated my company. I had not yet given up the hope that my parents would allow me to finish out the remainder of my high school there.

"You know they are never going to give you up." He smiled back in the direction of our parents' bedroom where we could hear them anxiously moving around getting ready for work. He poured two glasses of juice and came to sit next to me. I quickly gulped the juice and refilled my glass with water. I didn't shuffle my food around like most mornings. I was famished. Each bite tasted better than the last.

"Wow, you make it sound as if I am a puppy. No one would be 'giving me up.' Seriously, I would be less than two hours away."

"Even so...."

"I'll be heading off to college soon anyway, and it's not like I would be that far away. You could be there in less time than it would take you to watch a movie." Caleb was not the one I needed to convince. My argument was well rehearsed but rarely executed.

"You're just avoiding putting down roots again. Don't you want to be able to finally call someplace home?" He popped a crunchy piece of bacon in his mouth. I reached over and swiped a piece off of his plate. "Hey, I didn't even think you liked bacon?"

"I feel like I'm home when I'm there. It's the closest thing that I've had to one anyway." My words came out far too sentimentally for breakfast banter with Caleb. I tried to redirect the conversation. "Man, this is so good! I don't know why I am so hungry."

"Margo, home is where *we* are...all of us...*together*." Great! Now he was getting all sentimental with me. Crap! My argument was slipping. I declared defeat for now and changed the subject.

"Let's go. I want to get you there on time at least once this week."

"Um yeah! You gonna let me drive this morning?" He flashed a set of perfectly straight white teeth in my direction.

"No way! I thought you said you wanted to be on time today. If you drive, we'll never get there! Slow poke!"

"Not fair!" he called. "Get in the car!" I called over my shoulder. He grabbed our books and headed towards the door.

****

I couldn't concentrate on my schoolwork. Was it really gone? After an entire lifetime of the condition, how could the "eczema" be completely gone? I sneaked another peek at my arm when I was sure that no one was looking—smooth. Could it really be true? I had long ago resigned myself to the fact that if something out of the ordinary was going to happen, it was definitely going to happen to me. Yes, I finally concluded, I'm a freak!

At lunch I skipped the cafeteria and headed straight for the library. Our school library was quite short on books in general, especially medical books, but I combed the information available searching for something that could possibly give me some indication of what could have healed my skin. This was something that I'd done many times before, but this time I was looking for something pertaining to sea-salts…seaweed…sea-*anything*. Nothing really seemed to fit the bill as an "instant cure."

As I was leaving, I noticed the *Guinness Book of World Records* displayed on one of the library endcaps. I rolled my eyes, realizing that I was about to pick up a book that was by no means typical for a literary fanatic like me.

I flipped through the pages deciding what section to look under…running…no…track. Ah! Here it was! The world record for the 400 meters dash was 44.2 seconds. My time was 43.8 this morning. I laughed almost aloud! OK! That stopwatch this morning was most definitely broken! I instantly dismissed my running debut completely and headed for my next class.

Rain had begun falling sometime over the course of the day. All of the afternoon sports practices were moved to the gymnasium. Both the track team and the soccer team were running laps around the gym, while Jen was holding cheerleading tryouts on some large mats near the middle of one side. I sneaked in and sat at the bottom of the bleachers to wait for Caleb and pulled out a book, trying to be completely unnoticed.

I was there less than ten minutes before Jen caught sight of me. Her voice became louder and louder as she instructed the new trainees on the requirements of the audition. Then, as if she had just seen me sitting there, she addressed me from across the room.

"Margo!" Her voice was sugar sweet, but her intentions were obvious. She was going to try to embarrass me. "Try-outs are over here!" Her words echoed through the gym in an obvious attempt to humiliate me in front of most of the school. I refused to look up as an array of girls struggled to do some basic cheer skills and stunts on the mats. I could sense the attention in the gym shift towards Jen again. I tried to bury my face deeper into the book I was holding. *Uh! Why hadn't I waited outside for Caleb!* Heck, sitting out in the rain would be better than subjecting myself to Jen's humiliation. I took a deep breath. *How do I make this go away? Just be polite.* I could hear my mother's words ringing over and over in my head. *"Just kill them with kindness."*

"Um. No, but thanks." I looked up briefly and tried to send a genuine smile in her direction to try to defuse her growing animosity towards me. It didn't work.

She turned her attention back to the twenty or so girls auditioning and bellowed in a loud voice. "See girls, some people just don't have what it takes…It takes more than just talent and strength and poise. Some girls just don't have that 'it' factor."

My eyes moved involuntary from the pages of the book that I was no longer reading, to the faces of the girls who were now looking over at me. My heart began to pound in my chest, and I could hear the blood rushing in my ears. I could feel the heat of the color burning on my cheeks. I was embarrassed—no I was *furious*. My knuckles turned white as my fists were now clinched tightly to my sides. I tried to take a deep breath to calm myself, but the mixture of embarrassment and fury were a fierce combination to combat. My eyes narrowed. I felt out of control. Much to everyone's surprise, I exploded across the gym floor. The gymnasium had stopped, and all eyes were on me as I barreled toward Jen. Jen's perfect face showed panic in the split second it took me to reach her, and several girls gasped. Jen stumbled aside as my shoes reached the edge of the mat. I sprang forward, my hands reaching for the floor. My legs were perfectly straightened as they met together in the air and landed on the other side of the mat. My body whipped backwards in back handspring after back handspring, as I flipped perfectly over and over—clear across the gym floor. The gym floor stopped before I did, as my body tucked tightly flipping high into the air before gracefully landing against the wooden floor. I was someone else. The gymnasium stood completely immobile.

Luckily, I landed facing the gym exit door and instantly headed straight for it. I left immediately without turning back to face the reactions behind me. All anger was gone—replaced by something else…confusion…anticipation. What *was* that? Had I really just tumbled effortlessly across the gym floor? I wasn't even winded. Maybe, just maybe the stopwatch this morning hadn't been broken after all. What did this mean? What was happening to me? I was a freak. No, I corrected myself, I was an even *bigger* freak. I was halfway to the Jeep before I realized Caleb was running behind me with my book bag in hand.

"Margo! Margo—wait!" I turned to face him with tears welling up in my eyes. With one look at him, I was sobbing.

"What *was* that? How did you…how did you *do* that! Have you been secretly training for the Olympic gymnastics team or something?" He beamed with excitement and amazement.

"I…I don't know! Something just came over me. I was angry." I had no explanation suitable to give him or even myself.

"Anger doesn't give you moves like that! Good god! Margo, you were amazing! Every mouth in that room is still dragging the floor. You should have seen Jen's face! Some poor girl asked her if that was the "*it*" factor she had been talking about! Ha! Did you really not know you could do that?"

"No." It was the only answer I could manage to get out through the tears. I was thirsty; my throat felt as if it were on fire.

"Impossible—and in a skirt no less! Heck, *I* may not be able to get a prom date, but *you* will have them lined up at the door! Man, you should have seen the way Blake was looking at you!"

None of it mattered to me. None of those people meant anything to me. "Seriously Margo…how did you…I mean, I remember like three months of gymnastics when you were like seven—you totally sucked…where did *that* come from?"

"I can't really explain it," I cried. "I just *saw* it in my head. I knew what to do—like it was instinct. I know that sounds crazy."

"But how…," he protested.

"I don't know, Caleb, truly I don't! When the anger hit—it was like my body just took over. Just face it, your sister is a freak!" I sobbed harder burying my face in my hands. This would usually be the part when Caleb would agree and tease me relentlessly, but he knew that today I was spent. I needed him.

"No, you're not a freak. No more than any of the rest of us," he laughed and smoothed the hair back that had come loose from the top of my head back in place. "Apparently you just have some hidden talents that we are just beginning to discover. Late-bloomer maybe? Freak? Not a chance! I just hope you don't have too much ability! Heck—I'm supposed to be the athletic one in this family!" He wrapped his arms around me and pulled me to his chest. He pulled back from me. His tone shifted, but he still kept holding my arm. He put the back of his palm against my forehead. I could see the concern on his face. "Margo, are you feeling okay?"

I wasn't sure. I tried to calm myself.

"You are burning up! You have a fever!"

"I'm fine—I think." I lied. I wasn't fine at all. The adrenaline from earlier had begun to wear off. I spied the water bottle in his pocket and pulled it quickly to my lips consuming every drop. I felt weak, faint. I was extremely ill. In less than a few minutes, I had gone from a body so strong that I had wowed a whole gym, to feeling so limp and weak that I was unsure if I could make it to the car.

Caleb flung my book bag over his shoulder and put his free arm around my waist. I protested. "I am fine. I can make it!" Caleb didn't respond and continued to look concerned as he ushered me to the passenger seat of my Jeep. He propped my book bag up on the seat and began fishing out the keys. I was relieved that he had thought as much to retrieve it for me before coming after me.

"Oh no! There is no way I am letting you drive my Jeep home! You only have your permit." He located the keys and tossed my bag into the back of the Jeep. He caught his arm around me again helping me up in the seat.

"Um—actually, I really wasn't asking your permission." He didn't look over to me again as he jumped into the driver's seat. I was too weak to fight. Heck, I was barely strong enough to respond.

I felt myself growing more ill by the second. "Um—can you just promise me one thing? Don't say anything to Mom and Dad about what happened today. Okay?"

"OK—but why?" Caleb was not one to keep a secret.

"I'm not sure, but for some reason I just don't think we should talk about it with them—not right now."

"You have my promise." He looked over at me. He meant it. The concern on his face had turned to fear. I slumped down in the seat barely strong enough to keep my eyes open.

"All I know is that we need to get you home. You look awful!"

"Oh, and Caleb…I owe you a new stopwatch." My head became dizzy, and my words were so weak that I could hardly recognize my own voice. And then the world went blank.

****

I wasn't dead. I was almost certain anyway. I could still feel things: cold hands, warm blankets, gentle touch, and pain. Uhh…what hurt? Things were quiet, but there were sounds too; some that I could make out: my mother's quite sobbing, the low sound of my father's concerned voice, Caleb's gentle optimism. I even heard Lucy's quiet giggle once before she was hushed. I wanted to scream out, but I couldn't. My world was hazy, as if I were lost. I felt frozen—not unpleasant or anxious, just stuck. It could have been just a few hours, days, or weeks? Time seemed to lose meaning. My mind remained active, as if I were trapped in a dream, but unable to awake from the sleep that held me captive.

I listened for familiar voices and learned over time to pick out the voices that I thought were my doctors and nurses. I became accustomed to these voices. The deep firm voice of my doctor, the gentle voice of my favorite caregiver, I listened for them. Waiting. Always waiting to rejoin the world. But there was one voice that I could not seem to place. It was a voice that was familiar, but I was certain that I had never heard it before. He only came once. It had to have been late, since the voices of my family and doctor had stopped hours earlier. It was a man's voice—seemed older...gentle somehow. He spoke my name, and I felt his hand brush gently across the side of my face. I felt my arm being lifted as if it was being inspected, but his touch did not seem like that of a doctor: it was tender, more careful. The words of the people around me usually didn't register for long, but his low soft words were unforgettable.

"You will be protected Marguerite. No harm will come to you. My solemn promise is to secure your safety, to restore your health, and to guide you to what you were born to become." His words trailed away, and the room once again was quiet. It could have been a dream, or an angel maybe, as I did not hear footsteps as he left. Only silence.

****

A voice broke through the monotony. One that I instantly recognized, one that made me *want* to wake up. I could smell the faint linger of *White Shoulders* perfume as she walked into the room—Grandmother! But then there was another smell, a smell that I could only faintly remember. The strong smell of salt marsh as the sensation of a cool sponge as it gently rubbed over my body. I could feel my lips curl, as I knew my time for slumber had grown short. If her miracle potion could clear a lifetime of broken skin, surely it could wake me as well. Things became more lucid. I could feel the warm soft folds of a hand as it took hold of mine. No, I was not dead, but surrounded by the people that I loved. I wanted to join them, so *finally* I awoke.

The faces surrounding my little hospital bed were almost too much to stand. My face flushed with embarrassment, and for a brief second I actually wished that I *had* died. Any situation that put me as the focus of this much attention was more than an unwelcome event—it was torture. I smiled and pulled the sheets over my head. Nothing hurt. I felt weak, stiff, disoriented even, but no pain. My mother gasped with delight.

"She's back!" I heard Caleb's voice teasing me through the sighs of relief that had broken in the room.

"How long?" My voice was dry and faint. I hardly recognized my own words. My mother rushed to my side to bring some water. Her face was full of jubilance and relief. She was crying.

"You have been unconscious for just over a week." My father smiled down at me as the relief spread wide across his face. I saw him try to slyly brush a tear off of his cheek. He looked tired, older than I had remembered. The thought that I had caused them so much worry broke my heart.

"Are you okay honey? Can I get you anything? Don't do too much. I am right here if you need anything. You've been very sick. You've had us all worried!" All of her words ran together, and she was speaking loudly as if I was hard of hearing. I smiled at my mother. She was truly the most precious creature alive. I would humor her, at least for a while, and play the "good" patient.

"Some water would be great. I'm parched!" She leapt from her seat to get a nurse. I was extremely thirsty. "What happened? What was wrong with me?"

"There is plenty of time to get into all of that dear," my father said gently brushing back my hair from my face. Caleb sprawled out casually along the foot of my hospital bed.

"Please Dad. I want to know." The lines on my father's face deepened. The toll my illness had taken on him this week was evident, but even so, he was still the most handsome man I had ever seen.

"They aren't sure exactly. When Caleb brought you here, you were running a fever of about 105. The doctors immediately started running tests. Your white blood cell count was through the roof, as if your body was trying to fight off some awful infection, but amazingly all of your other vitals were perfect." My mother returned with the water, and I took a big gulp as Caleb continued, "They immediately thought of some type of cancer, but every test has come back perfect. They haven't been able to find the cause. They doctors can't seem to identify a rash that is on your arms and torso, but that's nothing too unusual with your history. No one is quite sure *why* you lost consciousness, but your fever broke last night, giving us hope you would be coming around soon." Leave it to Caleb to lay it all out for me plainly. I was thankful for his honesty.

My grandmother spoke for the first time. Her words were soft, and she had tears in her eyes. "You're going to be fine Marguerite. I'm here. I'll help you get through this." I smiled at her warmly. I was glad that she was here.

"Thank you for coming, Grandmother. I hate to have caused everyone so much trouble."

"We're your family, dear. Where else would we be but at your side?" she said with a gentle smile, but the worry still showed through her soft expression.

"Where is Lucy?" My thoughts raced to my little sister; I knew she would be asking for me.

"She is with the neighbors. We brought her up to see you yesterday. We didn't want to scare her, but she demanded to see you."

"When can I get outta here? I need to see her...to show her that I am alright!"

"Easy. Not so fast! You have been through a lot." My brother looked at me disapprovingly.

"They still want to run some more tests." My dad's words were tender and full of emotion. I knew all that he wanted to say to me. He was not a man of many words, but we were indescribably connected.

"That won't be necessary. She'll be fine." My grandmother came over to the hospital bed. "Caleb, go start packing her things. Marguerite is coming home with me." Although I had been waiting for years to hear those words, they still took me by surprise. My father looked surprised as well. I could see his mind racing in all directions as his eyes flickered between all of us.

"What? Mom, wait a minute! We need to talk this over. You know Christine is never going to let you take..."

"This isn't up for negotiation. Marguerite is going to need some constant care for a while. You and Christine have to work and take care of Caleb and Lucy. I am able to give Marguerite all the attention that she needs right now. She will be better off right now in my care."

"Mom, we can't just let her go! Not like this!" I saw the pain spread across his face at the thought of sending away his oldest daughter. I knew he would never agree to it unless...

"I *want* to Dad. I think it would be a good idea to try something new for a while."

"Margo, you just came out of a coma. You need some time to—to get back on your feet again. You don't realize what you are saying."

"I know exactly what I am saying. I've wanted this for years. Dad, things aren't working out for me so well in Florence. I think this would be good for me."

"But Margo, just give it a chance. I know this move has been the hardest one for you, but maybe, after some time, you would be happy."

"Dad, I think *this* would make me happy. You know how much I love it there." I could see the pain in his eyes as he thought about not seeing me every day. I felt the same way.

"Steven, Marguerite knows that you love her. She won't be far away, and you can take turns visiting each other on the weekends."

"That's not the same, and you know it Mother."

"Murrells Inlet is only a short trip from here. It isn't like I would be taking her across the country. We can just try it out for a few months, give her some time to get on her feet again, and if it isn't working out, she can always come back at any time." I could see her words were softening him a bit as he contemplated the proposal. "What do *you* say, dear?" She turned to me already knowing what my answer would be. I nodded.

"Yes, Dad. We could work this out. They aren't going to let me go back to school for a while anyway. Just let me try it there for a short time. Don't think of it as me leaving home. Just think of it as an extended vacation. Like summer, but not…." He scowled. I was reaching now, and I realized my chances would be better if I rested my case.

Caleb sat silently. He knew this is what I wanted, though I could read the pain clearly written across his face.

"Say that I was to go along with this, just for the remainder of the school year, what was I ever going to say to Christine to convince her?" I could see his mind churning. For twenty years this man had given my mother whatever she wanted. It was an extremely rare case when he would dare to go against her wishes.

"I'll talk to her, Dad." I began to feel stronger and pulled myself more upright in the hospital bed. "I'll take care of it." He looked skeptical, sad. The expression on my father's face almost made me change my mind…almost. I absolutely adored my father. I would fix anything that ever made him unhappy, but not this. I wanted it far too badly.

****

24

I waited until the next day to talk to my mother. My strength had improved enough to get up and begin moving around again. My arms and torso were still partially covered with the rash, but my vital signs were all good, and I knew I would be released soon. She, of course, flatly refused at first to the idea of me going to stay with my grandmother. I calmly explained to her my reasoning behind the notion, as I wanted her to know that I was by no means choosing my grandmother over her. My mother was my best friend, and I didn't want her to feel slighted. I watched her mind as she went over the options time and time again in her head. She couldn't disagree with the constant care that my grandmother could provide. She could see on my face that I had my mind set on this, and after a few tears, finally agreed as long as I promised to return every few weekends to be with the family.

It was decided. My courses would be completed by correspondence until I was well enough to once again attend school, and I was to leave with my grandmother a few days after I was released. Hiding my excitement was almost impossible, but I kept my emotions in check to avoid hurting my family any further. Being without them each day would be painful.

I was released from the hospital two days later. The doctors wanted to keep me a little longer, but they could find no logical reason to do so as test after test came back normal. I knew that I was far from normal. But whatever was going on in my body, no hospital would be able to cure. Finally, the doctors were forced to let me go. I spent several nights with my family before preparing to leave. I wanted to spend some time with Lucy, as I had been like a second mother to her since she was born. I would miss not being with her every day, but I knew it would strengthen her relationship with Mom, and I would see her as often as possible. The minute I arrived from the hospital, her little arms were around my neck in a huge bear hug. My face was covered with her tiny kisses.

"Margo!" she squealed. "Are you okay now?" She cocked her full face to the side and bit her bottom lip as if she had been worried. I fought back a laugh.

I buried my face in her soft hair and kissed the top of her head. "Yes Lucy, I'm all better."

"I was so worried!" She gasped a bit dramatically.

"I'm sorry I had you worried, but everything is going to be fine now." Apparently that was enough explanation for her.

"Great! So we can go read together?" She dragged me across the floor towards her room, her favorite book in hand, my old worn copy of *Anne of Green Gables*. I smiled and went eagerly. I brushed back a tear at the realization that I would miss so many of these opportunities together. Leaving behind my family would be a lot tougher than I thought. But somehow, despite the ache in the pit of my stomach, I knew I was stepping into the place I belonged.

2

———

"The cure for anything is saltwater: sweat, tears, or the sea."

Isak Dinesen

"Well, that's the last bag I can cram in there!" Caleb gave an extra push to the duffle bag stuffed in the back of my Jeep. "No changing your mind at this point I guess." He feigned a weak smile in my direction.

"No…hey, thanks for helping me pack." I couldn't look him in the eyes. "Guess I've made you late for school one last time." I smiled.

My grandmother returned home just after my release from the hospital to get the house ready for my arrival, but I remained for a few extra days to make the last preparations. I had already said my goodbyes to Lucy and my parents earlier, but long after they were off to work and school, Caleb remained. He scuttled around buying time, despite the fact that most of my bags were packed and loaded. It was as if he sensed a change that the others had not.

"Nah—I don't mind a tardy slip. Not today anyway. Guess this is where we part ways huh?" He shuffled his feet against the uneven driveway pavement.

"Caleb, you know it's not like that. Seriously, we will see each other all of the time." Despite my encouragement, I knew he was right in so many ways.

"Yeah, I know, it's just that…we have always been together…you know, at school and all. It'll be a little odd knowing that you aren't there. What I mean is…"

"I know." I wrapped my arms around my little brother, burying my face into his lean collar. His always-tanned skin smelled of fresh soap. I closed my eyes as if to make it a memory. *Whenever I would smell fresh soap, I would remember Caleb and this moment.* "You can do this you know…without me. This is the right place for you. I just have to find the right place for me too."

"Yeah, guess I've known deep down for a while now this was coming. I'll miss you." He playfully pushed me away, before grabbing me tightly for one last hug. Caleb opened the door of the Jeep hanging on it just a bit. It was rare that this type of emotion passed between us, but we both knew the significance of my departure.

"Me too. Take care of mom and dad—Lucy too." I climbed into the front seat of the Jeep, and Caleb reluctantly passed over the keys.

"Are you sure you're well enough to drive? I could drive you."

"I'm fine. I promise. I'll call and leave a message when I get there—love you." The engine roared as I turned the key. "Call me too…okay."

"Okay, now get outta here before I start crying. I have a reputation to uphold!" We both knew that we had reached a turning point. He was now on his own, and I was about to embark on my own adventure. It was the first time that we had ever been apart. "Love you too," he mumbled and turned away.

I didn't look back as I pulled out of the drive. I knew he was still watching from the curb.

****

The marsh air hit my lungs as I approached the bridge. The scent that was repulsive to most was intoxicating to me. I giggled. I was here! I checked the time on the Jeep's radio, as I never wore a watch. The drive had taken only about an hour and forty minutes. Not a bad drive after all! The air was remarkably warm for early March, but a cold bite still lingered in the air. I regretted not being able to let the top down. I looked out over Murrells Inlet as I made my way over the tiny bridge that connected Garden City to the mainland. Breathtaking! The sun was still high overhead, its blinding beams glistening across the water. The tide appeared to be falling as the reeds were barely beginning to trace the canals. There could be no place on earth more beautiful.

The Garden City pier marked my turn onto the beachfront strip. My heart raced at the sight of the ocean waves peaking between the beachfront homes. Just a mile to go and I would be there! The faded blue paint could be seen in the distance as the Jeep edged slower and slower in the direction of Grandmother's house, aptly named Inlet Joy. It was much older than most of the properties that surrounded the area. Amidst the large newly built vacation homes, it stood timeless—like a pearl amidst a collection of gemstones.

My grandfather, Steven Westley Sr., began building the Inlet Joy in the mid-1960s as a present to my grandmother. My grandmother, Sara Askins, had grown up just over the inlet on the far end of the creek. She was the daughter of a local fisherman, but much of her childhood was untold. All I really knew about her childhood was that her father saved just enough to help get her through college, a rare occurrence during this time. Apparently soon after she left for college, her childhood home on the inlet caught fire and burned to the ground. Her parents didn't rebuild. Instead, they moved to the upstate, far away from the coast. My grandmother never revealed the details behind the family's relocation, and we never pressed her on the subject.

It was during her time in college that she met my grandfather, a former army Lieutenant who had just returned home from WWII. He had already purchased a small farm and was doing quite well by the time she finished school and they married. The money he saved was wisely reinvested to purchase other properties in the area, which he rented out to other farmers for extra income. Sara worked as a teacher at the local elementary school. They were by no means wealthy, but lived quite comfortably. Sara rarely spoke of her life growing up on the inlet, but my grandfather could sense her love for the area and had repeatedly tried to take her to vacation there. She refused even to return for a visit. So eventually, after many years of hard work and saving, he finally had enough money to buy a large lot just off of the inlet. It was to be a surprise anniversary gift.

For almost a year, my grandfather helped in the building of the house. But when the project was complete and its name hung so prominently on the front of the house, no one could have anticipated

Sara's strong reaction to the surprise. She immediately burst into tears and left the place at once, refusing to return despite my grandfather's disappointment. She demanded the place be sold at once. My grandfather, not realizing the cause of her grief, agreed to sell it. It wasn't until his untimely death years later that she discovered that it remained unsold and untouched for many years. Much to everyone's surprise, she now left her home in the upstate and returned, alone, to Murrells Inlet to live in the Inlet Joy.

I breathed a sigh of relief as I pulled into the drive. My earlier observation was confirmed as I looked over the majestic inlet so perfectly settled behind the house—the tide was indeed falling. Perfect! High tide would be around sunset, the most beautiful time of the day. It had been seven months since my last summer stay, but everything was just as I remembered. The house wasn't large, just three small bedrooms and two bathrooms. Adjacent to the screened porch was a storage room that had been turned into a rather small bedroom for extra sleeping quarters. When Lucy arrived, I made my summer quarters this small room so that I would not wake her. Within the first summer I had fallen in love with the room, despite the inconvenience to a private bathroom. It was close enough to feel assured of my safety, but far enough to give me some sort of independence.

My grandmother was rocking on the front porch anxious for my arrival. She rushed downstairs to meet me as soon as the Jeep hit the shale drive. "You're here! I honestly can't believe it." She clasped her hands together in delight before hugging me.

"Yeah, pretty unbelievable huh?" I grinned back at her before opening the door.

"How are you feeling? I was concerned that you may not feel well enough to make the trip." She tugged loose a bag from the back of the Jeep.

"No, I feel fine." Actually I was feeling better than fine. It was remarkable how my strength had improved since my first taste of the salt air.

"Well, let's see if we can get some of this unloaded, but let me know if you start feeling tired. We don't have to unpack everything right away." She grabbed another smaller bag and headed toward the house.

"No, my strength seems to have fully recovered." I pulled out several bags and headed toward the steps. She proceeded up the steps and turned to open the door to the house. "Oh, Grandmother, I was planning to stay in my old room out here." I turned toward the tiny room off of the porch.

"Marguerite honey, it isn't practical for you to stay out here when we have other rooms inside."

"I know, but this has always been *my* room. I couldn't imagine myself anywhere else. Besides, my family will be coming so frequently now that I am here that they will need the inside space. I think it would be more inconvenient to have my space invaded by Caleb each time they come for a visit."

"Alright, alright—I suppose you make a good point. I had a feeling that you would feel that way so I put fresh linens on the bed just in case. Let me know if you change your mind." She smiled as she put the bags just inside the door, before returning for more bags.

My room, though small, was perfectly suited for me. It was decorated in the same oceanic motif as the rest of the house. There were a variety of shells from floor to ceiling, and a collection of mismatched nautically inspired treasures that she had excitedly unearthed down at the local market. In the center of the room was an antique metal bed covered with a white handmade spread. It was saturated, like the rest of the room, with the salty marsh air. There was a small nightstand table next to an old wooden dresser, with a corner closet built in across from the bed. But the most prominent feature of the room was a large double window that framed the breathtaking view high above the inlet. I quickly opened the sheers to allow the natural sunlight to stream into the space. *Who would trade a larger space for this magnificent view?*

My grandmother and I retrieved the remainder of the bags from the Jeep, and I spent the rest of the day getting my belongings settled into the room. Almost the entirety of my summers had been spent in this room since I was eleven. By the end of each summer, the room was distinctively my own with a variety of books, writings, and several unfinished paintings adorning the small space. When I left at the end of last summer, I took only my clothes and books. I was happy to find everything remained untouched since the previous summer. This room was my own personal haven—simple, cozy. It was where I belonged.

My grandmother thoughtfully occupied herself with other things to allow me the privacy. Thankfully she was the type who had a keen sense of when she was needed, and when I preferred to be alone. We had perfected this through the years. It was one of the many reasons we got along so well. There was no need for her to entertain me, and though I was sure my presence provided companionship, she seemed equally as content with solitude.

By dinner, my room looked as if I had been living there for ages. My books were once again returned to the shelf above my bed. My clothes were either neatly folded in the chest or hanging in the closet. All of my music and family photographs filled the new bookshelf in the corner, and everything else had been stored neatly in the bins under my bed. Perfect!

Dinner was, of course, all my favorites—a mix of my grandmother's specialties. The table was adorned with a seafood smorgasbord of sautéed shrimp, baby scallops, fried flounder, homemade slaw, and hushpuppies. For dessert she had prepared her prized pecan pie. She celebrated the joy of my arrival the best way she knew how—in the kitchen. I was touched. I ate as much as I possibly could to satisfy her, and then helped her clean up the kitchen.

After dinner I was anxious to walk over to the beach, but as soon as my face hit the cool evening air, I was reminded that it was still early March. The sun hung low on the horizon, and I knew that it would soon be dark along the beach without the benefit of the lights from the vacant summer rental houses. The temperature had dropped substantially, and a strong wind was blowing in from the north. I would have to wait until daybreak to venture to the shore but decided I could not wait for morning to head down to the dock. The covered quay and adjacent floating pier joined our property to Murrells Inlet. It had been built by my grandfather just after completion of the house and was well weathered from years of exposure. I carried my journal, scribbling my thoughts by the last light sunlight of the day.

> *"The old wooden boards moaned with the sway of the tide and creaked with each step I made along the planks. Such sounds played like music as if to welcome me back from my long absence. The sun was settling for the night, its rays slowly retracting their golden arms in preparation for slumber. I watched the majesty in blissful solitude as the sun finally dropped from sight. All doubt was erased. I was home."*

A gentle hum could barely be heard off in the distance, slowly growing louder at the approach of a small beautifully crafted wooden boat winding among the marsh canals. Through the dim shimmer of nightfall, I could see the driver. I recognized him immediately, as I had seen him often through the years but rarely up close. Since my childhood I could rarely recall being out on the water without a glimpse of the boy. He was always easy to spot in the small wooden boat that seemed to belong in a much earlier era. He never smiled as he passed but would often stare over at me through deep-green eyes that seemed to sparkle unnaturally from the light bouncing off the water. His dark tousled curls fell just above his ears and bronzed skin seemed to gleam through the quickly darkening sky. He was stunningly beautiful, but his reclusive nature left the impression that he was quite odd.

But as he drew near, it became quite obvious that this was no longer the boy from my memory. His childlike features had been replaced by the structure of a man. He spied me immediately but his boat did not slow as he passed. He looked over at me, his beautiful eyes piercing mine, but his expression was far from friendly. He didn't seem at all surprised to find me standing there and glared at me with an expression far colder than the evening air that had already begun to cool with the setting sun. And then, as quickly as he had arrived, he once again disappeared back into the canals as if the dark water swallowed him.

I sighed. *Great! I'm already making friends.* I was reminded of why I thought the boy strange. Each time I had seen him, his face always held the same cold expression. I wasn't sure if it were just me that he didn't like, or if it was everyone. I could not deny that I myself was far from a "social butterfly," but at least I wasn't rude. Wonder what it could be about my presence that seemed so offensive to him? I tried to brush him from my mind completely as I headed back toward the house, but I found that more difficult than anticipated. There was something in his eyes that seemed to stick with me far longer than I cared to admit.

****

After a few games of cards and a crime drama on the television, my grandmother politely headed to bed. I did the same, but I couldn't sleep. I wrapped myself in the ancient cotton sack quilt that adorned the base of my bed and quietly stepped on to the back porch. I cozied into my favorite of the four faded wooden rockers. The evening air wrapped around me, leaving me giddy—drunk from its heady scent. All was dark except for a few dim lights that stretched across the waterway and the moon that reflected beams of light across the smooth surface. The inlet had a beautiful eerie feeling in the off-season. It was too early for the vacationers, too late for the fishing charters. All was quiet except for the gentle lapping of the current against the seawall. The inlet's belly was so full that all of the marsh reeds were now completely hidden from the night.

The cool wind whipped through the thin screens that covered the porch as I wrapped the quilt tighter around my body. The adjacent homes were all vacant, as they were not rented out and rarely occupied by their owners outside of the warm summer months. There was one in particular that kept drawing my attention—the Merri Mac. All was quiet there—too quiet. I was reminded of the summers here before the Leighton's had arrived.

I was eleven when they purchased the house just two doors down from the Inlet Joy. It didn't escape my notice when we had first arrived that summer that the "For Sale" sign so prominently displayed had been removed from the Merri Mac. But after many days of curiosity, we had yet to meet the new owners. Their arrival had not gone unnoticed, as it was impossible to ignore the sudden boost of energy to the area. During the morning hours, all was quiet at the house. Occasionally someone would head out onto the large back porch or walk out to the dock nursing a cup of coffee, but most of the party did not stir until well after noon. But the house seemed to hum to life once evening fell; lasting well into the late hours of the night, the Merri Mac buzzed with activity that was uncommon for our quiet nest of houses. I was in awe of the energy that came with their arrival. There was always a wide variety of people and cars. I was usually too far away to recall any faces, but their laughter, energy and music seemed to sail in our direction through the salty night. Their world was completely foreign to me, and as a young girl whose entire household was asleep just after ten, I was more than intrigued by their late night parties. Beach music was the backdrop of bare feet shagging against the wooden planks of their decking. The dancing would migrate onto the dock as the evening progressed. I stood on the outside of this circle and watched like a spy in the night soaking it all up.

Some nights I would get enough courage to go down and sit upon the dock instead of the porch. The view was much better here, faces easier to detect; looking back toward the house I could see the entire place all lit and alive. It was wonderful. With only the dim post lamp, I was hidden. I was the shadow. I was the dark, and they were a fountain of light. I didn't know it then, but my life was destined to become intertwined with theirs. It had been six years since I had first met James Leighton, and once again I sat staring into the night wishing he were here. I missed James. Could I really survive being here without his company? Despite time and distance, we had remained the closest of friends. Aside from my family, he was the dearest person to me—my best friend. My first night here, and already I ached for my childhood companion. When I found James, any void from my lack of female friendship was erased, and despite our distance, my friendship with him seemed to transcend all other superficial relationships. We could go months without a letter or call, but whenever we were together again, it was as if we never had been apart. I adored him and he was the only person, apart from my family, that truly knew the real me. He was my cool breeze on a blistering day…or the rain when I was wilting.

Day after day I was off on some excursion with James, sometimes with Caleb in tow, but most of the time it was just the two of us. I showed him my father's prized fishing holes and how to maneuver the inlet canals to avoid the hidden sandbars during low tide. James desperately wanted to learn to surf, and I rolled with laughter from the shoreline as he and Caleb fumbled their way through the small Garden City waves. James' face was always red. It was hard to tell what colored it more: embarrassment, determination, or sunburn. It was clearly evident that he sought to constantly impress me, usually with hilarious results. And for the first time ever, I adored the attention and companionship of a friend. There was no finer person, or truer friend on earth than James.

Just a few days after James and I had first met out on the beach, I was issued my first invite to join the Merri Mac's evening festivities. I had never been more nervous as the evening I came to meet the Leighton family. But my nerves were short lived, as his family welcomed me into their clan wholeheartedly. The entire family seemed to rotate around the energy of James' mother Dolly Leighton. The words "larger than life" were created to describe such a person, as she was louder, funnier, and more endearing than any storybook character in all of my literature. She welcomed me with both open arms and a sharp eye, and I knew almost instantly that she saw me as a potential romance for her son. Her husband, Bobby, seemed to worship her. He was as outgoing and welcoming as she was, but was substantially more reserved. James was the oldest of the three Leighton children. Rebecca held the spot as the middle child. She favored James the most with lily white freckled skin and an abundance of copper curls. Though not traditionally beautiful, I thought her quite lovely. She was the closest in age to me at just six months younger. Upon first meeting her, I couldn't help but hope that we would become great friends. But though she was polite, I could sense she had little desire to form any close friendship with me. The youngest sister, Kitty, was about Caleb's age and by far the most beautiful of the Leighton children. Her smooth slightly tanned skin was accentuated by her blonde hair and bright smile. The blue eyes was the only trait that she seemed to share with the rest of the clan. She was by far the most eager to want to get to know me, but upon each attempt she was pulled away by one of the other family members. I did not see this as a slight upon me, but more of a courtesy to James. I was *his* friend, a title that I was blessed to be given.

I never tired of James' company. Despite my lack of coordination, he immediately took it upon himself to teach me how to shag. Just like the rest of the Leightons, James was a wonderful dancer. This was without a doubt, a product of Dolly's instruction. It would have been impossible for anyone other than James to get me onto a dance floor at all. But with countless hours of dockside practice, I eventually learned to follow his lead. As the crowds of guests would gather at the Merri Mac, James would now *find* me in the shadows and pull me from the dock into his lively world.

With a low sigh I turned away from the dark shell of the Merri Mac. It would be many months until summer, and when they would arrive once again. I knew that I would be just like that young girl again, waiting for signs of life until they returned. For someone who was supposed to be so fond of solitude, why did I miss him so?

I looked out over the moonlit waterway one last time before heading off to bed. I had often dreamed of living here, and now my wish was granted. But despite my excitement over my new life, I couldn't deny the feeling that something was missing—James.

Sleep did not come. I tossed and turned over and over begging for it to take me, but still I remained awake. Not a good start for my first night here in nearly eight months. Of course there would be some adjustments. I could have blamed my restlessness on the new room or even the feel of the bed, but I had slept in it for so many years that the old mattress wrapped around me perfectly. No, there was something else keeping me awake. It was as if some feeling buried on the back of my mind was preventing my body from relaxing, as if the mere ability to close my eyes had been stolen from me. I fought the urge to get up for hours before finally slumping on the edge of my bed in the dimness of the night. I looked over at my alarm clock—3:28 am.

The light from the moon radiated through the window reflecting off of the white-bedspread and illuminating the tiny room. The moonlight seemed to draw me to the window—closer and closer, until I was peering out over the smooth inlet water. The sky was black with only the moon and stars for light, much darker than I had remembered from summers past. My eyes scanned the panoramic view. Searching for what, I did not know.

It was then that I saw the shape of something outlined by the reflection of the moonlight. My heart began to race as I spied it from my view above. It appeared to be kneeling down in the shadows of the dock. My eyes narrowed and my heart began to pound as my eyes beheld something I had never before seen. The shape appeared to be human. But only in form, as it held itself in a manner that was nothing less than supernatural. The form looked large, too large to be female, but it was impossible to make out any other features at such a distance. It hunched motionless, appearing to not even breathe, completely faceless in the dark night.

I studied the creature carefully for quite some time, trying to convince myself that it must be a shadow—that my tired eyes must be deceiving me. Had my imagination gotten the best of me, and all that stood there was the cool dark folds of darkness? Despite my efforts to dismiss the figure—still it remained.

The pace of my heart increased as I felt my body heading towards the old door. Curiosity seemed to override any sense of fear or common sense as I gripped the doorknob. Or maybe it was more than curiosity. Maybe I was being helplessly drawn to the one thing that I should have feared—the one thing that could so easily seal my fate. I stepped forward with little reservation into the unknown dark cover of the night.

3

"It's time to start living the life you've imagined."

Henry James

My heart pounded louder and louder in my chest with each step, as my bare feet inched across the cold wooden porch planks. My eyes still fixated on the outline that remained motionless in the shadows of the dock. It would have been logical to remain safely in my room, but all logic seemed to have completely left me at this moment. The dark shape crouching in the night remained motionless. I thought it impossible for a human to remain so still, and yet the form still appeared to be human.

The screen door creaked as I slowly opened it, but it was nearly impossible to hear it over the whistling sound the strong wind made as it blew through the thin porch screens. I made my way down the stairs and began moving across the lawn. Each step brought me closer and closer to the unknown figure that remained hunched in the darkest corner of the dock. Its form was turned so that its back was the only partially in my direction. I moved without hesitation, without fear, as if I were being drawn in and was unable to stop myself. I had to get closer. The long wet grass wrapped round my feet, and the cold sand collected between my toes as I inched closer and closer. Logically, I should have been cold, as the northern winds continued to press down hard upon me, but I felt nothing but the burst of adrenaline that continuously pumped through my veins. I was just steps from the sea wall when the wind suddenly ceased. I stopped abruptly and remained still—frozen. I could hear my own heart pounding in my chest.

The shape on the dock lifted its head into the night air as if it were trying to smell something. My eyes narrowed as I tried to make out what was before me. In one swift motion and with a high-pitched hiss, it sprang from its crouch defensively to face me. Its body did appear to be that of a human male, but longer, more defined, leaner somehow. The fluidity of its movements, however, was completely inhuman. I searched through the darkness for the features of its face, but it remained covered in darkness except for its eyes, which seemed to cut through the blackness with a light very much like that of a large cat. Its defensive posture softened as it glared over at me, still completely frozen at the seawall. Even through the darkness I was mesmerized by its beauty. The seconds that passed between us felt like hours. Then, without warning, it sprung up and backwards into the air. Its arms reached outward into the night sky. Its legs were pressed tightly together, as it reached a height impossible for a human to obtain unassisted. It seemed to almost fly through the moonlit night, and plunged with virtually no disturbance into the frigid water at the midpoint of the canal.

And then—nothing.

I stood on the seawall motionless for quite some time, my heart pounding in my chest so hard that I felt breathless. I had been haunted with the memory for years, that there was something lurking beneath the waters. Something hidden there, to which I was drawn, yet feared all the same. Now, I was certain of its existence.

****

I passed through the remainder of the week in a daze. I tried to immerse myself in schoolwork, but my attention was once again directed toward the frigid waters just beyond the seawall. My days were endlessly spent on the dock in hopes of discovering something—anything that would explain what I had encountered. And my nights were tormented by a combination of restless sleep and the uncontrollable urge to return to look for the creature. Except for a few fishing boats that would occasionally appear, the inlet remained quiet. There was no sign of anything actually. Not even the boy in the wooden boat, whose haunting eyes penetrated my thoughts almost as much as the creature.

It had been raining for my entire first week at the Inlet Joy. The combination bad weather and the sudden cold snap that had delayed spring, compounded with the mystery of what was ever out in those icy waters, seemed to wear on my spirits. I tried to occupy myself by writing to James or walking along the strand with my grandmother. But my thoughts always seemed to carry me away, back to the events of my first night here. My distraction even seemed to seep into my phone conversations with Caleb, whose concern for me was also growing.

"Margo, are you sure you are okay? You know, you can always move back if you are unhappy. I know Grandmother would understand." Caleb's voice was reluctant, and I could hear the concern coming from the other end of the receiver.

"No Caleb. I am fine…really. Everything here is…great actually. I mean, I miss you guys of course, but seriously, I am completely happy here."

"Margo, I can hear something in your voice. What is going on? You don't sound very happy. You may be able to hide it from Mom and Dad, but I know you too well. Is there something you need to talk to me about?"

There was no way that I was going to tell Caleb what was really going on in my head. That I was now spending almost every waking hour staring out over the water looking for…well, I wasn't even sure what I was looking for. Caleb would think I had totally lost my mind if I told him that both my days and my nights were completely consumed with the possibility of "sea monsters."

"No. There really is nothing to tell. If I seem distracted it's just that I'm up to my eyeballs in all of the catch-up work that mom just sent from the time I was in the hospital. You know it just kills me to fall so far behind." My lie almost sounded convincing.

"Okay. But really, if you need me, I can be down there in a flash." He sounded reluctant to drop the subject, so I changed the topic quickly before he continued asking questions that I didn't have the answers to.

"I know. How is Lucy? Does she miss me awfully?"

"Sure she does. But Lucy is well…Lucy. I have to admit she is doing much better with your absence than we ever thought. She and mom have been spending a lot more time together. So, yes, we all miss you, but it is nothing you need to be concerned over. She's great." His words were comforting to me, and I was glad that she and mom had been spending so much time together. I had always worried that Lucy and I had been too close, and I was glad now that mom was able to fill that place.

"I am so glad to hear that. Give her a big kiss for me and tell her I will drive up to see her soon, okay?"

"Okay, take care of yourself. I'll call you tomorrow."

"Sounds good. Love you." I was anxious to get off of the phone as Caleb still had concern in his voice, and the last thing I needed was for his acute observation to be voiced to my parents. There was no way I was leaving Inlet Joy, not when there was so much that I was determined to uncover still hidden here along the coast.

I heard my grandmother setting the table in the other room, so I headed in to see her. "Do you mind if I skip dinner? I had a late lunch and I am really not hungry. Today is the first afternoon that it hasn't been raining since I had arrived. I was thinking about going out to the "point" before sundown." The truth was that I wanted desperately to get out of the house. The bad weather had made me a bit stir crazy. Maybe some fresh air was all I needed to clear my mind.

"Well, I suppose not, but I really think that you should at least eat something." Her words dripped disappointment and a scowl spread across her lovely face.

Mealtime was my grandmother's most prized part of the day. Her dishes brought cooking to a whole new level. The thought that someone may actually not be hungry was an idea that was almost impossible for her to accept.

"Everything smells incredible, but I am still full from lunch," I said heading for the door as my grandmother was still busy finishing up the last touches to the meal that she would now be eating alone. "I'll be back before sundown, and I will grab something when I get back," I promised reaching for my keys resting on the countertop. She looked up disapproving.

"You are looking exceedingly thin lately. You have me quite worried about you."

"Ok. Now that is virtually impossible with the meals you have been preparing." I shoved my hands deep down into my pockets to secretly pull up my blue jeans that were indeed hanging quite low on my hips. I hadn't noticed a weight loss, but now that she brought it to my attention, my clothes did hang off of my thin frame more than usual.

"I promise that I will eat twice as much tomorrow. Please…pretty please, let me go." I fluttered my eyes dramatically.

"Alright. Alright, but I don't want you out past dark. I expect you back well before then."

"I promise. I just need to get out for a while. Some fresh air and a good book will do me some good," I said pleadingly.

"You do need to get out more. I don't want you to feel stuck in this house all of the time. And you are looking quite pale, even for winter."

"It should be warming up in the next few weeks. I will have to start spending more time outdoors. I will be back in a few hours."

"Are you sure you are feeling okay?" I could see the look of concern in her eyes.

"I feel fine—perfectly recovered."

"Alright. Be safe…please be safe." She said with a look of concern.

I flashed a smile in her direction. "I always am Grandmother."

"Oh, and as long as you are out, would you mind grabbing some sugar on the way back?" She reached across the counter to pass a five dollar bill to me.

"Sure. No problem." I smiled and quickly headed for the door before she could have the opportunity to change her mind. I shut the door behind me and hurried downstairs. I grabbed a towel from the outdoor shower and my flip flops from the bottom step to go with my gray jacket. I tucked my gray book and my favorite novel under my arm and hurried out to the Jeep.

The sun no longer hung directly overhead. It had recently slipped just behind the clouds leaving a haze to the late afternoon sky. I sighed with disappointment realizing that my time would indeed be limited before nightfall. The wind had noticeably picked up, and I could feel the threat of rain just off the horizon. I slid both arms into my gray windbreaker and pulled up the hood before starting the Jeep. The shale limestone rocks ground under the tires of my Jeep as I pulled out of the driveway and headed south in the direction of the "point."

The "point" was at the mouth of the inlet. It was a narrow strip of water that connected the inlet area to the ocean. Large rocks called the "jetties" marked the gateway, and waves of sand dunes lapped out in all directions on both the inlet and ocean sides of the "point." The area was a nesting place for many of the wildlife species of the area because it was virtually cut off from the vacationers. The inlet side of the "point" could only be reached by boat, and could only be reached by those familiar enough with the channels to maneuver through the labyrinth of sand bars. There wasn't a public beach access at this end of the peninsula, so I pulled off of the road between two rental properties that were clearly deserted for the winter. I wrapped my book up in my towel and slipped unnoticed between the two houses. A narrow planked walkway led to the shoreline. The beach was much wider at this end, but it was cut off by a large seawall that separated the beach area from the jetties. I tucked my towel wrapped book into my zipped up jacked and hoisted myself to the top of the seawall, careful not to cut myself on the barnacles that covered the weathered posts.

The view from the top of the seawall was stunning. The beach fanned out in all directions with small tidal pools dipping in and out of the landscape. The gulls and sand lappers seemed not to notice my intrusion, as they darted in and out of the sea foam along the water's edge. There was a narrow lagoon that dipped towards a large gated home nestled just off of the jetties. The architecture of the house was quite different from the other surrounding homes. Unlike the other homes along the peninsula, this house wasn't lifted by pilings, but it rested along the dunes. The main house was a gray two story, with the center of the upper story encompassed by a large circular glass lookout, much like one would see atop a lighthouse. Inside the crow's nest, a large lamplight could be seen from the shore, but in my many summers here, I had never seen it lit. There were also three smaller bungalows that were connected to the main house by stone walkways. Bare pergolas encompassed each walkway. These cottages blended so easily into the landscape that one would barely notice them at all.

The wind swept through my hair sending it high into the air before it rested again, messily, around my shoulders. I giggled aloud. The smell of the salty air and the taste of the ocean spray against my tongue were intoxicating. The place seemed deserted, as was expected so late in the day during this time of the year.

With only my towel and book in hand, I made my way up over the dunes far out of sight, and found the perfect spot away from the main waterway. Hidden within the dunes was an almost magical spot that dipped and curved along the sand. A tiny inlet stream served as an escape or entrance for the water as it either swelled into, or emptied out of, the tidal pools trickling nearby. I carefully spread my towel along the embankment and lounged back against the dunes with one of my favorite books in hand. The small brown leatherette covered copy of *Pride and Prejudice* had been purchased at the flea market years earlier and was so worn that the binding had come lose. Its words, now read so many times, and its lines now so endeared, that I was able to recite each by heart.

I had been there no longer than a half hour, both reading and occasionally jotting down a few favorite passages when a shadow appeared over the dunes just several yards away. I recognized him instantly, as it was impossible to forget the features of the boy from the beautiful wooden boat. I had for some reason thought him much older, but as he grew near I became convinced that the person could not be much older than I.

He stopped a few yards away and just stared at me quite immobile for some time. In truth, the time span was no more than a few seconds, but it seemed to stretch for some time as I stared at him over the dunes. I was quite certain my heart had stopped altogether. His stature took my breath away. He was tall and slender with a bronzed muscular frame covered by a fitted blue baseball style t-shirt and shorts. Deep green eyes flickered in the light that had just peaked a bit through the clouds as it made its final descent of the day. His dark sun-kissed curls, framing a perfectly chiseled face, were tousled by the ocean breeze. His bronzed skin was perfectly smooth, too smooth to possibly belong to a teenaged boy, and the pale blue shirt he wore was pushed up at the sleeves revealing arms only seen on a professional athlete. He was tall. I guessed his height to be around six foot two inches, and his lean muscular frame was clearly closer to a Greek statue than that of a human. I had never laid eyes on a creature more perfect. I thought it impossible for someone to be so beautiful that had not been stripped from the pages of a fairytale. In fact, through the many books that I adored, I knew of no hero that could physically compare to him.

He looked over the water for several seconds, before he slowly looked behind him. For a moment I expected him to walk away—but he didn't. He seemed to take a deep breath and began walking in my direction. I sat as still as a stone statue, unsure if I should remain looking at him or if I should look away. He didn't seem to try to hide the apprehension in his expression as he made his way over the dunes. I tried to breathe, but my entire body was stone. He stopped just a few feet away from where I sat nestled against the white sand. I had not remembered him to be so remarkably perfect. He was clearly no longer a boy as his facial features were now angular and his body perfectly defined.

The sun now completely broke through the clouds just above the horizon framing him in golden rays as he stood on the dunes quite close to me. He looked more like some sort of Greek god as opposed to a local Murrell Inlet boy. He was without a doubt the most handsome creature that I had ever laid eyes upon. "I didn't realize anyone was out here," he said breaking the silence. His words were as smooth as cashmere. His eyes scanned the area protectively before looking down at the book that I held firmly in my hand.

"I was just looking for a quiet spot to read," I uttered, surprised that I was able to speak. I hoped that he could not hear my heart that was now rapidly pounding in my chest. He didn't smile. His eyes narrowed as he remained stationary on the dunes just above me.

"You are out here to read?" I wasn't sure if it was a question or a statement but his annoyance seemed to build as he contemplated my response.

"Yes, my 'escape from reality' I suppose," I replied looking up at him only briefly. I could sense my cheeks becoming more flushed with each passing second.

"And you chose to come here...alone?" Much to my surprise he moved closer to me stopping only a few feet away.

"Yes. It's quiet here. Peaceful, I guess...." He seemed to contemplate this before slowly nodded in agreement.

"True." He looked out over the water once again, this time as if he were searching for something, and then turned back towards me. His eyes bore into mine in a way that made my bones feel unhinged.

"Isn't often that I find a young women hiding out here in the dunes. Forgive me if I seemed a bit rude, I was just surprised to see you out here." He looked puzzled. I suddenly realized that I had planted myself quite a distance from the shoreline—too close indeed to the beautiful vacant property behind me.

"Oh! I'm sorry! I didn't mean to trespass. I didn't know anyone still lived out here?" I motioned towards the large house resting just off of the 'point'."

"I don't actually. That house has been deserted for years." He looked over to the large home that adorned the tip of the peninsula. I sighed, quite relieved that I had not literally "overstepped my boundaries."

"That's a shame. It is quite beautiful. It's kind of sad that no one lives there anymore. I prefer this side of the jetties. Sometimes during the summer, the south side can get overrun with tourists. I remember a time when only the locals and fishermen could find this place, but now it seem like there are people everywhere." He seemed intrigued by my rambling words and the corners of his perfect mouth turned up slightly on the edges. It was the closest thing to a smile that I had ever seen from him.

"True. But luckily there are very few during this time of year," he responded, in a voice so low that it could have easily been mistaken for the surf.

"I'm Marguerite Westly, by the way." I brushed my sandy hand off on my pants leg before extending it to him.

"It's a pleasure," he said looking down at my extended hand. He took one step forward and accepted it briefly. A bolt of electricity traveled through me as his hand touched mine. His skin was warm, much warmer than I had expected. I felt the blood rushing to my face, as his skin touched mine. I hoped that he didn't notice the change, but his lips curled again slightly at the edges. I could only come to the conclusion that he had noticed the blush to my cheeks. No one had ever made me blush before.

"William Avery," he said as our hands parted.

His name sounded familiar, but I couldn't place where I had heard it before. It suited him perfectly.

"I've seen you before I believe—over the years but only from a distance."

"Yes. You spend your summers at the blue house down the creek." I tried not to show my astonishment. I mentally gathered myself before replying.

"I do—the Inlet Joy…with my grandmother." He nodded.

"You come to spend your vacations with her." It wasn't a question. He eyed me curiously. Despite the ease of the conversation, it wasn't quite friendly. There was a wary edge to his tone.

"Every summer. But I am staying here for now."

"Really?" His eyes locked to mine and for an instant I felt as if I may faint. I wasn't sure if I were even able to speak, so I shook my head in response.

"Interesting. Why exactly are you here Marguerite?" He walked over to the dune closest to me. I tried not to stare directly at him, but it was almost impossible not to study the perfection of his features. I tried to steady myself before my reply, hoping my voice was steady as I once again tried to speak. "Well, I love it here. It's quiet—the perfect place to get away."

"Get away? What are you running from?"

"Nothing. I'm not running. I just prefer it here, the water, and the quiet—everything." He nodded, looking out over the water again. I surprised myself as I continued speaking. "It's just...well, it seems like everyone is always running around trying to do something—be something. I don't know; I guess I feel like they are missing the point of living. I feel alive when I am here." He turned and for the first time really looked at me. He seemed to study my features as I had studied his. I dropped my eyes nervously tracing my finger through the sand.

"I agree," he added at last, before looking far out into the horizon. He shifted his weight, and I thought he may walk away. I broke the silence.

"So...do you come here often also?" I said, trying to act casual—friendly even.

"Yes. Quite often, but this is the first time I have ever found company." His deep green eyes bore into mine. I blushed again under his stare, but this time found the courage not to look away. He now seemed intrigued.

"Where are you from?"

"Nowhere. Everywhere. My parents currently live in Florence. It is only about two hours away."

"Oh."

"Are you familiar with it?"

"I know the location but can't say that I've been there."

"Really? It's kind of odd that living so close you have never been there."

"I wouldn't call a two-hour drive close."

"I suppose not, but most people have to pass through it to get here, so I thought ..."

"I prefer the coast. I rarely travel inland," he snapped quickly.

I didn't respond. I thought this a bit odd but decided to dismiss the subject.

"Do you mind?" He motioned toward the dune just across from me. I stared blankly at him before realizing that he was asking to join me.

"Sure." My throat was dry. My words barely escaped my lips.

His lips curled at the edges, and for the first time, I saw him smile. It was enough to stop my heart all together. I stared at him as he situated himself on the dune across from me.

"So…tell me about Florence."

"There isn't much to tell actually."

"Weren't you happy there?"

I looked at him curiously, uncertain why this beautiful creature would be interested in me.

He seemed to read my thoughts. "I don't mean to pry. I am just curious as to your motive for being here."

"No motive. Florence is fine. It's nice enough I suppose."

"But you don't feel like it is home to you?" He continued to stare directly at me.

"No. Actually, my parents haven't lived in Florence very long. In truth, I guess we have never lived anyplace very long. I moved around a lot growing up."

"Oh. That must have been hard on you."

"No. Not really. I prefer to keep to myself anyway."

"You have never lived anywhere that you felt was 'home?'"

I shrugged. "When I am here, I feel like I am home. I guess I have always felt that way. Each year when I would come, I felt like I was returning home." I closed my eyes, a bit embarrassed at how my emotions seemed to flow out so easily talking to William. How very unlike me! "You must think that sounds silly."

He didn't speak right away but his eyes remained fixated on my face. My heart pounded louder and louder in my chest. I was relieved when he finally spoke.

"No. I don't think that is silly at all." He looked down for a moment before turning back to me. "So exactly how long are you staying?"

"Indefinitely."

"Indefinitely? What does that mean?" His words were flat and his expression even more curious.

"I don't know exactly. I moved in with my grandmother three weeks ago and really don't have any plans to return to Florence."

"You don't get along with your family?"

"Nothing like that, my family and I get along great."

"But your parents didn't move with you?"

"No, they are all pretty happily situated. I have a brother and younger sister that are both in school."

"Don't you miss them?"

"Sure I do, but my grandmother lives here alone. She needs me too…and the benefits aren't so bad either." I smiled and closed my eyes to soak in the breeze that had picked up.

His words and expressions changed.

"So the brown-haired boy that is sometimes with you—is he your brother?

"Oh yeah, that's Caleb. He is about to turn fifteen."

"Why doesn't he stay for the summer?"

"Soccer. He plays for several teams and has soccer camps throughout the summer."

"Do you play any sports?" I asked, turning the questions back on him.

"No," he replied curtly.

"Do you live close by?" I asked curiously.

"Just down the creek with my guardian Silas."

By his expression, it was obviously that he wasn't comfortable answering questions about himself. He quickly turned the questions back to me.

"And the older red-haired boy that I see you with sometimes?"

"James. Yes, we have been good friends for about six years now. He's my best friend actually."

"Ah."

"I feel at a disadvantage here," I said teasingly. "Why is it that you seem to know so much about me, and yet I know nothing about you?"

"I pay attention," he replied. He said it in a way that I was certain this was the only information about himself that he planned to surrender.

A misty fog began to settle over the waterway, casting a beautiful but eerie feeling to the area. The sun was falling fast. "You shouldn't be out here alone." His eyes looked deep into mine. His expression became serious.

"I've been coming out here since I was a young child. I'm not afraid to be here by myself." I was quite unprepared for this conversation, especially with him, but I had no desire for the interlude to draw to an end. I was drawn to him in a way that I could not explain.

"Well, things are different now. I mean—you know, the world is more dangerous. Just promise me when you are out here you will stay on this side of the dunes—away from the ocean, okay."

"Why?" My brow furrowed.

"It isn't safe for you to be here." He seemed to be carefully choosing his words. "I mean…just don't go out there alone, okay." His tone became quite serious. I thought his warning quite strange, especially for the short amount of time we had known each other.

"What do you mean by that? Your warning is kind of vague, don't you think?"

"Like I said. It isn't safe." He said firmly.

"You're out here by yourself." My tone had become slightly defensive.

"That's different."

"Thank you for your concern, but I am quite capable of taking care of myself."

Suddenly a strong wind swept up off of the water and caught hold of the old pages of my book. I tried to catch hold of the spine, but it was too late as the pages were tossed into the air in all directions. I gasped under my breath and jumped up to try to retrieve them, but as I did another gust of wind caught the sand as well. I tried to shield my eyes in time, but it was too late as the sand cloud blew directly into them. William had leapt to his feet as well to retrieve my pages but immediately returned to my side when he saw my hands over my eyes.

"Don't rub them!" I couldn't see but I could sense his body close to mine. Very close.

"But that was my favorite book!" I moaned. His arm instantly encircled my waist and was leading me over the dunes. His fingertips were hot to the touch, and my heart began to race so fast that I was certain it would just stop at any second. I followed blindly.

"Where are you taking me?" The irony of having a little sand suddenly render me helpless did not escape me. My cheeks flushed. How easy it seemed that I had proved his point so thoroughly. But he said nothing of the sort. There was only concern in his words.

"To the water's edge. We need to flush the sand out before it scratches your corneas."

When we reached the water he gently tilted my head to the side. His fingers were soft upon my jaw, and I hoped the he had not noticed the shiver of electricity that accompanied his skin as it moved against mine. He bent down and cupped water into his hands.

"Ok—open your eyes! The salt water may sting a bit, but no more than if you were swimming with your eyes open." I could not remember the feel of salt water on my face or my body for that matter.

"I wouldn't know. I don't swim," I said impulsively. I opened my eyes but surprisingly, the water did not burn my eyes at all. There was an instant relief as the sand was flushed from my eyes. Both the sand and the pain were completely gone. I turned to find him still next to me, this time so close that I could smell the crisp scent of his skin. It was a smell like no other, a perfect combination of sun and wind and salt and his essence that seemed to awaken parts of me that had remained asleep for my seventeen years. My heart raced in all directions at once.

"Thank you," I muttered, but my words were lost as I could tell he was deep in thought.

"Did you say that you can't swim?" He could not hide the astonished look that swept over his perfectly chiseled face. I instantly wished that I had not broached the subject—if only I could somehow divert the conversation away from me. But I knew the questions that were sure to follow—questions that I couldn't answer.

"I said that I don't swim, not that I can't swim." The words sounded ridiculous as they escaped my mouth, but William seemed unmoved. His fascination with me only seemed to intensify, and I suddenly wanted an escape. How could I answer his questions when I didn't have the answers myself?

"You don't swim at all?" I shook my head.

"Never?" He asked without expression.

"No"

"But you know *how* to swim"

"I suppose so. It's been many years. It's kind of a long story. I don't really talk about it." My eyes wandered to the water's edge as I carefully watched the water gently rolling up onto the sand before stopping just inches from my toes. I shivered and took a step back.

I felt a warm hand gently lift my chin. I raised my eyes to find his face just inches from mine.

"Something happened to you out there didn't it?"

I stared at him and became lost in his eyes. Whatever he asked of me, I would have no choice but to answer. I slowly nodded.

"Yes."

I hoped that he would let it drop, but I could tell from his expression that he wasn't about to let it go so easily. I turned my face as if to walk away, but his fingers caught the corner of my chin so tenderly that I thought that I may lose consciousness. He dropped his fingers slowly as my face turned to meet his. I was quite certain that I no longer had a pulse.

"Please." His face looked so genuine, so trustworthy, that I would have told him anything.

"You'll just think I've lost my mind."

"Try me." He wasn't going to give up.

I took a deep breath and searched for a way to reveal the memory without allowing myself to become emotional. Impossible. I tried quickly to come up with some sort of lie but quickly dismissed the idea. I was undoubtedly the world's worst liar. It was quite evident that someone as astute as William would be sure to pick up on any falsehood as soon as it left my mouth. I tried to put myself in a cold place emotionally, and after a long pause began a tale that I had never planned to revisit, especially not to someone who was practically a stranger to me.

"My father taught me how to swim when I was five. Right here in the inlet alongside of our dock actually. I was apparently quite a gifted swimmer. I loved the water so much that my family could hardly keep me out of it." I stopped unsure if I could continue. He was asking me to recount memories that no one spoke of, and I had no wish to have to recall.

'What happened?" He leaned closer to me.

"I don't really talk about it."

"Please. I want to know."

"I don't think I've ever talked about it."

"You can trust me." I don't know why, but for some reason, I wanted to tell him. Why after so many years did I want to share my most guarded memory with this stranger?

"Please," he repeated.

"Well, when I was eight years old I was out in the ocean swimming with my father. I kept swimming deeper and deeper as he protested for me to return. Anyway, something happened. I don't go out there anymore."

"What happened to you?" There was a strange protective tone to his voice. Strange, I was sure that my ears had to be deceiving me. Why would this beautiful creature ever care what happened to me.

"The truth sounds crazy." To continue my story would relinquish any amount of dignity I had left. But I quickly realized it was too late for dignity anyway. Besides, I would probably never talk to him again. Definitely not after he heard the rest of my story and declared me a nut job.

"I don't care. Please tell me." This time I didn't hesitate but continued with my story as clinical and unemotional as possible. At least after I was finished I could crawl back into my hole. He would be gone for sure.

"Well, I felt myself being pulled out to sea and began to scream. I don't remember all of the details exactly; I was pretty young. But I remember looking back and seeing a face. It looked human, but different all at the same time. Whatever the underwater creature was, it had a hold of my leg. Its eyes were like nothing I had ever seen. Its teeth were long and pointed, and its face seemed distorted with rage. But the main thing that I remember was its eyes. The evil in those eyes often haunt my sleep. Anyway, while I was under the water, someone grabbed my hand and pulled me free."

"Who was it?" he asked almost in a whisper.

"I don't know. Someone or something was there under the water with me. The sand and water was churning from the struggle—all I could make out was a hand. The hand was smaller, like a child or youth—like mine, but stronger and different somehow." I paused to look at William, unsure of what his reaction would be. He stared at me expressionless.

"What happened next—after you were rescued?" His emerald eyes remained fixed upon mine.

"My family claimed it had to be the undertow at first, but whatever it was, left its mark." I barely lifted my pants leg to reveal the scar above my ankle. "My family thought it was a shark or something, but I know it was something different."

He didn't say anything. I held my breath waiting for some type of response. At last the silence became unbearable. I shuffled my feet into the sand nervously. I waited for William to laugh at me, to call me crazy, even to just walk away, but he did none of the above. His eyes remained steady and his focus constant as he looked out over the water for what seemed like an eternity. At last he spoke.

"I believe you." His words were sincere. He turned to face me after another extended pause. "The inlet is safe for you. No harm will come to you here. But you must never go into the ocean again."

His words had a much greater impact on me than I could have ever expected. Most importantly it was the first acknowledgement that my instincts had possibly been correct. If there had been nothing to fear in my encounter so many years earlier, then I was quite certain William would have acknowledged it, dismissed my silly notions, and encouraged my return to the surf. As it was, he had surprisingly not done so, affirmed my fears, and opened a new book of questions.

"You believe me." It wasn't a question. I stood astonished that someone actually believed my account.

"Yes."

"So, there is something out there? I didn't imagine this creature, did I?"

"No." I suddenly realized that William knew more about what was out there than I did. This stranger possibly held the answers to the questions that had plagued me for so long.

"What is it? Please…I need to know. I need to know what really happened to me."

"I can't say."

"Can't or won't?"

"Both."

"What do you know, William?" I pleaded.

"I have said more than I should have. Go back to Florence, Marguerite. You don't need to be here." His expression had changed—his face now as hard as stone.

"I can't."

"Look, you need to get away from here—away from all of this! You are putting yourself in danger to remain here."

"I am not going anywhere."

"There is nothing I can do to insure your safety here." He looked out again past the jetties into open sea.

"My safety? I don't need anyone to keep me safe."

"Are you sure about that?" he responded, his eyes narrowing.

I suddenly shivered as I remembered the creature on the dock. What if he was right? Was there something here for me to fear?

"There is nothing holding you here." His tone added a new element—anger.

"Yes, there is. I don't know what it is exactly, but I can't go back. Not now."

"You say that you like to be alone. It isn't safe for you to be alone here."

"I am confused. What do you mean by "it isn't safe for me"?"

"I can't say. Just listen to me okay."

"That isn't very fair! You tell me to trust you, and yet you don't return the favor!"

"You are right. I'm sorry." His tone was anything but apologetic. His eyes flickered fiercely.

"I guess I thought we were becoming friends."

"Friends? I am sorry if I gave you that impression. I can't be friends with you."

"Why not? You say that *I* shouldn't be alone. Well, come to think of it, I have never seen you with anyone!"

"I choose to be alone."

"And I choose to stay here!"

"Fine. Have it your way, but I warned you. It's dangerous for you to be here."

"And yet you refuse to tell me what the danger may be." His tone softened as he realized that he had hurt me.

"You know. You've seen what is out there."

"What *is* out there?" He didn't respond.

"You know don't you?" I pleaded. He still said nothing.

"Tell me what I saw!"

"You saw something that you were never meant to see. Forget about it! Go home."

"You have to give me more than that. What are you keeping from me?"

"Trust me, you don't want to know. Leave it at that."

I didn't want to drop it. I was determined now to know the truth, but it was also clear that William was not going to share with me the information that I now so desperately sought. I turned and began to walk back up to the dunes to retrieve my things.

"Where are you going? Don't leave." His words pleaded with me. I angrily turned to face him.

"You asked me to trust you, and yet you refuse to trust me."

"I can't. I couldn't even if I wanted to."

"That makes no sense at all."

"I know."

"And you have said that we can't be friends."

"No. We can't ever be friends."

"Then there is really nothing else to say."

"Margo—I can't protect you, if you have no interest in protecting yourself." He turned away realizing that he had said too much. Him protecting me? Why would he feel any obligation to keep me safe?

"Well, if you're right, and I do have something to fear by living here, then I guess my number is up. I'm not going anywhere." The embarrassment that I felt tuned to anger. How was I so foolish to trust my story to someone I had just met! I grabbed my towel and the remnants of my book, and strode back across the dunes. I didn't look back, but I could feel two emerald green eyes watching me as I hoisted myself back over the seawall.

I was nearly home when I remembered my grandmother had asked me to pick up some sugar. Uh! I was still visibly upset and just wanted to be alone, but it was a rare occasion that my grandmother asked anything of me, and so I wiped my eyes with my slightly sandy sleeve and made the short trip down to the corner. The Beach Mart was deserted except for the cashier; I quickly plopped my purchase down on the counter, anxious to return home. It was then that I saw them through the large glass storefront windowpanes. Three guys and a girl were leaning against a black raised pickup that was parked just across the street from my Jeep. I had to do a double take as this group was nothing like I had ever seen before.

The first one was very tall and slender. Lean muscles seemed to stretch the entire length of him. His hair was a sun-kissed golden blonde. It would have hung just below his shoulders but was pulled back loosely at the nape of his neck. A few shorter pieces had come lose and curved around his angular face just below his chin. His bronzed skin was perfectly smooth. I couldn't help but to think he looked exactly like a younger version of one of the heroes that they put on the cover of romance novels.

The second was much shorter and stockier but still extremely handsome. His hair was dark and cropped very short. It fanned out across his round head like porcupine bristles. His muscles bulged out from the sides of his t-shirt and shorts. He reminded me of a young Hercules. His tanned round face had two very deep dimples on both sides of his mouth and a smile that seemed to stretch from ear to ear.

The third guy appeared to be the driver as he fiddled absentmindedly with a set of car keys off to the side. He wasn't as tall as the blonde boy, nor was he as muscular as the second, but he was by far the fiercest looking of the group. His hair was shaved so close to his scalp that it was impossible to know the color. His face was sharp and angular with high cheekbones and chiseled features so pronounced that he almost didn't look human. He had a small scar just above his right cheek bone that was visible even through the foggy glass of the doors. He looked more like he should belong as the lead in an action movie than hanging out on the corner in Garden City.

The girl was unmistakably beautiful with her dark curls hanging midway down her back. She neither needed nor wore any makeup, as her skin was the color of golden sand. Her cheeks and nose was naturally highlighted from the sun, and her extra full lips curved upward in a beautiful pout.

The group hovered in the parking lot as if they were waiting for someone. I pulled a few loose bills from my pocket to pay the cashier. When I looked up, I was a bit startled to see four pairs of eyes peering at me through the glass from across the lot. I couldn't help but think that they looked like the surfer version of a gang from *Westside Story*. Only, I was certain that no group had ever been as beautiful as this one. Were they waiting on me? The sky had begun to get dark, and I couldn't help but feel a bit nervous.

I took my package from the cashier and was slowly moving toward the door when I saw an old blue pickup truck quickly pull up and stop just between the group and my Jeep. I recognized the driver instantly as William quickly leapt from the old truck. I remained frozen as he appeared to be arguing with them, but the confrontation was mostly hidden from view by his truck. Before I even had time to process William's sudden presence, his truck sped off, and he was gone. My eyes followed his truck as it sped out of sight, and when they finally returned to where the crew had been standing, they had fled in the opposite direction—only a set of taillights racing off in the distance to prove their presence.

I absent mindedly slammed the screen door behind me, as I stomped across the porch planks. Why was I so angry? I didn't even know the boy whose face now clouded my thoughts! Why had he even entered my life! The evening's events had been both strange and frustrating to say the least. I thought back over meeting William at the "point," and to the beautiful group of magical misfits that had disappeared into the night as fast as William had. What had he said to them, and why was he there? For that matter, what were they all doing there, and why did it appear that they were waiting on me? I threw my jacket on the bed and went straight over to the chipped mirror that hung above my old pine dresser. I wasn't sure what had upset me the most, the fact that he wouldn't tell me what he knew, or the fact that he refused to be my friend. I wouldn't admit to myself that it was probably the later of the two.

I hardly recognized the tear filled hazel eyes staring back at me—plain hazel! Why couldn't I have been born with deep chocolate eyes like Mom, Lucy, and Caleb, or even better, rich blue eyes like my father? Why had I been the only one to inherit eyes with no real color—eyes that were neither brown, nor green, nor blue, nor gold. How plain they seemed in comparison to William's deep emerald eyes. Had those eyes mesmerized me? How could I have trusted this stranger enough to tell him my most guarded memory and greatest fear? I barely knew him, but he seemed to have the answers for which I had been searching.

I sighed thinking back over our argument. There was a feeling worse than thinking you have experienced something that no one believed—knowing you experienced something, while also knowing that the person who held the answers wanted nothing to do with you. I brushed back a tear that had escaped just as a soft knock was heard against my door.

"Marguerite? Are you okay dear?"

"Oh, yeah. I must have walked too far because I am suddenly pretty tired. Do you mind if I turn in early tonight?" I hastily opened a jar of moisturizer and began swirling it over my face in an attempt to cover my tears.

"Sure. Sure—are you sure everything is okay? Are you upset about something?"

"Oh—no. Everything is fine. I think I am just a bit overtired."

"Are you sure?"

"Yeah—No, I am fine."

"Alright. If you are sure everything is okay."

"I just need some sleep. I left the sugar on the counter for you. Goodnight."

"Goodnight dear." She took a long look at me, as I continued to ready myself for bed before shutting the door.

It was only then that I noticed the foot of my bed. Waiting there for me was a neatly placed stack of water stained pages—the very same pages that were blown from my book and lost just a short time earlier.

4

———

"There are all kinds of love in this world but never the same love twice."

F. Scott Fitzgerald

I t was Friday. Almost another week had trickled by with no sign of the creature—or William. I was in the bathtub looking over myself as the warm water washed over me. My relocation to Garden City had helped the red patches on the majority of my body, but it still remained on my arms and thighs. I kept them covered the majority of the time despite several days of warmer weather when shorts and a tank-top would have been my preferred attire. It no longer bothered me. When you spend a lifetime of waiting for something, eventually you forget what you are even waiting for.

The real question that remained was why had I not asked my grandmother for more of the sea salts that she had sent me just before I had become ill? I wasn't sure of the answer to this. Sure, it was amazing to awaken to skin as smooth as silk, but had it also contributed to my strange abilities? Could that concoction give an average person with even less than average athleticism such extraordinary abilities? How else to explain being able to run so fast and flip through the air like an Olympian. If so, was it also the cause of what had made me so ill? How strange that there was so much to say between my grandmother and I, and yet, our dinner conversation consisted of things such as books, the weather, and the local news.

Despite my grandmother's excellent cooking, my body remained quite thin from my stay in the hospital, an observation that did not go unnoticed by my grandmother whose main hobby was to create as many mouthwatering dishes as possible to fatten me up. I appreciated her efforts greatly, but aside from the seafood dishes that I tore into ravenously, I had little appetite for the rest.

Days passed. More rain. I spent the week landlocked, like I was waiting for something. I wasn't sure exactly what I expected to happen, but there was something out there, and I couldn't shake the feeling that I was somehow connected to whatever it was. William's words at the point only confirmed what I already knew in my heart—there was *something* out there.

I once again opened my weathered copy of *Pride and Prejudice*, carefully studying the water-stained pages that had so amazingly been returned to me. How had he been able to collect them all, and how was he able to return them to my room in such a short time without the notice of my grandmother. The fact that he knew where I slept should have freaked me out, but for some reason, it didn't. His presence in my sleeping quarters didn't leave me with fear, only intrigue. I spent many restless evenings going over possible scenarios. Nothing seemed to fit: the creature, the crew, William. There was something that I was missing. My life had become a puzzle with its pieces scattered about like paper in the wind, with no one there to chase them but me. If the answers weren't going to come to me, then I would have to find them myself.

I had spent the majority of the past week looking out over the water. The creature wasn't the only thing that consumed my thoughts. I found myself searching for the owner of those pair of emerald eyes that haunted my sleep. I masked my heavy thoughts with a constant book in hand, but in truth, every word that I read was now clouded with thoughts of William. I needed answers. It became evident that I was going to have to uncover them on my own. I knew now what I had to do. I dressed quickly and found my grandmother out on the front porch reading. I took hold of the nearest rocker and pulled it up next to her. She looked up at me and smiled closing her book as if she anticipated that I had something that I wished to discuss with her.

"So, just curious. Does Dad's old boat downstairs still run? I was thinking about trying to get it running." I hastily delivered my request, before I chickened out altogether. She took a deep breath and sighed.

"Well—Marguerite, I must admit that I am not surprised by your question. I suppose it was only a matter of time before this would come up."

"Do you think I could get it started?"

"I honestly don't know dear. The idea of you out on the water by yourself frankly scares me to death."

I shrugged. "I am seventeen. If I were a boy, there would be no reservations."

"But you are a young woman."

"*You* grew up on the inlet; did you have a boat?"

She nodded, and a faint smile crept across her face as she realized she was about to lose this debate. "I did," she admitted. "I actually worked for my father, so I spent almost every afternoon out there pulling crab traps and running lines for him."

"Well, I have a feeling that you were a lot younger than me when you first started going out."

"I was. But things were different then."

"Really? Are we seriously going to do the whole 'times were different back then' speech?" I snapped, barely giving my jury time to deliberate.

"Ah! So this is what it is like living with a teenager! I'd almost forgotten." She laughed. "Alright, I can already see that I am going to lose this debate. You're welcome to it if you can get it running, but I honestly can't remember the last time it was in the water." I grabbed her with both arms and gave her a big kiss on the cheek.

"You are the best!" I exclaimed excitedly.

"Why do I have a feeling I may live to regret this?" She mumbled to herself.

"So where do you think I should begin?" I went to roll up my sleeves, but stopped, pushing the thin fabric back down to my wrists when I was reminded of the red patches still on my arms. There was a new expression on her face that I had not seen before—fear maybe.

"Gosh, Marguerite, I honestly don't know what it needs. Your father brought that old boat down here the first summer I moved back. Not sure where he picked it up, but it was in pretty rough shape to begin with. The only time it has ever been used was during the summers when your family came to stay. It weathered out there for many years before I made your father finally put it back under the carport last summer."

"You've never had the urge to take it out?"

"Sure." She confessed. I could hear a bit of sadness in her voice. "But I live here alone, Marguerite; if that old boat had trouble, who would know to come looking for me?" My grandmother was an independent woman, but I was suddenly reminded of how difficult life must be living alone.

"I guess the first step would be to charge the battery to see if it's still good, then I'll go from there. But I just don't think this is a good idea! What if you get lost or…."

"Grandmother, my father and I would go out almost every day when we would come for the summer. I know the canals out there like the back of my hand. Seriously, if I am going to live here, I have to be able to get around the inlet." She looked at me tenderly, and I could see an expression of sadness come over her delicate blue eyes.

"Yes. You're right. If you're able to get the boat running, then it's yours, but Marguerite, be cautious love, don't let your sense of adventure override you common sense, the inlet harbors have many dangers. I just don't want you getting hurt."

"No. I know. I promise to be cautious." She looked at me then out at the ocean that peaked out between the houses in front of ours. She was suddenly distracted—deep in thought. I knew she had something she wanted to say to me, and she seemed to be searching for the right words.

"And whatever you do, promise me that you will never pass the jetties into the ocean." There was that warning again. The very same warning William had issued.

"I promise." She was the second person to tell me to avoid the ocean in the past week. Since arriving I could not help but feel like there was some big secret between us. She always seemed to be on the verge of telling me something, but always stopped herself.

As I pulled back the dusty, blue tarp that covered the old boat, reality quickly set in. It looked like it belonged in a trash heap more than skipping effortlessly across the inlet water. My father had carefully taught me the shift of the tides, the cut of the canals, and the dangers of the currents, but through all of my lessons, boat repair was not included. I knew nothing about the mechanics of this ancient, rust-coated engine. With a sigh, I stood there for a moment contemplating my next move.

Failure was not an option. I may not be able to repair this dilapidated relic, but I could try to clean it. I hustled into the storage room and within minutes returned with several steel brushes, scrapers, some detergent, several old rags, and a can of WD-40. I looked over the hull of the metal boat. The muddy army green paint had faded and rubbed off along the top sides, and there was a collection of dried barnacles that adorned the underbelly. But aside from the peeling paint and a few bangs and dings, the hull didn't appear to have any visible holes or spots in need of extensive repair.

My discouragement began to fade as I meticulously spent the remainder of the morning scrubbing and scraping. Around noon my grandmother brought me down a fish sandwich and a Coke, both of which I immediately devoured and quickly went back to work. Soon I was ready to spray off the vessel to ascertain my progress. I removed the blocks of wood from under the tires that appeared to be both dry rotted and flat. The hitch was angled such that I couldn't get my Jeep near it, even if I had previously installed a trailer hitch on the back of my Jeep—which I had not.

"Great," I thought to myself, "I'll never be able to push this scrap heap into the yard!" I got behind the motor and nudged it a little. Yes, it would roll alright. I pushed harder—the boat sprang forward! I had watched my father struggle to move the unhitched boat trailer, a task that seemed quite difficult. To my surprise, the boat began to roll out into the yard with surprisingly little effort. I barely had enough time to contemplate this, when out of the corner of my eye, I could see someone coming towards me from across the neighboring yards. The sun was almost blinding as I moved from the shade into the warm afternoon sunlight. I squinted and my heart leapt in my chest. I was certain that the figure coming toward me was most definitely not a mirage. I knew his stride too well to doubt my own eyes—James!

My feet were moving toward him before I could even make the decision to run. His face beamed as he saw me coming in his direction. In a fraction of a second, his arms clasp around so tightly that my feet were no longer planted on the ground but soared into the air with utter delight.

"You've come! I can't believe it!" I laughed and was suddenly filled with unfamiliar emotions. My eyes welled up with tears, and for the first time, I realized how much I missed my family. James was family. I did not realize how much I really missed Caleb and Lucy and my parents until I had my dearest friend's arms around me. He was here!

"Well, I heard Murrells Inlet had a new resident and had to come check it out for myself." He laughed as he put me back on my feet. "So you're really here for good this time? You crazy girl!"

"You know I never could stay away from this place! I finally found a good enough excuse to stay year round." If James noticed the tears in my eyes, he was far too much of a gentleman to call attention to it. "James! I have missed you so much. I am so glad you are here."

"Are you kidding? After I got your letter last week saying you were here, I have been counting the seconds until I could finally sneak away to come see you. I've missed you too, darlin'!"

"Gosh James, so much has happened!" I eyed him carefully. He seemed much taller than I had remembered—more handsome. "And look at you! You've grown!" I choked out, pulling my eyes away from him.

"Na, not that much. It has just been like six months since you last saw me. You must have forgotten what I looked like."

"Never! I could never forget you! You look exactly the same, just taller." I lied. The features of his face were now more pronounced. His frame seemed even more erect—stronger somehow. He looked great!

"Alright, fair enough." His eyes narrowed as the tone of his voice changed from jubilation to concern. "How are you feeling? I was concerned when I heard you had been sick.

"I'm completely fine. It must have been a virus or something."

"A virus?" he laughed. "You are undoubtedly the worst liar in the world. You were unconscious for a week! What virus does that?"

"The unconscious kind?" I teased.

"Nice. You came up with that one all by yourself?" He grabbed me by the shoulders and playfully ruffed up my hair as I lightheartedly pushed him away.

"I can't believe Caleb didn't call to tell me you were in the hospital. I was wondering why I didn't receive a letter from you that week."

"I'm sure no one wanted to worry you. Look, I'm fully recovered. You are here now! That is all that matters!"

"Margo, you know I would have been right there." he said tenderly.

I tucked a strand of hair behind my ear suddenly conscience of what my own appearance must be. I tugged at the sleeves of my shirt to be certain my arms were completely covered, and suddenly wished that I had actually known he was coming so I could have showered.

"I know. But seriously, I am doing great, especially now that you're here."

"Do they know just what happened?"

"Not really. I collapsed. It was most likely from the high fever, but what caused the fever is still a mystery. Actually, the doctors aren't really sure *what* happened to me exactly. But I seem to be fine now, better than fine."

"Well, I'm glad to hear it. I don't know how I would *ever* be able to fill my summers without you to show me the ropes."

"James, that's a lie and you know it! Sure, that may have been true five years ago when you first arrived, but you know this inlet now as well as I do, and more so in the fact that *you* will actually get *in* the water. Besides, I'm sure you could find some tan, beautiful blonde to take my place!"

"Ok, now I know you really *are* still ill. You know I could never replace you, darlin'." His eyes met mine. There was a brief silence as he looked at me intently. It was one of those rare moments that reminded me that James had strong feelings for me. It was rare that he allowed his feelings to surface, but I was uncomfortably aware that with age these moments were more frequently. It was without question that we loved each other. With so much time and history between us, love was inevitable, but I had refused to ascertain the depth of my feelings for James. He had been my best friend since I was eleven. I wanted to be with him whenever possible; I got butterflies in my stomach at the possibility of seeing him. He made me laugh—happier than I ever thought possible. There was no one in the world I could be myself with as much as James, and yet any romantic feelings seemed displaced. It was almost like any sort of romance would abate what was between us.

If James thought himself romantically in love with me, I knew that I needed in some way to discourage this emotion. But each time I saw him, my utter and true delight at his presence only fueled any feelings that he may have, and yet, still I was unable to stifle my jubilation. I was relieved when James suddenly broke away and noticed my latest "project" behind me in the sunlight.

"Margo, what are you up to you silly girl? Don't tell me you're trying to get this old thing running!" He laughed aloud as he looked at me from head to foot. James brushed away a bit of foam that still remained in my hair. I blushed remembering I was completely filthy covered with everything from engine oil to marsh mud.

"I most definitely *am*!" I admitted with a grin. "You'll be begging me for a ride when I succeed." I was able again to put aside my pride and try to joke back with him.

"Um, I'm not sure what I think about you out there on the water alone." James was usually game for any big adventure I had planned, but I could hear the apprehension in his voice. "Especially since I won't be here most of the time to keep an eye on you." *Great, now James too!* Concern for my safety seemed to be a running theme around here. I wasn't sure that I liked the new direction this seemed to be taking.

"Well good. Stay here with me, and I won't be out there alone."

"There is absolutely nothing in this world that I would love more than to be here. Especially now that I know you're here *indefinitely*. It kills me actually. But I have two months of school left until summer vacation. I can't exactly run out on it now that I have finally almost reached the end of my junior year. Besides, I'm not nearly as focused as you in regards to the whole correspondence thing. I think I could always come up with an excuse not to study. "

"I am just teasing you. Of course you need to finish with your class!" I looked down at the large camera hung around his neck. It looked much nicer that the one he carried last summer but older—vintage. "Besides, what would Conway High do without their most elite photographer?"

James had taken up photography a few summers back. It had gone from a hobby to a passion. Though I knew my opinion was completely biased, his photographs were amazing. He had a way of capturing the human spirit and expressing it on paper in a way that was breathtaking.

"Um no, my absence would be quite unnoticed I'm afraid. But be there—I must!" He paused for a moment before changing the subject.

"So, are we really going to try to get this thing running?" His smile was deep and calculating. He turned his back to me as he more carefully eyed the mechanics of the boat's motor.

"*We*…did I possibly hear you say *we*! Does that mean you are going to help me?" My arms playfully wrapped around his sides in a movement that was something between a hug and a tickle. James instinctive jumped, as he was quite ticklish, and let out a yelp that sent me hysterically laughing as I ran to the other side of the boat to avoid retaliation.

We spent the remainder of the afternoon catching up. The hours flew by more quickly than I would have liked as James' energetic words consistently filled the air. I mainly listened as he gave me a detailed update on each of the Leighton family. I savored every word far more than he realized. When the conversation switched to me, I would shift the spotlight to my family—Caleb's soccer abilities or Lucy's dance recitals. It wasn't as if I couldn't share myself with James; I knew that I could share anything with him, but there was really so few interesting things about my life to report. Well, things that I could share anyway. His life seemed so interesting compared to my own. I just couldn't risk bringing up the freaky things that had been happening recently. James would think I was crazy for sure!

When the sun began to fall over the marshlands, we shifted our reunion to the bleached out old Pawley's Island hammock hanging on the dock. We politely declined my grandmother's dinner invitation and opted instead to run out for pizza. We stopped on the way at the hardware store to pick up some fresh sparkplugs and a set of new tires for the boat. I took full advantage of my best friend's company, and didn't let him retreat to his own empty house until well past midnight, and only then under strict instructions that he would meet me in the morning around eight-thirty.

I was aware that his feelings for me had long since surpassed that of my own, and yet I so desired his company that I selfishly could not discourage his attention. If I had not hurt him already, I knew that one day I would break the heart of the friend I held most dear in the world. If I were a less selfish person, I would allow him to spend his summers perusing, and possibly even falling in love, with someone else. But I refused to give him up, despite my inability to supply the feelings that I knew he was patiently waiting summer after summer for me to reciprocate. We were no longer children, and I knew that it was only a matter of time before I would have to make a decision. He was my security, my laughter, and my dearest friend, but could he also be that lifelong love that I had always dreamed of someday finding? I mulled over the question relentlessly that evening as I restlessly tried to sleep. Was what I felt for James the forever type of love? And if so, why was it William's emerald eyes that haunted my dreams?

The sun had not broken through the clouds when a sound outside of my door stole me from my slumber. I rolled over to face the clock—not yet six o'clock. I wasn't scheduled to meet James until eight-thirty. My heart began to pound as memories of the shadowed figure upon the dock ignited my fears. I tried to calm my imagination, as why would anything that would cause me harm take the time to knock on my door. With rising courage, I grabbed the robe that I had messily discarded on the floor and stepped toward the door.

"Hello. Who is there?" I tried to steady my voice.

I was relieved to hear the reply was the familiar voice of my grandmother.

"Marguerite. The sunrise service begins in half an hour. Are you still planning to go with me?" Oh, crap! I forgot it was Sunday. All week I had promised to attend the sunrise church service with my grandmother, and with all of the excitement of James' visit, I had totally forgotten my promise.

"Oh, um yeah Grandma. Give me like ten minutes, and I will be ready. Okay?" I checked the clock again before quickly stripping off my sweat pants and t-shirt.

"Okay dear, just try to hurry. I will meet you downstairs in the truck. Are you sure you still want to go? It's fine if you want to sleep in."

"No, I really want to go. I just forgot to set my alarm. I will be down in a minute." I called back to her as I pulled on the khaki skirt that I had stuffed into my bottom drawer. With a thin navy sweater from the box under my bed, and my tan flats from the bottom of the closet, I was satisfied. I pulled my hair back into a ponytail, grabbed my silver hoops from my shelf, and swiped on a bit of pale lip gloss. I quickly grabbed my purse and hurried downstairs. Consistently, making Caleb late for school each day had conditioned me to dress quickly.

It was only a short drive past the pier to the service. I knew that after our late night, James was certainly still fast asleep, and I was glad that I was able to keep this promise to my grandmother. Sara Askins Westley's faith radiated from within. Her eyes were often quietly closed in prayer, and from her mouth came beautiful words of thanks before each and every meal. Each Sunday she attended a sunrise service held on the beach by the Garden City chapel, but aside from this service, I could not recall ever seeing her enter a church. She saw God through all that surrounded her. I admired her quiet devotion, not just her faith, but the connection she had with nature.

The service was small; about thirty people had gathered along the beach to listen to the short service and gather in prayer. I took my tan flats in hand before walking onto the beach. Many people chose to stand, but my grandmother moved to take one of the folding seats that had been transplanted onto the sand for the service. I would have chosen to stand too, but followed to the seat beside her. The air was much cooler than I had expected as it had been many months since I had experienced the shoreline at such an early hour. My thin sweater offered little protection from the morning air, but I wasn't cold. The purple hue of the morning sky became brighter and brighter with each passing minute as the sun began to make it's morning debut. The gulls and sand lappers scattered along the water's edge in search of their morning breakfast, and a small group of pelicans took to the water to begin their early morning fishing. The cool salt air was more intense in the early hours of the day, and with each breath, it filled my lungs with its brisk fragrance. I closed my eyes to soak it all in.

The minister had not long begun the service when I realized one side of my chair was slowly sinking in the sand. *I knew I should have stood in the back!* I slowly turned and lifted my weight to adjust the chair while trying to draw as little attention to myself as possible. It was then that I saw him. My heart stopped. William stood apart from the others off to the side. He was even more handsome than I remembered. He wore a pair of khaki slacks and a pale blue button down shirt. The morning sun pervaded his dark curls casting a golden tint through his windblown locks.

When my eyes finally rested on his face, I was startled to find that his eyes bore into mine with an intensity that took my breath away. His emerald eyes held a stare that was somewhere between anger and contempt. He did not look away, nor try to mask the animosity that was unjustly cast upon me. I quickly looked away, and succeeded in ceasing to looking in his direction for the remainder of the service, despite the certainty that his piercing eyes remained upon me. The words of the minister were now lost to me, as I spent the remainder of the service replaying every word of our last encounter. How had I offended him so? My heart began to beat again, but this time it raced so loudly that I was sure that those around me could hear its irregular rhythm. But I somehow remained steady until the last words of the service were spoken. Unable to contain myself any longer, I turned to face him only to find that the spot that once held him was empty. My grandmother could not help but notice my agitation as my eyes scanned the area in search of him.

"Are you alright dear? What are you looking for?"

"Uh, yeah. I just thought I saw someone that I knew."

"A friend of yours?"

"No. I thought it was a friend of mine, but I was mistaken." I said suddenly feeling quite foolish that the person who haunted my thoughts, could barely stand the sight of me? "It was no one."

James arrived at the set time, quite eager to see me, but my mind was still engaged with the morning's events. More specifically, I could not erase the memory of the eyes that pierced through me with an unexplained anger. Though I had passed him along the waterway many times through the years, I couldn't recall anything that I could have done to spark such emotion. What offended him so about my presence here? I was so lost in my own thoughts that the sudden struggling moan of the old boat engine took me by surprise. I turned and threw my hands over my mouth in utter surprise. A wide smile spread across James' freckled face.

"Well madam, looks like your chariot awaits!" He delivered an exaggerated bow in my direction.

"You did it! I can't believe it!" I shrieked in delight.

"No, we did it! All I did was change a few spark plugs and clean it up a bit. You were the one who did all of the real work."

"No James, I can't thank you enough—and you said you weren't a mechanic!" I squealed and threw my arms around his neck.

"Truly darlin' this is a first for me. I honestly don't know how she is even running! It wouldn't crank at all last night, and yet, this morning it started right up on the first pull!" My excitement temporarily erased any previous thoughts, and I was once again in debt to James for making things better.

"That's odd. These things are so finicky, who knows why it finally decided to run. Let's put it in the water." I motioned toward the old boat ramp at the far end of the property. James stopped the engine.

"Not so fast. We still have to replace these tires before we can get her in." I impatiently waited as James figured out how to change both tires. He struggled with the rusty bolts on his side, while I quickly removed the ones on the other side. When he moved to begin the work on my side he was surprised to find the bolts of the old tire had been removed.

"How did you do that so fast?" He looked up at me with an expression that was somewhere between shock and embarrassment.

"Oh, the nuts on this side must not have been put on so tightly." I shrugged, secretly wondering the same thing. He looked down skeptically at the rusted pieces and then back at me. I tried to ease his embarrassment. "So, what time will you have to be heading home?"

"Ah, so eager to get rid of me already? He said playfully as he slid the remaining tire into place and began to refasten them.

"On the contrary actually, I want you to stay. I just wanted to be certain you didn't have some big date tonight that would be pacing the floors waiting on your return."

"Date? Um no. The only thing waiting on me is a trigonometry assignment, and believe me, that one can just wait."

"Just checking. I didn't want to be keeping you from something."

"It isn't every day that I get to risk my life on the open waters with a beautiful girl by my side. The real question is will this baby float or will we be swimming back home." The familiar boyish grin that I loved spread across his face as we stepped back to view our project. Almost in unison we both burst out.

"Better get the lifejackets!" I was still laughing as I ducked in the storage room to retrieve the extra gas can, life jackets, and paddles. James hitched the boat to his blue Chevy Blazer and began to back the boat down our boat ramp and into the water. I stopped James as the hull reached the water, and taking the rope in hand, pulled out the pin holding the boat to the trailer. The tide was still rising, and it easily slid into the water as I stood along the bank holding the rope tied to it. James parked the Blazer, and we maneuvered the vessel down to the dock and tied it along the floating pier.

The midday sun had started to fall behind the clouds, and the wind had begun to pick up, as we loaded our sad lot of gear into the boat. I zipped up the thin grey windbreaker I had earlier retrieved from my room and climbed in. James was already waiting in the rear fiddling with the motor as I made my way to the middle bench seat. "No way Miss Westly! This is your boat, and you, my dear, are going to help me drive it!"

"Fair enough! If you're sure?" He nodded and slid out of the way so I could pass. I smiled as I stumbled to the rear and took my place beside James. I was delighted as the motor roared to life on the first pull, and James quickly untied us as the current swiftly drifted the light boat from the dock.

"All right. It's now yours. He said handing me the steering shaft. I reluctantly accepted. I glanced down at the handle and was relieved to realize that I remembered all my father had taught me. With extreme caution, I slowly turned the grip, shifting the engine from neutral to forward. The boat leapt forward and hastily began to cut through the water. I giggled at the brief moment of panic on James' face. Backing off, I slowed the boat to not more than an idle. Gradually I began to pick up speed until I was once again confident with my abilities.

"See you're a natural! I must admit, I was kind of hoping you would need me to jump in and take the reins. But as usual, I'm just the eye candy." He struck a pose as if he were a model and leaned back dramatically. I roared with laughter.

The water was quiet as we left the canals and made our way into the bay. There were several fishing boats off in the distance and another pulling into the marina, but aside from this, all was surprisingly still. I wasn't accustomed to the luxury of the inlet in the off-season. Sure, my family and I had been here many times during the winter and early spring months to visit, but I was always amazed at the undisturbed beauty that accompanied these tourist free months. It was magical. During this time, the wildlife moved undisturbed through the marshlands. I marveled at the variety of egrets and herons along the water's edge, and the beauty of the pelicans as they flew into the bay. The sunlight glistened across the water through the breaks in the clouds, and the cry of the gulls could be heard over the rumble of the engine. I thought it impossible that even heaven itself could be more beautiful. I felt a warm hand cover my own, now resting on the seat beside me, but James did not look over at me. He knew my thoughts well enough not to spoil the moment with idle chatter, as we toured the area we both knew so well. All was beautiful. All was perfect!

On the horizon, a small boat was moving with pace in our direction. I felt my heart skip a beat. I was certain of its occupant despite the fact that the boat was still only a shadow off in the distance.

It was William.

5

-----

*"Sit in revere, and watch the changing color of the waves
that break upon the idle seashore of the mind."*

Henry W. Longfellow

T he small boat upon the horizon came upon us much quicker
than even I could anticipate. It seemed incapable that a vessel
so small and beautiful could travel at such a pace without breaking to
pieces. The features that had clouded my mind seemed to manifest before
me like magic.

The boat sped directly towards us as it pounded effortlessly atop the
churning water. I was certain that James was watching the approaching
craft as well, though I could not tear my eyes from the nearing vessel long
enough to be certain. Neither of us spoke, as my hand slid from the
throttle bringing the craft to an idle. I froze, unable to decide what to do,
as the boat came charging upon us. It abruptly stopped at a distance that
could have been no more than twenty feet from us. The driver turned to
face us. With the sun reflecting off of his perfectly defined face and the
salty air billowing through his dark sun kissed hair, I could not be certain
that this creature before me was actually human. Was his presence simply
a mirage? Maybe I had completely fabricated his existence altogether.
Surely it was impossible that a boy so physically perfect existed. Could

James see him? With relief, I turned to find my passenger looking across the waterway at William, affirming that he was indeed real.

His eyes remained narrowed, and his countenance even more severe than when he had first looked at me upon the beach. But in his expression there was something else. His face appeared to be twisted as if he were concerned. Odd, apart from Jen's jealousy, I had never sparked much of a reaction from anyone. Why now with this boy? I had no time to try to make it out. His focus quickly turned to my passenger. The immediate fierce glare in his direction radiated with an intensity that was almost frightening. James sat virtually motionless on the seat in front of me—his arms crossed in front of him, his posture both astute and strong. His face held no reaction to the glares before him. William's expression seemed to change from concern to aggravation as he immediately shifted the boat in the opposite direction. He glared at us over his shoulder as the boat now moved against the current.

Then in one swift motion, as quickly as it had come upon us, the boat sped away. I remained speechless and was unable to draw my eyes from the boat until all that was left was a speck upon the horizon. He had once again vanished. The next few minutes that passed after his hurried departure seemed like hours. I luckily mustered up enough composure to kick the decrepit motor back into gear and turned the boat back toward the Inlet Joy. James remained in the seat in front of me with his back still turned so I was unable to read his expression. I thought it odd that my friend would remain silent after such an event. I wanted desperately to know what he was thinking. At one point, he turned to face me. His eyes refused to meet mine, and he opened his mouth as if to speak. No words were uttered, and he quickly turned away once again.

As we rounded the final bend, I slowed. James uneasily shifted without meeting my eyes. His courage seemed to rise as he moved to the seat next to me. His hand covered mine as he took hold of the steering shaft. I quickly removed my hand from under his, relinquishing control of the boat.

"So, are you going to tell me what that was about out there?

"What?" I pretended not to hear him in a sad attempt to gather my scattered thoughts.

"Out there. It appears things have been more eventful here than you've been letting on."

"Huh? Oh—that guy. Yeah. That was odd—wasn't it? He must have mistaken us for someone else." James didn't fall for it.

"Yeah, I don't think so. William looked like he was going to rip my head off out there for being with you."

"William? You know him?" I was dumbstruck!

"Actually, that was exactly the question I had for you." He raised an eyebrow and an odd look of jealousy spread across his face.

"No, not really." I fumbled nervously with the zipper on my jacket. "I only met him a few days ago." I confessed truthfully.

"You really don't recognize him?" The corners of his mouth curled up in disbelief.

"No. Should I?" I said absentmindedly biting my lower lip.

"That was William Avery. I'm sure you've seen him around the creek before." I nodded hesitantly. "He's a strange dude to say the least. His parents were killed in a boating accident about eight years ago. I think he had a sister that was killed as well." My heart ached at this revelation.

"That's awful!" I said under my breath suddenly feeling a bit faint. "What happened?"

"I don't know. We were so young at the time…all I've ever heard are rumors. The whole thing kind of messed him up I think."

"How do you know all of this?"

"Everyone around here does. It made all of the papers at the time—some type of explosion I think. William went to Conway High for a few months last year. We never officially met—he kind of stayed to himself. Like I said, he's a pretty weird dude. But even with all of that, it doesn't explain his reaction back there. "

"I have no idea. Honestly. Strange wasn't it!"

"He just seemed like he knew you that's all. Well, actually he looked like I had taken something that belonged to him, and he was trying to decide if he should come and get it back." My heart skipped a beat—maybe two.

"That's insane talk," I muttered. I think the idea of someone belonging to someone else only still lives in classical literature."

"I don't know about that. If you belonged to me, and someone else had you, I would come get you." James' tone remained casual, but I could see the seriousness in his eyes.

"Ok, well—he doesn't even know me. Who knows, maybe the guy was just having a bad day."

"Maybe so. He isn't known for being the friendliest person in the world to begin with, but that seemed a bit extreme, even for his standards."

"So how do you know of him?"

"I don't know much about him really, but it caused quite a stir when he first arrived at school. The girls all went crazy over him, but he hardly even spoke to anyone. I heard he transferred to Conway High from Socastee High last year. Not sure why exactly. He *was* a senior but must have dropped out or something because no one has seen him around for a while."

"But Conway is a pretty good distance from here."

"Yeah. Rumor is that he has been through quite a few schools. Didn't seem to be adjusting at Conway High either."

"He didn't make any friends?"

"None that I can recall. Pretty sad since his parents were killed and all." My heart instantly grew heavy in my chest. He was orphaned. "Of course, it is hard to feel too bad for the guy because every girl in the school flipped over him, but he rarely so much as spoke to any of them."

"Did he date anyone?"

"Not a one. Believe me, in a school as small as ours, if he had gone out with anyone it would have been all the gossip." My mind was racing. I wanted to ask more questions but decided that James had been through enough interrogation for one afternoon. I would have to learn more on my own.

I dropped my speed as we approached our destination and carefully nudged the boat along the side of the floating dock. James leapt to help, swiftly moving to the front of the boat to help ease the docking. My face turned red with embarrassment as I overshot the pier and circled around for another try. James was snickering as he turned to see my now blushed and frustrated face. He joined me in the rear of the craft.

"You know Margo, you are kind of cute when you're flustered. Here, let me help." He sat next to me taking charge of the steering.

"I can do it you know." I willingly handed it over and moved to take his place at the front of the boat. James turned the craft, this time moving against the current and easily lined it up against the old wooden planks and seaweed coated buoys that lined the dock.

"The key is to come in *against* the current. If you turn off the motor right as you are coming up to it, you should be able to glide up. The current should slow your speed enough to just coast in." I flashed a thin, tight smile in his direction.

"You knew that already didn't you?" He said rolling his eyes. I laughed, then reached to tie up the bow of the boat to the weathered bracket along the edge of the plank.

"Yes. Just out of practice I guess." More like my mind was preoccupied. I lifted the lifejackets out of the hull and passed them to James, who was already standing on the dock.

"Ah, I should have remembered there is nothing around here that is new to you—nothing that I could teach you that you don't already know." He reached out his hand to help me out. I took it as he wrapped his arms around my waist and hoisted me up. To an observer, the gesture would have appeared innocent enough, but James held on just a little too long—a little too tightly to simply be offering assistance. I had grown accustomed to his style of affection. What others would see as mere southern chivalry, I knew had another motive. James did not put his feelings for me into words, but I knew this was his way of wanting to elevate our friendship to the next level. What he sought to alter, I struggled to keep constant. I thought everything that existed between us was perfect just as it was.

"Actually, there is something that you could teach me." I said pulling away from him. I touched the camera suspended around his neck.

"Photography?" His face lit up as he suddenly picked up his camera and playfully snapped a few pictures of me. I buried my face in my hands.

"Come on! Don't be so stubborn!" he coaxed. I laughed and began making random silly faces for the camera. James was enjoying himself so much that I continued to play along and made some sad attempt at a sexy model pose.

"Ok Margo, now that's just sad. You're going to have to do better than that if we are ever going to get you in the *Sport's Illustrated Swimsuit Edition*." I stuck my tongue out at him and grabbed his camera.

"Alright tough guy! Your turn!" I snapped a few pictures of him laughing before his expression suddenly changed and he swiped the camera back. I relinquished it willingly, and we retreated to the upper pier. He leaned into the side rail and began to carefully focus the lens as he lined up a shot of marsh.

"The key is to view your subject in a way that no one has ever seen it before—to show a side or emotion in the subject that others may miss." I could hear the passion in his voice. I looked over the inlet trying to see what James saw through his lenses—the gentle ripples in the water, the changing colors of the marsh reeds as they swayed in the breeze, the tiny intricate tunnels of the fiddler crabs throughout the pluff mud. There weren't words that could describe its beauty. I didn't notice as James had once again shifted his camera in my direction, but this time I didn't protest as he captured the real me.

The late afternoon sun's rays shimmered across the inlet water. James peered over the top of the book he was reading across from me in the hammock. "Well, I don't know about you, but I am starving. Do you have time to grab a bite before I have to head back?"

"That would be great actually. Why don't we walk to the pier and grab a couple of burgers at Sam's Corner?"

"You took the words right out of my mouth darlin'. Maybe I can also convince you to play a few games of pool with me." I actually tried to avoid any game that required any sort of coordination, but if it meant more time with James then I would just have to try to be a good sport. I took a quick glance at my reflection in the water and found my appearance unacceptable. "Do you mind if I change and freshen up a bit before we go?"

"Sure. I'll meet you out on the beach in thirty minutes."

"Perfect!" I smiled and practically ran towards the house to change. I didn't look back, but I was confident James remained on the dock until I had closed the door behind me.

He was waiting on the beach just beyond the dunes as promised. James had showered and changed his t-shirt and had concealed his newly sun burned forehead with a ball cap. I thought he looked quite handsome. It was the nicest part of the day—the time of day when the sun hovered just above the horizon. A purple haze swirled among the clouds as the sun prepared to set for the day. It was the perfect time for a walk along the beach. He smiled as he saw me crossing over the walkway and eagerly came to join me.

"You look beautiful," he said, but I only shook my head. Earlier, I had quickly pulled on a thin gray sweater, some faded jeans that I had rolled to midcalf, and had tried to run a brush through my hair. I was anything but beautiful.

We walked side by side at the water's edge just as we did when we were kids. The pier was a little over a mile away. We talked endlessly along the way. No subjects were ever off limits. I loved these times with James. Whenever we were together it was just like we were kids again. But even as we rattled on about everything from current events to the weather, I couldn't knock the feel that someone was watching me. I found myself glancing over my shoulder every few minutes or eyeing the dunes cautiously. I even kept a close eye on the water's edge, afraid of what, I had no idea. I felt silly for allowing this sort of paranoia to distract me from my time with James, but it was unavoidable. William had warned me that the ocean wasn't safe for me. Finally, James brought it to my attention.

"Margo, are you okay?" You seem distracted—like you have been in another world all afternoon." There had never been any secrets between us. I wanted someone to confide in, and I knew that he was the one person in the world who would never judge me. Even with this knowledge it was still hard to open up. I took a deep breath and decided to take the plunge.

"James, I know this is going to sound like I am losing my marbles, but I guess I need to tell someone."

"You know you can tell me anything."

"Well, the night I first arrived, I couldn't sleep. It was late and I was looking out over the inlet. Anyway, I saw something out on the dock— something that looked human, but it didn't move like a human, and its eyes reflected the moonlight like some sort of animal. I know—I sound insane. Maybe I even dreamt it all up, but I guess I have just been a bit paranoid since then. I am sure it was nothing, but it seemed real. You think I am crazy now, don't you?" He smiled.

"Of course not! I'm sure there is a perfect explanation for what you saw. Actually, since the beginning of time everyone from seamen to scholars have claimed to see creatures among the oceans. Driftwood would often be mistaken as sea monsters, and even the manatee was thought to be a mermaid. The water seems to have a way to play tricks on the eyes down here."

I wanted to argue that what I saw was different. I had not seen a piece of driftwood, nor was there a manatee lurking on my dock at night. I could *not* rule out that whatever I had seen was not a monster. I was, however, intrigued with the mermaid idea. I played with that idea for a moment before dismissing it. Despite the dark night, I think I would have noticed a large tail diving into the water. Mermaids and monsters were the creatures that filled childhood storybooks, not the everyday world, and certainly not the South Carolina coastline. Even when I saw something in the water as a child I had not thought of the creature as a mermaid. Whatever it was, had remained in my memory as a monster. Mermaids, in my mind, brought thoughts of beauty. This creature had only brought with it fear—evil. I decided that there was no possible way that James could understand what I had seen unless he had been there.

"I'm sure you are right, James. I'm just being hypersensitive. I don't know why I am being so paranoid." I quickly changed the subject. I was relieved that James did not revisit it or bring it up for the remainder of our walk.

The sun had finally fallen just beyond the clouds when we neared the pier, but the sky remained bright enough to light the narrow path that led from the beach to the nearby shops and restaurants. Right across from the Garden City Pier was a quaint burger joint that had been there well before I was born. Sam's Corner sat next to the small beach stores that aligned the drive. There was an ice cream shop, a pizza parlor, several souvenir shops, a firework store, and a beach mart that carried everything from groceries to fishing tackle. Garden City had so far escaped the "tourist traps" with most of the stores still owned and run by locals. Over the years, I'd often wandered in and out of these stores on rainy afternoons always buying very little but enjoying the trinkets and baubles. Occasionally, my father would send me to the Beach Mart to pick up something that we had forgotten to pack or grab a little extra bait for his fishing trip. I always enjoyed the outing and volunteered whenever possible. It was called "the corner" by the locals. Not a very original name, but I suppose it was called that because the most notorious establishment of the area was Sam's Corner. James and I had been to the small diner together many times before, usually to stop in for a Coke after one of our early morning walks. Almost as a tradition we would lean on the old metal rails outside that lined Waccamaw drive to watch the waves rolling in or secretly make fun of the tourists darting about—but not today.

James picked a quiet booth in the back. When I was situated, he headed up to the counter to order for the two of us. I watched him up at the counter as he waited. He had grown up so much over the last few years, and yet, I had barely noticed. His hair had gotten darker and his features more chiseled, but I couldn't describe exactly what had changed the most about him, he seemed, well, more like a "man" than a boy, even past his years. He turned and smiled at me then returned to the man in line beside him who he had struck up a conversation. He was not traditionally handsome, but his confidence and humor filled any gaps that may have been lacking. He returned to our table shortly with our burgers, mine with no onions and extra pickles, his with chili and cheese.

"Looks perfect! Thank you," I said removing my food off of the tray and leaning back in the booth. "I always wonder if I should order something different, but once I find something that I really like, anything else seems to disappoint me. Maybe one day I will surprise you and become a vegetarian," James laughed.

"I know I should have asked you what you wanted first, but I think I have your taste buds figured out by now. The rest of you, however, remains a mystery."

"I think you know me pretty well—there isn't much to figure out I am afraid."

"On the contrary, at this point, nothing that you could do would surprise me. I wish that I could say that I've given up trying to figure you out. But the truth is, I spend more time than I care to admit still trying to unravel what is going on in that head of yours." I laughed.

"I know. And that's what makes it so much fun. True?" I shot him an innocent flirty smile.

"Yeah, yeah. You gotta stop doing that; my heart may not be able to recover." He put his hands to his chest as if he were having a heart attack.

"I think there is little chance of that." I threw a fry in his direction. "I couldn't get away with that stuff with you if I tried. You are too perceptive, and I am *too* bad at it."

"You? Bad at flirting? Seriously Marguerite Westly, you have no idea what you do to the male population just by walking into a room."

"Ok. That is so *not* true, and even if there was anyone interested, my best friend would just run them off." I took a sloppy bite of burger.

"Yes. You do have a point there. My time with you is limited enough as it is. I can't imagine also having to share it with some other guy. Besides, no one would ever be good enough for you in my book. I would have to run him off…for your benefit of course."

"Oh, of course," I admitted flatly. "You are forgetting the fact that someone would actually have to "put up" with me first. I can be quite difficult you know."

"Oh I know, God help the man who actually does falls in love with you!"

I hurled another fry in his direction. "Gee thanks, Rhett Butler!"

"Huh?" James looked confused.

"You stole that line from *Gone with the Wind*."

"No way! I've never even read that! That one is all me!" He hurled a fry back in my direction playfully. I ducked, and the fry went soaring onto the table directly behind us—narrowly missing an older lady who turned around and gave us a dirty look. We smiled innocently, unsuccessfully trying to conceal our giggles.

James leaned across the table almost in a whisper as not to disrupt the lady behind us again. "Well ok—Scarlett! I am quite certain that beautiful women were put on this earth just to torture guys like me. You just know you should stay away, but no matter how hard you try, you just can't." He pretended to sigh dramatically. I rolled my eyes at him.

"It goes both ways." I assured him, but this time, I was thinking of William, and how in just one day my world had completely been turned upside down.

"It's not the same, my dear, not the same." I wanted to argue with him, but I decided against it and let his comment go. I knew that this one was an argument that I couldn't win.

The pool hall was virtually deserted—much to my relief. I needed as little witnesses as possible if I were to play any game. There was a rather portly older man with shaggy gray hair and a round prickly face who appeared to be running the place and a middle-aged couple off to one corner nursing cups of coffee. James immediately led me to the pool tables closest to the jukebox and passed me a pool stick before feeding several quarters into the table. I picked up the blue chalk and rubbed it on the well-worn tip. In truth I was kind of unsure what actual function the blue chalk served but followed along to be a good sport.

James flipped through the songs on the jukebox before making a selection. He then turned to me with a smile and held up another quarter. "Any requests darlin'?" I made a quick inventory in my mind of all of the recent popular music, mostly lame stuff I had no desire to pollute the air by playing. I liked a wide variety of music, and James had excellent taste, so I was certain that anything he would chose would be fine.

"Anything is good with me." I smiled as I loaded the balls up on the table and placed them into the rack. "You pick."

"Alright, I will pick a few but you have to come up with at least one request." James again flipped through the song selections several times before loading several more selections into the jukebox. "Ok. Your turn to pick something."

I walked over to the jukebox as James rearranged the ball I had put in the rack. I caught him smiling to himself. I was sure it was because I had put them in incorrectly, but James was too much of a gentleman to point this out. I snickered to myself as I caught him racking and lining up the balls with painful accuracy. He was nothing if not thorough. I smiled as I watched him set up for his first shot, taking more care with his first shot than usual with a friendly game of pool. This side of James always cracked me up. He was the type of guy that wanted to be sure he completed every task correctly and by the book. I also was aware that this was also done in part as his way to impress me. Just to aggravate him a bit, I purposely ignored his first three shots. All three solid colored balls landed perfectly in the table pockets, as I fidgeted at the jukebox still unsure of my song selection. I finally settled on an all-time favorite as I turned back to the table just in time for James to narrowly miss his fourth shot. His face reddened and his jaw hardened. I knew exactly what he was thinking. *"Great! And she misses my first three shots I nailed!"*

James' music selections were primarily beach music. I smiled as *"Sitting on The Dock of the Bay"* echoed through the empty pool hall, reminding me of all of those many nights we spent together as he taught me to shag on his back porch deck.

"Alright, your shot beautiful."

I walked around the table trying to pick out an easy striped ball to pick off. A loud rumble suddenly grabbed my attention as it echoed through the pool hall. I turned to see a large familiar black truck pull up to the curb just outside. I was sure its tires were probably larger than my entire Jeep. A girl stepped out of the passenger seat. I instantly knew her as the girl from that day outside of the Beach Mart. She was even more beautiful than I remembered. Her long dark curls ran the entire length of her soft grey sweater, and her black jeans fit perfectly into a sleek pair of ankle boots. Her skin radiated with an uncommon glow that made it nearly impossible *not* to look at her. Her beauty wasn't like Jen's at all but a subtle beauty that seemed to require little effort.

Next a tall blonde guy effortlessly glided out of the back of the pickup. His golden curls hung loosely just above his chiseled jawline, and a thin expensive looking V-neck sweater hugged his muscles, giving him the appearance of a male runway model. A stocky dark-haired guy exited the back simultaneously. He was every bit as graceful as his friend, but his frame was so large that as his feet hit the pavement, I was surprised that the road remained intact beneath his feet. I tried to draw my attention back to James, but it was impossible to look away from them. The driver's door opened, and the shaved-headed one leapt out of the driver's seat. He carried the same fierce expression as the first time I saw him. The others seemed to be joking around with each other, but the driver remained rigid, as if he were watching out for something.

James moaned. "Great. Looks like the locals are here," he said, edging closer to me.

"You know them?" I questioned, still trying to pull my eyes off of the locals.

"No. Not exactly. But I know plenty *of* them for sure. I've seen them hanging out around here for the last few years. They surf the pier territory, so I prefer to stay further down the coast when I surf. Not the friendliest group, that's for sure! They all go to Socastee High, except for the guy with the shaved head. I think he graduated last year."

"Oh." It was all that I had time to mutter before the door swung open and the four entered the room. I looked away, but James eyed them closely as they situated themselves at a table in the back corner of the room. They neither acknowledged us nor looked in our direction as they floated past us. Their movements were fluid as the tides, and they seemed to carry a rare confidence.

"Alright, my dear. Looks like it's your shot." James flashed his signature smile in my direction. If he was the least bit uncomfortable with the extra energy that now permeated the room, it was impossible to tell. "Now try to take it easy on me. I would like to leave tonight with my manhood still intact."

I smiled. "Ah, so what are you saying? You are afraid you may get beaten by a girl?" I tried not to look over at them, focusing instead on the game that I had very little actual interest in playing.

"Exactly."

"Oh, I think you are *more* than safe when it comes to this one. You know I stink at pool."

"On the contrary, you've never been able to stink at anything you have ever tried to do—despite your most valiant efforts." My friend was unlike any other high school boy I had ever met. Who else would use words like *"contrary"* and *"valiant"* in the same sentence? His expressive vocabulary was one of the many things that were endearing to me. We spoke the same language.

I clumsily lined up for my first shot and was able to sink an easy ball in the corner pocket. James cheered, and my confidence grew leaps and bounds. I couldn't help but notice the four sets of eyes watching me from across the room. My heart began to beat faster. "See, I told you I'd be eating humble pie by the end of the night," he groaned. I rolled my eyes and located my next shot. My target should have been equally as simple, but the cue ball hit much lower than I was expecting sending my ball at a much sharper angle than I was aiming. The ball easily sailed past the pocket.

"Almost, darlin'!" He said as he crossed around the table and took my pool stick from me. James easily sunk his next two shots. On his third shot, he purposely overlooked an easy shot to attempt a super hard one near the far right pocket. The blood rushed to his freckled face as the cue ball cut to the left.

"Oops. Looks like you missed that one," I teased as he looked up across the table to signal to me that it was my turn. I loved this side of James. His competitive edge always made me laugh. There was no one on this earth that tried harder at everything than James.

I looked over at the locals for the first time since they had entered the pool-hall, finding four pairs of eyes watching me. The blonde was flirtatiously cutting his eyes at me; the stocky one stared at me with a friendly grin that stretched from ear to ear, while the shaved-haired one and the girl both looked at me as if they could rip my head off at any second. *"What a fun bunch!"* I thought suddenly wishing I had talked James into skipping the pool-hall. I leaned awkwardly across the table and missed my shot, also sinking the cue ball into the side pocket and ending our game.

"Alright Margo. I think you let me win that one."

"James, you should know that I have never *let* you win anything in your entire life. I told you. I just stink at pool."

"Nah. You just need to work on your form a bit. That's all. You will be beating me in no time. Up for another game?"

"Um, actually I thought maybe you should be heading back to Conway before it gets any later?"

"Nonsense! I have time for one more game at least!"

The "locals" racked up a game across the room. The blonde boy and muscled one joked amicably, occasionally looking across the room at us, while the girl and the shaved-headed one now neither smiled nor looked in our direction. I was relieved that the pair was no longer staring at me. "Alright, I am up for one more game." I agreed, as I was in no hurry for James to leave. A look of embarrassment flashed across James' already flushed cheeks as he dug into his pockets for more change.

"Huh? This is so strange. I know that I put a handful of quarters in my pocket before we left. I pulled out the five dollars I had stuffed into my shorts before we left the house.

"Oh, here. I have some money." I held out the bill, but he refused.

"No way are you paying for anything when you're with me. I have money." He pulled out several loose dollar bills from his wallet and located a change machine in the corner.

I noticed as James passed in front of me that the blonde haired local boy was now leaning on the bar with the gray haired man who ran the place. The beautiful blonde boy caught me looking over at him. He boldly winked at me, and a wide grinned smile spread across his smooth tan face. I quickly looked away with as little expression as possible, but I felt my cheeks flush. I knew his type all too well. He was evidently like Blake, expecting girls to swoon over him. One could hardly blame him—they were all unnaturally beautiful. Maybe it was something in the water here?

James appeared frustrated as he strode from the change machine to the counter. "Romeo" nodded as he walked by holding the two drinks the manager had just passed to him. I was standing at the jukebox mindlessly flipping through the vast array of tunes when James returned. His frustration had turned to anger, but James always seemed to have a tactful way for keeping his cool. "Apparently the change machine is broken, and the *manager* says he doesn't give change. I was going to run down to the arcade and get some. Do you want to come with me?"

"No, you go ahead. I'm fine here. Maybe I will have decided on some songs by the time you make it back."

"Are you sure?" James was uneasy. I could sense a protest coming so I tried to sound as assured as possible.

"Absolutely. I'll be right here." James nodded, and walked casually to the door. I knew that he wanted to make it back as quickly as possible. Since the place was deserted except for the 'locals" and manager, I hoped he would hurry back soon as well. The door barely closed behind him when I looked up to find the blonde boy already at my side holding out a drink. I was amazed that he was able to get over to me so fast.

"No thank you." I politely replied turning back to the jukebox.

"I think I must disagree with your friend." His voice was as smooth as warm butter.

"Excuse me?"

"About your form. I think it is quite nice actually." My face flushed. He eyed me from top to bottom in one purposeful stare. His meaning was quite clear by the sheer inflection of his velvet voice. I looked away, confident that my face was every shade of red imaginable. He held out the drink again, but this time I didn't reply. I shook my head, trying to hide my discomfort.

"Come on. It is just a Coke!" When he smiled his entire face was luminous. He beamed confidence.

"Thank you, but I'm not thirsty." I heard my voice crack, and my face flushed again.

"Are you sure?" He asked as his smile widened even further. As soon as the words escaped his mouth, I realized that I was indeed thirsty. I felt hot, very hot, and my mouth was so dry that I could barely swallow. Odd. I had not even realized that it was warm in here. He only smiled and once again stretched out his lean muscular arm. "I promise it won't kill you." His words were as smooth as velvet. I accepted the Coke and instantly took a much bigger gulp than I had intended. He laughed aloud. I turned to see the muscular one was laughing from across the room. The other pair did not smile but glared rudely at me.

"Thank you." I replied dryly. "I guess I *was* thirsty."

"I thought you might be." I turned away and began once again flipping through the jukebox.

"You know. I know it's none of my business, but he is all wrong for you." His lips now pressed firmly together curled up at the edges. I looked up at him, still confused at the very demeanor of this stranger. I'd never come across someone so brazen in my entire life!

"You are right. It *is* none of your business. And we are just friends— old friends actually."

"I didn't mean the red haired boy. I was referring to William."

I felt like I had been hit by a bullet. I was quite sure that my shock shone clear across my face. "You must have me confused with someone else," I mumbled. He studied my face curiously.

"William Avery?" He asked, suddenly quite intrigued. It was the second time I had heard the name in one day, first from James, and now from this guy. How ironic that the name was now associated with the very same face that consumed my thoughts.

"You are mistaken. I hardly know him."

"Really?" He seemed amused by my response. "I can see that you are sincere. I must admit that I am quite astonished."

"Why is that?"

"Perhaps you could enlighten me then, on why someone you have met only once, someone who has never had an interest in anyone that I am aware of, has taken such an interest where you are concerned?" My heart raced faster in my chest.

"I don't have an answer for you. I've only just met him. You must have me confused with someone else."

"You *are* Marguerite Westly aren't you?" I turned to face him quite startled that he knew my name.

"I'm sorry. Have we met?" I searched his face again but was completely certain that I had never seen him before. His face, though not my type, was one that would have been impossible to forget. I tried to mask my discomfort with another large gulp of Coke.

"No, not exactly. I'm Kirby Winslet—one of the locals here. Anytime we get a new resident I know about it—especially if she is as beautiful as you."

"That still doesn't explain how you know my name." I chewed on my lower lip anxiously waiting James' return.

He chuckled. "We have our ways."

"We?"

"The local crew. We keep up with everything around here." I looked over his shoulder at the group—each member of the party with features more perfect than the other. It was impossible to say who was the most stunning. I had never felt as inadequate as I did at this moment. I was sure that in the entire history of the world, a more perfect group of people had not existed.

"Oh." My mind raced. In truth, I didn't know how to respond. I had too many questions.

"I'm making you uncomfortable. That is quite odd as I usually have quite the opposite effect on people. How strange." He seemed to be studying me now. Uncomfortable was an understatement! I felt a bit dizzy.

"No. I'm not uncomfortable. You aren't making me feel anything actually." I lied. I was surprised that my feet were still supporting me. He laughed.

"Alright princess, if you say so. William has threatened the very life of any one of us who so much as talk to you. Since William has never taken an interest in anyone before, that makes you interesting. As you can see, I'm unmoved by his threats. In fact, I am quite intrigued." I went numb. That must have been what I had seen that day outside of the Beach Mart! So they had been waiting for me and had left because of the altercation with William! He had threatened them! But what would they want with me, and why would William want them to stay away from me?

"I can assure you that there is nothing what-so-ever intriguing about me. You are mistaken. The boy that you speak of has only ever greeted me with disdain. Actually, I think he hates me, though I am not sure what I could have done to him?"

"Really?" Kirby laughed again. "Now I am even more intrigued." He said slyly. "Well, not all of the locals here behave in such a way. Please allow me to make it up to you this coming Saturday. Let me show you the ropes around here!"

"Actually, I know the area quite well. I have been coming here since I was a child."

"I am once again astonished. Alright, then allow me...*us*, to get to know you." He said motioning to the others across the room.

"I don't think so...."

"Come on! Come hang out with us! Just one night—since you appear to be one of *us* now—a local, I mean." I began to protest again. "I won't take "no" for an answer. Meet us on the beach down below the pier this Friday night—ten-thirty!" I didn't have a chance to respond. James opened the door to the pool hall and smiled in my direction before detecting my company. His smile faded, and the quarters slid from his hands to the floor. We both bent to our knees pick them up, but Kirby remained unmoved.

"Is everything okay?" He said to me as he retrieved the last quarters that had fallen around us.

"The only thing wrong is you monopolizing the most beautiful creature on the strand." Kirby's words smoldered as he held out his hand to help me off of the floor. As if in a daze, I took the offered hand. James looked bewildered. Kirby kissed my hand, just like in one of those old sappy black and white films.

"I will meet you at the pier Friday evening princess. I hope it won't be past your bedtime." I opened my mouth to protest, not just to the hour, but to the entire invitation, but I was too late. He had turned again to rejoin the others. I had no intention of meeting him anywhere!

"You want to tell me what that was all about?" James said when we were once again alone. His voice was calm and friendly as usual, but I could easily detect another emotion just beneath his cool surface. Was it anger, or hurt?

"Is everyone living here crazy?" I whispered, partially to myself.

"I don't know, but it looked to me like you've been making new friends."

"I have no idea what *that* was." I said, trying to calm my nerves enough to sound normal. "But I can assure you, they are no friends of mine." James held out one of the pool sticks; I went to take it realizing my hands were shaking a little.

"Um—if you don't mind, I think I've had enough pool for one night. I'm feeling a bit tired." James smiled.

"Actually, you took the words right out of my mouth." I felt his hand guiding the small of my back as we turned towards the door. "Let's go—*princess.*"

"Very funny," I said, as he escorted me out of the door. "But if you ever call me that again, I may kill you." He chuckled. I refused to look back, but I could feel the four pairs of eyes watching as the door closed behind us.

The walk back to the Inlet Joy was too quick, as I knew that when we returned, James would have to return to Conway. James suggested taking the sidewalk instead of the beach route. I could rarely remember us taking the sidewalk. I would have objected, but a storm front was moving in and the usually bright skyline was now covered in a thick cover of clouds. The dimly lit street lamps provided ample light, but the return trip proved awkward as we both were consumed with thought. He took my hand in his. Summer after summer things had remained the same; we both could feel the winds of change blowing in from all directions.

Upon arriving, he didn't come up, nor did he make any advancement to further extend our evening together. I wasn't sure if my disappointment streamed from the fact that James was leaving or the fear to be alone with my own thoughts. I think it was both. My mind ran rampant...of Kirby...of the locals...of William. But it was late. He was going to leave. He turned to me with a barely audible sigh. "I have to go." He didn't look at me. His eyes remained fixed upon the waterway. I wanted to say something to try to get him to stay, but I knew that any attempt to do so would be far too selfish.

"I know. Thanks for coming to hang out with me this weekend."

"There is no other place that I would rather be, darlin'." He turned to me with the same familiar smile that had warmed my heart since we were children.

"I wish that you didn't have to go. I'll be lonely here again without your company."

"Ah—and sadly, I am aware that you will survive somehow without me." He scooped me up into a bear hug, and held me for several seconds before planting me back on my feet.

"Survive? Sure. But hurry back when you can, okay? I'll miss you." He smiled again, this time with a strange hope in his eyes. I quickly added, "I mean, seriously, you seem to be the only friend I can drum up around here." He sighed.

"Just be careful about the friends that you *do* make." He looked out across the waterway again. "I mean, with the locals and all. I guess...I just don't want you trying to fit in where you don't belong."

"I think you know me well enough by now to know that the last thing I would ever do is try to fit in anywhere."

"Just whatever you do, don't get involved with those guys we ran across tonight. Okay?" He climbed into his Chevy Blazer and turned back to me for a response. I nodded as he shut the door and smiled back in my direction one final time before driving away. I watched until the red taillights faded out of sight.

The thought of James leaving resurrected the feelings of isolation that had crept over me during the last week. I wanted him to stay. As much as I thought I craved solitude, I couldn't ignore the fact that I equally sought companionship. And with that acknowledgement came the awareness that there was no other person whose company I enjoyed more than James. Despite this, it wasn't James' face that now consumed my every thought.

It was the perfect face of a stranger.

6

"I stand, and wait among the sea foam. I swim in my own tears—I sing without my voice, I do not reach for higher ground, because I have lapped in the churning water."

Marguerite Westley

The sleep that came was restless. I was dreaming again. In my dream, I was on the beach alone searching for something along the water's edge. With each wave that rolled onto the shoreline, I became more and more upset that I couldn't find what I was searching for. I called out frantically for assistance. But the shore was deserted. No one could hear my cries. I tore through the water in desperation splashing through the breaking waves and pushing aside the sea foam, but it could not be found. As I desperately pushed away the foam, there just beneath the water peered two glowing eyes such as one would see on a cat at night, but evil and ready to pounce like a snake. With tears streaming down my face, I tried to make it back to shore, but long fingers were wrapped tightly wound around my ankles, slowly pulling me deeper and deeper into the sea. I screamed out through the darkness, luckily waking myself up in the process. Wiping the sweat off of my brow, I pulled the disheveled covers back around me. I had dreams such as this over the years but never one so vivid. I sat up in bed and took a drink from the glass of water. The large numbers on the clock flashed 6:45 am. I was relieved when the filtered sunlight began to illuminate my room, to escape the dark dreams that had kept me restless throughout the night.

My stomach began to growl as the aroma of my grandmother's breakfast seeped under my door and permeated my tiny room. I grabbed my favorite blue flannelled robe from the foot of my bed and made my way into the main house. To say that my grandmother had been cooking was an understatement. The long table sat adorned with every type of breakfast food imaginable.

"Good morning." I said as I swiped a piece of sausage right off of the serving platter. It was no mystery that my grandmother went overboard with the cooking when she was either nervous or excited. "Are we expecting company or is all of this just for the two of us?"

"Morning, sweet pea." She looked over her shoulder and smiled as she flipped an oversized pancake. "No. No company. I just want to be sure you are taken care of properly."

"There is enough food here for an entire family. You do a perfect job taking care of me." I prepared a rather large plate of food taking a small helping of each dish to satisfy my grandmother. She looked over at my plate and smiled. I picked up the newspaper that was unfolded on the counter. The bold headlines on the front page immediately caught my attention.

Search Party Continues off the Coast of Pawley's Island for Two Missing Fishermen

My eyes quickly scanned the article. There really wasn't much information as the article was quite short on details. Two fishermen from North Carolina had charted a 32-foot Boston Whaler the previous morning, supposedly headed toward the reef just two miles off the coast in search of Spanish mackerel. When they had not returned by nightfall, the Coast Guard sent out a search party. The Whaler had been easily recovered near the reef, but there was no one aboard. So far neither fisherman had been recovered. The article continued with a brief interview of the distraught families of the men, but I could read no further. The thought of something happening to my own father brought tears to my eyes. I quickly pushed the paper across the table and forced down another bite of scrambled eggs.

"Tragic isn't it?" My grandmother said picking up the paper and taking another look at the headline.

"Awful," I said pushing my eggs around on my plate.

"It's the third disappearance we have had in the area this winter."

"The third disappearance?"

"The first was just before you arrived. A girl down in Surfside drowned early one morning. A storm blew up out of nowhere, and she was knocked overboard during the high seas. Luckily the other two of her friends somehow made it back safely, but the missing girl's body was never recovered." A shiver went down my spine as I remembered William's warning to me.

"Guess it is easy to forget the dangers out there." I murmured, still thinking of the missing girl.

"You must never forget, Marguerite. Promise me that you will put safety above everything else, stay in the inlet waters, and always keep a close check upon the weather. Even if there's the slightest chance of a storm, promise me you will never go out there."

"I promise you have nothing to worry about," I said, trying to convince her. But why did I now have an aching feeling that her concerns were justified? I looked over to the counter and saw that my school assignments for the week had arrived like clockwork. I realized that my morning plans to further explore the inlet would have to be postponed for schoolwork. I caught my grandmother watching me from across the room.

"I don't like you out there alone on the water."

"Are we seriously going to go down this route again?" I said, a bit more agitated than intended. "I will be super careful and promise not to go out without letting you know where I'm going and when I will return."

We spent the remainder of the early morning together cleaning up the kitchen. My grandmother rattled on about everything from her favorite television shows to her evening plans. "Oh, Marguerite! I almost forgot. Be sure you have tied the boat down well this afternoon. There are thunderstorms expected this evening, so make sure you bring the lifejackets and gas can into the storage room. After shopping, I'm going to Becky's house for bridge with the ladies, so I will be out for the evening. I put leftovers aside in the fridge for you…or I can prepare you something before I go." I had forgotten it was bridge night. My grandmother went every week like clockwork.

"No. Leftovers sound great. I'm sure I will still be full from breakfast anyway."

"On second thought, maybe I should cancel my evening plans. I don't want to leave you alone with a storm on the horizon."

"Please go. There is no way I'm going to let you change your plans just to stay home and baby-sit me over a silly thunderstorm. Seriously, I'm just going to finish my schoolwork, then curl up with some reading I have been waiting to get to since before James arrived. I'm looking forward to it, and if it rains this evening, even better. There is something magical about reading with tapping rain against the window panes." She smiled.

"You are very much the romantic Marguerite! Only our heart and your head reside in two different worlds." I rolled my eyes and covered my face with a throw pillow. She laughed. "Alright, I should be home about 10:30 pm. Call me at Betty's if you need anything. I have her number in my address book on the counter."

"Got it. I'll be fine." I mumbled.

"Oh, and why don't you go ahead and get some of your schoolwork completed this morning? I would love to take an afternoon walk together, as the beach is the most beautiful just before a storm." I giggled.

"And you say that I am the romantic!" She smiled.

"Guess we were both cut from the same piece of cloth."

"A patchwork quilt." I laughed. "A piece in progress."

I spent the late morning trying to focus on my studies. It was hard to concentrate. William's face invaded the majority of my waking thoughts. His eyes haunted even my daydreams. I gravitated to the literature first. This semester's focus was on eighteenth century literature, one of my favorites. I was pretty sure that I was as knowledgeable on works and authors as the teacher of the class, maybe even more so. I quickly and eloquently answered the essays with little more than the expected generic answers and moved on. The next one was Calculus, a subject that I loathed, and I quickly made minced meat of the assigned work. I tackled the remainder of the subjects, knocking them out within the next hour. By mid-morning I had already completed the majority of the week's work.

A call from Lucy helped to break up the monotony of the day. She was the top reader in her class at school and excitedly read me three short books before passing the phone off to Caleb. I desperately missed her. A mixture of longing and guilt swept through me as I realized I wasn't there to share such a big milestone in her life. Caleb was cheerful and talkative. His team had won the last three games and had big plans to go to the playoffs. He had also begun dating a new girl that had recently moved to West Florence. Despite some relentless teasing on my part, he sounded extremely happy to talk to me. I promised to come home to see them soon.

In the late afternoon I joined my grandmother for her afternoon walk along the beach. It was much cooler along the shore than I was expecting. I had forgotten the cold front that was expected to start moving in throughout the day. Luckily I had thought enough this time to remember my gray windbreaker. With each step I remembered the countless walks we took together when I was a child. Life was so uncomplicated back then. I sighed. There was something magical about the beach just before the weather began to warm up for the spring. The usually cloudy water was translucent during these months. It rolled onto the strand as crystal clear as an undisturbed mountain stream.

"So you and James were able to get that old boat running after all! I am quite impressed! I never thought that old boat would make it back onto the water."

"Yes, James did all of the hard work, I just supplied the manual labor. Funny how the motor cranked up first thing the following morning after we had unsuccessfully tried to start it all day." I eyed her face wondering if she would admit that she was the one behind it. I had noticed a small amount of grease around her cuticles that morning but decided not to call attention to it.

"Sometimes I guess some things just fall into place like that." She winked at me.

"Especially when there is a good mechanic behind it." I said cutting my eyes in her direction. "Thank you." I added softly.

"You are welcome." She said squeezing my hand. I know you were glad to have James' help as well. He is a very smart young man."

"I couldn't agree more. He's great."

"Any budding romance between the two of you?" She teased.

I was sure my cheeks had turned red.

"Romance? Me? I don't think I am the romantic type." My grandmother laughed aloud.

"Marguerite, why do you think you always have your face buried in one of those books that you love so much?"

"Because I love to read?"

"That may be true dear, but one day you will know exactly what I am talking about. Some young man will sweep you off of your feet, and you will be smitten."

"Ok. Now just the word "smitten" sounds like something from a sappy 1920's black and white film. I have no desire to be "smitten" with *anyone*." Darn it! William's perfectly chiseled sun-kissed features crept into my mind. Was I *smitten*? I was completely put out with the idea that I could actually have a "crush" on some random guy that I barely knew. How illogical. How insensible. How completely unlike me! I was intrigued. That's all!

"Alright, I think I have teased you enough for one afternoon. Just be sure you keep your heart open when that time comes along. Love is one of God's greatest gifts to us. I just don't want your logic to override your heart."

I gulped before trying to find a response. "That is easy for you to say. You found grandpa."

"Yes, I loved your grandfather very much. He was a wonderful man and everything I could have prayed for in a husband. But he wasn't my first love."

She instantly had my full attention. "He wasn't?"

"No dear, he wasn't. Does that surprise you?"

"Yes, I guess so. I never really thought about...."

"About the fact that I was young once too?" She smiled, but I could see even after all of these years how difficult it was to talk about it.

"Who was he?" I asked curiously.

"He was a boy that lived just down the creek from us growing up. We were hopelessly in love; we planned to marry one day."

"What happened?"

"We were forbidden to be together."

"Forbidden? By whom?"

"Let's just say that part was complicated."

"I don't understand. If you loved each other...."

"We kept the relationship a secret for many years."

"Years?"

"Yes, but when we were discovered, everything fell apart."

"Oh."

"We were separated."

"But I am sure you tried to...."

"Sure. We tried everything that was in our power, but there were other...more important things that took priority."

"What could be more important than love?" I blurted out without thinking. I sighed as I realized she was indeed right; I was a hopeless romantic. She smiled, but I could see the tears still tucked in the corners of her eyes.

"And you say you aren't romantic. Sometimes love just finds you whether you want it to or not or sometimes it is right under your nose and you let it pass you by until it is completely out of reach. But sometimes, like in my case, love just isn't enough to overcome what the world throws at you. You will understand one day." Her soft smile faded. She shook her head as if to wash the memories from her mind. "Anyway, everything happens for a reason. I met your grandfather, and we had a very happy life together."

My courage began to rise. "But not here. Why did you let this place sit for so many years after Grandfather built it for you?"

"Marguerite, being here brought back too many memories for me. Some were very painful. I wanted to separate myself from the past, and I wanted to protect your grandfather from that."

"Oh." Suddenly so much made sense.

"It wasn't that I wouldn't have been happy here with your grandfather, I would have been happy with him anywhere, but the memories this place held already belonged to someone else." She wasn't talking about the house that my grandfather had built for her, she meant the inlet…the creek…the waters here held her memories—and her heart. Of course I wanted to know more. But she had given me more of herself than she had intended. Despite my curiosity, I respected her privacy enough not to push any further. She would tell me more when she was ready. Over the course of my life, I had spent many memorable walks with my grandmother, but none proved to be as unforgettable as this one.

After she left for the evening, I showered and slipped on a white tank top and my jeans, which were now permanently creased from being rolled just below my knee. I still rarely showed my arms, even around my grandmother, as the red patches had grown worse in the last few weeks. I grabbed my favorite patched quilt and writing tablet before heading down to the dock. The early evening was spent curled up in the hammock on the dock thinking and writing. It was a perfect setting as the sky was dark and billowy from a storm brewing in the east. The reeds of the salt marsh swayed in unison as the wind swept through the inlet. The air was alive with flocks of gulls, pelicans, and herons all rushing about searching cover.

Off in the distance an occasional thunder rumble could be heard, but the storm still seemed quite a distance away.

The gray pages of my writing tablet were well worn, as I took it everywhere, but before meeting William, it had been many months since I had written. Now material seemed to flow more easily. I winced realizing the source. In truth, I loved to write as much as I loved to read, but the words would rarely come without inspiration. How quickly things had changed! I was now flooded with thoughts and feelings.

The tide is rising—
These waters hold my heart, my soul, my love.
He is lost in the waves—He is drowning.
These currents hold my laughter, my soul, my memories.
They are consumed by the waves that devour
I search for them along the water's edge,
But they are consumed. Stolen without mercy—
Taken without remorse —
And still I stand, and wait among the sea foam.
I swim in my own tears—I sing without my voice,
I do not reach for higher ground,
Because I have lapped in the churning water.

I was satisfied with my poem, but less so with my penmanship. I despised my handwriting, but had long ago given up all hopes of improving it. I gently tore the page from the tablet and began to copy the words over again this time with extreme care. I had only recopied a few words back into my tablet when the wind suddenly picked up, sweeping under my shelter and ripping the page from my loose grip—not again! My page rose into the sky is if it had wings, swiftly traveling across the canal before becoming trapped in a bed of reeds quite a long distance away. I was barely able to see it wedged among the tall grasses.

Logically, I should have dismissed the page and tried to recreate the poem again on another page, but I have never been accused of logic. Within seconds I had slipped into the johnboat and was frantically trying to untie the nautical knots that held the ancient vessel in place. With one swift pull, the boat motor came to life, and I pushed off to retrieve my page.

The water was extremely rough. The glassy surface of the previous afternoon had been replaced by a mixture of strong winds and swift currents that bounced the small boat in all directions. I was too determined to entertain fear, as I could still see the page flapping against the reeds in the distance. The tide was quite low. I was concerned that I wouldn't be able to get to it through the maze of canals and sandbars, but I somehow managed to maneuver the boat through the labyrinth of marsh grass. I reduced the speed to an idle as I pulled just ten feet away from where the page hung, and gently ran the boat right upon the oyster shell that covered almost the entire muddy creek bed.

I slipped my bare feet into the old large pair of men's boots added to the bow earlier for shell hunting. The oyster shells crunched as I stepped out with caution toward the bank of reeds. But as I neared, the wind shifted, sending my work once again into the air, this time in the direction of the waterway. I watched helplessly as the paper tumbled through the rough winds, finally dropping into the rough waves and disappearing into the clashing water.

Thunder rumbled again, this time much closer, signaling that the storm was blowing in quicker than I had anticipated. I needed to get to shelter soon, but as I turned back to the boat, my right boot plunged deep into the pluff mud. I struggled in vain to pull it out, but as I did, my left boot lurched even deeper into the marsh bank. Panic began to set in as I sunk deeper, the mud now coming up to my thighs, covering and seeping into the interior of the boots, as well completely encasing my feet. I was completely stuck. My heart pounded in my chest as I realized with each louder rumble that the storm was getting closer. The more I pulled to free myself, the deeper I descended into the mud.

I searched in all directions, but there were no other boats in sight. The waterway appeared to be abandoned. I brushed back the tears that had escaped the corners of my eyes and were now rolling slowly down my flustered cheeks. I had to find a way out! I pulled and struggled for quite some time as the sky continued to get darker. The clouds continued to swell, and I knew a massive storm was heading in my direction. I closed my eyes and prayed.

From a distance I could hear the gentle hum of a boat engine. A flicker of hope was ignited as my eyes scanned for signs of a rescue. With each passing second, the sound grew louder. At last, a small boat appeared on the horizon heading swiftly towards me. I knew the beautiful boat instantly. It was William.

As the boat neared, his eyes met mine. His expression was hard with no apparent concern, as he seem to calculate my current situation. His eyes shifted from me to my boat. It was now turned sideways and knocking against the oyster beds harder and harder with each passing swell. I stood there in my former white tank top afraid of my only options. Was my rescue worth the embarrassment of having to ask for help? I could see the headlines now, **Teen Drowns in Storm Trapped in the Mud Wearing a *White* Tank Top**.

"*Oh great,*" I thought to myself sarcastically, *"This is just how I want to be remembered!"* White—why in the heck did I pick the white one? The absurdity of the color choice made my situation borderline hysterical. How embarrassing! Neither option looked very promising, but the death option seemed at least less painful. If he stopped I would probably die of embarrassment anyway.

But it soon became quite evident that he wasn't going to stop. His jaw tightened, and he turned the boat away from the marshland that had now had me captive for quite some time. The boat and driver passed as if I did not exist. Tears began to run down my face uncontrollably. *Did he not see that I was in trouble? He did see me! I was sure of it!* He knew that I needed help, and yet, would not stop. I didn't even try to wipe the tears away. How stupid had I been to contemplate this boy as any form of hero!

Fatigue began to set in my legs, as I began to realize the gravity of the situation. My pale body was frozen and covered with goose bumps. Once again I shifted my weight onto my right leg trying uselessly to pull my left leg out of the mud. My efforts were futile as any exertion proved to only further the problem. A small sharp piece of oyster shell slid into my boot with the mud, and as I pulled uselessly, the piece slipped to the bottom of my foot slicing into my left foot as my weight came back down on it. I gasp in pain and with the realization that my predicament had gone from bad to worse. The sky seemed alive as the dark clouds were now moving in at an alarming pace, totally blocking out the sun.

But suddenly the boat that was now almost out of sight, abruptly spun around and began to make its way back toward my direction. The tiny boat grew larger and larger with each passing second, as I painfully fought once again to free myself. Was he actually coming for me this time, or would he ignore me again? I would not allow it! I would not give him the satisfaction of returning to me as he had left me, still stuck and helpless! I began shifting my legs and feet back and forth pulling them up a little at a time. But I had sunk too far down by this point, and my legs were beginning to shake with fatigue.

As his boat neared, this time I was certain that he was undeniably coming for me. A tear of joy ran down my face. He glided his boat up onto the oyster bed about five yards ahead, and tossed the anchor into the nearby shallows. My heart was beating so fast I was certain it would stop at any second.

"Digging for clams?" His words were playful, but his expression was as hard as ever. His eyes found mine briefly, but he did not smile despite his joke.

"Yes, but I think they got the upper hand." I smiled, still relieved that I was going to make it out of my predicament. My dignity would be lost, but at least I would escape without drowning.

"Are you hurt?" His voice sounded concerned, but his face remained as cold as stone.

"No." He slid into a pair of boots that had been resting in the bottom of his boat. His boots were more on the line of hiking boots but the laces had been removed. He leapt out of the boat with ease and paused a moment to look at me. Despite his hard expression, I couldn't help but notice that his eyes carried a genuine look of concern. My cheeks, arms, and forehead were streaked with a combination of fresh and dried mud. My hair had now escaped my earlier ponytail and was now blowing into my face, and my clothing appeared to be unsalvageable. My face was red with embarrassment.

The old oyster shells crunched under his weight. He was more beautiful than I had remembered, so stunning that even my dream could not recreate his perfection. I search my brain for something clever to say but I came up empty handed. I was speechless. "Are you strong enough to put your arms round my neck?" I nodded. "How long have you been out here?" he said. He positioned himself so that he too would not also get entrapped.

"Not long." I lied.

He looked at me doubtfully, "Grab hold around my neck. Hold on tight." He leaned into me, and I wound my arms around his toned golden neck. The intoxicating smell of his skin caused me to nearly lose my balance, but his arms instantly caught my waist to steady me. His hand was warm on the small of my back. A lightning bolt flashed across the sky just above us. "We need to get you home. The storm is almost here," he said looking over my shoulder into the dark sky. The loud roar of thunder broke the silence. He easily scooped me up into his arms. My arms were still hanging around his neck. It felt wonderful as my feet slid out of the muddy boots that were still submerged in the mud.

"Thank you," I said sheepishly as he carried me back to his boat and gently placed me on the bow. He looked down at me, his expression now not angry, but frustrated, then quickly turned away to pull in the boat anchor. I took this opportunity to quickly assess myself. I was coated from head to toe in mud. My humiliation was short lived as I noticed a red puddle quickly forming by my foot in the hull of the boat. My foot was injured far worse than I had originally thought. He must have read my expression as he was back at me side in an instant.

"You're hurt!" he said, his cold demeanor turning to concern.

"No, it's just a cut." I tried to reassure him. But he was unmoved. He carefully rolled the leg of my mud splattered jeans that had fallen loose earlier and gently rinsed my foot in the salt water. My body shivered as his skin touched mine. My feet tingled at the feel of the saltwater. It was the first time since I was a child that my feet had touched the inlet waters. When my foot was clean, he took off his white tank undershirt and easily ripped it into long strips of fabric. The beauty of his body was beyond words. His chest was tan, hard, and fit. He observed me looking at him; I looked away trying to hide my embarrassment.

Another flash of lightning crackled; he quickly eyed the skyline. His hands moved even more quickly as he wound the fabric tightly around my foot. I had no time to protest. A bolt of lightning popped so close this time that I gasped aloud, unsure if we had been hit. Instantly the sky opened up and the rain began to pour from the sky on us. He left me then, grabbing a rope from the rear of his boat and hurried over to mine, securing it behind his own.

"I'm fine, really." I shouted at him through the rain as I realized now what he was doing. "I can drive myself back." As I attempted to stand, my legs shaking from fatigue, collapsed from under me. I sat again feeling completely helpless. He didn't look up but finished securing my boat behind his.

"You aren't in any condition to tackle this sort of weather. If you're going to trying to kill yourself, it won't be on my watch. You shouldn't be out here alone in the first place. I would have left you there if I would have thought it would have scared some sense into you." I didn't respond and remained still as he finished tying my boat to his. I fought back the tears that had begun to well up in the corners of my eyes. *So he had contemplated leaving me out there—to teach me a lesson!* I winced at the thought. The cold drops of rain were now pelting my face. I shivered. He jumped into his boat and threw a thin blue button down shirt in my direction that had been thrown across his rear bench seat.

"Put this on!" he said. I went to shake my head, but the stern look glaring in my direction stopped me. I slipped my arms through the shirt and wrapped it around me. The wind was whipping all around us, and the surf was now coming in over the bow of the boat. "You can't sit up there." he insisted. "The surf is too rough." He pushed off the boat and jumped in beside me. He was right of course. I would get soaked by the waves in this kind of weather and bounced around relentlessly. He offered up his hand to help as I tried to move to the middle seat.

"No, I've got it," I said stubbornly, once again almost falling. I moved to the wooden bench seat in the middle of the boat trying to hide the pain in my foot. He shrugged, and what could almost be described as a grin swept across his face. William moved effortlessly to the rear of the small boat and in one motion slid on a light blue t-shirt tucked behind the seat. With one pull, the engine came to life, and we cut through the ever-brewing storm in the direction of the Inlet Joy.

The trip home would usually take only minutes, but as the storm intensified, he was forced again and again to reduce his speed to maneuver with my boat in tow behind. The surf pounded into the front of the boat, and with each new wave, the hull slapped down violently against the inlet water. The rain began bearing down harder and harder, becoming slightly painful as it hit upon my face. I pressed my chin against my chest for protection, but it was of little use. The lightning began popping closer and closer, and I was glad that he had insisted on me riding with him. His wooden boat was far safer in a lightning storm than my aluminum one.

William moved the bow of the boat from side to side trying to reduce the impact as the storm surged harder against the vessel. The surf swelled higher, blowing and beating against us. A large wave caught the front of the boat sending me off of my seat falling backwards. He seemed to anticipate this, as he leaned far enough to grab hold of my arm and pull me backwards onto the seat at his side. His arm now wrapped around my waist pulling me against him to shield me from the relentless elements. He body felt so warm against my cold, wet skin that I couldn't help but lean my face against his shoulder for shelter. He pulled me closer.

Through the wind and rain, I was still able to smell his warm salty, skin. I felt dizzy, intoxicated—wonderful. I knew that I should pull away from this beautiful stranger, but I was unable to. I pressed tighter against him without thinking. I refused to contemplate what was happening, afraid that it would be too much for my mind, or maybe my heart, to take.

"Looks like we might make it after all," he said. I could feel his eyes look down upon me through the rain. I looked up when the rumble of the motor slowed to an idle as we approached the Inlet Joy; the rain, still falling heavily from the sky, no longer stung as it hit my body. I reluctantly pulled away from him as we slowed next to the dock. He first pulled his boat alongside of the floating pier and shut off the engine. He released his arm, still tight around my waist and went to tie up the front of the boat. I located the rope in the back of the boat to also fasten it safely.

"I really don't know how to thank you. I don't know where I would be right now if you hadn't…hadn't turned around." I shouted towards him as another strike of lightning crackled across the sky. He didn't respond but paused long enough for our eyes to meet. His eyes looked tenderly upon me, but only for a moment before his jaw tightened once again. He leapt upon the dock and moved to help me out of the boat his eyes careful not to meet my face again.

It was at that moment that I remembered my grandmother and looked up anxiously at the blue house. Luckily she was still away and had no reason for worry. I was fortunate that she had gone out for the evening and would be oblivious to this whole event.

William finished tying his boat and was leading my boat around to the other side of the floating pier to secure it. The storm once again seemed to catch up with us as the rain began to beat down so hard that I could scarcely see in front of me. The lightning split through the sky. "Go! I know your grandmother must be worried." He shouted over the rumbling storm, pointing me towards the house. He did not look up at me as he continued securing the items within my boat.

"She isn't here actually. She is away for the evening. Let me get a towel for you."

"No. I'm fine. Go Marguerite!" he said firmly. Another very close bolt of lightning brought me back to reality. I would have to sort all of this out later. I turned and began to head towards the safety of the house. The distance from the dock to the house suddenly seemed greater than usual. My injury had been all but forgotten to me until that moment, but I was unable to put any pressure on my foot without extreme pain. The white shirt was still wrapped tightly around my foot now soaked with blood. I painfully limped towards the house, struggling to make it through the wet grass, all the while hoping that William was not watching me. I stumbled, and in an instant, he was at my side. I felt his hands slip around the small of my back, and in one swift motion he was cradling me in his arms again. My body tightened in protest.

"I'm here. I've got you." he said. Through the pelting rain, his eyes met mine as he looked down upon me now cradled in his arms. I felt helpless, nervous and wonderful.

"I thought you left." I said uncomfortably. "You've already done…you have *really* done too much for me already." He shook his head.

"You're shivering. I need to get you out of this weather." he said rushing me in his arms through the rest of the yard, my eyes fixated on his beautiful face. I looked away from him when I realized that the rain no longer fell upon my face. We had reached the breezeway under the Inlet Joy; I expected him to release me, but he carried me up the stairs to my bedroom. My heart raced as he held me in his arms. I barely noticed as my feet were slowly and gently lowered to the floor, his arms still wound tightly around my waist. I tried to steady my footing but realized my legs were now trembling.

"I wanted to see you—to tell you *'thank you'* for returning my book pages. I don't know how you recovered all of them." My words were soft, barely more than a whisper.

I looked up to find his eyes fixated on my own, his face once again now serious. He didn't look away from me, nor did he respond to my words. One arm traveled from my waist so that his hand could brush away the water still rolling down my cheeks. His hand moved up over my cheek to brush back the wet hair that had fallen onto my face, then moved gently to my chin. He cupped my face in his hand. I had stopped breathing altogether as his face moved closer to mine.

And then he slowly began to pull away from me. His face went suddenly stiff, cold. I stared at him blankly as my confusion turned to hurt. He turned towards the door. "No wait! Don't go! Not like this. What have I done? Why do you hate me so?" The words flew from my mouth before I was able to stop them. He stopped, but did not turn back to face me, his head facing downward.

"I don't hate you." His voice was stern. "I am sorry," he added quite unapologetic. "This isn't about you."

"Ok. Well, the least you could do is explain to me what this *is* about." I pleaded.

"I owe you nothing. You were in need of help—and I helped you. You shouldn't even be here. Go back where you came from Marguerite!" His words were like ice and stung harder than the coldest rain. I wanted to cry, but my tears were pushed away by my pride. If he wanted nothing further to do with me, than I would not try to stop him from leaving.

Within seconds he was out in the rain again darting across the lot in the direction of the dock. His stride was long and quick as he headed across the yard. He didn't look back as his boat disappeared through the pelting rain.

7

"The pure and simple truth is rarely pure and never simple."

Oscar Wilde

Reality eventually set in—at least as much as it ever would again. Whatever had just taken place between William and I had altered me permanently. My heart no longer felt as if it belonged to me. It now felt as if it had been stolen, torn from my chest by someone who wanted no part of it. Up until this point, I had only read about this kind of emotion, and now I realized that no written words could ever be able to describe the turmoil inside that plagued me like a curse.

I checked the clock and realized my grandmother should be returning anytime. A quick assessment of my appearance was shocking. I was covered in mud and wet from head to toe. How could I ever explain this to her? She would never let me out in the boat again if she knew what happened. I stumbled to get in the shower and to get myself together. My hands were still shaking, and my heart continued to pound so loudly in my chest that I was certain it was audible. Just a short time earlier I would have thought it impossible for anyone to have this type of effect on me.

I hardly recognized the girl staring back at me through the bathroom mirror. It was worse than expected. All the blood in my body rushed to my face in utter humiliation. I was horrified that he had seen me looking like this. I buried my face into my hands wishing this all to be another one of my nightmares. Surely, I thought myself logical enough, careful enough, not to lose my heart so carelessly. It had to be a dream, a horrible, wonderful dream.

Out of the corner or my eye, I caught a glimpse of his pale blue button down still clinging to my wet frame. I still wore his shirt, an undeniable reminder that William was as real as my feelings for him. I turned the shower on as hot as it would go. The steam filled the small shower stall. I rinsed my hands and forearms thoroughly before unbuttoning the shirt and carefully folding the wet garment as if it were my own most prized treasure. *Silly girl!* I thought, staring at the neatly folded shirt. I picked it up again and wadded it up, tossing it into the corner of the bathroom. I would refuse to allow myself to give into such ridiculous girly emotions.

As I had earlier expected, my mud splattered tank top was unsalvageable. I tossed it into the small trashcan in the corner, and then I remembered my injury. I had been so distracted I had hardly remembered the cut from the oyster shell in my boot. I sat on the edge of the wooden benched seat to inspect my wound.

I slowly unwound the bloodstained strips of fabric on my foot. I was sure that the gash I had seen earlier would require numerous stitches. But as I unwound the last bloody strip of fabric, I stared in disbelief at my foot. Earlier, William had carefully washed it free of all mud and dirt before applying the make-shift bandages. During that time I had clearly seen a sizable cut, no less than two inches in length. The pain had been severe, and the pool of blood in the bottom of his boat was proof of the seriousness of the injury. And yet, all that remained of my injury was a faint scar line where the wound had once been.

How was this possible? I studied the spot of the injury closely, gently pulling at the faint brown scar line. The wound appeared weeks old, not hours! My hands covered my mouth in disbelief, and my head began to spin so rapidly that I had to hold onto the bench for support. What could this mean? I thought back to how William gently rinsed the wound before wrapping it.

I picked up the blue button down, studying it more closely as if it would in some way reveal the mystery of the boy who had worn it. No such luck, just a common blue shirt. I folded it again, this time putting it over by the stack of clean towels.

I slipped out of the remainder of my clothes and into the hot shower, hoping the warm shower would help to clear my thoughts. The warm water felt divine on my tired muscles, but not even the steam could settle my rattled nerves. So many strange things had happened to me recently that nothing seemed out of the realm of possibilities anymore. Had William healed me? Over the course of my life, I had had many cuts and bruises, but none had ever healed like this. It had to be him! Was he magical? Maybe he wasn't even real. And then, through the steam I stared in disbelief at my body; the rash that had covered so much of my body was gone. My soul leaped! I was stunned! I barely had time to process the revelation, when I heard the sound of truck tires pulling into the drive; my grandmother was home.

I wrapped one towel around myself and the other around all of my things—to hide the evidence. I quickly mopped up any mud or blood around the shower stall with an extra towel and hurried to my room to slip on some comfortable clothes. I would sneak down later to rinse the muddy towels and blood stained cloths out, before hiding them in the washing machine. William's shirt, still wrapped in a dry towel, was quickly crammed under my bed. I had just finished slipping on a long-sleeved t-shirt and sweat pants, wrapping my hair up in a wet messy bun, when I heard the truck door shut downstairs. I grabbed a random book off of my dresser and rushed into the house grabbing an old quilt from the back of a chair and flopped onto the couch.

"That was quite a storm this afternoon!" My grandmother said as she opened the door. She wore a faded yellow rain coat and was carrying a large bag of groceries. "I was worried about you here alone. Bridge was completely out for the evening. And I was trying to make it back to you before dark, but the rain was so bad that we had to pull over and wait it out at the ice cream shop—you know the one out on Highway 17." I nodded.

"Need any help?" I asked leaning up to go help her with the groceries.

"No, no. This is all of it." She brushed back a piece of hair that had fallen out of her grey streaked ponytail. Even at her age, she was still beautiful.

I put down my book and nodded as my grandmother sat in the rocking chair beside me.

"It was an awful storm. I'm glad you made it back safely."

"I couldn't decide if we should try to fight the rain or wait it out."

"Well, if you had to wait it out, the ice cream shop wasn't a bad place to be." I tried to act relaxed and casual. I could picture my grandmother there with a large butter pecan ice cream piled in a waffle cone, while I was out in the worst thunderstorm I had ever experienced, stuck thigh deep in mud. I smiled.

"So how was your afternoon? Did you get very much reading done?"

I swallowed hard and tried to come up with an answer that wasn't a complete lie.

"A bit—but I mostly wrote poetry."

"You have so many fine talents dear. I can't wait to read it." I frowned.

"Sadly that won't be possible. I walked out to the dock before the storm hit, and a gust of wind carried my paper away." I was pleased to be able to tell at least part of the truth.

"Oh, I know that must have been disappointing. I hope you were able to rewrite it." She pulled a variety of fresh fruits and vegetables, as well as a few canned items out of one of the bags, and I began to help her put things away.

"No—not yet. Maybe I will try again tomorrow. Guess I just became frustrated when it was lost—I haven't had the heart to try again."

She sighed. "Well, I know it's not much consolation, but think of your poem as a lost love letter that was cast into the sea. I always thought it would be romantic to find a message in a bottle. I remember during the war hearing stories of sailors writing letters to their loved ones—casting them into the waves in hopes that someone would find them and they would one day be delivered.

"That is a pretty romantic notion. I wonder if any of the messages were ever delivered."

"On occasion, perhaps, but most probably still belong to the wonders of the sea. Some seamen would actually write letters and poems to the sea itself, in hopes of finding safe passage and good favor with the creatures living there." Her words struck a chord with me, and suddenly she had my full attention.

"Did you say creatures? Like what?" My voice cracked—I hope she didn't take notice of my uneasiness. I turned away stocking another can of tomato paste into the pantry.

"Oh, for ages people have been writing accounts of creatures from the sea—mythology and folklore is full of stories." The word "creature" caught my attention. I stopped dead in my tracks and turned to face her.

"Creatures? Like mermaids?"

"Yes. Mermaids, water nymph, sprites or *sirens*."

"Sirens?"

"Well, they have been given many names, but throughout time, there have been many sightings and stories of human-looking creatures living in, and around, the sea."

"Yes, but, no one actually believes that stuff. I mean, except maybe kids reading fairytales. I mean, they would be pretty much hard to miss— the tail would sort of give them away." I suddenly wished that I had paid more attention when we were studying Greek Mythology in the fifth grade. It was never a favorite of mine, and I only vaguely remembered any stories about sirens.

"Actually in many stories they don't even have tails. In some accounts sirens have wings, and in others, feet just like you and I. And who says they have to just be female?"

"Mermen? Really?"

"You have to remember who is recording the stories. Sailors would much prefer to see a beautiful maiden—wouldn't you think? But that doesn't mean that men wouldn't exist."

"I guess I've never thought about it." Suddenly it was all that I could think about. What if there actually was such a creature.

"Well, the stories of sirens were often used to explain things."

"Like what?"

"Everything from storms to missing crew members." I was beyond intrigued.

"So they thought the siren had special powers?"

"Well, that part would vary too. Inhuman beauty was always the first to make the list. Sailors claimed to be completely captivated by their beauty and songs. But also there are claims of other powers as well such as: speed, strength, controlling the weather, and healing properties."

"Like being able to heal someone?"

"I really don't know all of the specifics, dear. And like I said, the folklore varies from story to story."

"Folklore, you say? Do you have any books on that kind of stuff?" I looked behind me to my grandmother's vast collection of books on the back wall. Surely there were some books on oceanic folklore in the collection. She paused for a moment, and in that brief second, I noticed her eyes briefly shift to a large old leather-bound book high on the top shelf. I was certain the book had been in that very spot for years, and yet, why did I notice it only now? Her eyes shifted away so quickly that most people would never have even noticed the glance in the first place.

"Um, I don't think so. Of course you are more than welcome to look through anything up there that you find interesting. Most of these books I haven't read in years." She followed behind me as I moved toward the shelf. "However, it is probably best that you go through them tomorrow. It is getting pretty late and I'm exhausted. I think you have done enough reading for one day, so it's best if we make an early night of it." She gently took my arm and seemed to usher me off to my bedroom, making small talk along the way. Odd. Was there something up there that she was keeping me from, perhaps something in a large leather-bound book? It was possible my suspicion was only in my mind, but the only way to be certain was to get my hands on the book.

Alone in my room, I unwrapped his pale blue shirt from the towel that I had stowed away earlier. Despite being slightly damp from the rain, it smelled of him. I foolishly unbuttoned the top buttons and slipped it over my head. I flung myself onto my bed burying my face deep in my pillow and curling up under the cool clean sheets.

The entire day had been some sort of mixture of heaven and hell, delight, pain and now mystery. It was too much. My heart still beat rapidly with both excitement and pain when I thought of the events of the day. I once again ran my fingers across the spot that had earlier been filleted open, but now was healed so tightly that even the small scar seemed to be disappearing. I lay down and closed my eyes. Nothing made sense anymore.

My grandmother's words echoed in my thoughts. Was it a siren that had come after me as a child? And if so, was it also a siren that had saved me? Is it possible that creatures from folklore existed? I had spent so many years trying to dismiss the occurrence when I should have been searching for answers. If they had once come after me, would they again? William had been quick to warn me about the dangers the ocean held for me. What could he know about what was out there? I wanted answers. I would wait until my grandmother went to sleep and sneak back to retrieve the book.

There had been a knock on my door at one point, and I had not answered it, pretending to be asleep with my book on my chest. The door had been slowly opened and quietly closed again as I lay immobile, my eyes tightly shut. I had assumed it had been my grandmother coming in to check on me and to tell me "goodnight." I waited impatiently. It was after 2 am when I crept rather noisily into the dark house. I was clearly no Sherlock Holmes. I tripped over the door jam and tumbled quite noisily onto the grey shagged carpet. I stumbled back to my feet and tried to regain my composure. Perfect. If that didn't wake her, then nothing would. I smirked to myself realizing that I was the worst thief ever. I scanned the room. At least her door was closed.

My original plan was to quietly retrieve the book, read it, and return it before morning. I had once again grossly overestimated my skills. I stood in silence rolling through a variety of possible excuses I could give my grandmother when she opened her bedroom door and discovered me creeping around in the darkness. But much to my surprise, as the minutes rolled slowly by, her door remained tightly shut. I proceeded cautiously, pulling a tiny flashlight out of my pocket and positioned the narrow beam in the direction that the book had been earlier. The spot now sat empty. I scanned the light around the shelf, carefully reading each of the familiar titles, but clearly the thick dusty book had been removed. Where had she moved the darn thing? Surely it had to be here somewhere. I continued to search the shelf until I was adequately certain that it was no longer there.

I crawled into bed confused and frustrated. But soon my mind drifted back to William. Even the mere thought of his perfect face made my heart beat faster in my chest. I hated the fact that he had that effect on me. I convinced myself to try to forget him, but logically I knew that would be impossible at this point. I had never felt so confused. I sighed, burying my face deep into my old feathered pillow. Two things were obvious. First, I *was* clearly the worst actress ever. My grandmother noticed that I had seen the book and had removed it before I could get the opportunity to come for it. And second, and undoubtedly more important, I now knew that there really was something that she was hiding from me, something that she didn't want me to know.

The answers were in the book.

The sun broke through the slats of the inexpensive vinyl blinds that covered the window of my room. I was anxious for the relief from the darkness that had mercilessly held me prisoner throughout the entire night. I had once again gotten very little sleep. I tossed and turned recounting every moment of the earlier evening and night. Who was William Avery? And why had he entered my world? I reluctantly began to open my eyes and took my first deep breath of the morning. The scent took my breath away, and once again, my mind was clouded with his smell. His scent still filled my senses. Maybe I was still dreaming. I pulled myself out of bed, and began untangling the sheets that had been twisted and balled up, as I tossed and turned over and over throughout the night. Had the previous evening been only a dream?

I couldn't erase the feel of his skin against my face or the way my blood rushed through my veins as he had pulled me tightly against his chest. His unforgettable scent stirred feelings inside of me that I could never imagined possible. Of all the boys I had even known, no one had even so much as turned my head in this way. A twinge of guilt spread through me as I thought of James. If I had ever cared for anyone in such a way, I had always assumed it would have been James.

I sleepily made my way over to the old mirror that hung above the oak dresser. My hair sprung out in all directions, proving that I have indeed been quite restless throughout the night. But that wasn't what captivated my attention. The pale blue button up still hanging from my shoulders proved that the events of the previous day had not been a dream. I gently ran my fingers down the buttons of the cotton shirt. It was well worn and soft against my tired body. My thoughts drifted to an image of William sliding into it and buttoning the shirt against his lean muscular frame. I lifted the edge, brought it to my nose and inhaled. The essence was not that of any type of cologne, but of the sweet smell of his skin, blended with only the most alluring elements of earth and the water and the sun. Intoxicating! Such a boy couldn't be captured in storybooks. All of the beloved gentlemen from my classical literature failed miserably in comparison to his godlike features. My mind could not create such perfection. Nor, was it even capable of describing him with mere words.

The night had been blissfully painful. My rare moments of sleep were even more disturbing, as I restlessly dreamed of his lips pressed gently against my own. My unconscious thought perfectly recounting his arm wrapped around my waist holding me tightly. This was the recollection that my conscious mind would not allow, and yet I could not avoid it each time my eyes closed ever so briefly. I dreamed of seeing him again, except this time his eyes looked softly and tenderly upon my face with no signs of cold glares that had been directed to me each time our paths crossed.

I felt confused, and though I tried not to admit it, I was hurt at the contempt that he constantly threw in my direction at every turn. I could not forget the coldness in his stare or the obvious reluctance to come to my aid in the first place. And yet, all I could think about was seeing him again. I had only known this boy for such a brief amount of time and was utterly mystified by my own feelings. Why should I remotely care what he thought of me? I had never in the past sought anyone's good opinion. How odd that I should start caring now. I was angry with myself to allow anyone to invade my thoughts in such a way.

I could not deny that there was something that linked us together. What was between us? I felt somehow strangely linked to someone that I barely even knew! As if our paths were destined to cross. I had sought nothing from him, expected nothing of him. He was beautiful for sure, but I had never before had my attention captivated by a face. I knew the answer. There was more to this boy than just a beautiful façade. Whatever it was, it was obvious he was privy to the connection and planned to keep me completely in the dark. Could it be that he wasn't even human at all, but something more?

And then it hit me—was he a siren? I wanted to slap myself for the absurdity of such a thought. *Sirens aren't real!* My throat felt dry and hot. To think such a thing was ridiculous, and yet the insane pull he had over me was undeniable. I was well aware from my childhood storybooks the consequences of a mere mortal falling in love with someone that was not of this world. Was this why he refused even so much as a friendship with me?

William was a stranger to me—a stranger who had made it crystal clear that he wanted nothing to do with me. He had warned me to go home. He had even thought about leaving me in the storm. Whatever he was, I knew that it was impossible for me to stay away from him at this point. I needed to see him again. I wanted some type of explanation. He walked away leaving me with so many unanswered questions, and yet, why did I also now fear the answers.

8

"There is no use trying," said Alice; "one can't believe impossible things." "I dare say you haven't had much practice" said the Queen, "… Why, sometimes I've believed as many as six impossible things before breakfast."

Lewis Carroll

I awoke the next morning to the sound of a boat engine puttering down the creek outside my window. I practically leapt out of the bed and rushed to the window to check to see if it was William. It was not, but there on the dock awaited my lost boots from the evening before. My boots had also been rescued—not exactly Cinderella's glass slipper, but another impossibility for sure. I had awakened several times during the night for no reason other than to stare out my window into a dark nothingness. I searched for fairytales, waiting for something, but found only an abyss—a starless abyss.

I couldn't stop thinking about him. I studied. But the pages could not hold my focus. I read. I saw his face in every character. I combed the beach constantly looking for signs of him. It was no use. With each new figure that appeared on the horizon, my heart rose and broke with disappointment. He was everywhere and nowhere. Three days turned into four with no sign of the little wooden boat that was now perfectly etched in my mind. My heart ached with a dull pain that I had never before experienced. The water seemed empty without him, and I knew that his total absence could only be for one reason. He was avoiding me—but why? Surely the presence of a single teenaged girl would not alter his routine so substantially. I began to question myself. What was so wrong with me?

My frustration turned to sadness and sadness to anger. I wished for James. I needed my best friend to be here with me to help sort through it all. James had promised to try to make it down on the weekends, and I longed for his companionship now more than ever. But as Thursday rolled around, I received a disappointing call from him to let me know he would be unable to come down this weekend after all. He had been asked to shoot a large local event and couldn't turn down the money or experience that went along with it. I couldn't fault him for not dropping his life in Conway just to keep me company. He had his own talents, own hobbies, and own school and friends there. But I couldn't deny that I missed some type of companionship. As much as I adored my grandmother, I missed the rousing from Caleb, the tenderness of my mother, and the entertainment James provided. I missed the joy Lucy carried and the security my father held.

But I belonged here. I didn't regret my decision to leave school early and to complete the year through correspondence. Most of my real learning came from my own love of books anyway. I could be supplied no greater teachers than Dickens, Chaucer, Whitman, and Shakespeare. Alcott's women were my friends and Austen's gentlemen my suitors. With their company, I was never before lonely…until now. Something had changed—I felt alone.

I had all but given up searching for the mysterious book. Its absence only proved that whatever material it possessed was precisely what my grandmother did not want me to discover. I lacked the courage to simply confront her and ask her directly, but I couldn't let it go either. Maybe my answers could be found elsewhere. I spent the entire morning at the local library combing through books on siren and mermaid legends, but as the small library branch mainly catered to sunbathing tourists looking for Grisham and Steel novels, it lacked a large supply of books that contained any real substance. The information that I uncovered, mainly centered on contrasting stories of folklore. The constant traits that seemed to be shared between stories were: speed, strength, and an inhuman almost alluring beauty.

Towards the end of the week, I decided to take the boat out, trying to convince myself that it was only to soak in the beautiful inlet sunshine, but no matter how hard that I tried to fool myself, I knew that I really wanted some excuse to run into William. I wanted to see him again. I pulled on a light grey tank and some khaki shorts from my drawers, slipping them over a black one-piece swimsuit and headed into the house for some breakfast. I grabbed a couple linked sausages and some scrambled eggs that were barely still warm, still waiting on the stove for me. The house was still. I knew without a doubt that my grandmother was already out on the strand claiming the evening's shells that had been washed up by the tide.

The day was warm and the sunshine a welcomed change from the cool April winds. It was by far the warmest day since I had arrived. Much to my dismay, the red patches had begun to reappear again on my body. I was sure that the warm sunshine would be beneficial to my tender skin, but my self-consciousness over the patches caused me to grab a long sleeved shirt off of the clothesline for cover. The thin white shirt had once belonged to my grandfather. It was my favorite shirt as it held the only real memories I had of him. I planned to remove it for some sunshine as soon as I was sure that I was alone. Today I was simply out to enjoy a beautiful Friday, or at least that is what I kept telling myself. I refused to allow myself to think about William. It didn't work.

"So where are you off to today so chipper?" I turned to find my grandmother at the picnic table with a bucket of olive shells, a foam ring, and what appeared to be some type of epoxy. I hardly thought that I looked "chipper" but I guess the warmer weather had at least put me in a better mood.

"I thought I would go out to the 'point' for the afternoon—take advantage of this nice weather before another cold snap hits." I picked up a towel that was hanging over the banister and draped it over my arm.

"It's about time." she continued, taking another olive shell in hand. "You've been moping around here for the past few days. I never thought I would say this, but I will be glad when James finally gets down here for the summer. You need friends. When is he arriving?"

"He isn't able to come this weekend, but promised me to come as soon as he can." She looked surprised.

"Ah, well I am proud of you for not letting it get you down. I was wondering if possibly you should register for school here after all."

"But there are only a few months of school left for the year." I protested.

"I'm aware of that, but I was thinking it may help you make some friends for the summer."

"James will be here!"

Yes, but you need other friends as well. Besides, I don't know if it is good idea to miss, next year, your entire senior year I might add, by taking correspondent classes. Marguerite, it's not right for you to be alone so much. You are missing more than just poorly executed lectures by not enrolling in classes. I just want to see you happy."

"Look, I know I have been moping around a bit this week, but I'm truly happy here. And as far as being alone, I like it that way. Really…I do." I was at least partially telling the truth.

"Alright, I concede for now, but just think about your options for the fall. School may be a good thing."

"I promise to think about it," I said, suddenly anxious to get out on the water. "Does this mean that you aren't planning to send me back after the summer?"

"This is your home as long as you want it to be. In fact, I've grown so accustomed to having you here, that I would be terribly lonely without you."

"I'm not going anywhere." I quickly changed the subject. "So, what are you making anyway?" She hot glued another shell onto a large ring.

"It's an olive shell wreath. Do you like it?" She held the partially completed craft up and one of the shells dropped onto the table below. I giggled and rolled my eyes.

"Nice. We could use some more shell decor around here," we both laughed. "Maybe I'll see if I can find some more olive shells to contribute to that fine piece of art you are sculpting." She laughed.

"You better hurry off before I grab another foam ring and put you to work."

"I'll be back before supper." I called back to her as I almost had reached the dock.

"Be safe!" She called back to me as I slid into the driver's seat of my old john boat.

Adrenaline rushed through me the moment I smelled the salt air churning beneath the boat motor. The thought of an afternoon out on the water nearly took my breath away. The sun now hung high into the clear sky sending rays of light sparkling cross the gently rolling waves. The afternoon air still carried a slight chill as the boat bounced along the top of the water creating a wonderful conflicting sensation over my body as the brisk air contrasted with the warm afternoon sun. The gulls called out to each other as they swooped into the waves looking for a midday meal, and tiny sand lappers seemed to dance along the sandbars that had just begun to peer out of the falling tide. It was as close as this world could come to heaven; I could not imagine anything more perfect.

I didn't go to the "point" after all but traveled further south for about another mile before pulling the boat up upon the sandy embankment. Never had I traveled this far south of Murrells Inlet before, but my adventurous side trumped any safety concerns that I might have felt from traveling to a new place alone. I knew the risks associated with the unfamiliar canals and sandbars, but the tide was still quite high and I managed to find a safe place to stop without any difficulty. The sand along the waterway was much wider on this part of the inlet, and I couldn't help but question why I had not ventured here before. It much resembled the sands along the beach during a calm low tide and would easily be mistaken as such if not for the lack rolling waves that incessantly accompanies the ocean shoreline. The inlet coastline remained peacefully still as the water ever so slightly dipped into the white sands as if to kiss it.

I pulled up to a low spot on the deserted shoreline and effortlessly tossed the boat anchor onto the sand. Much to my surprise it soared the entire extent of the rope before falling abruptly onto the sand. I looked down at my hands, a bit surprised by my own strength. *Cool!* Playfully, I picked up one of the oars from the bottom of the boat and hurled it into the air. It soared well past the sandy shore and out of sight over one of the dunes. So, I *was* stronger!

I thought back over the legends I had read earlier and some of the changes I had noticed over the past few months. Could any of it apply to me? If the siren creatures were out there, was I somehow connected to them? I looked down at the scar just above my ankle remembering the incident. Was it possible that the creature had also somehow changed me that day—given me these abilities? I thought of my speed on the racetrack that night and my agility in the gym that day. How easily I had pulled out the boat trailer with two flat tires—and now this!

I kicked off my worn leather flip flops and slipped off my shorts, dropping them next to them in the sand, before heading out to retrieve the oar. But as I looked out over the dunes, I saw someone heading in my direction carrying it. William appeared as if he were a mirage sauntering over the dunes, oar in hand. I tried not to gasp at the sight of him—impossible! His skin glistened as if it were made up of tiny glimmering pieces of sand, and the sun radiated off of his tousled hair giving him the appearance of an angel.

"Loose something?" He asked with a smirk as he seemed to eye my stripped down attire. Embarrassed, I blushed pulling the thin white shirt tighter around me.

"Um, yeah. Thanks." I responded, my words barely audible.

"Wind catch it? Never know when these wind gusts can pop up." He said suddenly scanning the area with a concerned look on his face. He once again looked like he was ready to pounce at the first sign of danger, and yet his words seemed as if he may have been trying to cover something up. I had no time to come up with an explanation.

"No. I threw it." His expression instantly changed, and I had his complete attention.

"You threw that?" He asked reserving no effort to hide his astonishment. "Why?"

"Yes." I admitted softly. "I just wanted to see how far it could go." I felt the blood rushing to my cheeks. He didn't seem surprised at all by my strength and made no reaction to my admission.

"Do you think you are capable of throwing it farther than that?" He asked curiously. I nodded, taking it from his hands and hurling it a seemingly impossible distance. He looked impressed. "What else can you do?" He eyed me carefully as if he were seeing me for the first time.

"I'm fast—I can run fast, very fast actually." *I didn't really know how to describe the whole tumbling part, so I decided to leave that part out of my confession.* He bit his bottom lip as he analyzed me.

"Can any other members of your family do these things?" He asked curiously.

"No—not like me. I appear to be the only one in the family." I shuffled my feet along the cold sand trying to avoid his analytical stare.

"Let me see your foot." I barely had time to process his words when I felt my feet sweep out from under me and I was in his arms. I completely lost my breath as William effortlessly swept me up in one quick motion. However as strong as I had become, he was obviously much stronger as he lifted me as if I were a feather. The sweet familiar smell of his skin suddenly filled me, the smell much stronger, much sweeter than the scent from his shirt. His hands gently lifted my foot, and a charge of electricity swept through me as me thumb gently rubbed over the completely healed spot that had been filleted open just days earlier. He gently returned me back to my feet and took a step back away from me and looked away as if he were contemplating something.

"Did *you* do that?" I asked breathlessly. "Did you heal my foot?"

"No." He said flatly. The wind picked up carrying the thin white shirt off of my shoulder with it. I reached to catch it, but it was too late. William had seen the tender patches that adorned my shoulder and most of my arms. I tugged the shirt back in place over my swimsuit too embarrassed to speak and once again turned to head back towards the boat. I hoped he would not follow as I had reached my limit of mortification for the day. I was wrong as his long stride quickly caught up with mine. He firmly caught hold of my hand and slowly spun me around to face him. Deliberately he unbuttoned the top two buttons of my shirt and slid it from my shoulders. I stood motionless, and his fingers stroked along the inflamed patches of my shoulder blades. His touch was a fusion of fire and ice as his fingers brushed against my skin.

"How long have you been like this?"

"I don't know. Since childhood I guess. It gets better then worse." He looked away, and I could see something in his face that led me to believe he possibly knew more about what I was than I did.

"What am I?" I pleaded wanting for someone to finally tell me the truth.

"I don't know." He looked into my eyes tenderly.

"So I'm a freak?" I quickly pulled my shirt together, realizing that even if William *did* know something, he wasn't about to share that information with me.

William gently eased my fingers from the buttons. "No. You are not a freak." He said in a low soft voice. His fingers slowly unbuttoned the last few buttons on my shirt, and it fell to the sand.

"Come with me." He grabbed hold of my hand and led me to the water's edge. Panic washed over me.

"No I can't! Really, I can't." I protested softly as we neared the inlet water. I tried to pull away but he held firm to my hand.

"I want to try something. You have to trust me. I won't let anything happen to you. I promise." I opened my mouth to protest, but as I looked into his eyes, I couldn't, all of my fears were subsided as he began to lead me into the icy water. "You are safe with me. You know that right?" His eyes remained fixed on mine. Oddly enough, I did feel safe. He took hold of my other hand as he slowly walked backwards into the cool canal.

The water rose passed my ankles and headed toward my knees as he gently led me deeper and deeper into the cool water. My breathing quickened as his hand slid to the small of my back for support. The sensation was unlike anything I could have imagined—the warmth of the sun rays against my closed eyes, the coolness of the water against my feet, and the current of adrenaline that charged through me each time his fingers moved against my skin. He stopped just as the water reached my thighs. His right hand remained firm against my waist as his free hand dipped into the saltwater. He cupped the water in his left hand and carefully brought it up to my shoulder.

"This may sting a little," he said as he slowly poured the water over my tingling skin. It did sting, but only for a moment, and then I felt nothing but an odd numbness where the patches had been. I remained immobile as time after time he moved his hand into the canal, cupping the water and bringing it to different parts of my shoulders, arms, and back. My body shivered each time his fingers swept against my skin, not from the coolness of the water, but from the exhilaration of his fingers brushing against my body.

When his hands reached my face, I opened my eyes to find him staring intently into mine. The gentleness of his wet hands moved over the lines of my face, first to my jaw, then beneath my chin as he seemed to carefully trace every part. He slowly dipped into the water again before running his thumb across my brow. The tips of his fingers next moving to my eyelids that closed once again with his touch before gently moving across my lips. They instinctively began to part beneath his fingertips. My body responded in a way that it had never done before, as it impulsively pressed against his, my hands stroking the curves of his muscular back. And then in an instant, he was gone—beneath the cool water so fast that I didn't see him move. I only felt the absence of him around me.

I turned to the shore, then out across the water, searching for him—searching along the water's edge as I had done only days earlier. But he was gone...disappeared. I took a few steps toward the shoreline before turning toward the sea again. My heart now raced so quickly in my chest that I was all but certain I would collapse at any moment.

And then I saw him among the dunes. He stood as still as a statue, his back to me. His hands balled tightly into fists held at his hips. I took a few steps out the water and caught sight of my body. My skin was once again as smooth as silk with no sign of the red patches that were there just moments before, but it was more than that. My skin seemed to radiate with the same luminosity as William's. Not in an unnatural way, but in a way that only appeared in the airbrushed covers of magazines. But it was *more* than that. My entire body felt different. I couldn't quite describe the feeling. I felt strong, alive, invigorated.

As I reached the sand, I immediately reached for my discarded cover-up. But I stopped and did not put it on; there was no need now, there was nothing that I needed to hide. Shirt in hand, I turned to see William watching me. He stood motionless as his eyes moved over the unmistakable glow of my skin.

"I don't understand. How is this possible?" I said charging up to the dunes. "Did you do this?" Tears were now welling up in my eyes, but I didn't know if they were tears of joy or tears of embarrassment from his rejection.

"No. I have no magic."

"But you have knowledge. Knowledge of what I am! Knowledge that you won't share with me!" He turned away, his jaw hardening.

"*Can't* share with you!"

"William you have to tell me what is going on!" He didn't respond. My words softened. "Why have you been avoiding me?" I found the courage to look into his emerald eyes. "Tell me that you have not been avoiding me?"

"Just because you haven't seen me, doesn't mean that I haven't seen you."

"You watch me?" He nodded. I was stunned by his confession and instinctively reached out to touch his arm. He pulled away.

"I am sorry if I have given you the wrong impression. I watch you out of duty, and duty alone." His words pierced through me like hot daggers.

"But why?"

"Because you are in danger." He whispered.

"So the day James and I were out along the waterway...."

"I was caught off-guard. I had to be sure you were safe."

"What is after me?" Several seconds passed and still he didn't respond. "Is it the thing that I saw underwater as a child? Some sea creature, a siren or something?"

He looked up at me. "You need to get away from here—away from all of this. The more you know, the more dangerous your life becomes."

"Did I *become* like this because of what happened to me as a child? Did the siren do this to me?"

"No, it came after you in the first place because of what you *are*." A look of frustration spread across his face. "I have said too much already." And with that, he turned from me, and before I could stop him, he charged into the icy surf, disappearing beneath the water with not so much as a splash.

Astonished, my head spinning from all I had just seen, I went back to the boat. I headed away from the sandy shore, but I couldn't go back to the Inlet Joy. Not just yet. Instead, I sped toward the "point." I dropped the anchor as I glided into the familiar shore. No hurling, not this time. My mind was spinning as if it were a top out of control. I pulled the towel out of the bottom of the boat and found a secluded spot to gather my thoughts. I smoothed each ripple of the towel against the sand before lying back. The faint scar just above my ankle was now the only blemish on my skin, skin that didn't feel as if it belonged to me—it was like a silk robe covering flannel pajamas. I ran my finger along the scar line trying to remember every detail of the attacker, but as I closed my eyes, all that I could see was the hand that reached out for me beneath the water, the hand that took hold of mine and had pulled me to safety, the hand that had once again taken mine today and led me into the water. I gasped as I realized that William had been there that day so many years ago. He had been my protector even then. My heart ached, but I could not admit the reason for it, not even to myself. The world no longer made sense.

If there was something unnatural—or should I say supernatural—existing along our coastline, I had spent an entire childhood oblivious to it. But in truth, isn't that exactly what childhood should be—shielded from the uncomfortable realization that the world isn't this perfect place of "happily ever after?"

Well, at least that as what being a child was in my world. It was for Caleb and I, and James as well, but I knew for William and possibly others it was different. How different I did not truly realize until my eyes were suddenly opened to a whole new world that I never dreamt existed. I was no longer a child. Any drop of childhood that had lingered within me had been washed away by the same salt water that had healed me.

With William's words, I was now forced to question everything that I had learned over the last seventeen years of my life. I finally had an explanation for his behavior towards me; he wanted to protect me, but it had come with a cost. He could never reciprocate the feelings that I had so obviously developed for him. I closed my eyes tightly in a failed attempt to fight back the tears. I was trapped between two worlds, neither of which I truly fit in. The world I knew, and had spent a lifetime unsuccessfully trying to adjust to, and this new world that I never dreamt existed.

There was no question at this point that the feelings I had for William were real. I could no longer deny the emotions I had been fighting against. But what was he? Too perfect to be human, and yet, so unlike the monster I had encountered beneath the surf. I didn't belong with him; I didn't belong anywhere. I was finally able to see what he had seen from the very beginning. How could I ever fit into his life when our worlds were so very different? How could he ever love me? He was unlike anything I had even encountered—or would ever encounter apart from these churning waters of the coast?

I *had* to learn what I was—what William was. If he were not completely human, then maybe there were others, others that knew the truth. I did not have to think long before four inhumanly beautiful faces flashed into memory, the distinctively striking features of the three guys and stunning girl from the pool hall. Almost a week had passed since I had last seen them, a week since the tall one, Kirby, had so gallantly issued his invitation to me. Maybe they had the answers I needed. Maybe, with an ounce of courage, and a gallon of stupidity, I would accept his invitation after all.

I would take him up on his offer and meet them tonight beneath the pier.

9

"The moon gazed on my midnight labors, while, with unrelaxed and breathless eagerness, I pursued nature to her hiding—places."

Mary Shelley

It was just after eleven o'clock when I arrived at the Garden City Pier. I was sure my grandmother would not approve of the late hour, so I decided not to tell her. She checked into her room about ten, and I waited almost a full hour before leaving. I clearly didn't think this whole "sneaking out" thing through as she would most definitely be awakened by the sound of my old Jeep. So with an expired pepper spray in my jean pocket that my father had given me years earlier, I darted down the sidewalk towards the pier. I would have preferred to take the mile walk down the beach instead, but heading William's warnings, I took the sidewalk.

My nerves began to get the best of me as I reached the boardwalk beneath the pier. I took a deep breath and started down the pathway, not knowing what I would find at the other end. Perhaps they wouldn't even be there? But as I neared the beach, it became quite evident that someone was there indeed. Off in the distance, I could see the faint embers of a small driftwood campfire. It danced through the darkness with an unnatural blue flame. I had heard that driftwood produced a blue flame due to the salt in the wood but had never actually seen one before. Was nothing ordinary here?

I was pretty sure they knew I was coming, as before I even made it down the boardwalk, four sets of eyes seemed to unnaturally glow against the flicker of the blue flames, one set moving toward me at a rapid pace. I didn't have time to become afraid. I didn't have time to turn back.

"I told them you would come." Kirby appeared out of the darkness, taking hold of my arm. He led me down the path and over the sand dunes. His golden curls seemed to sparkle in the dim moonlight.

"I'm late." I said, barely audible over the sound of the surf.

"No worries. Time doesn't matter too much to us around here."

His face was beaming as if he was a child on Christmas morning, and his steps moved so lively it was almost as if he were skipping. His long, thin legs glided easily over the boardwalk as I struggled to just keep up. I stumbled a few times, but he kept his grip firm on my arm. "My, my, you are a clumsy little thing aren't you? What will we ever do with you?" He said with a chuckle that made me wonder if he was flirting, or if my growing fears were warranted.

"Maybe I shouldn't have come?" I replied as we made our way closer to the campfire.

"You'll be fine. Don't be afraid. *We're* not the ones you need to worry about." Kirby replied briefly looking over his shoulder as I was once again lagging behind.

"What do you mean by that?" I asked directly.

"Oh, don't pay any attention to the things I say. The crew is always getting on my case about babbling on so much."

"The crew?"

"My buds! Come and meet them. Promise we won't bite!" I eyed him skeptically. "Well, most of us anyway." He chuckled again. His eyes danced in the moonlight.

"I hope they won't mind me being here with you." My words ran together nervously.

"Aw, don't worry about it. They knew you were invited—didn't think you would come—but knew you were invited none the less. Besides, you are with me tonight. I'll take care of it if anyone has anything to say." His words were of little comfort to me and only increased my anxiousness.

"Well, I don't want to intrude, I mean, it's getting kind of late and…." I suddenly had the urge to run, to run like I had done that night at West Florence, as fast as I could away from here.

He stopped and looked back at me his eyes looking directly into mine. Strangely my fears began to subside. His hand slid down my arm and he took my hand. "Like I said, you're with me tonight. I am not *about* to let you go off anywhere else." I didn't pull my hand away. I wasn't even sure that I could even if I had tried. What an odd effect this boy had on me.

He turned and with a few more steps we were over the last dune and onto the beach. We made our way under the dark pier. I was shocked at how dark and damp the air became as we traveled beneath it. The old logs creaked and groaned as each wave knocked against the old pillars. I was glad when the moonlight once again cut the darkness as we appeared on the other side now just a few yards away from the blue flames. Just north of the pier two guys and a girl were seated on several pieces of logs and driftwood that surrounded the fire. They were all even more beautiful than I had remembered from the pool hall.

The stocky one rose to greet me. I liked him immediately. His dark spiky hair framed his smiling face. His white undershirt, clearly too small for even his stocky frame, hung over his faded red trunks. He immediately jumped over to introduce himself. "What's up Margo?" They appeared to do some type of handshake thing that only the two understood. I smiled suddenly more at ease from his friendly nature. He stepped back to look me over.

"Margo, this is Tobie. He's my wingman I guess you would say."

"Oh, *your* wingman…oh, I see how it is dude," Tobie playfully punched Kirby in the arm.

"Not in front of the girl, man," he said punching him back even harder.

"Dude, this one is pretty! What'd ya have to do? Kidnap her to get her to come with you!" They both laughed and were in an instant rolling around in the sand tackling each other in a playful romp. They both appeared to be out of breath after only a short time, Kirby pinning Tobie. Tobie feigning defeat, then easily flipped Kirby onto his back pinning him completely immobile.

"Alright, you win dude! Enough already! Let me up!" Kirby chuckled as Tobie released him. Within seconds they were at my side again brushing off the dry sand that covered each of them. They more closely resembled rambunctious children more than young men standing before me. The other two remained seated as Kirby led me to the campfire. He picked up a mason jar filled with an odd smelling drink and tossed it to the fierce looking one with the shaved head.

"Marguerite, this is Mace."

"Hello." My voice trembled.

He nodded curtly in my direction but was obviously not pleased with my presence. Despite the cool temperatures he stood shirtless with dark colored board-shorts that hung low upon his thin chiseled frame. He was built much like Kirby, resembling a male underwear model. He was slightly unshaven, and his blue eyes matched the flames from the fire in front of him. I looked away pretending to look down at the drink that Kirby forced into my hand. I quickly took a swig of the greenish substance before I had even realized what I had done. The taste was awful, as bitter as raw cocoa, but with an organic texture as it slid down my throat. Evidently, my displeasure was quite evident, as they all seemed to get quite a kick over my scowled expression.

"What *is* that?" I said as Kirby passed me a soda to wash it down.

"I guess you would say it is *our* version of an energy drink. Don't worry; it won't hurt you." He chuckled. Kirby then walked over to hand another drink to the girl. Her long wavy brown hair had been pulled up high in a pile on top of her head, and her golden skin glimmered against the campfire. Her lips were full, and her eyes an even brighter shade of blue than Mace's. She was the most beautiful girl that I had ever seen. She had a natural radiance that required no makeup or embellishment.

"Margo, this is Aria." Kirby said, and for the first time his confidence was shaken. I could tell through his demeanor that even he was a bit unsure of this introduction between us. She didn't nod or acknowledge my presence at all. She stared at me intensely with no attempt to hide that my presence was unwelcomed.

"Nice to meet you." I muttered. She glared. I was sure that I was staring back at her as well but for a different reason. Her beauty was such that one could not help but stare.

"Aria, since Margo's new around here, she might need some of your girly input. Ya know, girl power and all that…to make her feel welcome." I felt anything but welcomed. Kirby's failed attempt at trying to lighten the mood went over like a wet blanket.

"So, you say you are new to the area?" She responded, her eyes narrowing as if she were sizing me up.

"No, not exactly. I've spent my summers here since I was a child…every summer of my whole life actually." I could hear my words stupidly flowing from my lips and suddenly wished I were in my nice warm bed. *What was I doing here? I didn't belong with this crew any more than I did with the students of West Florence.* Her eyes narrowed and she leaned in towards the fire. "So, you aren't really local then?" Her tan skin glistened in the moon light, and one of her straps from her overalls had fallen onto her shoulder revealing part of a brown knit bikini top almost the color of her skin.

"I am now." I said mustering up a bit of courage.

"But you didn't grow up on the water at all?" She smirked.

"No, only during the summers."

"Surely you had a lake, pool or something?" I thought the question odd but answered anyway.

"No pool, but *who* really swims in the winter anyway." I regretted the comment the moment it escaped my lips. They all laughed. I didn't see what was remotely funny about the comment. *So glad I can be their amusement.* And with that, the entire crew charged through the darkness towards the water, shirts flying off, as they whooped towards the surf. I watched in complete disbelief as each soared with unnatural height into the waves, disappearing almost immediately into the black water. If there was an ounce of me that still questioned if they were human, it was gone.

Kirby was the first to return, carrying an armful of clams, with Tobie just behind him toting six of the largest blue crabs that I had ever seen, and Mace carrying a large snapper. Aria returned bringing back several wide pieces of sea kelp.

"Hungry?" Kirby asked as he pulled out a pot that was stashed in the dunes and filled it with seawater. I was too shocked to answer, as Tobie dumped the clams and crabs into it and slid the pot into the bond fire. Aria took a large stick and thrust it through the still flapping snapper, then wrapped it with the kelp and propped it over the flames. I stood frozen. I had gone looking for fairytale characters, but now that they stood before me with all embers of a human façade erased, I was shaken.

"So tell us about yourself Margo," Tobie said as the group settled around the fire. I looked around at their faces; no one appeared to be cold despite the frigid water. In fact, they hardly even looked wet.

"Not much to tell actually." I tried to keep my voice from trembling.

"Well, for starters, you could tell us why you've come." Tobie said with a smile.

"Well, my grandmother lives here—she grew up here as a child but left in her late teens. She moved back after my grandfather passed away and now lives alone."

"You don't have a family?" Mace uttered.

"My family lives elsewhere…but to make a long story short, I got sick, and she thought it would be a good idea to come live here with her for a while."

Mace looked up at me. "You say you were sick?" His eyes narrowed.

"Yeah, they weren't sure exactly what happened, but I'm better now," I added, not wanting any sympathy. It was clear none would be given anyway.

"You're a fool to bring her here." Mace hissed at Kirby. "I told you to stay away from this one!"

"Come on Mace! Aren't you even a bit curious?"

"William warned us to keep clear of the girl." A stab of pain swept through me at the sound of his name. "He is no friend of mine, but we steer clear of *this* kind of trouble." I stood frozen, unsure if I wanted to cry or run. *So William was warning them to steer clear of me the first time I had seen them outside of the grocery. But why? And why had they been waiting for me in the first place?*

"She seems harmless enough to me." Tobie added flashing a brilliant smile in my direction.

"Come on Mace! Look at her! What trouble could she possibly be? Besides, any day when I can ruffle William's feathers is a good day." I liked Kirby a little bit less at this point. Had he just brought me here to anger William? Why would William even care? William offered me no friendship or answers. What right did he have to choose who I would spend my time with?

"I don't like it!" Mace hissed again.

"Look at her Mace, she is just a girl, a regular human gir…" The words barely come out of his mouth when Mace's drink hurled through the air towards my face at an unimaginable speed. I had no time to realize what was happening, no time to be afraid, only time to try to protect myself. I unconsciously reached my hand in front of me, catching the jar just inches away. Not a drop was spilled.

They all stared at me stunned as I held the jar. I began to tremble as I realized what I had done.

"Damn it Mace! Have you lost your mind?" Kirby exclaimed, still not taking his eyes off me.

"No. I knew she would catch it. I had to prove that...."

Over the dune came a dark shadow whose eyes glowed fiercely as he charged. It was William. The crew was on their feet immediately, crouched in some defensive posture as if they were ready for an attack. William went straight for Mace, grabbing him by the wrists and literally hurling him into the air like a rag doll. Yet Mace landed with unimaginable grace, crouched on the sand like he was ready to spring. I stood in awe and fear of the entire exchange. William charged again, but this time Mace landed a punch to the center of William's chest knocking him backwards into the dunes. William sprung forward again, but this time Kirby and Tobie stepped between them. The crew stood ready to defend Mace—all except Aria, who stood off to the side with a torn expression.

"Party's over!" Mace exclaimed to Kirby as he pushed them out of the way and headed back over the dunes. William remained ready to attack until Mace was completely out of sight, then he turned to me, completely ignoring the others. His eyes met mine with a look that was surprisingly tender. "Are you okay?"

I nodded. Still completely shaken by what I had just witnessed.

"Will, now it just isn't like you to crash a party! I didn't even think to send you an invite!" William turned to glare at Kirby.

"Don't worry. I won't be staying." William said furiously. "Let's go, Marguerite," he said crossing towards me. My heart skipped a beat as he put his hand on the small of my back. I took a step in his direction, and we turned to leave.

"William, please..." Aria interjected and for the first time, I caught the look in her eyes as she stared at him. She looked at him the way that I looked at him. My heart sank deeper in my chest.

"This is *not* the time Aria!" He cut her off before she could say anything else. Whatever history was between them, it was more than obvious that she harbored some type of feelings for him. Kirby was instantly there facing us. "Ok, Will, I am not sure what *this* is exactly or what gives you the right to come over here and just take my date, but

Margo is with *me* tonight. I'm not *about* to let you just come and take her away."

"I warned you all to stay away from her!" He growled.

"And what gives you the right to decide who her friends are?" Kirby shot back.

"Yeah. You all seem to be quite welcoming." William glared over at Aria—she looked away.

"She didn't get hurt now did she?" Tobie shrugged. William picked up the same jar that I had caught just inches from my face and hurled it at the pot that was still roasting in the fire, just narrowly missing Tobie's head. The speed of the impact caused the glass to disintegrate into fine sand like powder that flowed down the pot and into the flames. At first I thought he had thrown it in anger at Tobie, but I realized he was demonstrating what would have happened to my face if Mace were wrong and I had not been able to catch the jar.

William took my arm and once again began to lead me away. Kirby once again stepped in front of us.

"You are *not* taking her Will!" His words were more forceful this time.

"Um yeah, Kirby. Actually, I am," he snapped.

"Answer one thing for us then," Aria's beautiful voice echoed over the sizzling fire. "Is she one of us? Is she like us, William? You owe us…me, at least, that much."

"She is like no one."

And with that he led me down the beach away from them all.

I didn't look back at the others, though I was quite certain that all eyes were on us as I was willingly ushered down the beach. His hand had moved from the small of my back to my elbow as we passed under the pier and into the shadows. He didn't so much as look at me, and I was still too much in shock to speak.

The sky was clear, and the moon lit up the beach perfectly as it reflected off of the evening tide. There was a gentle breeze blowing in from the water. The tide was rising, but there was still a large part of the beach uncovered. I was quite surprised when he didn't lead me up the path to the parking lot on the far side of the pier but continued walking down the beach. It was hard to breathe with Will so close. I was relieved when he spoke first.

"What were you thinking going out there tonight?" he said after we were quite some distance down the beach. His hand brushed against my side as we walked.

"I was thinking that I needed answers, and as you haven't given me any, I thought possibly they could."

"Did you find what you were looking for?"

"No. Not really. More questions than anything else."

"Like what?" He seemed a bit amused.

"Well, I guess the biggest question I have is…what *are* you?" He smirked but didn't answer the question.

"Next question?"

"Are the others like you?" He pondered this for a moment.

"Yes and no. Each of us have certain things that make us unique— certain *talents*, I guess you would say."

"And what would yours be?"

"I guess you would call it intuition. I can sense things…anticipate things before they even happen. Plus it doesn't hurt that I have heightened senses, which seems to compliment my…talent."

"So you knew I was coming out here tonight?"

"No. You are highly unpredictable—and human, which makes things more difficult. I had no idea that you had even left and was extremely worried when I realized you were gone."

"So I *am* still human?" He laughed. I was temporarily mesmerized by his smile.

"The fact that you have to ask me that is quite comical."

"But something *is* happening to me, isn't it?"

"I can't say for sure, but that appears to be the case."

"Has this ever happened before?"

"Not that we are aware of." He said flatly.

I tried to ignore his reference to "we" and pressed on as I finally seemed to be getting some answers from William. "So essentially, you were stuck with the task of watching over me until they figure out what I am?"

"In a nut shell."

"And yet, you won't tell me what you are?"

"You know what we are," he said taking my hand and turning to face me.

"I don't."

"Yes, you do, but your mind is telling you that it's impossible. Marguerite, you aren't ready for this. You won't be able to grasp any of our world until you allow yourself to move past all that you assume is impossible, and believe that just maybe, another world out there exists within your own." He gazed out over the dark ocean water.

"That sounds crazy."

"Crazy, but not impossible."

"But, if this were true, how do I fit into your world?" I pleaded.

"I don't know. I honestly don't know. I don't have all of the answers that you are looking for. But it is important for you to understand, that we aren't all good."

"Were *they* going to harm me?"

"No. Not intentionally. They are like me, they are protectors, but they are still untrained." He turned towards me and took my hands in his. "Look, you can't just wander about out there. There are those among us who would try to harm you because of what you are and others for what you could be. They aren't strong enough to protect you from all that is out there. Even I am not strong enough. The world that I live in is not safe for you. You need to stay in your own world and try to forget all of this. Try to live a normal life!"

"So the group I was with tonight is like you?"

"You need to stay away from them. They are reckless; they draw attention. The last thing you need is to draw attention to yourself."

He stopped and looked up at the dunes.

"Your house is just through there," he said motioning to the boardwalk. "Goodnight," he said curtly.

"Wait, I have more questions!"

"The less you know about all of this the better." It was I that caught his arm this time. He looked down at my grasp and seemed surprised by my strength. I released my grip.

"Reverse the situation. Suppose you could sense something was happening to you…that you were changing in ways you have never dreamed possible and that there was a group that just might know what was happening—a group that could even possibly be like what you were becoming. Wouldn't you do everything in your power to find out the truth?"

"That is quite a lot of hypotheticals." He said with a smirk. I wasn't amused.

"I have to know."

"I am sorry. I can't offer any answers for you."

"Can't or won't?" I shot back in frustration.

"Both." He said flatly. His emerald eyes glistened against the light of the moon. "Like I said, goodnight Marguerite." He turned and disappeared through the darkness.

But I knew, somewhere not too far away, hidden in the night...he was still there.

10

"To die would be an awfully big adventure."

J.M. Barrie

Constant rain proved to be my enemy as I spent the next three days a prisoner to the weather. I occupied myself as much as possible by writing, reading, and painting, but each word I composed somehow related to him, each character bore his face, and each brushstroke carried his likeness. To say that I was miserable was an understatement. All that had once held my interest seemed trivial with such mystery just out of reach. There was no physical sign of him anywhere, and yet, I saw him in everything.

I left the Inlet Joy only a few times throughout the week, just to run to the Beach Mart and for another unsuccessful trip to the library. The library provided little insight, as these myths and legends of sea people all ran together. Nothing truly seem to fit these "locals" that I had met. I found a small bookstore, searching for records, sightings, or some account of humans "changing" into something. But each source led only to comic books or fairytales.

By Thursday afternoon the skies had cleared enough to venture outdoors once again. My grandmother was equally as stir crazy, so I joined her for an afternoon walk along the beach. It was much cooler along the shore than expected, as another cold front had started to move in. I zipped up my grey windbreaker, burying my hands deep in the pockets. With each step I remembered the countless walks we took together when I was a child. Life was so uncomplicated back then.

The smell of the salty air once could clear my mind, but now it only escalated all thoughts of William. Frustrated, I tried to think of something else, but my heart pounded harder in my chest at the mere thought of him. I hated being in love. I loathed the days that passed uneventful with no sight of him and wished that I could somehow forget that he existed. I had spent seventeen years quite content with reading of love with little desire to know it firsthand. The sonnets and love poems made it out all wrong; for though I could not deny its power, no words could ever describe the agony of unrequited love.

"Is something on your mind Marguerite? You have been unusually quiet this afternoon." I felt her fragile fingers take hold of my hand as we were walking.

I smiled. It had been years since she had taken my hand on our walks. There was always comfort and safety in those hands. The cool touch of her soft hand against mine made me feel like a young child again. "Do you know a boy by the name William Avery?" I tried to keep my voice steady and my eyes did not venture from the long stretch of strand ahead.

"Avery you say?" I gave no verbal reply, but nodded. "Huh, I haven't heard that name in quite some time. No, I must say that I don't know him personally, but I do remember reading about the Avery tragedy in the newspaper a few years back."

"Tragedy?" I asked curiously. James had told me his parents had died in an accident but was short on the details.

"Yes, a sad situation for the entire area at the time."

"What happened?" I took a deep breath.

"The Averys were a fairly young couple, quite new to the area about eight years ago. The couple began a small ship design business that they turned into a rather large and profitable company. It made a big stir at the time as they moved the entire operation just outside of Conway, bringing many new jobs to the area."

"Do you know where they were from?"

"They moved here from the Charleston area with their son, about ten years old, and a very young daughter. The boy's name *was* William, I believe."

"What type of accident?"

"Like I said, their company built boats, beautiful large sailboats. The family was on one of their sailboats a few miles off the coast and something went wrong. There was an explosion. The media reported that the entire family was killed, but the boy was found a few days later hanging onto a piece of wreckage." I was speechless. "Where did you hear the name?"

"I met him the other day—down at the pier." My pulse raced at even the smallest of lies.

"Really? The accident happened many years ago; I didn't realize the boy was still in the area."

"He is. Lives down the creek past the 'point' a ways with someone named Silas." Her expression instantly changed. She looked ill. "Do you know of anyone by that name?" Her face had turned as white as sand.

"The name sounds familiar," she uttered breathlessly. We continued in silence for only a short distance before she turned to me. "I am suddenly not feeling very well. Do you mind if we head back to the house? I think I have had enough walking for today."

Alone in my room I couldn't stop thinking of all that my grandmother had revealed. The tragedy that William had been through should never have to be felt by anyone. Very few people could ever understand what it would be like to lose an entire family. Was that why he pushed everyone away? Was that why he had refused my friendship? It was quite evident that the crew were not friends of his. Sure, there appeared to be history between them, especially with Aria, but clearly friendship was not part of it.

My grandmother had hidden away in her room since our walk, only appearing briefly to check to see if I had eaten something. I couldn't decide if something that I said had upset her or if she truly had taken ill. I decided to take a shower to clear my thoughts, but as I undressed, I scowled at red patches starting to resurface on my skin. Whatever I was, or whatever I was becoming, I now knew what my body needed—the one thing I feared the most.

After my grandmother had settled for the night, I crept out of the house heading toward the sound of the crashing surf. It was much darker than I realized. The narrow steps leading over the dunes were dimly lit by a single street lamp several houses over. I was by no means a stranger to the beach at night. James and I would often walk along the coast after dark, but this night was different. The vacation homes sat unoccupied and abandoned from the winter. It felt odd to encounter the area so void of the lively summer occupants that monopolized the area. But there were no tourists scampering around with flashlights searching for treasures or drunken frat boys on spring break. There were no fireworks off in the distance or catcalls from the balconies. Even the constant hum of the cars passing down Waccamaw Drive was void this time of year. Without the illuminating glow from the row of houses nestled just behind the dunes, the shoreline was darker than I had ever dreamed possible. It was also more beautiful that I could have imagined—beautiful, but isolated. I had realized how isolated the beach felt at night walking home with William.

My heart pumped faster in my chest as I neared the water. I thought of turning back but brushed all fear aside. I had been continuously warned of the dangers of the ocean but had seen nothing remotely threatening since I arrived. The waves seemed to call to me, they beckoned as the salty water was my cure. I took a deep breath as I crossed over the last dune. The clouds from the earlier bad weather had passed, and the moon now loomed high in the sky casting the image of a brilliant silver orb across the water. Beautiful!

I pulled the thin oversized white sweater around my shoulders, fastening it with the loose belt that was now blowing behind me. The wind was usually stronger along the beach than along the marsh, and tonight was no different. I regretted my poor choice of attire and wished that I had opted for a heavier jacket instead. How surprising that a place so familiar could feel so foreign with just a change of season! I stashed my flip flops on the last step of the wooden walkway at the edge of the dunes. The cold sand between my toes was quite a different sensation than the smoldering hot dunes of the summertime.

I sat amongst the dunes for quite some time trying to build up my courage. I remembered how effortlessly "the crew" glided through the icy surf. That night had been no less cold than this one, and yet, the possibility of getting in the water seemed insane. If my body needed the saltwater, then I would have to face this fear. How much easier had it been with William at my side! To the left just over a mile in the hazy distance was the Garden City Pier. It was now completely dark except for a single faint light at its end, serving as a mark for any maritime vessels venturing out in the night. The familiar structure now eerily stretched out through the frigid water.

To the right, the coast spread with no interruption of piers or rocky erosion dams. Through the light of the moon, I could see the bend of the water's edge as it curved gently ahead for miles. It surprised me the distance that I could see with only the moonlight for illumination. There in the distance was where it cut into a dead end by the jetties that surrounded the mouth of Murrells Inlet. The small canal that joined the inlet to the ocean and surrounding beach, which we called the "point," was in my opinion the most beautiful part of Garden City, now even more beautiful to me as it was where William and I had first met.

I slipped off the grey sweatpants that covered my swimsuit and untied the white sweater, leaving them both on the dunes. The cold air instantly covered my body with goose bumps. I would just go out a few inches— just enough to cover my feet, then I could scoop the water over the rest of me as William had done.

The surf was quite calm as I approached the shoreline. The water took my breath away as the waves rolled onto my feet, then ankles, instantly sending the same exhilarating feeling throughout my body that I had experienced in the inlet. I bent down and cupped the water into my hands as William had done, gently pouring the cold water against my skin, first my legs, then arms, then body and face. As before, I could begin to feel the red patches disappear. All fear was gone as I edged deeper into the surf. I felt alive—invigorated. I wanted to go deeper, but through the bliss could hear William's warning playing over and over in my mind. I walked back to the dunes, slipping on the clothes that were still waiting for me. I couldn't go back to the house, not yet. I felt too wonderful. I would walk—surely there could be no harm in a walk! I turned away from the pier and began walking against the wind towards the jetties.

The tide was quite high leaving only a narrow stretch of dry sand. I giggled, realizing I no longer had the urge to avoid the water. It was a part of me that I could no longer deny. I quickly walked about a half a mile up the deserted beach, the icy water spreading around me like icing on a cake. I was in the water—walking in the water! I began to giggle. My giggles turned to uncontrolled laughter as I spread my arms out on both sides of my body and spun circles round and round like a small child in the ankle deep water. I felt intoxicated.

The wind began to whip hard around me, and waves churned out in the water just off the beach with a force that was almost frightening. But I was too distracted by my own new found joy to notice. I leapt along the water's edge as the tide, now stronger than ever, *pushed* the water against my feet, circling around me with each wave that burst onto the shore. Through my utter delight, I exploded into a sprint running faster and faster along the shore. I ran as I had only done on one other unforgettable occasion. I closed my eyes and let the moment overtake my senses. I was reborn.

How long, how far, or how fast I had traveled was completely lost to me, but without warning, my body came to a complete stop—tumbling into something. I did not fall. I gasp, dazed from the impact. It only took a fraction of a second to realize that I had not run into something, but someone and that someone had a hold of me. No sound escaped from my now trembling lips. Lean hard arms had wrapped themselves firmly around my waist. I thrashed about ridiculously, trying to free myself, but all my efforts were in vain.

"Marguerite! Stop!" His words smoldered through the darkness in a voice too perfect to be human. My arms fell limp by my sides. By the light of the moon, I looked into the same face that I had been unable to clear from my mind for weeks now. His features, just inches before me, were even more exquisite than my mind could recreate. I gasped in relief. But my heart raced even faster, as his closeness took what was left of my breath away. I looked up at him like a child—still immobilized as his arms did not release their firm grip.

I realized he wasn't looking at me at all. His beautiful emerald eyes glared past me. His piercing stare did not waver as he growled furiously into the darkness, and for the first time, I realized that we were not alone. I turned around and saw her. She stood approximately ten yards from us—motionless against the backdrop of the surf. I had not realized that anyone had been behind me, but there she stood—a creature like none I had ever before seen. Or had I?

Her form was undoubtedly human; her limbs were long and seemed to glisten in the reflection of the moon. Her hair was as black as the night itself, falling into loose curls just above her waist. To call her beautiful would have been an insult, as I had only seen a woman so physically perfect in an illustration. But her high sculpted cheekbones and full lips were only a temporary distraction from her sinister green eyes, which seemed to glow in the moonlight. I *had* seen her before, not only in the surf as a child, but also in the years of nightmares that would follow. The creature was before me once again.

She didn't take her eyes off of me, glaring at me with a stare so intense that I began to tremble. The arms around me shifted, but only to grip me tighter. I was too afraid at this point to even utter a sound. We stood there motionless with the only sound of the waves rolling onto shoreline. It was the second time in my short life that I knew: I was looking death in the face. The silence was broken by deep songlike laughter that bellowed above the crashing waves. She spoke in a rich, flowing tone that I was certain could not be human. "And so she *does* exist! Remarkable!" She smiled devilishly through perfectly white teeth. "Theron will be so pleased to know that she has returned. Come here, dear!" Logically, I knew to fear her, and yet I felt my body unconsciously step towards her. "Remarkable! She responds as a human!" She took one fluid step in my direction, but before I could move another step forward, I was off of my feet. William had instantly shifted to place himself between us, keeping one arm still tightly secured around my waist.

"She's not going anywhere with you Maris." He hissed back at her with a sound unlike I had never heard before. "Leave the girl alone!" Her laughter once again broke through the night air. I stood motionless realizing that they were negotiating my fate.

"William, now you know that I can't do that." She said in a sultry songlike voice that I was quite sure no human male would be able to withstand. "There are rules. Even *you* cannot prevent the inevitable."

"You won't so much as touch her!" he hissed.

With that, her beautiful face was transformed by an expression of pure evil. Her mouth seemed to spread apart to reveal dagger like teeth behind her human façade, her smooth skin now glistened as if it belonged to a serpent. Her eyes glowed wickedly against the water. She sprang at him, and instantly he tossed me far from the water's edge, nearly halfway up to the dunes. I felt my body land with a thud against the firm sand, but there was no pain. I watched helplessly as this creature attacked William. He appeared "transformed" as well—his frame larger, stronger, and his teeth also glinted with dagger-like sharpness. But unlike her transformation, he remained beautiful, only fiercer, like a tiger protecting its kill. She sprang at him, but he was too quick and blocked her advance in midair. She tumbled along the sand and rolled into the surf. She leaped again, this time angling so that she landed on his back, her teeth plunging for the veins of his neck, but he easily tore her away again. Suddenly, she redirected her attention to me, lunging onto the beach with a bloodcurdling screech. But as she reached the water's edge, she came to a snarling halt and retreated back toward the water.

"Stay where you are!" he shouted. "She has no strength out of the water. She needs it to survive!" I stumbled backwards, further into the dunes.

Even as she slithered backwards into the surf, she appeared to be weakening. William was right! This creature, as evil as she was, could only sustain life out of the water for a very brief period of time. William returned to my side, encompassing me into his arms. She hissed at me one last time before her eyes shifted to William. Her monstrous features seem to once again become majestic and beautiful, just as she had first appeared.

"Be very careful, William. Theron's patience is growing quite thin in regard to your "activities." I would advise you to choose your causes wisely," she warned. Her tone was a twisted jumble of threat and sultry invitation.

"I answer to no one—least of all Theron!" He hissed. He was not only beautiful but also brave. I felt my heart leap in my chest.

"Such a declaration, I fear, will not be well received. Treaty or no treaty, you are *all* simply tolerated. You can all be done away with as easy as this girl." Chills ran up my spine as she once again turned to me. I remained frozen.

"I think you have said quite enough Maris. Tell Theron the girl is off limits." Her evil laugher resurfaced.

"That is not your decision!" her eyes narrowed.

"She is under our protection. We will not negotiate nor will we be bullied into submission."

Maris fumed at William's audacity. "Suit yourself. Your protest is adequately noted. I am quite disappointed it has come to this and over this…girl! You would do well to reconsider, William. The Protectors have been on thin ice since breaking with Theron's Legion. I am actually quite surprised he hasn't terminated all of you already." William hissed. Her thin lips curled up on the sides. "Are you sure she is worth it? You are *more* than aware of what happens when someone disobeys Theron. I always thought it a pity that you were forced to learn that lesson at such a young age."

The sound that escaped from William was beyond frightening. It pierced the night air with such intensity that the crashing waves were whispers in comparison. His eyes now green burning embers glaring out across the water. He was so filled with anger, I was certain he had all but forgotten my presence. Maris only laughed as she disappeared into the dark waters as quietly and as mysteriously as she had come.

William was instantly at my side. "Are you alright?' He asked tenderly? His arm now gripped my waist so tightly, I was certain it was bruised. I tried to stand, but my knees felt weak. I felt sick. My head began to spin so rapidly that I felt my legs become unsteady. It was all too much; I was falling.

The last thing I remembered was the warmth of William's body against mine.

****

I felt warm all over—except for the stinging in my feet. Through the darkness, I reluctantly began to open my eyes and pull my face from my cozy blanket. Ouch! A sharp pain moved up my leg. My feet were freezing! I reached for the blanket to cover them. But I was not in the safety of my bed, and there were no blankets. I pulled my legs toward my chest, holding tight to the arms that were wrapped around me. I opened my eyes to see the lines of William's perfect face. My heart began to pump so hard that I was afraid I was going to pass out again. I looked around, realizing we were on my dock near the edge of the floating pier. William sat with his feet dangling into the cold inlet water. His arms were still draped loosely around me, and his eyes looking down into mine.

"You're here," I muttered, unsure if I were awake. He looked down at me tenderly and nodded. "So, that wasn't a dream?" My lips stumbled through the words with trembling lips.

"Would you believe me if I said it was?" His mouth twisted on one side in almost a smile.

"No." I said quickly. He smiled.

"I didn't think so." He produced a small towel and covered my wet bare feet. I suddenly remembered Maris' face and began to pull away from the water.

"It's okay. She is not here. They can't come into the inlet."

"What happened?"

"I carried you here from the beach when you passed out. You wouldn't wake up. I thought this might help," he said motioning toward the dark inlet water.

"Oh." Not only had I passed out, but he had carried me for over a mile back here? The blood rushed to my cheeks. I would have been more embarrassed if I hadn't just seen him fight a *sea monster*. I wanted to question him further, but I just couldn't seem to gather my thoughts. His voice made me dizzy.

"Thought your feet would be a better choice than splashing ice cold salt water on your face." The edges of his mouth curled into a half smile. I couldn't help but smile back at him.

"True." I agreed, then looked away still embarrassed.

"Do you do that often?"

"What?" I looked back confused.

"Pass out." I could read some type of concern on his face.

"No. Not usually. Guess the first time was about two months ago after I had been running."

"And tonight you were running again?" He raised his perfectly arched eyebrow.

"Yes, I guess I was…."

"On a dark beach."

"Yes."

"Alone."

"Um. I suppose so." My actions seemed ridiculous.

"Maybe you shouldn't run?" He smiled, and for the first time, I realized that there could possibly be some sort of connection between the odd changes that seemed to be happening and my recent loss of consciousness. "And has it ever occurred to you that maybe a young girl shouldn't be out alone on a dark, deserted beach?"

"It *wasn't* deserted. *You* were there," I teased.

"You don't even know me. I could be dangerous." His face became serious.

"Are you?" I looked over at him doubtfully.

"I could be." His face was unreadable.

"I don't think that's true."

"You saw things tonight that you should have never seen—things that humans don't live to tell about." I shivered, suddenly recalling the details of events. Through my fear, I tried to make sense of things that made no sense at all. I nestled tighter to William's chest.

"What did she want with me? Who is Theron, and how does he even know who I am?"

"The less you know of all of this, the safer it is for you."

"But you keep me safe, don't you." I said looking up into his emerald eyes. My hand slid to the nape of his neck, and my fingers tangled into his soft hair. He didn't pull away, but instead his hand gently brushed the side of my cheek.

"It isn't right for you to be around me. I'm not safe." He said as his fingers ran across my lips.

"Should I be afraid of you?"

"Yes." I looked up at him and even through the darkness our eyes met.

"I will take my chances," I said softly. Neither of us would give in. He tilted my chin up to his face as if to kiss me. My eyes closed and my lips trembled, but his lips did not meet mine. There was a pause. He studied my features in the moonlight. Then his expression softened as he released me.

"It's getting pretty late. You better head up to the house before you're missed."

"No. Not yet. You may disappear again. You seem to be pretty good at vanishing into thin air."

He smiled. "I kind of have to be." He gently guided me to my feet and released me.

"Don't go." I said softly.

"I have to. I have a job to do." He said pulling away. "But, would you agree to one thing for me?" His eyes pierced mine, and I would have agreed to anything.

"Yes."

"I need for you to go back to your parent's house," he said firmly.

"I can't leave—not now!" I protested.

"Please—just for a week or so." I wanted to protest, but he put his warm finger against my cold lips. "I need some time to make sure the area is safe—to throw Maris off of your scent and possibly make them even believe you've gone for good."

"But I don't understand any of this."

"If you do this for me, leave for a short time, I will talk to Silas and explain to you as much of this as I can when you return."

"Why do I get the feeling that Silas is more to you than what you have led me to believe?"

"He nodded. "Silas can give you the answers that I cannot. I just need a little time."

"A week?" I asked. I had not seen my family in quite some time. I had promised to visit weeks ago. I wanted to see them. "And then you promise you will explain all of this to me."

"Just a week." He promised. "And I will tell you all that I am able." I scowled.

"What if that isn't enough."

"This is all I can promise." I looked into his eyes and saw something different. I saw a tenderness that I had not seen before. William would be true to his promise. I nodded, and within seconds, his body soared off of the dock and into the dark water. It was a sight that I had seen before—the evening I first arrived. I now knew exactly what I had seen that night. I had not feared the creature then, but as he disappeared this time, I was suddenly afraid. Not a fear of harm, but that somewhere in the frigid water, he took with him my heart.

I tried to regain my composure as I walked up the steps leading to the back to the Inlet Joy. I clearly was in danger. But what would this creature by the name of Theron want with me? And the woman, Maris, or whatever she was, surely there could be no logical reason that she could wish me any harm. Why me?

All fear was cast aside at the thought of my protector. I could not leave William, even if I wanted to. The sweet smell of William skin still lingered on my shirt, and I could still feel the sensation of his strong arms wrapped tightly around me as I crawled into bed.

****

My grandmother was washing dishes when I finally made a morning appearance. She looked up and smiled as she heard the door close behind me. "Well good morning! It isn't like you to sleep so late. I was starting to get worried."

"I'm sorry. I stayed up a bit too late last night." I needed to talk with her. I needed answers, or at least some information. If she had grown up here, then she must know more than she was telling me. But after her reaction yesterday at the mention of Silas' name, I couldn't find the courage.

"I approve of your love of literature—but you really should go to sleep at a descent hour. The pages will remain unchanged by morning," she sighed.

"Caleb use to get onto me about that all the time. Guess old habits die hard." I knew that logically I should have told her the truth, but I was unsure how to say, *"I am in love with someone who I am pretty sure isn't human, and I think someone who I have never met is out to kill me for reasons I cannot explain."* Part of me wanted to break down and tell her everything. I wanted to tell her about the dark shadowed figure on the dock, and the woman-like creature on the beach. I wanted to tell her that I knew that I was in *some* type of danger, but that I had never felt more alive in my entire life. I wanted to tell her that my skin seemed to miraculously be healed by the salt water, and I was now stronger and seemed to be able to run as fast as the wind could blow. Most of all, I wanted to tell her about my feelings for William. But I couldn't.

I couldn't risk being sent back home before I had the answers that I needed. I now know for certain that there was something out there. My childhood experience in the water had not been my imagination. If she knew the dangers facing me, she would never let me stay. No. I would have to find the answers on my own. If my grandmother had anything that she was hiding from me, then I would find it without confronting her. Her words broke through my inner monologue.

"Is James coming down again to see you soon? You always seem more cheerful when he is around."

"Oh…uh, yeah…I am hoping he can come this weekend."

"Too bad the Leightons aren't here year round. A bit of company for you would be nice. I worry about you being here alone all of the time."

"I am sure they will be down more once the weather starts getting warmer. And besides, I don't mind being alone. I have my books and art to keep me busy. I prefer the solitude actually."

"True. True. You never did need anyone to entertain you dear. Just let me know if you feel isolated. I am so thrilled to have you here, but only if you are happy.

"I am quite happy."

"I just want to make sure you feel like you made the right decision in coming here." Her eyes panned the room and stopped on my face. I immediately bit my bottom lip in an attempt to keep it from trembling.

"I do." I offered up too quickly, still hoping that she didn't see that I was still physically and emotionally unstable. She then looked hard at me. I could see that she was aware of my shuffled state.

"Marguerite, is everything alright?" This time it was her voice that seemed rather unsteady.

"Yes…fine. Just realized this morning how many weeks it has been since my arrival. I was thinking it might be a good idea if I go see my family this week." It was true. I ached to see them—especially Caleb and Lucy.

"I'm sure they would love that!" she admitted, "Though I'm pretty sure I'll be completely lost this week without you!"

"I'll miss you too!" I admitted truthfully.

"Should we call and let them know you are coming?" She picked up the phone and handed it to me.

"Nah! I think it will be more fun to surprise them." I smiled. But my thoughts began to drift away once again to the deep emerald eyes I would be leaving behind.

11

"For truth is always strange, stranger than fiction."

George Gordon Byron

To say my family was excited to see me would have to be an understatement—they were ecstatic! My surprise homecoming was more than I expected. Returning to Florence was like waking up from a long fairytale. All of the monsters were gone, but so were all of the beautiful creatures. All of the fantasy that I scarcely believed existed was now erased, everywhere but in my mind. I felt as if I were privy to some amazing secret, another world that I was in some strange way connected to. But which world was the dream; this world that I had known since childhood, or the world that was slowly opening to me, revealing itself one layer at a time?

I surprised Caleb first. He was just getting out of practice when I pulled into the school parking lot. He raced across the parking lot grabbing me in a big bear hug so strong that it could have easily broken a rib. "Hey sis! I was wondering if you were ever coming back!"

"I know, right! Not sure how those two weeks so quickly turned into four." I could also see Blake Lakely walking to his car on the other side of the parking lot. The way he looked at me made it obvious that his interest in me had not diminished during my absence. He smiled and waved, so I politely returned the gesture. I could sense his confidence rising so decided we needed to get out of here before he decided to come over. Jen's wrath seemed quite mild in comparison to what I had witnessed just the evening before with Maris, but after just surviving an altercation with an evil sea monster, I thought better than to tempt fate with a jealous cheerleader.

"Well, the main thing is that you are here now! Does the rest of the family know you are home?" Caleb asked as he threw his gear into the back of his Honda. Out of the corner of my eye, I saw Jen's cherry red convertible squeal into the parking lot. Her head spun around as if she were possessed when she saw me. Huh? On second thought maybe I would fare better against the sea monster.

"Not yet," I replied, trying to remember his question. "I was waiting for them to get off of work to surprise them, but let's go pick up Lucy from daycare early!" And with that, we hauled out of there before the blonde cheer monster could attack.

I spent the next few days soaking in as much family time as I could. Caleb rarely left my side, and Lucy was a much needed distraction. But when my family was once again off to work and school, I was left with ample time for my thoughts to run back to the shore, back to William. I couldn't seem to escape the effect that his unnatural emerald eyes had on me. I began to feel ill, what I was sure was heartbreak. I tried to hide it from my family as much as possible. That is, until the third day.

After Lucy had gone to bed, I curled up on the couch next to my mother. She excitedly rambled on for the next hour about any and everything she could think of. I was also anxious to spend time with her, so I eagerly listened to all of the news I had missed during my month-long absence. The news was quite uneventful, but I listened with as much enthusiasm as I could muster up. The mothers in Lucy's class had set up a weekly play group, giving my mother a new social group to further occupy her time. Caleb had been dating several girls from school, some of which my mother approved of, some of which she did not. My father had several large projects at work that had been monopolizing his time. I mainly listened. It pleased me immensely to know that my mother's time was so well occupied. But as the evening rolled on, my head began to throb, and I became so sleepy, that I could barely keep my eyes open.

As I washed up for bed, I couldn't help but notice that my face looked quite tired, more tired than usual, and a bit flushed. As I touched my face, my cheeks were warm to the touch. I took a washcloth off of the towel rack, submersed it in cool water from the sink, and laid it across my face. Even after just a few seconds, the coolness of the washcloth was gone. I undoubtedly was running a fever. The very last thing I wanted to do was alarm my mother, so I crept off to bed in hopes that my illness was just a virus and that I would be fully recovered by morning. Convinced that a good night's sleep was all that I needed, I crawled up into my childhood bed and was soon fast asleep. But a good night's sleep did not come.

In my dreams, I was alone in the ocean at dark. I was quite a distance from the dimly lit shoreline. The ocean water was warm, very warm. I kept calling out for William. But I received no response. No one was there. I could feel something under the water brushing against my legs and bumping into me. With each bump I would gasp, but the water was so dark that I couldn't see below the surface. The water became so warm that it burned against my skin. I became frantic. I began to paddle to shore, but the harder I paddled, the further I drifted out to sea.

My bedroom was still dark, but a narrow strip of sunlight broke through between the curtains, streaming across the foot of my bed. It was much later than I had intended to sleep. My bed was drenched with sweat, and my entire body burned painfully. As I attempted to stand, a tear rolled down my cheek as the discomfort was tremendous. I turned on the lights of my bedroom; I gasped in horror at the sight before me. Aside from my face, my entire body was covered in blisters. The red patches that once appeared on my arms and legs were nothing compared to this.

My skin was so tender to the touch it was difficult to dress. Pants were completely out of the question, so I found an old sheer tan slip dress in the back of my closet. I wrapped an ivory throw blanket around my shoulders and began packing the few articles that I had brought with me. I wasn't expected back at the Inlet Joy for another day, but I knew that if I waited another day, I would end up in the hospital again. I also knew that my condition was not one that any doctor could fix. The single thing that I needed couldn't be found here.

As I picked up my bag to leave, I heard the back door open. "Oh Crap! Someone was home." I checked the time again. It was 9:40, well past the time when the entire household should be at school and work. I thought about hiding. I couldn't let anyone see me like this, but there was no time. "Margo. It's just me." I heard Caleb's voice coming down the hall. "I forgot my clothes for soccer, so I had to run ho—" As he turned the corner and faced the entrance to my room, he stood frozen with a horrified look upon his face. Jeez! Margo! What is wrong with you?" I thought the worst of it was hidden by the slip dress and throw blanket, but my neck and legs were still exposed.

"Caleb—I'm sick again." I bent down to grab my bag, but Caleb's hand was over mine in an instant.

"Why is your skin like that?"

"I am not sure." I grabbed another bag.

"What do ya think you are doing? We have to get you some help! Let me go call…."

"No Caleb. We are not calling anyone. Can you just help me to my Jeep?"

"Have you completely lost your mind? I am not about to let you drive anywhere! Margo—you are sick! We have got to get you to the hosp…."

"No. No more hospitals. They can't fix this, Caleb. The doctors don't know *how* to treat this. But I know what to do."

"What is it exactly? What is causing this to happen to you?"

"Honestly, I don't know the exact cause. I think it is something genetic or something, but I know the only cure."

"Well let's go get you some help." He scooped up my bags and began to gently usher me from the house.

"There is someone who can help me."

"Well, let's go! Which doctor?"

"I need to get back to the coast."

"The coast? We need to get you to the hospital! I am calling Dad."

"No Caleb! You aren't calling anyone! You have to trust me on this one. I know this sounds crazy, but it's the water—there is something in the water that can heal this. No, even more than that, it is like there is something in the water that I need—that my body needs. "

"So what? You have turned into a mermaid now?" he said with a mix of sarcasm and anger. "Margo, you don't even go anywhere *near* the water."

"Look, I don't understand a lot of this, but there is someone who does, and I think he can help me if you can just get me there."

"He?"

I nodded.

"Why do I have a feeling that there is more to this story than you are telling me?"

"Now's not the time." I felt myself slipping. My temperature spiked, and I stumbled a bit.

"Can you walk?" He gripped my waist with one hand and my bag in the other.

"I think so." I tried to sound as healthy as possible, but my words sounded labored.

"Fine, but you have to let me drive." He closed and locked the door behind us in one swift motion.

"But my Jeep…!"

"Forget the damn Jeep! I will get it back to you later. We're taking my car!" I frowned as I eyed the blue Honda CRX in the drive but obediently was led into the passenger's seat. I was quite dizzy and was in no condition to argue.

The drive took much less time than had anticipated. I wavered on the edge of consciousness through much of it as his small car weaved in and out of the traffic along the way. Caleb didn't bother with small talk, but would occasionally ask me a random question, just to be certain I was still holding on. He tried to mask his concern, but he nervously flipped through the radio stations, and I would occasionally hear him mumbling something quietly under his breath. I was jolted back to consciousness as the little CRX hit the bridge heading to Garden City. Both nervousness and relief washed over me as I opened my eyes to see the marshlands spread out across the inlet just over the edge of the bridge. Just as we passed over the inlet, a ray of sunlight broke through the wintery clouds and caught the side of my face.

Caleb barely hit the brakes as he rounded the turn towards Inlet Joy.

"Go to the 'point,'" I muttered with a voice barely audible.

"What! I don't understand. What is possibly there that can…."

"William."

Caleb didn't ask any other questions, possibly because he knew I was just too weak at this point to answer. He quickly pulled the car off to the shoulder of the road once the road ended at the large gated property that encompassed the entire "point."

"Nice. Does he live here?"

"No. But he'll find me here. I know he will be here." My voice was so weak that I hardly recognized it as being my own. I pointed in the direction of the icy surf.

Caleb got out of his seat and quickly opened my door.

"Margo! Have you lost your mind! I can't believe I let you talk me into this. I am getting you to a doctor now!"

"Just help me out. I can walk from here." I went to stand, but it was as if all of the strength had drained from my body. I began to crumple against his side. Caleb caught me before I hit the ground, scooping me up into his arms. His strong hands burned against the tender skin that felt as if it were ripping from my body. I screamed out in pain.

"Oh gosh! Margo, I'm hurting you."

"I will be alright. Just get me just over the dunes. There is a path just through there." Caleb hoisted me up as careful as possible into his arms. I let out another gasp as he adjusted me into his arms. My entire body felt as if it were on fire. Caleb pushed aside the sea oats and stumbled onto the hidden pathway between the dunes. As the salt air filled my lungs, it was as if I were breathing oxygen for the first time. I closed my eyes and inhaled deeply.

"Good lord Margo, you are heavier than you look." Caleb stumbled as he carried me down the pathway. "Margo! Are you okay?"

"Yes. I'm here," I mumbled, now barely conscious. I looked over Caleb's shoulder to see William's perfect form sprinting towards us at an unnatural pace. He could have been a mirage—a beautiful mirage. I grimaced in pain as my entire body was burning, blistered, and withering away rapidly. William was the one person who could save me. I was dying of thirst, and my last drop of water was at last in reach.

Caleb saw the corners of my mouth curl upwards and turned to see William now just a few yards away. "I am assuming this is the guy?" I nodded. William approached carefully, his face twisted with concern as he looked over me. Caleb slowly pulled back the blanket with one hand to show the extent of my ailments. "So you're the guy, huh?"

"How long has she been like this?" He asked frantically.

"It must have started last night. I found her this morning and drove straight here. I kinda sped a little."

"You were right in bringing her here."

"She really didn't give me another option. She said that you would know what to do." He nodded. "Is she going to be okay?"

"This is one of the worst I have seen, but I think you got her here in time. I will take it from here. Thank you Caleb." William swiftly and carefully removed me from Caleb's arms, and in an instant I was pressed firmly against William's hard chest.

"So, you just expect me to leave her here with you…like this?!?"

"Yes."

"I don't even know you!" Caleb threw his hands in the air exasperated. I was frozen. Speechless. I wanted to reassure Caleb, but I barely had enough energy left to speak.

"Yes." William turned to face my brother, who was clearly visibly upset at this point. "Caleb, your sister is safe with me."

"How do you even know my name?"

"It is my job to know."

"Your job? What are you talking about? Who are you? And how is *my* sister *your* business?"

"There will be time for explanations later. Caleb, I need for you to cover for Marguerite for the remainder of the week, just until I can get her well again. "I will call you and leave a number to reach her as soon as she is stable. You can call as much as you need to, but I need for you to trust me."

"And why would I do that?"

"Because Marguerite needs you to. Tell your parents she has returned unexpectedly to Garden City, your grandmother is still expecting her in Florence for the remainder of the week—is that correct?"

"Yes, but this is all crazy. I am not going to just...."

"Intercept any calls in both directions and take care of anything that may become an issue. I will have your sister well and returned to the Inlet Joy by the end of the week. If something unexpected arises, I will contact you directly."

"She's my sister! If it were your sister in danger, you would understand!" William went frigid, as if someone had shot him straight through the heart.

"She is safe with me."

"And how am I to believe that? What are you—her boyfriend?

"I am her protector."

I heard myself softly gasp—the last sound that reached my ears before my world went black.

****

When I awoke, I was lying in a warm bath. The world slowly began to come into focus. I looked around, finding my surroundings completely foreign. I was in the most beautiful bathtub I had ever seen. The tub was a white porcelain claw foot tub shaped like a slipper, with a very feminine small white chandelier that dimly burned just above me. Fragrant foam with an oddly familiar smell covered my body. I was relieved to realize that my skin no longer felt like it was on fire. Where was I? The bathroom was a beautiful soft blue grey with dark antiqued planked floors. There were few accessories, other than several exotic sea shells, and a mountain of neatly folded white towels stacked beside an antique table that held a small basin sink. A woman's voice could be heard in just the next room. She seemed to be humming an old hymn, but one in which I was unfamiliar.

"Hello?" I faintly called, nervously unsure of who would be responding.

"Oh, hello Miss! You're awake! You had us all worried." A lovely dark skinned woman that appeared to be in her mid-forties came swiftly around the corner.

"Um…hello." The blood rushed to my face as I realized this stranger had obviously helped me into the tub. She quickly comprehended my embarrassment.

"Now don't you go on getting all bashful, Marguerite! I can promise you don't have anything I haven't seen before." She knelt down beside the tub and lifted my arm out of the water eyeing the faint red patches carefully before reaching for a bottle of mineral salts on a tray next to the tub. As the salts hit the water, a shock went through my body, and I jumped almost knocking the entire bottle into the water.

"Easy Miss, not too much of this stuff. William has been anxiously waiting on you to awake." My heart skipped a beat at the mention of William's name. I thought back to my very last memory before everything went black. William had told Caleb he was my "protector." What was that exactly? My head swarmed with questions and all of the events of the past few weeks flooded back to memory. I felt dizzy and suddenly sick to my stomach. The woman quickly put the cork back into the bottle and put it back onto the tray.

"Um, where am I exactly?"

"You are at Knoxx Point."

"Oh." I knew exactly where I was. It was the beautiful abandoned gated estate that sat just off the jetties. "Why am I here exactly?"

"Why William brought you here of course. Knew we could get you all fixed up in no time!"

"Thank you," I said meekly, suddenly wondering how long I had been here and what all this kind woman had done for me. She smiled and opened another bottle of something that smelled strongly of lilac. She poured a small amount onto my head and began to hum again as she lathered it into my hair. Soap bubbles swirled into the air, and I heard a high pitched little girl's giggle from around the corner. Two tiny eyes peered at me through the crack of the door. She giggled again as I looked over at her.

"Olivia, You know you are supposed to be in there reading, girl!" This time she laughed aloud in a cackle that was infectious. I smiled. "Alright, you might as well come in here and meet Miss Marguerite." Two tiny eyes peered around the corner, followed by a rambunctious, beautiful little girl. She was about the same size as Lucy, but thinner, with deep rosy cheeks atop her dark chocolate skin. She had two dark braids bound tightly to her scalp and wore an exquisite hand-smocked pale yellow dress. I couldn't help but smile. "Marguerite, this is my daughter Olivia. She just turned five on Sunday. Please forgive me for not introducing myself sooner, but I am Sadie. My husband, Henry, and I are the caretakers here at Knoxx Point.

"Nice to meet you both. I can't thank you enough for what you have done for me."

"Any friend of William is a friend of mine." She took the sprayer and began to rinse my hair.

"Will has never brought anyone to see us before mommy! She is very pretty." I felt the blood once again rise to my cheeks. I knew I looked just horrid." I genuinely smiled at the tiny girl. She walked over to the edge of the tub and caught a bubble that had escaped into the air.

"Olivia, I have a little sister just your age. Her name is Lucy."

"You have a sister? I would love to play with her! I have always wanted a sister!" She said, her face beaming with excitement.

"Well, I will have to bring her to meet you next time she is in town." She smiled and giggled as she ran out of the room again. There was a long silence as she continued to rinse my hair.

"Olivia is right. William has never brought anyone here before."

"I thought Knoxx Point was deserted?"

"No, but we don't get a lot of company. The owners have been gone for a very long time but continue to keep us here to take care of the place."

"Oh. How do you know William?"

"We have known him since he was just a little boy; we were friends of his parents I guess you would say. He's always so good about checking in on us from time to time. Such a devoted young man he is."

"Yes, he always seems to be there for me at just the right time."

"Well, there must be something very special about you. William doesn't keep many friends." She held out a fluffy white robe for me. As I stood, the foamy water rolled down my legs. The lesions were still present, but the redness had faded, and the pain was gone. My fever had diminished.

"Actually, all I seem to cause him is trouble." I stepped into the robe. It felt like heaven against my tender skin.

She smiled as she handed me a hairbrush and a dryer. "There are lots of different ways to look at trouble. Trouble isn't necessarily a bad thing. The Lord sometimes gives us challenges to make us stronger. I guess we will just have to figure out just where you fall in all of that."

I smiled halfheartedly and stepped into one of the most beautiful bedrooms I had ever seen. There was a large ebony four poster bed in the center of the room covered in a billowy pure white down comforter. The bed was adorned with an eclectic array of white pillows with a single black velvet neck roll in the center of the bed. The walls and sheers were also white. A dark antique-looking dresser stood prominently in front of the bed, and above it hung a mirror that was completely encompassed with bleached corral. One of the owners of Knoxx Point must have been an artist as I could have never imagined a room more elegant.

"Do you like your room?" Sadie said with a full smile.

"It's just beautiful."

"Good. I am very glad that you like it. It suits you. I will have dinner for you and William in an hour. I bet you're starving."

"That sounds wonderful. I am pretty hungry actually." That was an understatement. The sick feeling from earlier had subsided, and I was very hungry. My stomach let out an embarrassing grumble. "Forgive me. I was in such a hurry this morning that I forgot to eat anything."

"This morning? Oh no, Miss Marguerite, you arrived here *yesterday* morning. You have been unconscious for quite some time now."

"Yesterday? So I stayed in here last night?"

"Well, no actually. William had you down in the tidal pool for most of the day yesterday and throughout the night too.

"Tidal pool?"

"Oh yes, a healthy dose of salt water is the best thing for what you have. Henry tried his best to get William to let him take over for a while, but he would have none of it. I've known that boy his whole life, and I've never seen him so worried. He only brought you up here to me after your fever broke and you were starting to come around. He wanted you to feel clean when you woke, so I took over to clean you up in private. William was raised a gentlemen you know."

I only nodded.

"What do I have Sadie?"

She looked over at me dumbfounded.

"Why Miss Marguerite, you don't know?"

I shook my head. She looked suddenly uncomfortable. Her eyes shifted from side to side, and I realized she was contemplating her response.

"Well, I don't know how to explain it exactly. You'll have to talk to William or Silas." She began to fidget around the room straightening up the already completely cleaned room. I suddenly had a million and one questions, but they stuck deep in my throat. I would find my answers in time. Sadie had shown me too much respect and hospitality for me to press a subject she clearly wished to avoid. My mind drifted over her other words. Had William really held me in his arms for such a length of time and in a tidal pool of all places? He knew the salt water acts as some sort of healing agent for me. Could I be any more of a freak? "I took the liberty of hanging clothes up for you in the closet, and I placed some toiletries in the bathroom drawer. You may want to put on something nice as you are expecting company."

"Company? Are you sure? I don't think anyone even knows I am here."

"All I know is what William tells me."

"But I don't think I packed anything nice." There was a bit of panic in my voice as I thought back over the two old pairs of jeans, several worn knit shirts, and one pair of PJs had thrown in the bag to go see my parents for the week."

"I thought as much Miss Marguerite, so I rounded up a few things that we had in the closets around her, and also hung those alongside your things. Wear whatever you like. No one has been here in many years, and it's a shame to have so many pretty things go to waste."

"Thank you for being so kind to me Sadie." She nodded.

"If you need anything else, please let me know as I want your stay as comfortable as possible."

"Oh. I will be staying here?"

"Yes, William thinks it is best. For a few days at least. He wants to be certain you are fully recovered from your, um—ailment."

"Are you sure the owners won't mind me being here?" The very last thing I wanted to do was impose on anyone.

"Actually Miss Marguerite, the owners of this home would be delighted to know you were here…more than you know." The last part was mumbled as she left to give me privacy, but my ears caught it none the less. Later there would be more time to decipher the day's events. William was waiting on me.

Suddenly, his face was all that I was capable of thinking about. I thought back on the look on William's face when Caleb brought me over the dunes. His concern was obvious, but there was something else in his eyes. There was an emotion there that I had not seen before—something more than concern. Did he care for me? Surely my fever had caused this hallucination. I wasn't naïve enough to believe it could possibly be true. There was nothing about me that could hold the affections of someone like William.

I hurried to the bathroom to dry my hair and saw the remainder of the mineral salts on the tray by the tub. Whatever treatment was in that bottle did wonders to my skin—to my entire body actually. I lifted the bottle carefully studying the product inside. The mixture was shockingly familiar. I was sure that it had to be the same product that my grandmother had shipped to my parent's house months earlier. I bit my bottom lip so hard that it broke the skin. How frustrating that I was once again left with so many unanswered questions. What could be the connection with this substance and my grandmother? I was tired of questions. I wanted answers.

Just as Sadie had promise, all of my toiletries were stored in the bathroom drawers. It was then that I caught the first glimpse of myself in the mirror. Even with wet hair, I could not deny that I looked substantially different. My skin glistened without imperfection, and my eyes appeared brighter and lighter in color. My lips were much fuller than I remembered, and my face held a rosy glow unlike anything I had seen. My fingers traced the creamy lines of my face. I stared in awe of the creature facing me in the mirror. Who was she? My hair seemed to glisten like spun strands of gold. Was it possible that it appeared three shades brighter and several inches longer? How strange. Surely this was all another dream! When my hair was dry, I located my small cosmetic bag and pulled out a small compact of powder blush. But there was no need to apply as the colored powder looked pale in comparison to the color that now flushed my cheeks. My lips were also more red than usual, and so I swiped a quick coat of clear gloss across them, before tucking away my cosmetic bag altogether.

But what to wear? The armoire in the corner of the bedroom contained five dresses and two night gowns. There was a tea-length, dark blue dress with covered white buttons going down the back, a simple short A-line white eyelet dress, a pale yellow dress with a fitted top and flared skirt that fell just below the knee, a casual tan dress that was fitted at the waist with natural buttons made of shell going down the front, and the final dress was a black glossy cocktail style dress. The owner of these dresses had impeccable style. As the cotton robe hit the floor, I was shocked to see that my recently marred skin now looked as smooth as silk. I pulled out the tan dress and slipped it on. I felt like Alice as she entered Wonderland. How quickly everything kept changing! I fastened the brown belt around my waist and eyed my appearance in the floor length mirror in the corner of the room. The dress fit my frame perfectly. Of course it did! *This is a dream!* I hardly recognized the creature looking back at me in the mirror. The girl couldn't be me! There was nothing average about this girl. Her hair shone as if sunlight radiated from it, and her skin was as smooth as fresh milk. Her face was illuminated with rose colored cheeks and lips, and her eyes were set with long lashes that seemed to curve back towards her brow. She was beautiful—definitely just a dream. I pulled a pair of tan sandals from my bag, and took one more glance at myself in the mirror before heading for the bedroom doorway.

The interior of the estate was breathtaking. The upstairs rooms ran in a horseshoe pattern with a long balcony that overlooked into a large living area. The kitchen and dining room were on the opposite end. The floors were made of aged teak, and the staircase that wrapped around the upper level was made of carefully woven driftwood. The lower story was encased with large picture windows that seemed to stretch from one end of the house to the other. The sun falling down over the inlet sent orange and yellow hues dancing around the room. But by far the most stunning aspect of the house was the large glassed domed ceiling in the center of the house. My jaw dropped as I looked up into the colorful evening sky. Surely such views had never been seen inside of a private home before! I knew from the outside of the house that there was a crow's nest just above the dome that harbored a large light such as one would see in a lighthouse.

I spied a narrow staircase and small door just off of the second floor that undoubtedly led to it. I was contemplating if it would be rude to ask Sadie for a tour, when I saw him looking up at me.

William was on the far end of the room near the entrance to the kitchen propped up on a large window box. He was perfectly still. The book in his hands slowly slid to his side as he watched me descend down the grand staircase. He stood, but remained frozen in place as I sheepishly crossed toward him. My eyes remained on the long wooden planks of the floor, as I did not have the courage to look him in the eyes. He spoke first, "Sadie told me you were well."

"I am quite well actually, though my appearance seems altered a bit." My voice trembled a bit with each word.

"It suits you." But his casual tone could not hide the uneasiness that seemed to be mounting inside of him. Had I once again offended him in some way?

"I'm quite confused by all of this." I picked up a golden lock of hair that hung several inches longer than it had just two days earlier.

"I know. Silas will be arriving shortly. He will explain."

"I want *you* to."

"It isn't my place to do so." He looked up into my pleading eyes. His expression softened briefly before his guard was up once again. "Sadie has prepared an excellent meal for you, as I am sure you are quite famished. You can wait for Silas in the dining room."

"You aren't dining with us?"

"No. I only stayed to be sure you were well."

"Stay." I said as my eyes met his.

"I can't," he said looking away. "I have something I have to take care of." My heart sank. He turned to leave, as I tried to hide the mounting disappointment. I called after him.

"William?" He turned back to me, his eyes once again meeting mine. "Thank you—for what you did for me. Sadie told me. I just wanted to say…"

"You don't have to say anything." And with that, he turned and exited through the large double doors leading from the house.

Well, there he goes again, I thought, as the pain of his apparent rejection swept through me once more.

12

"We must be willing to let go of the life we have planned, so as to have the life that is waiting for us."

E. M. Forster

The room was silent. Not knowing what to do, I wandered about the space. The array of objects in this home ranged from antique paintings, to a variety of artifacts that seemed to belong in a museum instead of a private home. Many were nautical in nature and appeared as they could have come off of a sunken ship. There were seashells as well, but unlike the shells from my bedrooms, most were odd shaped conchs I had never seen before. There was a large replica of a letter whelk in the corner, almost the size of a coffee table. It was unbelievably detailed and looked authentic, but a shell of that size would be impossible. A large bookshelf adorned the entire wall under the balcony. Many of the books were familiar classics, some were travel books of exotic destinations, and others looked to be very old collections of ancient legends and folklore.

But one book especially drew my attention. Its size and cover familiar to me, as I had seen it before. I instantly recognized it amongst the collection of other books. It was almost identical to the book I had searched for on my grandmother's bookshelf.

I carefully removed the book from the shelf and examined its antique binding. In old English script, there was something written that I couldn't quite make out. But just below it, the word "Sironian" was etched into the ancient leather. I walked over to the window seat that William had occupied earlier. The book he had been reading rested on the seat, an old version of *The Castle of Otranto*. I had never read that one. I quickly filed it on my "next to read" list. I tucked his book next to me and once again opened the ancient looking text. Not knowing where to begin, I simply turned to the beginning. I was quite startled when I realized I was reading the familiar words of the creation story, as one would expect to find in Genesis. While the text didn't follow the chapter and verse format of a Bible, the content was unmistakable. I had attended enough Sunday school classes in my seventeen years to know Bible stories when I read them.

Why would my grandmother have gone to such lengths to remove a book of Bible stories? I quickly skimmed the familiar story of God's creation of the Earth and of Adam and Eve, but as I flipped through the thin pages, new details were present that both captured my attention and confused me greatly. Written before me was how God had indeed intended Adam to rule over the land and Earth, but Adam's love for his companion, Eve, and vast duties throughout the land, left the sea in disarray. God saw that Adam was also physically unequipped to protect God's ocean creations, and so God created Adam another partner, Siron, to help rule over the sea.

God was quite pleased with the physical qualities he had given to Adam and created Siron to be Adam's physical equal, but as Siron was to rule over the sea, God also gave him physical attributes that would allow him habitation among the sea. I was entranced at this point and kept reading as swiftly and carefully as possible.

Just as God had created Eve as a partner to Adam, God had intended to create a partner for Siron as well, but after Eve's betrayal in the Garden of Eden, God saw how easily his creations could betray him for love. God chose not to create a partner for Siron.

Over time Siron grew jealous over Adam and his relationship with Eve. Desiring a partner himself, he became infatuated with one of Adam's daughters, Amelia. Siron began to neglect his own duties throughout the ocean as his infatuation for Amelia grew. One day, Siron, snatched Amelia from the shoreline and took her far out in the sea. God was angry and created an immense storm. As Amelia could not survive underwater, Siron struggled to get the girl to safety. Siron was strong and was able to find shelter for the girl, but as soon as Siron went to steal a kiss from the girl, God punished Siron for his disobedience once again. Through his kiss, Amelia's own life energy was sucked into his body, giving him unimaginable longevity and strength but leaving the girl dead among the rocks. Out of guilt and shame Siron tried to kill himself, but because of Amelia's life energy that now coursed through his veins, Siron was unable to do so. As God's punishment, Siron would be incapable of death, thus making it impossible for him to ever enter heaven.

Siron pleaded with God, and through His mercy, God made a deal with Siron. He agreed to give Siron a partner, but no love for her, as God wanted Siron to never again love another more than Him. God also gave Siron and his newly created partner, Clarissa, the ability to procreate, but as soon as their children reached their tenth birthday, their children were to be immediately separated from them to a different part of the ocean. This was Siron's punishment for taking Adam's daughter and also God's way of spreading his creation throughout the Earth. God promised Siron that after a thousand years of obedient service, God would allow Siron the chance to enter heaven, and Siron's first born would take over the protection and leadership of the sea.

Siron obeyed God, but with each generation, it became more painful for Siron to give up his offspring, because though he was incapable of physical and romantic love for Clarissa, he loved his children very much. Siron became bitter as the years progressed and made a law declaring that all Sironians could only have one child, and that child must also be separated from their parents on their tenth birthday.

The Sironians soon discovered that they too could gain longevity, strength, and physical gifts from the consumption of human life energy, and some of the more rebellious ones began abusing this power by seducing humans. Siron, trying to remedy the situation, created another law that a Sironian could only take the life energy of a human if that human was already in a situation where death among the sea was certain. Lastly, he created a law separating Sironians from humans and prohibited Sironians from exposing what they were to humans.

I felt my hands trembling as I turned page after page. Could this be true? I frantically turned the pages skimming for more information, but the remainder of the book seemed merely to recount all too familiar Bible stories with no twists or tales of Sironians. I flipped back to the end of the

Creation story and reread the last line I could find that pertained to the Sironians.

"And so Siron named his people for himself and they dwelt deep within the waters apart from the humans." I had become so consumed with the book that I hadn't noticed I was being watched from the corner of the room.

"Are you finished, dear?" I gasped completely taken off guard. "I am sorry. I didn't mean to startle you. I am Silas." I looked up to see a very handsome gentleman watching me from across the room. His voice was kind and soothing, and his expression gentle and concerned.

"Hello, I am Marguerite Westly."

"Yes dear, I have known of you for many years. I am a friend of your grandmother's."

"You are?" I gasp, realizing that my grandmother had indeed not told me the entire truth when I had asked if she knew William or Silas. "William said that he lives with you?"

"He does. I took over his guardianship just after his parents passed away."

"How do you know my grandmother?" He paused and took a deep breath.

"I will answer all of your questions, but first I need to know if you are finished reading."

"I don't know. I finished skimming the story of creation, or I suppose the version of creation written in the book. Is there more?"

"If you mean, is that all of the book that pertains to Siron and our kind? It is. However, our history far exceeds the pages of that text."

"So, all of this is true? I have never heard of any of this before."

"Yes, it is all true. The account of creation, including the creation of our race as depicted in the text, was handed down and preserved by Sironian scribes since the beginning of recorded history. I can assure you my belief, as well as that of our people, in the truth of the Sironian text is absolute."

"When you say '*our* history', you mean?"

"I am referring to our kind—myself, William, and you too Marguerite."

"Me? Silas you must be mistaken."

"No. You are Sironian Marguerite. Well, at least to some extent."

"But I'm human!"

"Yes, you are human. But you are like us as well."

"That can't be true!" I buried my face in my hands. He moved closer and gently pulled my hands from my face.

"It's alright. You haven't done anything to make this happen to you; you were born with the gene."

"That's impossible."

"We all thought it impossible as well. Don't you see, all of the changes that have been happening to you? You are the first half-human, half-Sironian known to exist."

"I don't understand," I said, suddenly realizing if this were a dream that I wanted to wake up.

"I know how confused you must be by all of this, but I can assure you that I speak the truth."

"But how can this possibly be true? My parents are both human!" I protested.

"Your mother is human, but your father is not. He is part Sironian."

"But my grandmother is human as well!"

"Yes, his mother is human, but his father was Sironian."

"My grandfather was a farmer. I *knew* my grandfather."

"I am sorry to be the one to have to tell you this Marguerite, but the man married to your grandmother was not your biological grandfather."

"What?" I wanted to cry.

"Your father has never met the Sironian who fathered him." He took the seat nearest to the bench and pulled it next to me.

"That can't be true Silas."

"My father doesn't even live near the water."

"I know. As there are no known documented cases of a Sironian and a human creating a child, this is all uncharted territory. We have laws against physical relations with humans, and until your father's birth, we never thought it possible."

"So is that why she left Murrells Inlet?"

"Yes. Your grandmother took your father far away from here before he was born to protect him. It would have been his certain death or worse if he had been discovered. We were unsure what his abilities would be or even if he would survive, but as his tenth year passed and there was no physical changes noted, we were assured that the gene would remain dormant within him."

My thoughts were filled with every possible memory of my father growing up. Sure, he was handsome, but aside from that, I could think of nothing unusual that could set him apart from any other father. I didn't remember him being an exceptional swimmer, though I had rarely had the opportunity to observe him around water. He seemed to have no extraordinary strength like I had been exhibiting over the last few months, and really no abilities that seemed to blend him into the Sironian world. Silas knew so very much, and my thoughts had been so consumed by putting this puzzle together in my mind that I had forgotten the biggest part. Suddenly my mouth went dry and I looked solemnly into the eyes of the older man in front of me.

"Silas, are you my grandfather?" He didn't smile but looked away briefly before turning to face me once again. His deep blue eyes met mine.

"Marguerite, I loved your grandmother very much. She and I were very close and very much in love. There isn't anything in the world that I would want more than to be your grandfather, but you are not my granddaughter." My heart beat so loudly in my chest, I was certain he could hear it.

"Who is my grandfather?"

"That is not my place to say. I am sure your grandmother will reveal that information to you when she is ready." I thought back over the many conversations I had had with her over the course of my life, all of those walks together. She had seventeen years to tell me about all of this, seventeen years to tell me the truth! I became angry.

"Because she has been so forth coming with information up until this point?" I snapped.

"Do not be angry with her Marguerite. Everything that she withheld from you was solely done for your protection, for the protection of your entire family actually." My family—I would never want anything to put them in danger. I had not thought of that. My anger began to soften.

Could my family be at some type of risk because of all of this? Lucy's round face and dark curls flashed through my mind and suddenly there was an ache deep in my stomach. I would do everything in my power to protect her, to protect my entire family. All anger drained out of me as I realized that this feeling was exactly the way my grandmother felt about us. She had done what was needed to protect us. I looked over at Silas. How deep had my grandmother's sacrifice been? Had she given up her true love to protect my father?

"So who is coming after me?"

"William told me about your encounter with Maris."

"Yes, she mentioned another name—Theron."

"Theron is the current ruler of the sea. Like you read earlier, each ruling descendant of Siron is in power for a thousand years. During Theron's rule, our people have become segregated due to the laws brought forth by Theron."

"What laws are these?"

"Theron shunned the laws of his predecessors, enforcing his own agenda through extreme measures. He divided our people into different areas of service, specifically designed to insure his reign."

"Area of service? Like what?"

"We have many sects of Sironians throughout the world. Some are designed for Theron's protection such as the warriors and defenders, some provide safe travel for humans, while other protect our waters from your pollution and overfishing, some are specifically tasked with ensuring peace among the different Sironian sects. There are even sects specifically designed to enforce and carry out punishment for those breaking Theron's laws.

"His laws? What kind of laws?"

"There were very few laws for our people until Theron came to power, but he rules through manipulation and fear. He has taken to arranging unions between Sironian couples as a way to strengthen his power—to create a stronger race by pairing those with special talents he finds desirable. Also, families caught with more than one child are often put to death; such was the case with William's parents. Most children are now taken from their parents at birth to be raised by other Sironians, usually those in whatever future area of service the child is expected to follow. This is done specifically for the purpose of weakening family bonds."

"But how could he do these things! These clearly are not the laws of God!"

"No. They are not. This is why our sect broke free from Theron's harsh rule about thirty years ago. Our group is different. We made Murrells Inlet our home because the inlet is large, yet completely divided from the ocean by such a narrow mouth. The mouth can easily be guarded from Theron's forces and also from any Sironian outlaws that could threaten the group or humans living along the peninsula. We can train and live here comfortably. You see, the protectors are the only group evolved to sustain life on land for short periods of time. Most Sironians cannot survive out of the water more than a few minutes. But there are a few of us that can withstand life out of the water for several days at a time. Those born with that gift were once chosen as the 'protectors.' We were chosen because we are the only sect that could live undetected among the humans, to watch over them, and protect them from the sirens who threaten them."

"What do you mean?"

"Well, you see. There are those among the Sironians who have broken away from our life and Theron's regime altogether. They hold no value for human life and take advantage of benefits of consuming the essence of humans. Despite Theron's extreme laws, he does still respect human life as a whole. Our sect was created to protect humans from those that do not share our beliefs. These outcasts once lured the humans in with their beauty, only to suck the life from them in order to gain longevity and strength. Most no longer consume in this manner, but rather select lone swimmers, those from shipwrecks or accidents. These are the sirens your legends are written about. These are the sirens that put human life in constant danger. Some are still very beautiful, while others have mutated in the deep depths of the sea into what you would call monsters, having little resemblance to anything remotely human." I shivered thinking that such creatures existed in the world.

"Are these creatures coming for me?"

"No, but these creatures would consume anything in the water with a human heartbeat. Maris was the one who first discovered you. It was she that first attacked you in the waves as a child. It caused quite a stir among our world at the time. She is also the one who discovered you on the beach last week. Maris is Theron's daughter-in-law. Theron's son was of one of the western warrior sects and was killed about fifteen years ago in battle. Maris has been his right arm ever since. " My throat grew dry, so dry that I could barely swallow.

"But I thought the monsters were the ones that consumed the humans?"

"We are all capable of this Marguerite. We are all the monsters of your childhood stories—all capable of destroying God's finest creation. You see, we all crave the human essence, but some of us are able to control it better than others. Our type, the protectors, seem to have better control in this area. We can at least remain in close proximity to humans. Kirby is the best at this type of self-control; he is the only Sironian that I have known other than myself to be able to have prolonged physical contact with humans."

"By physical contact you mean?"

"Let's just say, I am pretty sure there isn't a girl along this coast that his lips haven't had contact with."

"Oh." I felt my face begin to blush.

"Most of us, even the protectors, don't have this control. So you see, not all of Theron's laws are bad. If Sironians were permitted to mingle among the humans, the Sironians would succumb to the powerful temptation to feed, essentially living forever, and the human population would truly have monsters living among them."

"So Theron wants to kill me because I am half-Sironian, half-human?"

"In theory, but your existence is quite debated since Maris first reported your existence." I glanced down at the scar that still was quite visible on my ankle. "As soon as your blood hit the water, they could detect the abnormality." They have been searching for you for the past ten years, heavily patrolling the area hoping you would return."

"And they know that I am here now?"

"Yes, they know. But do not be afraid, just cautious. William was assigned by me as your protector."

"My protector?"

"Yes, under our Sironian law, as I explained, children are removed from the care of their parents at the age of ten to begin training for their duties. For a very long time, it has been my responsibility to train and supply the "protectors" for the entire East Coast. William was placed under my care just after his parents' death to be trained as a protector.

"But you said you were part of a group that broke away from Theron. Why would he still trust you to train his people?"

"First, I am very good at what I do, as I have served in this role for a very long time. Second, Theron knows that our group does not have the numbers to overthrow his rule or start some kind of rebellion. Our loyalty is not with Theron, but we have not the strength nor the lineage to challenge his power. As long as we don't directly oppose Theron, he tolerates ours existence. Theron is too crafty of a ruler not to utilize the tools he has available to strengthen his rule, including my service as a trainer for the protectors along the seaboard."

I still couldn't understand the intricacies of the relationship between Silas' sect and rest of the Sironians, but it was enough for me to know that

Silas and William wanted me safe. Figuring out the rest could wait. "So, you assigned William to watch over me when I arrived last month?"

"No, William was assigned to you when you were a child. He has been training to be your 'protector' for the past ten years." I was pretty sure my entire body was into shock with this revelation.

"He was there, wasn't he? When Maris first attacked! A hand grabbed mine, helped pull me to safety." Silas seemed surprised that I was so quickly able to put these pieces together. He didn't respond. "You've known of me even before Maris discovered me! You've always watched over me and my family, haven't you?"

"Like I said, I loved your grandmother very much."

"But William? All of those years—for me?" I muttered, barely able to speak. "Why was he chosen for me?

"William was extremely talented, even as a young boy. He was smarter, stronger, and faster than the others. Some of the other young Sironians have special gifts, but William was exceptional in almost every area. He has an amazing gift of intuition. He can't see the future but has a strong sense of what an opponent is thinking. It makes him very powerful in combat. "

"You chose your best protector for me? Why me?"

"Because you will need him. They will come after you Marguerite. Your very existence breaks their laws. But they are after you for other reasons as well. You are a mystery to us, and as you carry both human and Sironian genes, you may be exceedingly gifted."

"I have no extraordinary gifts."

'Are you so sure about that?"

"I am nothing of any significance. I am clumsy and awkward. I have no grace nor beauty." But even as I spoke, I began to doubt my own words.

I thought back to West Florence High School and of Jen's flawless beauty. High school seemed like ages ago and then I remembered my last day there. I had seen the girl flipping across the gym floor, and by some miracle, I was able to duplicate and surpass her skills. I was contemplating this when the incident at the track flashed across my now bewildered mind. I had thought the stop watch was broken, but it was not. Then, as if my mind was suddenly going in all directions at once, I thought back at how easily I had pulled the john boat out into the yard for repairs that day. It should have been difficult with two flat tires to pull it through the sandy soil. These things should have been impossible, and yet because I had willed myself to be able to accomplish them, I had done so.

"What are you remembering Marguerite?" I had not thought my reaction had been so obvious, but Silas was observant.

"I do recall a few things actually, that may be of some interest to you."

I spent the hour telling Silas not only about these events but also about my life thus far. He explained to me that as I was growing into adulthood, the Sironian gene was growing stronger within me, taking over what I once was, becoming more and more like them with each passing day. I was growing faster, stronger, more agile, and as much as I scarcely believed it, I was becoming more physically beautiful as well. I had never thought myself as beautiful, so this was the hardest part to accept. Silas agreed that I must have a talent for being able to watch someone's actions and mimic or physically recreate those actions in a way that I could recreate and surpass their skill.

Silas also explained to me that the red patches that had plagued me for my entire life had not been a skin condition but had essentially been my body's reaction to a lack of nutrients derived from the sea. Just like Sironians, I needed sea water and all of its properties to survive. The more I talked with him, the more familiar Silas seemed to me. It was if I had met him before but could not place where. And then I remembered. "It was you at the hospital, wasn't it? It was your voice that I remember?"

"You were dying. The gene had begun to take over, and your body needed nutrients that a hospital could not supply."

"How did you save me?"

"I replaced your glucose with the actual minerals your body needed. I was unsure if it would save you as you were pretty far gone, but I hoped that it would."

"And this weekend, when I became sick again?"

"We had not realized the extent to which the gene had progressed. Like I said, this is all new to us as well. Marguerite, it appears as if you are no longer able to sustain life apart from the sea. You need the nutrients the water provides to survive."

"But I don't even swim. I don't even touch the water."

"The waves and the wind carry many of these nutrients around you—the sea spray, the wind blowing across the marsh reeds, the sand between your toes. What you need to survive is all around you, but no one will know your full potential, your strengths, and your gifts until you are submersed. This is what you are Marguerite."

"But mermaids and sirens are of myths!"

"We are not like the creatures in your fairy tales, though your legends were acquired from careless Sironians who were seen by humans. We have no tail, but our rate of speed and water swiftly moving off of our legs and feet could easily be mistaken as such. Physically we are built like humans—well, most of us anyway, but we have our own genetic differences.

"Genetic differences?" He nodded as I thought back over the recent changes that were happening to me. "I cut my foot badly on an oyster shell, but it healed quickly after William cleaned the wound with saltwater."

"A perfect example. The salt water he poured over you rejuvenated your body. Not only does your body crave the sea, the water heals you. It has the capability to heal the Sironian body quite quickly, but we had no idea of what its effects were on you. I was quite delighted to learn that it carried its rejuvenation properties within you. William was very upset that he had sent you away and blamed himself for your condition. We were quite relieved that your brother had enough mind to bring you to Knoxx Point. You were lucky that you weren't so far gone that the water couldn't revive you. William spent many hours with you in the tidal pools, but when your pulse and temperature returned to normal late last night, we were reassured that you had made it back in time." This image of William made my skin flush. I thought back on the day at the oyster beds when he had held me in his arms and then the faint memory of his arms around me in the tidal pools. He blamed himself. I ached to think I had been the cause of any guilt he felt.

"There was a bottle of sea salts…."

"Yes, a concentration of sea minerals I have perfected over the years. I sent it to your grandmother when she wrote to me of your condition. It had been many years since she had written, so I had a feeling the gene had passed to you. The salts were first created for your father when he was a baby, but as he grew, it became evident that he did not require the nutrients. As your skin condition worsened, we hoped it possibly could help. We had no idea that such a small amount would expedite the gene process within you."

My face flushed. "Um—I spilled it actually. The entire bottle fell right into the tub."

"The entire bottle? Good Lord!"

"Yes." I bit my bottom lip.

"Well, that would explain a lot I guess. It was extremely concentrated and would elevate and quicken whatever processes were beginning inside of you."

"Like allow a girl who has never run track before be able to run a world record time or flip clear across a gym floor with no training other than watching someone else do it?"

"Yes, that would explain much of it and the coma as well. Your body being given such a high dose of the substance, and then nothing at all could have easily killed you. You are very lucky to be alive Marguerite."

"Wow." It hardly seemed like an appropriate response. There were so many questions that I had—about myself, about who I really was, or what I was going to be, but what I really wanted to know about was William.

"I know this is all a lot to take in at once, but if you will work with me, I will help to unravel any questions that you may have. I don't know all of the answers, but I will help you as much as I can."

"You said earlier that William is my protector?"

"Yes, since you were a young child. He has been dedicated to watch over you here."

"But he doesn't seem to want the job. Shouldn't he be allowed to do what he wants to do? I mean, it doesn't seem fair that he should have to sacrifice all that he may want in life just to protect me?" He sighed.

"I understand your concern, and I know it is hard concept to grasp Marguerite, but this has been our way of life since our creation. More importantly, it is our law. This is what we were designed to do."

"But he doesn't even want to be around me."

"You have to understand. Since his parents died, William has put up walls around himself. He hasn't allowed anyone to get close to him. Even I don't know the extent of what William experienced. William's parents were killed by Theron before his very eyes. But he still believes his younger sister could be out there alive somewhere. As you have learned, family bonds are not something that we are permitted as Sironians, but William carries her in his heart despite laws or reason. He has spent many years working on a boat that would allow him to go search for her."

"But he is Sironian—couldn't he just swim?"

"If she is alive somewhere, she is very far from here. The only way he could travel such distance undetected would be by boat. They would be less likely to detect a Sironian traveling by boat. He will go someday."

"But my existence prevents that?"

"One could presume that. But you have to understand that this is what we are, what we were designed to do."

"But what if I released him of his duties? What if I told him he was no longer bound to protect me? Then he would be free to go and search for his sister."

"That is not how it works. He is assigned to your protection for life."

"But what if I didn't need protection?"

"You do. Marguerite, now that they are certain of your existence, they will not stop until they have you. Their strength is very great Marguerite, and William is the best protector that we have. Once assigned to you, not even you can dismiss that vow."

"But I don't want to be the one thing standing in the way of finding his sister. No wonder he feels the way he does about me!"

"The chances of his sister being alive are very slim. We have our own people out there. We have our own people on the inside keeping track of Theron, and no one has heard of her survival."

"But William still has hope, doesn't he? If this is what he wants, I won't be the thing stopping him from searching for her."

"It is remarkable that you care so much. What has brought this about?"

"William has already saved my life on more than one occasion. I am indebted to him, and this is my opportunity to give him his life back. I want you to help me Silas."

"The only way to break the bounds of his vow of protection would be to replace him with another protector. The protector would have to challenge him for you, mentally and physically outwitting him to take over your guardianship. It is really the only way around the law."

"Has this ever happened before?"

"Only once in our history."

"Then that is what I will have to do." He smiled at me, very touched by my gesture.

"I think you underestimate William's skill. He was chosen for you because he is the best. I have no one more skilled than William."

"Train *me* Silas." I said firmly.

"You? Marguerite, it isn't possible!"

"But you say that I may have gifts, skills that even I don't know about.

"Even so Marguerite…"

"Will you train me Silas? You made a vow to protect me as well. I heard you—in the hospital."

"True."

"And what could be a better way to protect me then to teach me how to defend myself?" He contemplated this for quite some time before slowly responding.

"I have a small group of protectors still in training. You may train with them if you desire, but let me say in advance, that I know each of this group well, and not one is as naturally gifted as William. William is the most skilled protector that I have ever seen. He is the best." Determination began to swell inside of me.

"Then I will have to be better."

****

I didn't return to the Inlet Joy immediately. Rather, I decided to follow Silas' wishes to remain at Knoxx Point for an extra night. In truth, I was hiding out in a way. I needed some time to absorb all that Silas had explained to me. Everything that I thought I knew about the world had changed in an instant.

I also wasn't sure how to address my grandmother. I needed time to think. I was angry for being kept in the dark, but I also felt sympathy over her having to carry such a heavy burden. There were some serious conversations that needed to take place between us. I wasn't quite ready to have those conversations, but I knew that they would be inevitable upon my return. I was different both physically and emotionally. She would know that my Sironian heritage had fully surfaced. She would notice the changes.

After Silas bid his farewell for the evening, the estate was quiet. I was alone. I couldn't help but wonder where Sadie and Olivia had gone. I continued my earlier exploration of the estate, and it soon became quite clear as to why the property required a permanent staff for its upkeep, as each room proved more magical than the next.

There were eight bedrooms. Five were on the upper level and three on the lower level. Each room was meticulously decorated in a fashion quite unlike a beach house, as each piece seemed specifically chosen for each room and artfully designed. I thought whomever the designer had been, they were a sheer genius as each room was both inviting and warm but with both elegance and style. The master bedroom was on the ocean side of the house. The large French doors opened up to a private stoned paved ocean terrace.

The kitchen was open and carried the same lightness that spread throughout the entire house. The counter tops seemed to be of a material that I was unfamiliar with, a beautiful swirling grey stone inlayed with tiny shell fossils and tiny stones that caught the light like gems. The sink itself was organic in nature, as if it had grown straight from the ocean bed. The smooth hollowed out stones encrusted on the sides by bleached coral in an array of different natural shades.

I wandered to the back of the estate down a narrow passageway that led to a heavy old door. I gasped upon opening it, as I had never seen anything so breathtaking. The solarium was filled with an array of exotic plants that filled every inch of the surroundings. Exotic rare birds hung from the branches, most of which I had never seen. The center of the room contained a large deep saltwater pool surrounded by large dark rocks. In the shallows, smooth seats were carved into the rock. Urchins and starfish adorned the rocky sides and a few small fish could be seen swimming just at the water's edge. It appeared to be bottomless though the water level seemed to rise and fall slightly, so I predicted this was some sort of underwater passageway to the ocean. It was all magical, a fantasy even I could not dream up—a place I never imagined existed.

I kneeled by the shiny stones that encompassed the pool. This must be the tidal pool Sadie was talking about. I had been here the night before. William must have taken me here because it was safe; he held me here to save my life. My chest burned with a new emotion, an intense gratitude unlike any I had ever felt. How could I ever show enough gratitude for William's sacrifice? I thought of the many times I had been out on the water over my lifetime, first with my father, then with James. Even though I didn't swim, I was constantly out in the boat, roaming the "point," or strolling along the beach. William had been there each time watching over me, protecting me from dangers I never knew existed. I could vaguely remember seeing him from time to time when he was a boy, always alone. I never knew his presence was for me. He had always been there, and I had never known the just cause.

I ran my fingers across the cool water. My fingers began to tingle, and then my arm. This time I did not need the explanation. I was Sironian. Well, at least part Sironian. My body craved this salty water as it craved the air to breathe. It had never been a mystery that I was different. I had always feel like I was a freak of nature, but the knowledge of what I truly was presented a whole new set of problems.

I opened the double doors that led to the inlet side of the estate. The salty night air rushed into my lungs. The moon was bright tonight. I peered out over the moonlit waterway. The familiar waters were suddenly a mystery. A mix of emotions brought a tear to my eyes as for the first time in many years, I wept openly. Could all of this really be true? Even as I questioned, I knew undoubtedly that it was so. And yet, it all seemed unbelievable! I wasn't a true Sironian but some sort of half breed. William would never accept me into this world! He would never accept someone like me into his life! I looked out over the dark row of houses spying the dim lights of the Inlet Joy in the distance. I no longer belonged to that world either. What would I tell my family? The changes within me were now obvious—I could never go back, never stay away from the coast for more than a very short amount of time.

All was quiet. The only sound was the inlet water gently lapping onto the sand. I closed my eyes and stretched my arms out wide. I wanted to dive off of the long pier into the still water—dive as the creature had done that night off of the dock. The creature that I now knew was William. He had been there even my first night back to watch over me—to protect me. He was my guardian, despite his desires to be free of me! I opened my eyes and scanned both the water and the dunes around me. I couldn't see him, but he was there. I knew William was there looking over me somewhere.

I stayed outside on the terrace much longer than I should have. I was chilled to the bone. The estate was dark when I made my way up the staircase to my assigned room. My room was dark. I mentally scolded myself for not leaving a light on. My teeth chattered, and my hands were shaking as I tried to warm them up. A lamp dimly lit the beautiful bedroom, where Sadie sat bedside reading.

"Oh, Marguerite, you look frozen to the bone!" She rushed over to me, wrapping me in a quilt from the base of the bed.

"I am alright. Just a bit tired."

"This should warm you up in no time at all! I saw you outside but didn't want to disturb you. I waited to make sure you were settled in your room comfortably for the night."

"Thank you Sadie. You shouldn't have waited up on me. I apologize for being out so late. I just have had a lot to think about today."

"It's perfectly understandable miss. I laid out a fresh gown for you to sleep in on the bed and a glass of water by your bed. Can I get anything else for you to make your stay comfortable? A snack maybe?"

"I appreciate your kindness, but I am not hungry."

"Well, I won't be far away, so you just let me know if there is anything that I can get for you." I took the gown and made my way to the bathroom to change.

"Thank you. Goodnight Sadie." As she turned out the lights, I caught a glimpse of her eyes glowing through the darkness. I pictured the green glowing eyes on the dock that night—William's eyes. Sadie was Sironian. It had not occurred to me that the caretakers of Knoxx Point were Sironian. There was still so much I needed to know. I would have to start with my grandmother tomorrow. Why did it seem like the more I learned, the more I was left with unanswered questions?

Despite all that I had learned over the course of the day, what baffled and frustrated me the most was the image of William's perfect face that appeared each time I closed my eyes.

13

"You can never let the waves take you. You have to resist the undertow before it truly grabs hold of you. Move with the current until you can escape with steps so firm that it could never take you back."

James Leighton

I arose and dressed just as the sun was coming up. I had caused enough trouble for the caretakers of Knoxx Point. I carefully packed the few clothes I had with me, and returned the ones I had borrowed neatly in the armoire. I scribbled a note of thanks to Henry, Sadie, and Olivia, and placed it on the bed pillow. Taking one final look at the beautiful room, I gently closed the door behind me.

The estate was completely quiet. I had half expected to find William watching over my door as I slept, but both to my relief and dismay, he was nowhere to be seen. I had fully intended on walking back to the Inlet Joy, as it was less than two miles away, but was surprised to find my Jeep waited for me in the drive—keys in the ignition. William had done so much for me. How could I ever really thank the person who was responsible for literally saving my life?

As I drove into the Inlet Joy, my grandmother's truck was in the driveway. My nerves began to get the best of me as I turned the door knob that led into the house. But the house was empty. I realized that she was not expecting me and was taking her morning walk. I was glad, as it gave me a chance to call Caleb. I knew he must be out of his mind with worry. Both Sadie and Silas told me he had been calling every few hours since my arrival demanding to speak to me. I took a deep breath before dialing the familiar number. He picked it up on the first ring.

"Hi Caleb! It's Margo!"

"Crap Margo! Do you have any idea how worried I've been! Seriously! I thought you were dying! I have been blowing up the phone trying to reach you, but some lady or that William guy was always telling me you were asleep!"

"I know! I am so sorry Caleb. Looks like I dodged a bullet with this one. I was pretty sick."

"But you are alright now?"

"Yes. Perfectly alright. I am better than before actually." I heard a sigh of relief on the other end of the phone.

"So, are you going to tell me what is going on now?"

"It's pretty complicated actually."

"Try me!"

"Are you alone, I mean, is anyone else around?"

"No. Mom has taken Lucy to school, and Dad has already left for work."

"Huh? What day is it?"

"Friday! Jeez Margo! You don't even know what day it is? What happened to you?" I could hear the anxiety building again in his voice.

"I was unconscious for a while, but it won't happen again. I finally know what has been happening to me...."

"Well, you better fill me in on what is going on, because I have been covering your butt with both the family and Grandmother for the last three days! Each time the phone rings I am bouncing back and forth making excuses for you, The last time I set eyes on you, it looked like you were on your death bed, and I am the dummy handing you over to some stranger!"

"William isn't a stranger. He is my protector actually?"

"What the heck is that? Protector?"

"Like I said, it's complicated."

"Well, you better start explaining, and you can start with, why my sister needs a protector and who exactly is he protecting you from?"

"I am still figuring out the basics myself Caleb, but the short of it is that I am a bit genetically different than most people." I was trying to be careful not to reveal too much all at once. The phone line went silent.

"That's ridiculous!" Caleb finally uttered.

"I know. I could scarcely believe it myself. But it's true. I'm different."

"Like how different? I mean are we talking about your skin condition?"

"Well, this is more like sci-fi movie different."

"What the heck are you talking about Margo?"

"Well, I know this sounds strange, but my body needs salt water to survive. It's a gene that I carry. Apparently in the past few months the gene really started to take affect. I have been changing. I look different; I feel different. It explains my skin, and why I keep getting really sick."

"Do you realize how crazy you sound?"

"Yes. Grandmother has known what was happening to me; this is why she brought me down here to live with her."

"And the flipping across the gym?"

"Well, apparently, it also gives me certain abilities as well."

"Are you serious? My sister is some type of mermaid superhero?"

"Very funny. No, Caleb, I am not a mermaid or anything approaching a superhero. Why do I have a feeling you are never going to let me live this one down?'

"Because I'm not! Cool! Do you have a tail?"

"Very funny!"

"I am being serious! Well, you said you look different!"

"No. I don't have a tail. It's nothing like that. I look different. I am…," I could barely say the words. "I'm pretty." Caleb burst out laughing at the other end of the phone.

"Your special super power is being pretty? Margo you have always been pretty."

"No not like, cute girl at school. I'm pretty like—siren pretty. I think genetically I am changing into some kind of siren." He laughed again.

"Knowing how you love attention, I'm betting you are digging this!" He said sarcastically. "Um. Ok—what's a siren?"

"Jeez Caleb! Don't you read at all?"

"Not if I can help it!"

"Well, Google it then!"

"Ok. Ok. Do Mom and Dad know about this?"

"No. It's best to keep it that way for a while."

"Why? If this is really all true, then it's really cool! I would assume you would want everyone to know. You would be like famous and stuff."

"Actually, that is exactly why I need protection. There are certain people who already know about me, and I am in danger because of it."

"Oh good lord Margo, what does that mean?"

"There are others like me that want to make sure no one knows about this. You all could be in danger—even Lucy. You have to keep this a secret Caleb—for everyone's safety." At the mention of Lucy, Caleb seemed to begin to understand the severity of the situation.

"This could put Lucy in danger?"

"This could put all of us in danger. You must promise to keep this a secret for now."

"Ok, I will…for now. But if you go missing again, I'm telling Mom and Dad. Now you said there were others. Like who? This William dude—is he one too?"

"Yes. And there are others, but they're different from me too. They are called Sironians. The Sironians and regular people aren't supposed to be able to genetically mix, but somehow, it happened through Grandmother's side of the family."

"But dad isn't one?"

"I know. He still has the gene but it's dormant in him or something. Look, I don't fully understand all of this stuff yet either."

"Do you think I have it? I mean, it would be pretty cool if I could do super hero stuff."

"I don't think so, but I guess we won't know for sure for a couple more years when you begin to mature."

"I'm mature now."

"Yeah, in your dreams!"

"Oh, crap. Look at the time; I am going to be late for school. Gotta go Margo! You can tell me more later! Next time I call answer the dang phone!" Leave it to Caleb to be worried about a tardy, when I just told him there was a new race of people that potentially places our entire family in danger.

"OK, but wait. How did you get my car to me?"

"That William guy…or whatever he is…told me as I was leaving the beach, to drive your car to school so Mom and Dad wouldn't be suspicious. He said to leave the keys under the mat, and he would get it to you from there. So I did, and when I got out of school, it was gone. I assumed he got it."

"He did. Thanks Caleb…thanks for everything!"

"Are you sure you're okay Margo? This is some pretty freaky stuff. Maybe I should come down there?"

"No, now that you kind of know what is going on, I need you to be at home to keep an eye on things there—especially Lucy!"

"Got it! And you do whatever you mermaid—siren people do down there. But don't get too freaky on me Margo. You know I have a weak stomach for that kind of stuff. Gotta go! Love you!"

"Love you too!" I said still holding the receiver as the phone line went dead.

I turned to find my grandmother standing in the doorway. She gasped as she caught sight of me. "You heard?" She eyed me carefully from across the room, and I knew exactly what she saw—the new me.

"I know. It is kind of freaky huh?" I ran my fingers across my cheeks and down the golden strands of hair that hung several inches longer than when she last saw me. She swallowed hard and crossed to meet me with tears in her eyes.

"No, just different. You're beautiful." I felt the blood run to my cheeks. "I'm sorry. I knew what was happening to you, but I didn't know what to expect."

"Why didn't you tell me?" I said, my voice suddenly pleading with her. I tried to keep my expression as neutral as possible. I could see on her face how drastically my appearance had been altered.

"I wanted to tell you, but I couldn't. Both out of secrecy and…honestly, I just couldn't find the words. I had hoped the gene would remain dormant as it did with your father, but the closer you came to maturity, the smaller that chance became. Even as a baby, I thought this was likely to happen; you seemed different from other babies—even then! But it wasn't until you were in the hospital, that I knew for certain."

"And that's why you were so insistent on me coming to live with you?" I already knew the answer. I wanted for her to explain.

"Yes, I had hoped to keep you hidden, like I had kept your father hidden, but you were going to die if I didn't get you to the coast. The gene is stronger in you than even I had imagined. You are truly special."

"But how did this happen? You have to tell me how this happened to me!"

"What do you know?"

"Silas explained to me what I am, but not how I came to be this way. He told me nothing of how this could have happened." I could see how her expression changed at the mention of his name. Silas wasn't just someone she was once in love with, he was someone she was still in love with.

"You were with Silas?" Her voice began to shake. I nodded. "I'm glad that it was Silas who told you."

"Everything but your part. He said it wasn't his story to tell." She smiled with tears in her soft blue eyes.

"Of course he did—ever the gentleman. But you *do* know of what you are now? You know the Sironian history?" I nodded.

"I just don't know how I am linked to it?"

"Did he tell you about the protectors?

"Yes. But he told me nothing of how we were originally linked to them." A tear rolled down her face.

"This has never been told to anyone, so forgive me if this is hard for me." The older woman took my hand lovingly and led me to the couch. She carefully studied the obvious changes in my appearance.

"I suppose it is time you know the truth, as clearly this is part of your life now." I nodded. "Silas is from a long line of protectors. He was the most gifted of them all and was assigned to be over the entire East Coast. He fell in love with Murrells Inlet and chose it as his home. There were very few inhabitants here during those days, and he could reside here without raising any alarm. I was a young teen at the time, and my father was one of the only fishermen who lived in the area. He sold fish and crabs for a living, and we had a small house just over the creek. It is pretty overgrown with trees now, but you can still see my mother's daffodils blooming next to the creek bed in the spring.

"I worked for my father on the fishing boats, and one day when I was out working alone, the boat sprung a leak. Silas appeared out of nowhere just as the boat was about to sink and rescued me. At first he was standoffish, but soon we became very close. He had a place just down creek. In the beginning, I had no idea what he was, and to be honest, I wouldn't have cared even if I had known. He was the most handsome thing I had ever laid eyes on, and the most amazing young man I had ever met. At first he was gone for weeks at a time. I knew he had some job that kept him traveling, but the more time we spent together, the less time he seemed to travel. And then it seemed like he was rarely ever gone.

"I suppose I first knew for sure that there was something very different about him when I was about your age. I was supposed to set and tend to the crab traps here in the inlet while daddy was out in the larger boat in the ocean. Silas desperately wanted us to spend the day together. He told me to wait on the dock, and he took out the boat. He returned about thirty minutes later…the entire boat was running over the top with large blue crabs. There must have been a thousand of them! I stood there in amazement, but Silas just smiled and said, "So *now* can you spend the day with me?" Ironically, both my father and I never came home again without a very large catch. The money helped to pay for my college, and for my family to start a new life after we had to leave the inlet."

"So Silas really is my grandfather!"

"No dear. He is not. Silas and I did not have a physical relationship. He actually thought it impossible. You see, a Sironian can draw the life from a human with a single kiss, even unknowingly. When I finally learned of what he was, I told him, I would live without physical romance, if only we could still be together. But relationships between Sironians and humans are forbidden.

"Silas, being a protector, did not want to leave my side, and in his absence the feeders moved into the East Coast. The feeders were a sect of Sironians that broke away from the laws and lifestyle that had been set by the Sironians. They have no respect for human life and would consume as many humans' life energies as possible. They began wreaking havoc along the East Coast's fishing communities, sometimes taking entire fishing fleets. Silas still refused to leave my side, but his childhood friend Aaron volunteered to guard over me in his absence.

"As with all Sironians, Aaron was extremely beautiful, but he carried an arrogance that Silas did not possess. Aaron was egotistical with a quick temper and a strong sense of entitlement. Though he and Silas had been childhood friends, Aaron was always jealous of Silas, especially when Silas was given the position as guardian of the East Coast. Silas would only return briefly before having to return to the seas again, all the while leaving me in the care of Aaron. But Aaron grew jealous of our relationship, and quickly set his sights on me. As weeks turned into months, he convinced me that Silas did not truly love me, that he was away from me because he wished it. At last Aaron wrongly informed me that Silas would not be returning. I was young, lonely, and brokenhearted.

"One evening, Aaron seduced me. The pull he had over me was unbreakable, and once he had taken all of me, he left me for dead in the ocean shallows. Though many miles away, Silas caught my scent and somehow managed to get to me. Ironically, the seed inside of me was the one thing that kept me alive. The ocean water kept it strong—it seemed to heal me in order to protect the new life that was forming in my womb.

"Aaron burned my childhood home, and reports were made that my entire family had perished. But Silas was able to rescue my parents and was able to hide me away in secret until I was well enough for travel. We wanted to keep Aaron and his family from learning the truth, that I was alive and that I now carried his half-breed child.

"My parents were somewhat aware of the Sironians by this point. They knew I was in danger, and my father luckily had saved enough money for me to go away to college and for us to relocate elsewhere. Though, I suspect, Silas covered much of the expense. We moved out on a farm, but my father never officially had to work again as large sums of money were randomly delivered to us. He knew it was from Silas but mistakenly thought it was to care for his child that I was carrying. The day we left for upstate was the last time I ever saw Silas. To assure my safety he broke all contact with me and my son, so not even a letter passed between us. I was once again heartbroken.

"I married your grandfather just out of college. He loved my son as his own, and there was never a need to tell your father the truth. The gene miraculously remained dormant in your father, and so we were able to live away from the coast peacefully and undetected. It wasn't until after your grandfather passed and your father was safely living elsewhere with his own family, did I dare to venture back here to be near Silas. I have not seen him except from afar. It is still unsafe for us to be together, but I am assured just to feel his presence from across the canal."

We were both crying. Whatever I imagined my grandmother's story to be, I had never dreamed of her sacrifice.

"But you still love him?"

"Yes, dear, true love doesn't fade from time or distance. But if Aaron discovers I am alive and that I have born a half-breed, our entire family will be at risk."

"The Sironians *do* know of me. I was discovered that day as a child in the surf. It was a Sironian that took hold of me, when her fingers pierced my leg—she knew."

"I have suspected this. They know you are a half breed of some sort, but they do not know of your linage. No one aside from Silas and myself is aware of how your father came into the world or that Aaron was responsible. If any of the Sironians found out this secret, your father would be killed. Our entire family would be killed. There is no where we would ever be safe."

"I have a lot of questions, but I need some time to process all of this." I said burying my face in my hands.

"Of course you do dear." She said stroking her hand across my head.

"I am going to go for a walk okay?"

"Sure. Just be careful. You know the dangers now."

"I do."

When I made it out to the beach, I didn't walk. I could barely stand. My mind raced in every direction at once. I felt the extreme heartbreak of my grandmother and the loss of the innocence of the girl that I use to be. I saw a world that had been transformed instantly into a fairytale, complete with its own villains and monsters. My biological grandfather was a monster.

I sat on the dunes as if in a trance, watching the waves roll onto the shoreline. Were those churning waters actually my home? Did I belong among the breakers covered in sea foam and bathed with sunlight, or did I belong nowhere at all. I could not deny that I had lived an entire seventeen years feeling consistently out of sync with the world, and now that I knew what I was, I only felt more out of place. I watched wave after wave until they all seemed to run together. Their crests seemed to be reaching out to me, and their faces seemed to be calling my name. I stood and moved closer and closer to the water's edge, and the closer I got, the more it seemed to call to me. Its call became a pull, as if its hands were on my shoulders pulling me closer and closer. My eyes closed and with each step I was drawn nearer and nearer to the choppy breakers. It sang to me. It called my name. I stepped into the surf and let myself go.

Instantly someone firmly grabbed hold of my arm and pulled me back to the shoreline with so much force we both went tumbling backwards onto the wet sand. The trance was broken. Was I alive? I gasped in shock at what I had almost done. I had not realized that someone had followed me. But this time, it was not William's face peering down on me. It was James.

"James!" I wrapped my arms tightly around his neck. He was still out of breath. James tried to keep his tone light and friendly, but I could hear the concern in his voice.

"What ya doing girl? Thought you didn't swi…?" He looked at my face, and I knew what he saw, someone that resembled his friend, but was now different. He moved his hand to my face tracing the lines almost as if he were in disbelief that it was really me.

"It's me," I said pulling his hand away.

"You look *different*. I just saw you two weeks ago, but now you look…."

"I know. Thought it was just time for a makeover."

"I don't think so. No, there is definitely something different about you. What's going on here?"

"It's me James! No aliens have taken over my body. I promise!"

"Alright. Prove it! How did I get this scar?" He pointed to the scar on his knee. I smiled.

"Well, you were thirteen…and we were walking one morning. I climbed up on the rocks to look for starfish. You *had* to come up after me despite your very poor sense of balance and tripped catching your knee on a barnacle. Then you tried to play the whole thing off as if I couldn't see the blood dripping from your leg for the next hour."

"Ok. You're Margo." I shrugged and nodded. The less I said at this point the better. "But why were you going out there? You don't swim."

"I—I thought that, I might need to work on that." I was not convincing. I could tell he was trying to size up the truth. How could I even try to explain when I barely understood any of this? Something had taken hold of me, called to me from the shore. It had almost succeeded. They were after me, and I now knew that they had more than just physical powers. I had no idea that they were able to draw me emotionally like that—the siren's song. It had to be Maris! Her powers were stronger than I had imagined. I would have to be more careful.

"Margo, I am not about to let you go out there darlin'. Do you see how the water is breaking to the west? Even if you could get out past the breakers the undertow would pull you right out to sea." I knew this—he knew that I knew this.

"Yeah, guess it isn't a good day for swimming after all." I tried to secretly brush back a tear without notice. James was too observant.

"Especially not in thirty degree water. So what's really going on here? I'm gone two weeks and you are now running out to sea?" He brushed back the tear that had escaped from the corner of my eye.

"Something like that." Another tear slipped out. This time, I didn't bother to try to hide it. In the many years we had known each other, he had never seen me cry. He thought I was trying to kill myself or at the very least, I had gone crazy. His tone changed, and a tender side that I had never seen before broke from his playful exterior.

"Look at me!" He took my face between his hands. "Whatever has happened, you can never let the waves take you. You have to resist the undertow before it truly grabs hold of you. Move with the current until you can escape with steps so firm that it could never take you back."

"It's not what you think...." I wanted to reassure him that I was alright. But couldn't help but wonder if I would ever truly be alright.

"You know you can always come to me...about anything." He wiped the tear from my face with one hand, before helping me to my feet.

"I know." I forced a smile for his benefit. But all the while knowing I couldn't share this with James. It would be selfish to put James in danger. I wanted nothing more than to tell him everything that had transpired in my life over the past few days. I longed for my confidant! But I couldn't do that to him. How could I tell him that the life he'd known was in fact a much different reality? "It's kind of complicated."

"There wouldn't be a guy involved now would there?"

"What?" His response took me off guard.

"I saw William again, just over the dunes as I was running after you. He looked like he was about to come after you, but changed his course when he saw me running toward you. He isn't behind this is he?"

Of course William had come. James had saved me from running into the water, but if he hadn't, William would have prevented it. He wouldn't have allowed any harm come to me—he couldn't. It was his job. My faces twisted at the thought that he was bound to my protection. How he must hate playing my babysitter.

"No. Of course not! We aren't even friends actually."

"Well, that's good, because I still say that guy is trouble. If he had hurt you, I would have had to teach him a thing or two." He flexed his lean arms, and a small firm bulge appeared. The wall had slipped back into place, and his playful exterior had returned. I almost giggled at the thought of James "taking on" William. Mere mortals never seemed to fare well when put up against the supernatural. I had seen William in combat, I knew why he was feared by the other Sironians. He was chosen as my protector because he was the best. I quickly changed the subject, fighting the urge not to look back over the dunes to see if William was still there.

"So what are you doing down here on a Friday morning? No school for you today?"

"Well, I actually came to see you. I figured missing one day wouldn't kill me, and I thought I'd get a jump on the weekend—especially since you were gone last week to see your folks." My time in Florence seemed like ages ago—I lived in a different world back then.

"I am so glad to see you!" My words were sincere and true, but I wasn't quite sure how to fit James into this new existence—into this new world that I was just beginning to discover.

"I'm the one who is happy to see you, darlin'—and apparently thankful to have you alive." I tried to smile. I knew there was no way I could explain to him the truth.

"Actually, I should probably go change these wet jeans before I freeze to death." My rolled up jeans were wet from the thigh down.

"That makes two of us." James' jeans were also wet. Had I put him in danger as he rushed through the surf to stop me? What if the Sironians had grabbed the both of us? I shuttered to think about what I had almost caused to happen.

"Oh James! I am so sorry." I blushed at the thought of my friend being uncomfortable due to my stupidity.

"It's no problem darlin'. How about let's both go run back up to the house and get ourselves cleaned up? I will meet you out on the dock in about an hour, and we can go grab some lunch." He put his arm around me as we made our way back over the dunes. When I was with James the world almost felt upright again. *Except for the fact that I wasn't fully human, but a Sironian half-breed being lured toward an underwater civilization where the majority of the inhabitants wanted me dead.*

I knew that it was wrong, but I nestled my head against James' chest as we made our way closer to the Inlet Joy.

14

"The mind is its own place, and in itself can make a heaven of hell, a hell of heaven."

John Milton

I **decided it best** to avoid my grandmother for a while. I knew there was still much to say, but I was emotionally drained and still a bit in shock. I needed a moment to be alone with my own thoughts.

My bags rested against the salvaged wooden door leading to my bedroom. I felt as if I were coming home. The room was just as I had left it. My paintings, books, and music remained just as I had left them. So much in my life had changed since I last stood at this threshold a week ago. But as I stepped through the door, I began to cry. The room's contents belonged to a person who no longer existed. That girl was gone.

In the mirror was the face of someone I could hardly recognize. I had changed; even more so than I had remembered at Knoxx Point. My features, though the same, were softened and my skin radiated in hues of rosy porcelain. My glossy hair hung an extra half inch longer than it did just this morning. The hazel of my eyes was now displaced by the rich emerald color that I had seen in my dreams. The "me" that I knew was gone, replaced by this beautiful creature that only bore a resemblance to the girl I once was.

I wrapped myself in the old quilt that hung on my bed and curled myself into a ball on the edge of my bed. The tears that flowed this time were for the girl who was lost—the gangly, clumsy girl with the sandy blonde hair who was gone. I wept softly and mourned her loss for quite some time, and then—there were no more tears left to cry.

There was a gentle knock, and my grandmother entered the room. She looked older than I had ever seen her, as the creases on her face were more pronounced and the circles under her eyes were a dark purplish. She had been crying as well. She looked around my room, finding me curled in a ball on my bed. She knew me well enough to guess my thoughts. "You know, you are still the same girl that you have always been, at least on the inside. Don't let this rob you of who you are Marguerite. This is what you were born to be; you just didn't know it until now." She slowly entered the room and sat next to me on the bed.

"I don't even know what I am anymore?"

"I admit that part of this is my fault, but I just wanted you to lead an ordinary life for as long as you could. But you are far from ordinary. You are extraordinary—always have been. Yes, you are Sironian, but you are also human. Don't you see? They fear your creation because you carry inside of you the strengths of both humans and Sironians. This *is* who you are, and it is time for you to start living the life you were born to lead."

"But I'm scared. For the first time in my entire life, I'm scared."

"And I am scared too. I'm scared for your safety, your future, and your happiness, but you aren't going to be able to hide what is inside of you any longer. Let them help you. Let Silas train you and show you a world that people only write stories about."

I nodded as her thin arms wrapped around me. She cradled me in silence for several minutes before releasing me with a faint smile. "But you know, it is never a good idea to keep a fella waiting." Her lighthearted words lightened the mood.

"What?" I was confused.

"That poor boy has been waiting out there on that dock for you for over an hour."

"Oh shoot! James!"

"A bit of advice dear—he will have some questions, and I know you will handle them as well as you did with Caleb, but we don't want to put any more lives at risk. Tell him as little as possible, for his own sake."

"I agree. James should know as little about all of this as possible."

"That being said—keep your friend close dear. You will need all of the support you can get to adjust to all of this. It is just what you need to have a bit of normalcy around you."

"Thanks Grandmother."

I hurried and pulled out my other pair of jeans from the bag. They smelled wonderful. Sadie must have washed all of my clothes while I was at Knoxx Point. I pulled a thin pale brown sweater from the closet and quickly pulled back my new shiny mane in a ponytail. The change would be less noticeable if it were pulled back. It would be best to tame down this transformation as possible. I removed my tan flats from my bag, also freshly polished, and hurried out to the dock to meet James.

James looked amazing. His baby blue striped button up brought out the blue in his eyes, and the mid-day sun reflected the copper tones of his short wavy hair. "Well darlin', you know how to keep a guy waiting, but when you look like *that*, you are more than forgiven."

"I am so sorry. I was resting and lost track of time." It was all the explanation that I was going to give, and James was enough of a gentleman not to push the subject. I could tell by the way that he looked at me that he was once again studying the changes in my appearance. I knew it was only a matter of time when I would have to come up with some type of explanation—not an easy task for someone who was the world's worst liar. I would have to get better at it. Covering was now going to be part of my daily life.

"Ready to grab some lunch?"

"I am starving actually!"

I was a bit surprised when James' car drove past Sam's corner, our usual hang out, and opted for a nicer seafood place just over the waterway. I had never been to Sara J's Seafood but had driven by it many times on the way into Murrells Inlet.

"Do you mind if I get a table that overlooks the water?"

"No, that's fine."

"Great."

The afternoon sun had warmed the temperature, so other guests had chosen to eat outside as well. The waitress ushered us to a table on the far end of the patio, took our drink orders, and promptly brought us a big basket of hushpuppies. I caught James staring hard at me again. I knew he was trying to find a way to bring up the obvious.

"So, you haven't told me what you think of my new look?" I blurted out at last.

He fumbled with his napkin nervously. It was quite unlike James to act nervous around me. I hated it. I wondered what could have caused this change. He had never seemed nervous around me before. "New look, huh? Well, you seemed like you were in a pretty bad place today, so I decided not to push the subject."

"Yeah. I meant to tell you that I was sorry about all of that...."

"Margo, I want you to know that you can tell me anything."

"I believe that."

"You could start by explaining why you suddenly look like a supermodel."

"Ha! Very funny."

"I didn't mean that as a joke. You are stunning—I mean, you have always been beautiful, but there is something remarkably different about you and I can't exactly put my finger on what has changed—or should I say, what hasn't changed." He reached across the table and took my hand. He had reached for my hand many times over the years, but this time his hand felt different in mine. I squeezed his hand affectionately, before pulling it back into my lap.

"I thought it was time for an updated look." I popped a hushpuppy into my mouth casually and shot him a squinty smile in a failed attempt to change the mood.

"No. No way are you passing this off as a simple makeover." James wasn't going to let this go very easy. I tried again.

"Um—vitamins. You know, they really do wonders for your complexion." I had no explanation that was safe to offer.

"Have you even looked around you? Do you not see it?" He was getting a bit flustered. I looked casually around the room, and suddenly I *did* see what James was talking about. People were staring at me—some quite obvious, others more subtle. I had somehow captured the attention of all that were around us.

"Why are people staring at me?"

"Because you're beautiful."

"That's absurd."

"No. It's true. Not just beautiful—absolutely stunning." That couldn't be the reason. There had to be another reason that they were looking at me. Did they know I was Sironian?

Suddenly, like a lightning bolt it hit me. I was a siren. It was more than beauty; it was what I had become. Whatever alluring qualities that the sirens possess were passed through the gene as well. I was a monster now—a beautiful monster. Could I so easily take a human life like the "feeders" I had just recently discovered existed?

"I'm the same person I have always been, I just look a bit different, that's all. It's like a genetic thing."

"Genetics? Instant genetics?" He raised an eyebrow skeptically. I racked my brain for the right words. Maybe James could become privy to just enough to satisfy his curiosity and still not become aware of the Sironians.

"Ok. A caterpillar only knows how to be a caterpillar until he falls asleep and awakens as a buttery. I think I have just woken up, and I now have to figure out how to fly." *It sounded better in my mind.*

"Very poetic, darlin'!" He smiled, "But what does that mean?"

"I can't really explain all of it, but I need you to trust that it's me, the same me you have always known, just different. More than anything, I need your friendship right now." He reached across and took my hand, but this time I didn't pull it away.

"Well, if that is all the explanation you can offer, then that is all the explanation I am going to ask for. I'm not going anywhere. Don't you know by now that I couldn't even if I wanted to?" I couldn't help but wonder if it was the human part of me that kept him close, or the siren I had become that was keeping him by my side. I prayed for the first.

"So are you up for a walk on the pier this afternoon?" He asked when the check finally arrived. I didn't want our day together to end yet. The longer he stayed, the longer I could pretend that things where how they once were. I could just pretend, pretend like he and I were just kids again. Life was much simpler then.

"Sure—sounds great! We haven't done that together in ages."

James easily found a parking place under the Garden City Pier. We both slipped off our shoes and left them on the boardwalk. The wind sent my loose pony tail in all directions, as the chilled wind seemed to only be stronger than earlier that morning. The surf pounded hard against the wooden pilings as if it were trying to beat them apart. We were alone, except for an older fisherman packing up his gear to leave. The reason was quite obvious. Not even a weathered fisherman could stand this type of wind, and no fish would bite in surf so rough. How quickly the beauty of the afternoon had faded!

"Guess this is my second bad idea of the day." He took his jacket off and wrapped it around my shoulders. I laughed. He put his hand on the small of my back, as we walked slowly to the end of the pier.

"It's just a bit windy, that's all. I don't mind it if you don't."

"Darlin' a little wind couldn't keep me from enjoying an afternoon with my favorite girl." I smiled and playfully leaned into his side.

We had stopped just shy of the end, when we heard them barreling onto the beach. The crew reminded me of an Indian tribe storming into battle, except the battle field was the beach, and their horses were surfboards. Their battle cry rang through the air as they charged into the icy surf. I recognized them all immediately as they were each etched carefully in my mind—the short stocky one, the lean beautiful one, the fierce muscular one, and the girl—each more beautiful than I had remembered.

They each paddled out at different rates. Tobie arrived on the line first, Kirby arriving just behind him. Aria paddled through the angry surf at a slower pace. I watched her in amazement as she, ever so gracefully, made her way through the wall of pounding waves. Mace stood upon the shore for several minutes. He protectively eyed every part of his surroundings, as if he was standing watch over his motley group. And then he saw me. He stared right into my eyes. He recognized the change in me. He knew I was now Sironian.

He was also aware, in just one look, that I now know the truth about what they were. How could I have missed it when I was first introduced to this crew of locals? How could anyone not see that this group was each too utterly unique to be human? Their skin radiated with energy, and their eyes sparkled like rays bouncing off of the water. Their features were too strong, yet each completely unique. They were all utterly beautiful. And I was one of them. Well, at least partly like them.

Mace tore his eyes from mine and bolted into the surf like a rocket. Neither he nor his surfboard could be seen under the surf until reappearing on the line with his friends. Then they all saw me—even at such a distance the change was obvious to them. They knew what I was. If they had questioned before, they were aware now that I carried the gene. I thought back to the pool hall that night. They always suspected it, even before I had known. This knowledge frustrated me a bit—to know that others knew "what" I was even before the knowledge came to me.

James remained next to me looking out into the surf, and yet, he didn't exist to them. He was human—just human. I finally understood! How easy was it now to see through their eyes? Humans were of little importance to this crew. James was human.

Aria caught the first wave. She sprang up upon the board with such grace and ease that it was almost easy to forget that she was in the middle of the roughest surf I had ever witnessed. Her wave was unbelievably large, and yet she maneuvered the board atop the wave with no less ease than a professional surfer on his best day. Her board glided from deep in the curl to the tip of the white caps, catching air as she soared from base to tip.

Tobie was up next. His board was a wide longboard. As soon as the board met the wave, he was atop of it, his feet high into the sky with his entire weight supported by one hand. As the wave peaked, the front of the longboard was sent high into the air. He did a backflip, gracefully landing back onto the board.

"Wow, what are these guys, circus freaks? I had no idea these goons could surf like that. They shouldn't even be out there with surf like that— and without wetsuits!"

"Yeah—kind of crazy, huh?"

Kirby caught the next wave. His red surfboard was shorter—more streamlined. Apparently it was built for speed, as he sprang onto the wave like a racehorse coming out of the stock. He bolted from wave to wave launching from the crest of one wave to the whitecaps of another. He made something so difficult look effortless. But before his run had ended, as if by magic, Mace appeared from behind him, his sleek black board just feet behind. Mace crested the wave without Kirby even noticing, and then the dark board and rider flew high above his friend landing no less than ten yards in front of him. Through his laughter, Kirby leapt from his board, a seemingly impossible distance, onto the black board, playfully tackling his friend sending both surfers barreling into the churning water. The playful brawl continued into the shallows until both friends regained their boards and headed out for another run.

Each one took another turn at the waves, each with skills and athleticism that outshone the one that had just gone before. I was quite certain that on any other day, the crew would never be able to perform in this manner. It was only because the beach and pier were deserted that they were able to so openly display this exhibition—deserted except for James and I. Clearly they would think nothing of displaying their skills in front of me, but I was surprised that with James at my side that they would put on such a display. They saw us but didn't care.

Kirby's handsomely chiseled face looked straight up at me after finishing an unbelievable run and he winked. With that, James had had enough and promptly suggested we head back to the Inlet Joy.

As we turned to leave, I saw Aria walking out of the choppy surf and gait over to the dunes. There was someone else out there watching. Despite such a distance, I could easily make out William's features. His light colored clothes blended perfectly among the dunes and sea oats. Had I not noticed the girl tearing towards him, I would have never noticed him sitting there. I desperately wish that my heart did not skip a beat at the sight of him. Of course he would be out here watching over me. It was his job to babysit the half-breed. I became even more convinced to one day relieve him of the unwanted commission.

Aria appeared to be angry, as she seemed to be scolding him relentlessly. He promptly dismissed her. I pulled my eyes away when he had disappeared back over the dunes. *Why was she scolding him so adamantly? And why did it make me feel immediately jealous? Perhaps he had been there to watch Aria instead of me?* My insides began to ache, as James took hold of my elbow and ushered me towards his car.

James and I spent the remainder of the afternoon in the hammock reading. It had been quite some time since I had been able to concentrate on a book at all. My life had shifted from reading of mystic tales, to living a story as bizarre and fantastic as any that my beloved authors could have created. I contemplated the history of the Sironians and how it intertwined into my own family's story. How had the tapestries been woven to put me in this extraordinary tale?

I randomly flipped the page every so often despite processing very little of what was on the page before me. I wondered if James was doing the same. He sat across from me in the hammock, and looked almost as distracted as I was. I caught him staring at me over the pages on more than one occasion. His presence brought me comfort, and yet, I knew exactly what was on his mind. James wasn't oblivious to the changes taking place in me. Nor could he ignore the display the crew had put on in the ocean. Was he seeing the link between the two? Any information that linked James to the Sironian world could put his life in danger. I couldn't risk that. He meant too much to me to ever lose him.

I took out my grey tablet and began to write. Writing had been my only source of sanity over the past week. It was as if I could not believe what was happening to me unless it was laid out with pen and paper. I had been writing for only a short time when James looked up at me.

"What ya writing over there?"

"Different things. My thoughts, ideas—sometimes quotes…poems or passages that I like. Things that speak to me."

"Is there anything in there about me?" His crooked grin broadened as he leaned forward reaching for my tablet."

"Oh no! There is no way I am letting you get your hands on this! And yes, there are many things in here about you."

"Now that is almost criminal to tease a guy that way." He said crossing his arms and leaning back in the hammock. He pouted dramatically. I laughed. It felt good to laugh.

"Alright beautiful—I think I'm up for some exercise. What do you say about a walk before dinner? We could ride out to the "point" and walk along the rocks at the jetties." The wind had calmed a bit over the course of the afternoon but was still coming in pretty strong. James snapped his book shut and leapt from the hammock.

"That sounds great actually." The jetties were two long lines of old cement and rocks laid along the mouth of the inlet at its "point." They created two walls separating the inlet from the ocean and lead to a narrow mouth. Each jetty had an asphalt walkway on the top that could be used to walk some distance out to the very edge of the inlet as it meets the ocean waters.

The events of the morning should have left me drained, but quite the opposite was true. I felt stir crazy. It was still light out. The jetties should be safe during the daylight hours, at least with James with me. But from now on, I would have to avoid bringing James to the beach or near the ocean's edge while he was with me after dark. The last thing that I would want would be the Sironians alerted to my presence with James at my side.

I love the inlet in the late afternoon. It was practically magical the way the sun bounced off of the water. The sky was painted in purples, pinks, and an array of golden hues. The short boat ride from the Inlet Joy to the point was a nice respite from the madness that had become my reality. I could sit back and inhale the thick heady air, filled with the very essence of the sea that my body seemed to crave. There was no sign of

William, but I was certain that he was out there somewhere. Just knowing he was there brought me security.

As we walked along the asphalt pathway atop the jetties, James and I talked continuously. This time he did not attempt to hold my hand, but I would sometimes feel his hand on the small of my back. I hoped that William did not see this or the way that James tenderly touched my forearm as he periodically helped me over an eroded area in the path.

I shoved my hands deep into the pockets of my pale grey wind breaker. My jacket offered little relief from the winds and seemed to be picking up by the minute. I was relieved when James suggested returning. I was eager to get out of the elements and also to get James a safer distance from the open waters of the ocean. The sun was setting deep behind the dark cloud, and daylight was quickly slipping away. While the rocky wall of the jetties offered the inlet protection for the open waters, I didn't want to push our luck by staying so close to the water this far away from any real civilization. Luckily, our boat ride back to the Inlet Joy provided to be uneventful, other than the cold wind whipping up the waters of the inlets and providing a chilly reminder of the season.

Our return home was met with the wonderful aroma of my grandmother's cooking. My grandmother had fried up crispy flounder fillets for diner with a large pot of creamed potatoes and asparagus. James had a double helping of each, which pleased the chef exceedingly. Her mood seemed much improved as if a weight had been lifted off of her shoulders. There was finally no need for secrets between us.

After dinner, we played cards for nearly an hour before my grandmother dismissed herself to her room. James and I grabbed a couple of old quilts and moved out to the rockers on the back porch.

A thick blanket of clouds covered the moon casting an eerie shadow over the inlet. The marsh reeds danced back and forth with the perpetual wind that had plagued the coastline for the majority of the day.

"I must admit, I had hoped for a more pleasant evening." James pulled his quilt under his chin and leaned back in the old porch rocker.

"You know, any other girl might just get offended by that comment." I smiled teasingly and wrapped my quilt a bit tighter around myself.

"You know what I meant. Of course the company couldn't get any better, darlin', but I hadn't expected this weather front to push through on my weekend here with you."

"I'm just teasing you a bit. I agree about the weather. It's been cold, windy, or raining almost every day since I made it to Murrells Inlet."

"It feels a bit strange being here with you when the weather is like this. I guess I just associate you being here with the warm months of summer."

"I know." James grew quite. The wind whistled as it blew through the metal porch screens.

"Look, I know it's not like me to get all sentimental, but I have to say that those times with you were some of the best times of my life." I smiled, thinking back over our many summers here together.

"Mine too."

"I guess what I am trying to say… is that… I don't want those times to end." James nervously fiddled with a string that hung from the quilt.

"I know. Me neither. Just promise me something. No matter what changes, promise me that you will stick by me—ok?" I needed James. What would he think if he knew that I was less than human? "Promise that no matter what, I will still have my best friend."

I knew the term "friend" was not the word James wanted to hear. I could see the pain in his face each time I spoke the word. But I couldn't let James envision anything else between us. If we became more than friends, then inevitably one day we would break up, and then I would lose him forever.

"Of course—there is nothing in this world that would keep me from that promise." His tone was more serious than usual, and I knew he was contemplating the conversation that I was avoiding. He grew silent. I knew he wanted to say more, but I was relieved that he didn't.

James looked out over the dark waterway. I was tucking the quilt around my feet when he arose abruptly. He stared intently into the night.

"What is it?" I asked. I could feel my heart begin to pump harder.

"I don't know. Do you see that? Oh, there it goes again!"

I did see it. Just beyond the dock something was thrashing violently in the water. It was extremely hard to make out what it was, or what was going on, but the water sprung high into the air as a geyser erupting. The struggle moved just down the waterway and seemed to escalate. The moon peaked beyond the clouds just long enough for me to catch a shadow of a figure I had seen once before. But this time it was not alone.

The two creatures were intertwined twisting and clawing briefly before emerging forcefully once again to the surface. Even through the howling wind, I could hear the thrashing as they tore back and forth through the water. Like a rocket, one creature sprung into the air, as I had seen it do before, twisting into the moonlight before gracefully diving into the waves. And then, as abruptly as it had all began—there was silence. The only movements were the marsh reeds blowing, and the flow of the current as the rising tide continued to fill the creek-beds.

"What in the world was that?" James continued to stare out over the marsh in search of something that I knew was gone.

"I have no idea—maybe a porpoise was being attacked by something." My heart felt like it was going to beat right out of my chest. It was William. I knew now that the creature was William. But what could have been the cause for such action? Then it struck me as if I had been hit hard in the face. They had found me. The Sironians now knew where I was located. Someone had come after me, and William had been there to stop it. A cold chill ran up my spine.

"Whatever that was it was too big to be a porpoise. I suppose it could have been a large shark after a porpoise, but I have never seen a shark leap into the air like that. It's rare to have large sharks like that make their way into the inlet canals, but not impossible. We will have to take the boat out in the morning to check it out and see if we can still see a trace of anything that might clue us in to what was out there. I'll meet you down at the dock at daybreak."

I hardly noticed as James quietly shut the screen door behind him. They had come for me—to my home! What William was sacrificing for my safety suddenly became very real. I had no doubt that William had stopped whatever had come for me, but there would be others. I pulled out the remainder of the ponytail that hung loosely at my shoulders and stared blankly at the dark waters of the inlet. The girl that I once knew was gone. My options were simple. Let them take me as I had so foolishly contemplated earlier this morning or fight.

I went into my room and stared into the mirror of my dresser. They would not take me without a fight! I saw my own features changing before my eyes. The innocence from my face now replaced with a fierceness of a warrior. The softness of my cheekbones became hard, and my eyes only recently opened to this new world became keen and sharp. I would learn to protect myself! Not just to relieve William of his duties over me, but because I wanted to survive. If they would come for me, then they would eventually come for my family as well. The blood in my veins ran cold. I could feel it. No! I would never let them touch my family.

I thought back over the abilities I seemed to be developing over the last several months. These were the things that I could use to protect what was most precious to me. I thought back to that dark West Florence track—*speed*. I remembered Jen and the embarrassment that she caused, bringing out the skills I never knew that I possessed—*agility*. Next, I had a vision of myself so easily pulling out that old john boat, despite the trailer hosting two flat tires—*strength*. I thought back over how others' perception of my appearance had changed—*beauty*. I turned to see two deep emerald eyes staring across the room from me—eyes that glared through the darkness. I gasped. My astonishment only intensified as I discovered that the eyes starting back at me through the darkness were my own.

It was my own reflection.

15

"I had hoped for you to have a normal life…but the changes in you have gone too far. You can't go back now."

William Avery

I **met James at daybreak.** I welcomed any excuse to escape another sleepless night. The rising sun brought with it a renewed hope for a future. I would go through with my plan to train as a "protector" and somehow find a way to ward off the forces that were after me. I refused to think about the impossibilities of either part of that challenge. I would somehow find a way to accept what I was and utilize my new gifts, if not for my own sake, for William's.

James was waiting for me as usual, the john boat gassed up and ready to go. There was a gleam in his eye that left little question what was on his mind; he wanted to discover what had mysteriously played out before us last night. Anything that we could possibly find would lead him to more questions, bringing him closer to danger.

He adjusted the old camera that hung around his neck before helping me into the boat. "Morning beautiful! Care for some adventures out on the open waters this morning?" It was difficult to adjust my "new" eyes to the bright morning sunlight.

"Sure. I'm up for anything." I tried to sound energetic, but my nerves were on edge. Was it even safe to be out on the water? Was I continuously putting James' life in danger? William had taken a vow as my protector, but I was pretty sure that his obligation did not carry over to the copper haired boy next to me.

"Great! Will you untie the front for me darlin'?" I quickly untied the ropes off the bow, and James started the motor. Each time I ventured out into inlet it seemed to prove more beautiful than the time before. The air was still chilled from the night, but the weather front had finally pushed through and the water was as smooth as glass.

James idled the boat through the canals as he casually peered along the creek beds. I mainly watched James. His face beamed just to be out on the water, and the morning sunlight accentuated the array of freckles just over his nose. He belonged atop the water.

"Gosh, it is beautiful out here!" I nodded, looking out over the open water. James looked up at me with his famous crooked smile and brushed his hair up under his hat. He smiled again, this time to himself. I wondered if he could read my thoughts or if my expression continued to give me away.

"So what exactly are you looking for?" My acting skills had not improved despite the drastic changes in other areas.

"Well, I was up half of the night thinking about it, and I just don't think that was a shark last night."

"What do you think it could have been?" We had gone past at least a dozen houses with no sign of anything out of the ordinary. I was relieved.

"I don't know. I really couldn't see much at such a distance, but I thought we may run upon some type of clues or something." I was relieved that James was unable to see as well as me. Apparently, my "new" eyes offered more than just an eerie glare at night. We traveled on for about a mile or so before James turned the boat in the opposite direction. I had hoped that James would dock when we reached the Inlet Joy, not that I didn't enjoy his company, or the beautiful morning on the water, but I didn't want to find anything that would further peak his interest. The less James was involved into the Sironian world, the better for everyone. But James hardly slowed when we reached the Inlet Joy. I felt my body begin to tense.

We had traveled just a few houses down towards the south side, when a white egret flew out of the marsh and rested along the creek bank just ahead of us. James quickly grabbed his camera for a few shots before the magical bird took flight once again. It was there that we both saw the very large tracks along the creek bed at the water's edge.

"Do you see those Margo?" James motioned toward the very large tracks in the pluff mud just over the side of the boat.

"That just looks like someone walking along the bank. I can't think of anything else that would make tracks that size. They probably belong to a fisherman or someone shrimping."

"No, I don't think so. See how the front fans out and the back is extremely narrow. The toes almost look webbed." James took his camera once again and snapped numerous pictures from different angles.

"Well, maybe these were made by a large bird or something." I was a bit concerned as these footprints along the creek side most definitely did not belong to William. They were much larger, and William most definitely did not have webbed feet.

"How many birds this size do you see around here?" My eye sight may have improved, but my acting still needed some work—that sounded ridiculous! He continued taking photos and looking for more evidence of the struggle. I studied the direction of the tracks in relation to my house. They lined up in direct view of my house. Yes, something had been there last night. It had been waiting, or watching for me.

I needed to talk to William. Something was out there! Something may still be out there looking for me. I needed to get back to the Inlet Joy. "Um—James, I am not feeling very well. Do you mind if we head back." I didn't have to pretend this time. I felt as if I were going to be sick.

"Oh, Margo! Sure!" I could sense his disappointment. "I hadn't realized you weren't feeling well today darlin'. You should have told me sooner." His full attention turned to me and away from the tracks.

"No, I'm okay. Think it is just a touch of motion sickness—that's all."

"I forgot you get seasick sometimes."

"Yeah. I had hoped I'd grown out of that." My face turned red as I recalled the time four years earlier when I had gotten sick over the side of the boat while fishing with James and his family. "I am sure I will be fine after I lie down for a bit."

"Sure. Let's get you back. We can meet up later when you are feeling better."

When we reached the Inlet Joy, I immediately excused myself under the promise that I would rejoin James after lunch. He reluctantly agreed and headed over to the Merri Mac to shower and grab some breakfast. As soon as James was out of sight, I flew up the stairs to my room. I had to figure out a way to contact William without alarming James.

As soon as I entered my room, I could sense something was not right. The clothes that I had left hung across the chair were moved to the floor, and the white shirt I had worn earlier today appeared to me smeared with something—something red. Was it blood? The towel that had been hung across my closet door was missing. I slowly closed the door behind me, but as I did, I felt the presence of someone beside me. I gasped aloud before realizing that the "someone" behind my door was William. The missing towel was wound tightly around William's right hand and was soaked with blood.

"Oh my gosh! Are you okay? What are you doing here?" I exclaimed. But no sooner did I get those words out did I hear footsteps walking across the porch towards my room. William held his index finger against his mouth and shook his head to silence me. He pointed toward the door. My heart was racing so fast that I felt dizzy. I nodded. My grandmother caught hold of my door just as I was closing it.

"Oh! Hi." Even with two words my voice cracked. *I tried again.* "Uh, you're up early." *Not much better.*

"Well, I was about to say the same for you dear."

"Oh. Yeah. James and I got an early start. We took the boat out just at sunrise so he could get some pictures of the landscape at daybreak." It wasn't a complete lie, so my words flowed a bit more natural. Well, as natural as possible considering the most beautiful creature I had ever seen was just inches away from me...*in my room*...dripping blood all over my carpet. I needed to get rid of her—and fast!

"Yes, I have been hearing quite a bit about James' photography lately. He has had quite a few photos published around town lately. He seems to have a noteworthy talent."

"Uh, yeah, he is doing well for himself and seems to really enjoy it."

"Well, how are things progressing between the two of you? He really does seem to be hanging around a lot lately. I was just wondering how he had accepted the new changes."

"Oh, I didn't tell him much, and he seems fine with everything...Do you mind if we talk about this later. I got a bit sea sick out on the boat and was thinking I would lie down for a while."

"Maybe you should eat something?"

"No, I think my stomach needs to settle. I thought I had outgrown my motion sickness. I just need to rest for a while, and I will be as good as new. Besides, James and I ate something out on the boat."

"If you're sure?" I could hear the skepticism in her voice. "I will be back later this afternoon. Becky and I were going to go shopping and to lunch, but I can cancel my plans if you aren't feeling well."

"No. Go! I'm fine. It is nothing really. I'm going to take a nap, then catch up with James later."

"Are you sure?" I nodded. "I'll be back to check on you then."

I couldn't get the door closed behind her fast enough. I turned to find William less than a foot away, staring at me with eyes that made me completely weak in the knees. I opened my mouth to speak, but William gently put his finger against my lips. He crossed to the window to check that my grandmother was completely gone. I just stared at him in shock.

"Sorry, looks like I owe you a new towel." He looked down at the thin blood soaked cloth covering his hand. His beautiful features remained, but his face looked utterly exhausted.

"Oh my gosh! You're hurt!"

"I needed to come talk to you." Our eyes met—I quickly looked down at his injury.

"This looks pretty bad. Wait here okay. " Before he could protest, I slipped out of the room to fetch the first aid kit from the kitchen. Upon returning I did a double take to be sure I wasn't dreaming. I wasn't. He stood near the foot of my bed—his presence filling the tiny room. Neither of us spoke. He watched me intently as I placed the kit on the edge of the bed and pulled out several items. He crossed towards me and our eyes locked. I somehow found the courage to reach for his injured hand; he allowed me to take it. I unwound the bloodstained towel and was shocked to see that his injury was worse that I had originally thought. There were two large deep cuts that shredded the inside of his left palm. It was badly in need of stitches as his palm was sliced almost to the bone. I turned back to the first aid kit pulling out a large bottle of Betadine. I put the towel against the backside of his smooth palm and carefully poured it over his hand to clean the wound. It should have been quite painful, but William did not even flinch.

"You are very good at this. Practice much?" I nodded without looking at him.

"My skin has needed constant care since birth. I had no idea "why" until now. Who would have thought that a little salt water was all that I needed?" I smiled, but William did not. I could see the seriousness in his expression.

"The water will heal this, but it will take some time, it is been bleeding through the night, so I am pretty weak."

"I'm glad you came here." I said tearing my eyes from his and back to the wound. His brow furrowed.

"You should have as little contact with our world as possible. I had hoped for you to have a normal life, the less contact with our kind the better. But the changes in you have gone too far. You can't go back now."

Yes. I've figured out that part." I picked up a piece of golden hair that now hung lower than yesterday. "But even if I could, I wouldn't leave."

"I know." With each heartbeat, the deep cuts on his palm filled with blood.

"You need to get to a doctor. These cuts need to be stitched up." I padded his palm with gauze and taped it tightly to keep the bleeding to a minimum.

"No, it will be completely healed in a day or so—one of the perks of being Sironian. We heal much faster than humans. If the injury is small enough, sometimes it can happen within hours. I am surprised you don't already know this Marguerite, especially with how fast the cut on your heel mended after your oyster bed scare." I had completely forgotten about that.

"Oh, right. I wiped the blood from his fingertips. It was impossible to deny the electricity that surged through my body as I touched his hand."

"Thank you." His words were surprisingly tender and seemed genuine. "You didn't have to do that."

"After the many times you have saved my life lately, it's the least I could do."

I cleaned up the blood stained towel and returned the gauze and Betadine to the first-aid kit. The very last thing that I needed was for my grandmother to start asking questions. I looked up to find William staring at me again. I blushed under his stare.

"So, a Sironian half-breed that isn't at all faint at the sight of blood but gets seasick eh?" I nodded. Was that a smirk on his face? "Well, I guess now I have seen it all."

"Only from time to time—I wasn't actually sick this morning, I just needed an excuse to return home."

"You aren't a very good liar you know."

"I know. I am pretty awful at it."

"Luckily your grandmother believed you about the other part." I blushed, wishing I was a more skilled liar.

"Which part was that?"

"The part where you said you ate on the boat." The sides of his perfect mouth turned upward.

"How did you know I was lying?" He took a few steps closer.

"First of all, your pulse beats faster when you are lying." He reached down and picked up my wrist and stroked his thumb across my veins. I hoped that he didn't notice how I shuttered under his touch. His smirk turned into what was almost a smile.

"You can hear my pulse?" He nodded then gently released my hand. A low growl could be heard clear across the room.

"Secondly, your stomach keeps growling." I was certain that all of the blood in my body had rushed to my cheeks at this point.

And finally, I didn't see you eat anything all morning."

"So you *were* watching me?"

"I am always watching *over* you, if that is what you mean."

"You were hurt protecting me?"

"There is no cause for worry. There was a breech last night, and something got through the mouth. I have been fearful that there may have been others, and so I was unable to go to Knoxx Point to treat my injury sooner." A wave of guilt swept over me."

"And that means you haven't slept either."

"We don't require as much sleep as humans and rarely during the night. We usually sleep no more than three hours a day, and normally it is in the late afternoon."

"But I sleep more than that."

"Do you? You forget my job. You are awake at night more than you realize."

"And how would you know that? Do you have a built-in radar or are you hiding in my closet?"

"Something like that…but I came to talk to you about something."

"Well, it's fortunate that you're here because I was trying to figure out how to get in touch with you. Last night, there was *something* out there in the inlet. Then this morning James and I found these strange tracks along the creek bed. I was wondering if you could tell me what it could be?"

"Actually, that's my other purpose in coming. I had hoped not to scare you, but I need you to take extra precautions until we can do a full sweep of the inlet."

"What was it?"

"Well, just as many species have evolved over time, Sironians in many parts of the world have evolved as well. There is a deep water sect that is rarely seen and that primarily resides near the Artic polar region. They are more animal than human. Their blood runs as cold as ice, and their skin is as white as snow. Their eyes are not emerald but as black as night. They have very poor vision but can swim extraordinarily fast due to their web feet. Their main defense is a sharp barbed backbone that they expel during combat." He looked down at his hand.

"That was *you* last night!" I gasped. He nodded.

"I have been watching over you since your first night here." I caught my breath. He is always out there somewhere. It seemed impossible.

"But why would those creatures come?"

"This kind of Sironian is called an Obyascon. I am not positive as to why such a Sironian would come here, but we have laws forbidding foreign Sironians from entering assigned marshlands. Silas has had guardianship over this area for the past one hundred years. No Sironian can enter this area without his permission. The Obyascon feeders do not respect or follow the laws of Theron. They have been enemies to our kind for thousands of years, but it is very strange to have one breech into this area." A shiver went down my spine as I tried to visualize the creature that William described. "It couldn't be here by accident, it had to have been sent here."

"Theron sent it after me?"

"That's one theory, but like I said, the Obyascon are enemies with Theron's regime. It could have been a rogue creature, or it could have been passing through and caught your scent."

"I have a scent?"

"Yes. A very attractive scent. The human scent is quite appealing to us, and your hybrid fragrance is more powerful than any human I have run across thus far. This is also why Maris was so drawn to you the first time she came across you as a child."

"Are you attracted to it?" I asked, my face turning every shade of red. "More than I care to admit. But you are safe with me, as your protector, no harm will come to you—despite your appeal." I pushed those thoughts aside, redirecting back to the monster.

"But what if it returns?" I was afraid.

"It won't return."

"And how do you know that?"

"Because I killed it." I stood in astonishment.

"You—you killed it?" He nodded. I knew that William was my "protector" but I never fully knew the danger involved for him. He would kill for me if necessary. It was difficult to keep my composure after such a revelation. "Are there others?"

"I don't think so, but Silas has the other protectors doing a sweep of the inlet as we speak."

"The others?"

"Your 'buddies' from out on the beach. Mace's group."

"They are the other protectors?" *Of course! It began to make sense now!*

"Yes. I must say they are quite intrigued that you are here. I believe they thought you were imaginary."

"They knew of me before I came?"

"Sure. Everyone has been watching for you since you were first discovered years ago. Silas essentially has had the entire waterway on lockdown for the past ten years…just in case you returned."

"For me?"

"You are a 'one of a kind' which makes you quite valuable. We are trained as 'protectors' to guard human life against the 'feeders,' or in your case, against those determined to enforce the Sironian law that prohibits your very existence."

"They will try to kill me again?" My words got caught in my throat.

"Possibly—but more than that, they want to know what you are and what you are capable of doing. It has been proven that it is physically impossible for you to survive away from the coast at this point, and our only options are to either defend you or to hide you." My mind began to run away with me. There could be worse things than death if they "acquired" me.

"I don't want to run, but I don't want to put any of you in danger either."

"This is what we are trained to do. We will keep you safe until another solution can be reached, or until they realize that pursuing you is a futile cause and move on. Either way, we can keep you safe, but you have to be smart and not put yourself in risky situations.”

“You said the others are searching the inlet?”

“Yes, they are relatively inexperienced as a whole but extremely talented. Some are very new protectors such as Aria; others have trained longer such as Mace and Kirby. They are capable to watch over things until Silas and I are sure the inlet is clear. Last night was the first breech we have since you were first discovered.”

“Oh. But the others—are they the ones Silas is training now?”

“They are—all except for one. Mace trained under another group but was relocated here a few years ago. Silas will be working with him as well, but he has surpassed basic training.”

“And their families all live here?”

“No Marguerite.” He sat on the foot of my bed. “Sironian law removes offspring from their parents at the age of ten. They are then chosen for a particular role and given to people who will raise and train them. Any true family relations are prohibited, so offspring are constantly shifted around. This crew were each shifted around through different sect before coming here.” I remembered Silas telling me of this, but it was hard to encounter its effect firsthand.

“Age ten! But they are still children! That’s awful! Why would they have such a law?”

“I agree. They are taken away to learn independence but also to have as little emotional attachments as possible. These attachments are felt to interfere with whatever role they have been chosen for.”

“But what if one refuses?”

“Those who don’t abide by Sironian law are killed or forced into hiding like Sadie and Henry. Their first child was taken from them—a boy, but when Sadie unexpectedly became pregnant with Olivia, they went into hiding. They would be killed if discovered.”

“Is that what happed to your family?” My words struck him like a dagger, and I instantly wished that I had not spoken about them. I was surprised when he responded.

“Yes, my parents fell in love, despite the laws. They were hiding to protect my infant sister and me when they were killed.”

“I am sorry.” I said faintly, unsure of what to say next.

The room went silent. I studied William’s perfect features. Despite his beauty, his eyes carried a purplish hue underneath. It was evident that he had not slept in many nights.

"Well, now you know what Theron is capable of." He sat on the edge of my bed. I could tell he was utterly exhausted.

"When was the last time you got some sleep?"

"I don't need to sleep."

"Yes, you do. I can tell it has been quite a while since you got any rest."

"I am fine. If I sleep, they might breech again." His tone was solemn, and his words sincere.

"But how can you protect me if you are injured and unrested? Look, you said the others are guarding the inlet, are they not?" He nodded. "And you are with me now—I am safe with you, aren't I?"

"You are," he acknowledged.

"And your fear is that something may happen to me while you sleep. Is that correct?" He nodded. "Well, I'm safe as long as you're with me, asleep or not."

"What are you saying?"

"I'm saying that you could sleep here," he laughed aloud. It was the first time I had heard him laugh and it took me by surprise. "What? You say that I am not safe if you are away, and you are badly in need of sleep. What other solution is there than you sleep here."

"That's ridiculous."

"Why?

"Because ...."

"You need rest." I could see him contemplating the offer.

"And say I decided to take you up on this. You would promise to stay right here—in this room—with me."

"I would."

"But I haven't showered."

"That is no excuse. There is one downstairs, and besides, you forget I already have one of your shirts you could change into." He sighed, still contemplating the decision. I knew that he must be on the verge of total exhaustion to consider my offer.

"Fine, but you have to promise not to leave. The crew hasn't finished checking out the area, and until they are certain it is clear, I have to stay extra close. You have to be prepared for anything Marguerite!" I took his blue button up from my drawer and passed it to him along with a clean towel from my closet. He accepted them both and bolted down the stairs toward the shower.

I paced impatiently for several minutes fidgeting with the pillow on the bed. Gosh, I wished I had cleaned my room. I took the clothes off of the floor and crammed them into my bottom drawer, straightened my books, and pushed my paint set under the bed with my foot just as he was headed back up the stairs.

"Wow. That was fast." I exclaimed. The room filled with the scent of soap mixed with the delicious scent of his skin. I felt light headed.

"I am not about to take any chances." William lay on his stomach across the double bed. His bare feet dangled off the side. He propped his head up on one of my pillows and looked over at me. I could only hope that my mouth found some way to close. He was breathtaking.

"So what are you going to do, since I am holding you prisoner here?"

"I—uh—have some reading I need to catch up on for school." I took my large English text book from the corner of the floor and sat in the chair next to the bed. He continued to stare at me as I fumbled through the pages."

"You know, that looks like the most uncomfortable chair in the history of chairs." I smiled.

"It's not so bad, I guess." The wooden upright was hardly an ideal place for reading, but it was the only chair that would fit in the tiny room. It's primarily purpose was to harbor the clothes I was too lazy to hang up.

"I think I'll survive," I laughed.

"Why don't you come over here? I promise I won't bite." I had to catch my breath at the thought of lying next to him. He closed his eyes. His outstretched body was brilliant. He was glorious. I shifted my weight in the old wooden chair. He opened one eye and looked over at me.

"It truly isn't fair that I am comfortable and you are in that torture chair."

"I'm fine."

"I can hardly sleep when I am concerned about you? What kind of gentleman would I be?"

"Guess you have a point."

I lay across the other end of the bed, careful not to touch him. I propped myself up on my elbows to read, but decided after only several minutes not to even bother to try to turn the pages. It was impossible to concentrate on anything other than the gorgeous creature beside me. I tried to shut my eyes and not look at him, but it was impossible. I tried to hold my nose so that I couldn't smell his skin. It was to no avail. I couldn't resist—he was intoxicating. I had been close to death more than once over the past few months but never as close to heaven as this very moment. After some time he spoke.

"Thank you for today. It has been many years since someone has done such a thing for me. Forgive me if I have forgotten how to show gratitude."

"You owe me no gratitude—but I would like your friendship." His brow furrowed.

"The one thing that I cannot offer—"

"And why would that be?"

"Because I am your protector, I cannot be your friend. It would compromise my abilities—it would compromise my judgment."

"Well, I don't believe that. It seems like the opposite would be true. It seems like if you *knew* more about the one you had to protect then you would have a better understand on how to guard them." He turned and propped up his godlike physique to face me.

"I have been watching you nonstop every summer since you were ten years old. I know that your favorite color is green, and that your favorite author is Jane Austin, that you bite your nails when you are nervous, and that you love to take walks in the rain. You love to paint, but only when truly inspired, and you are constantly writing in that grey tablet. I know that you prefer solitude, but that you are extremely loyal to your family, and that you vastly enjoy the company of the copper haired boy.

"James."

"I know his name. It is my job to know." Everything got really still. I could see that William was concentrating on something—waiting on something. Then he smiled. Very quickly I realized what he had been waiting for.

I was surprised when raindrops began to hit against the window panes. The droplets quickly went from a trickle to a steady rainfall. I turned to William. "Did you know for certain it was going to rain today?" I was astonished that it could be raining after such a beautiful morning.

"Sure. I could smell it coming off of the water from the east."

"Will I be able to do that?"

"Sure. You probably can now. It's all about practice." I relaxed allowing the air to fill my lungs. It wasn't long before I could smell the rain as William had predicted. I smiled to myself. Maybe this Sironian thing wasn't so bad after all.

It wasn't very long before his breathing slowed. He was asleep. The rain continued to fall steadily against the roof. I closed my eyes and this time breathed *him* in. How much had my sense of smell heightened since the change! The soap was the strongest smell. It mixed perfectly with the fragrant musk of his skin. But there were other wonderful smells as well: fresh sawdust, saltwater, marsh reed, and sunshine. There were also smells that I never knew existed—intoxicating smells that were impossible to describe.

The air grew thick and the rain fell harder. I could feel my own breathing slowing, my own eyes closing. My body scooted closer and closer to his, until I was nestled against his side. I tried to fight it but I couldn't. I was drawn to him in a way that was more than unusual; it was supernatural. I felt dizzy from his essence, drunk with his presence. Within just a short time I fell fast asleep at his side.

"Margo? Knock knock?" There was a gentle tapping upon the door that woke both William and I from our slumber. I knew the voice instantly. It was James. William seemed virtually unfazed, so he must have heard him coming. Why would William not warn me? Did he want James to find us together?

Before either of us could react, my door slowly opened, and James was standing there soaking wet from the storm. "Margo…?" His eyes swept over William and me lying there next to each other. The look on his face was a mixture of unbelievable shock and immense pain. He turned on his heels and was out of the door and down the steps before I could move. The screen door slammed as he moved quickly down the stairs.

"I have to go after him," I said to William as I hurried out of the room. I didn't wait for a response. I ran across the yards through the rain, James reached the Merri Mac before I could catch him—at least catch him without showing myself as a supernatural freak.

"James wait! Let me explain." The rain beat down harder, leaving us both drenched. Before I could reach him, he disappeared to one of the back bedrooms then reappeared with a duffle bag in his hand.

"What do you have to explain Margo? Why you told me that you barely knew the guy, or why you lied to me about feeling sea sick so you could go spend time with HIM…IN YOUR ROOM!"

"I didn't lie to you—well, not exactly." *Crap! Bad at lying again!*

"When you didn't meet me, I was worried because I *thought* you weren't feeling well. I had no idea that you were with HIM! COME ON

MARGO, THE GUY IS A FREAK!" James had never raised his voice to me before, but he didn't hold back.

"It isn't like that. James, you know me better than that!"

"Do I? Gosh Margo, I use to know everything about you. We shared everything. But I am not stupid! I see that something is going on with you that you aren't telling me about." I followed James as he headed out of the door locking it behind him.

"Please let me explain." He turned to face me.

"Alright go ahead—explain away." His sarcasm was hurtful.

"Well see—actually I can't really explain everything, but…."

"Can't or won't? And don't try to deal me any more of that caterpillar crap." His face was flushed and his eyes watery. I didn't respond. I couldn't respond without telling him everything. We stood there in the rain. The water droplets ran from my forehead to the tip of my nose. He was waiting for an explanation that was impossible for me to provide. Finally James opened his car door and tossed in his duffle bag.

"Where are you going?"

"Home—anywhere but here!"

"Please don't leave like this." I pleaded with him. It was then that I realized James angrily looking over my shoulder. I turned to find William watching our exchange from the dock.

James shot him a look that could kill before jumping in his Cherokee. I couldn't help but notice the final haunting look of hurt in his rear view mirror as his tires spun out of the drive.

As I turned back towards the Inlet Joy, there was a splash. Multitudes of ripples fanned through the rain kissed water. They were both gone.

16

"Never to suffer would never to have been blessed."

Edgar Allan Poe

It was Sunday. The sun remained hidden from sight, and the rain continued through the morning hours at a steady pace filling the belly of the waterway. I hoped the morning to produce James' blue Chevy Blazer parked behind the Merri Mac, but he had not returned. Nor had William reappeared, though I knew without a doubt that he was near.

I began just as the sun was coming up with an array of charcoals, paints, and pastels fanned out on a tray beside my old easel. An old tin can harbored my aging brushes. My hands could barely keep up with the pictures in my mind as I sketched and painted image after image. My new senses and skills seemed to carry over into my work as I produced sketches that far surpassed any artwork that I had previously done. The charcoals hardly left my hand, as I worked at a tremendous pace through the morning and well into the afternoon. A multitude of sketches soon filled the tiny porch. Many were nothing more than the hard, perfect lines of William's face, all without expression, and all without emotion. Some were just of his hands, others his feet. I sketched each part of him from memory, as if I were holding on to each memory of him, each part of him.

But there were other's sketches as well. James too was represented, one in particular carrying the expression I had seen on his face just the day before as he drove off. It caught my eye over and over, reminding me of the pain I had caused my dear friend. I crumpled it up and tossed it into the trashcan.

After lunch I moved into the oils, blending layer upon layer, and shade upon shade to capture the many seasons of sunlight as it passed over the inlet. Such majesty was impossible to fully capture in any painting, but I was quite pleased with my effort.

By late afternoon, I began to tire a bit. Of course I would tire during this time. I was Sironian and acknowledging my genetics, I curled up to slumber for a few hours of rest. Sleep came much easier now that I knew exactly what my body was expecting, and I woke ready to continue. My late afternoon pieces were primarily landscapes of the inlet, the waterways, and finally the beautiful Knoxx Point. I was surprised at how easily I could remember even the smallest detail about the place, and wondered if this acute remembrance of even the finest details was also a product of my transformation. As the sun began to set, the painting continued in my room throughout the night. I no longer dreaded the black sky, as there was no need for sleep. My fingers continued to work, and as the sun began to rise, I completed the final brush strokes on my finest work thus far. The portrait was of William. Though I knew it impossible to capture the perfection of his features, I was able to recreate the depth of his expression.

Just after daybreak, I heard a gentle knock at the door, and quickly covered the piece with an old towel. "Marguerite?" I opened the door to my grandmother's smiling face. "I was wondering if you wanted to head down to the market with me after breakfast."

"Oh, I was hoping to go out to the 'point' today and get a jump on some reading. I thought the fresh air would be good for me." It was Monday. Silas would be training "the crew" today, and he had promised to train me too. I wanted to be among them. I would learn to protect myself. I would challenge William for my guardianship. And I would give him his freedom back.

"Alright. Probably a good idea—as long as you are getting some fresh air today. You have been moping around here since James left, and I was getting a bit worried. Did the two of you have a fuss or something?"

"Yes. I think he is angry with me. He probably just needs some time to cool off. I'm sure he will come back next weekend." I hated that James was upset. I wanted to explain, but how could I ever explain this sort of situation to him?

"I had a feeling this may happen. His feelings for you are quite obvious. You are both changing, growing up. You are a beautiful young woman, and feeling were bound to develop."

"Do you mind if we not talk about this." I buried my face into a bed pillow.

"Alright, but just be easy with him. The change to adulthood is hard enough without the girl you are in love with becoming a siren."

****

The sun finally crept over the horizon, but a hazy fog remained over the marshlands. I slipped on a navy scooped-neck tee, jeans, my grey jacket, and sneakers—hardly proper Sironian training attire. I hurried down to the dock, still unsure where I would be heading. The gas tank was full. Ironically, my gas can was always full since William came into my life. I turned from untying the boat and was startled to find that I was not alone.

"Nice boat," The boy smiled, as water dripped from his lean tanned body. He was shirtless, wearing only a pair of army-green cargo shorts that hung low on his slender waist. Kirby smiled perfectly at me from his position on the front of my boat. "Wow! You look fantastic! Sironian seems to fit you!"

"What are you doing here? You startled me! "

"Silas sent me early this morning, but I wasn't sure exactly how to go about that…you know between your boyfriend and grandmother and all." His golden ringlets rested just above his ears, and his eyes sparkled an unnatural shade of blue. His most prominent feature was his extremely high cheekbones that were offset by his slightly crooked smile.

"James left a few days ago, and he isn't my boyfriend." I stammered. Kirby grinned from ear to ear.

"I wasn't talking about the red haired dude I saw you with the other day. I was talking about William."

"Once again, he isn't my boyfriend." It was becoming evident that Kirby liked to push my buttons. Kirby liked to push everyone's buttons.

"Yeah—whatever you say princess. Man, that guy takes this whole "protector" thing to a new level. I've never seen someone so mad as when he heard I was being sent for you today."

235

"So he knew I was coming to train today?"

"Silas told him last night after we did a final sweep of the waterway just after sun down. He was fuming. I've never seen him talk to Silas that way. Said you had no business being around any of us, threatened me to stay away from you, then he stormed off. I assumed he went to find you to talk you out of it, but there was no sign of him this morning." A twinge of angst spread over me at the knowledge that William was not there. Kirby must have picked up on this.

"Don't worry princess. You're as safe with me. I'm a protector too you know. We still may be going through training, but our little group is every bit as competent as William." He winked at me. I quickly turned my attention back to the boat.

I wasn't scared that something would happen to me, I was afraid that William may not return. That was what I wanted, right—to give him his freedom? I watched as the water droplets ran off of Kirby's shoulders and into the boat. "Aren't you cold?" I asked, trying not to look at his amazingly chiseled body.

"Me? Nah—thought the cat was out of the bag with all of this Sironian stuff now?"

"Guess I'm still learning the ins and outs of it all."

"Ah—well, unlike humans, our blood is more like an amphibian. Our blood runs the temperature of our surroundings making it possible to adjust to both hot and cold conditions comfortably. That is how we can swim in cold water without turning to a chunk of ice." A cold wind swept through the boat, and I pulled my jacket tighter around me. "Guess, when the genes were being mixed, you didn't get that part—eh?"

"Guess not."

"Interesting! I must admit that of all of us who know about you, I seem to be the most fascinated. Who would have thought that a human and Sironian could produce a child!"

"Not me, that's for sure."

"Guess we better get going as I am sure everyone is waiting on us, but you have to promise to tell me more about yourself later." I nodded.

"Do you want to drive?" I said, still looking away from him.

"Na. This is your boat. I'll navigate!"

When we neared the "point," the dunes were uninhabited. Kirby motioned toward a small canal just off the side that I had never taken before. I thought it impossible to travel through as the canal looked too shallow and narrow for passage. He smiled back at me, as if to read my thoughts, continuously urging me through. I followed his insistent directions as we meandered through the marshlands for nearly a mile. The canal twisted back and forth along the backside of the inlet. I had been up and down these waters my entire life, and yet, I had no idea that this area existed. When we finally reached the embankment, it became evident as to why this spot was chosen. The entire area was fully cut off on the ocean side by very large dunes, and completely hidden off from the inlet side by an array of marsh weeds, scrub trees and undergrowth. It was only accessible by the narrow canal we had taken, or by swimming. As there were no other boats in the area, it occurred to me that the others must have taken the later mode of transportation. Kirby helped me out of the boat, and easily pulled the vessel into the marsh reeds. There was no visible trail to the embankment, but I could barely make out a steep footpath through an array of overgrown vegetation. He offered his hand, and I readily took it as he pulled me through the underbrush.

The embankment was breathtaking. This hidden expanse had to be the last untouched place along the South Carolina coast. There were a variety of birds nesting safely along the outer banks, and other larger animals such as deer and rabbit were visible just along the brush line. All seemed completely unafraid of our presence. It was a perfect mix of ocean, wetland, and wildlife, but there was something else—a feeling. It felt magical as if it were pulled directly from a fairytale.

"Pretty cool, isn't it?"

"Why aren't they afraid?" I motioned toward the birds and animals that seemed to surround the area."

"Animals don't fear Sironians. We are not their natural predators, so they are comfortable around us. We only eat fish, mollusks, crabs—things from the ocean." I thought of the bacon I had eaten for breakfast. Oops. Guess that didn't carry over either."

"Oh." I was relieved that the animals didn't seem to acknowledge my presence despite my fondness of meat.

"Come on. Let me help you." He pulled me through the last of the brush so that the entire embankment was now visible.

"Thank you for coming for me."

"Princess, I volunteered." He smiled his crooked grin and led me into a large clearing.

"Wow. I had no idea a place like this existed."

"Yeah. And we had no idea someone like you existed, so I guess you are a perfect fit. Come on. Everyone is waiting." There were no unfamiliar faces among the group, but aside from Silas who eagerly came to greet me, no one else budged.

"Marguerite, you decided to join us indeed!"

"I did Silas. It is a pleasure to see you again."

"Likewise dear. You are very welcome here." I looked at the other faces among the group. Their expressions left me quite unsure of how far that welcome actually extended. Looking over the group as a whole, I was surprised that anyone who had seen them together believed they were human. Their faces too perfect, their bodies too chiseled, and their eyes all deep unnatural hues of blues and greens.

Silas took over the introductions. "You have met Kirby." Kirby winked at me. I blushed. At least I had one fan. "And this is Tobie." He motioned toward the short, muscular boy. I was relieved when Tobie shot me a dimpled smile of recognition. "This is Aria." The beautiful dark haired girl briefly looked in my direction, but her eyes were as cold as their ice blue color. I quickly looked away. "And this is Mace." He studied me hard, but his face carried no expression at all.

I was startled when he spoke first. "So, *this* is what all of the fuss is about." He took a few steps towards me this time eying my changes. "She is much improved, I suppose, but hardly worth the effort." I felt as if I wanted to cry.

"Mace, she is important because she is the first actual hybrid. She is the first of her kind. She is valuable because they don't know the extent of her abilities or how they could use her. It could be unsafe for humanity if she were capable of extraordinary things and used for the ill of mankind." My mouth fell open. Surely Silas wasn't talking about me? I thought his protection was only a favor to my grandmother or because of his obligations as a protector. I had no idea that he thought that there could be more to it than that. Aria spoke next.

"Come on Silas! A resource such as William protecting this human? Just look at her! I can see nothing extraordinary in her. We should just let them have her and end this!" I felt the tears welling up in my eyes. I balled my hands into fists trying to fight back the tears.

It was then that I saw William step from the wooded underbrush. His countenance took my breath away. Despite the beauty of the others, they paled in comparison to him. His face was hard, his body rigid as if he was prepared to fight.

"Enough! The next one to speak ill of the girl will have *me* to contend with." The others seemed unmoved by his presence, but not another word was spoken against me. A flood of relief swept through me. He had not left me.

"Glad you decided to join us after all William."

"I go where she goes. You know that Silas."

"Yes."

"Let me take you home Marguerite." William's words were firm.

"I—I can't." My eyes met his.

"What?"

"Silas has agreed to train me—with the others. I want to learn to protect myself." He looked at me for a split second as if he were going to hoist me over his shoulder and carry me back to the boat. He eyed me closely, then looked back over at Silas who nodded in affirmation of my words. I kept my expression firm. After a long pause, he seemed resigned to my wishes.

"Fine. I will wait for your training. Then *I* will take you home." He glared at Kirby. William crossed the embankment and leaned against one of the scrub trees.

"Are we done here?" Mace turned and tossed a large black duffle bag to each of his crew. One bag remained. Silas walked over and handed the final bag to me.

"This is yours my dear." I took the bag. It was extremely heavy. Even for my newly acquired strength.

"What is this?"

"Weapons." I felt a knot well up in my throat.

"But Silas ..."

"Marguerite, you said you wanted me to train you."

"I've never even shot a *cap* gun."

"We don't use guns Marguerite." Silas unzipped the bag and pulled out something that looked quite similar to a cross bow except it was longer with two separate arms. There was a hand grip with a variety of knobs that appeared to have some effect on its operation.

"Ever shot a bow?" He asked.

I thought of summer camp and suddenly wished that I hadn't faked a stomach ache the day we had done archery. I did remember shooting my brother's plastic archery toy once—in the fourth grade. Even then, I think

I almost took out the neighbor's cat. "Um—once or twice." It wasn't a total lie.

"This is called the dousie bow. I designed it years ago as one of the protectors tools of the trade."

"Looks kinda complicated." I pulled my hair back tying it in a knot at the nape of my neck.

"It's a fairly simple design once you get the hang of it. The strings vary in tension and can adjust for distance or depth. The bow is specially designed to use both in and out of the water. Arrows can be shot from each arm, allowing two shots in succession or from both simultaneously for those who are really skilled.

The others had already removed their weapons and were crossing the embankment towards a large target on the other end.

The large saucer was made out of tightly woven sea grass striped in lighter and darker shades to mark accuracy. The target itself was a work of art. The crew stopped at quite a long distance from the target and began taking shots one by one. As the others practiced, Silas showed me how to work the dousie bow's two arms. He explained to me the different tensions and how to properly utilize the features of the weapon. I lifted the bow in front of me and loaded a bolt onto the weapon. With a pull of the trigger, the first bolt soared for the target, only to fall just off to the side of the saucer into the brush below. I sighed, embarrassed. I knew the more skilled Sironians were silently laughing at me.

Under Silas' instruction, the crew continued to practice. They each seemed to value Silas' advice immensely, and as they improved I realized the quality of the instruction that Silas was providing. There could be no finer teacher on land or sea. Soon most everyone's shots landed on the target, each arrow inching closer, but falling short of the center bull's-eye. My arrows, though coming close to the target, repeatedly missed it altogether. I became more and more frustrated as the morning began to wear on me both physically and emotionally. Once again, I was thrust into a world in which I didn't belong.

Silas moved the targets further back. Kirby looked over at me with a wink, but in trying to impress me, he missed the entire target all together, with the bolt landing far off in the underbrush on the side of a tree. I thought of Blake falling over the hurdles trying to grab my attention months ago. How strange to find two creatures from two different world that were so similar. As he missed, I heard a snicker. It was William. Kirby heard it too.

"Ah, so you think that is funny do you? I don't see you over here."

William didn't speak, but slowly walked over toward me, and took the bow from my hands. He turned and walked clear across the entire clearing with his back completely turned from us. I thought he was going to leave, but as he reached the very edge, he sprung around at lightning speed and two arrows soared through the air, one flying from each arm of the bow. In less than a second, both arrows protruded out from the very center of the target.

There was no response from the crew. William crossed back to me and returned the bow back to my hands.

"Target practice is over Silas." He said before disappearing back into the moss covered trees nearby. I closed my jaw that had become loose at the hinges.

"Let's move onto phase two." As Silas spoke the words, I stood there not quite knowing what I should do. The others seemed to know exactly what he was talking about, retrieving their bows and plowing over the dunes towards the shoreline. I didn't look back, but I knew William was still close. I crossed the dunes onto a completely isolated beach. The water was as smooth as glass. The sands seemed almost untouched by the gentle waves coming to shore.

The crew lined the shore and began firing crossbow bolt after crossbow bolt into the smooth waves. "What are they shooting?" Silas only motioned for me to watch.

Tobie turned to me with his deep dimples. "Lunch." It was then that I saw Aria shoot an arrow into a large wave. Instantly a medium sized sailfish leapt into the air pierced through the side by her arrow.

"Wow! But how will she retrieve it?" I asked dumbfounded.

It was then that Aria slid off her top and pants, revealing a simple black bikini, and leapt from the shoreline into the wave. She put even the most beautiful of swimsuit models to shame. I thought back to the older one piece suit that William had seen me in, feeling suddenly embarrassed and inferior to her physical perfection.

At that moment, the human facade was dropped, and the group began their descent into the water. They leapt through the air at unimaginable heights and bolted through the water at inhuman speeds. Each retuned with a collection of fish in hand that ranged in size from the very small to very large. Tobie returned with a very large shark—just to show off a bit.

"Look what I got." He laughed as he effortlessly tossed the unharmed hammerhead back into the surf.

"Oh" I gasped, realizing that the shark must have weighed over three hundred pounds.

"Tobie is the strongest of our trainees." Silas said. They are *all* quite unique actually. Aria is the fastest and most agile. Kirby has the special gift of communication—he seems to be able to persuade those around him, both human and Sironian. And Mace can actually manipulate the ocean, such as being able to drum up larger wave swell and intensify ocean currents."

"You're joking right?"

"No. I am not. We have talents, just as many humans have talents and things where they uniquely excel. But like many other things, these talents are a little more extraordinary with us. Sects are chosen at a very early age to be able to pair a role with their talents. We are stronger this way."

"And William?"

"William is the most gifted young Sironian I have ever met. He excels in most every area. He is faster than most, stronger than most; he has abilities that even I am still trying to understand. But what seems to set him apart from every other Sironian I have trained is his intuition. He seems to sense things before they are going to happen. This makes him my best protector, because he is always one step ahead. He can sense when danger is near and make adjustments."

"Can he see the future?"

"No. It is more a sense than a vision. He doesn't *see* things; he *feels* them."

"Feels them?"

"Like intuition, but stronger. I know. It is difficult to comprehend."

"There is just so much for me to learn, Silas. It is like my entire world is like a dream."

"No, not a dream Marguerite. You were dreaming before. You are waking up to reality now. You will begin to view the world differently, but only when you allow yourself." I looked back again to see William atop the largest dune looking out over the sea. I hoisted the bow up to my chest. I focused my new eyes upon the water and within seconds could see a large shadow swimming in and out of the waves. I focused harder and could see the yellow belly of a tuna. I quickly released the arrow and watched as it pierced the water narrowly missing the tuna.

"The loser has to retrieve all the missed crossbow bolts." Kirby joked. I smiled, reloaded, and once again focused. This time the fish was longer, more sleek. Its silver scales danced in the reflection of the sun through the water. I recognized this one as a mackerel. Silas coached me.

"You have to let your senses go Marguerite. Don't think—feel." I closed my eyes and released. This time as before, the bolt soared through the water, once again barely missing the target. I sighed.

"Don't worry my dear. This is all very new to you. You will get better. It will just take some practice." I looked over at the others who were busily building a fire to cook their catch. They had long since shifted their curiosity from me and had now totally written me off. I would have much preferred the teasing to this callous indifference. I watched as they skinned and sliced several of the large fish piercing them with long wooden spears before putting them over the open flames. Silas and I stayed off to the side as the crew merrily cut up with each other. Kirby brought us both over a large section of fish. We sat together upon a large piece of drift wood and ate.

We had been there only a short time when I sensed some movement just below one of the dunes nearby. I sat in amazement as tiny sea turtles made their way to the surface of the sand one at a time. I gasped and giggled with delight as each baby turtle slowly wobbled through the sand and into the surf.

"It's amazing Silas!" I exclaimed! I had never witnessed anything more magical. The crew seemed amused by my reaction to the baby turtles.

"Yes it is, Marguerite. Our world is not all terrifying; it is also incredible. This is your world too, if you can accept what you were born to be."

William lingered down the beach quite a ways, still looking out over the ocean.

"I wish he would come join us."

"William is a young soul with a very old heart. He has had more pain to bear in his short existence than most have in a lifetime. "

"I cannot imagine the pain he must feel from the loss of his entire family."

"Yes. That is a loss that no child should have to bare. But there is more. I had not planned on telling you this, but I think it may explain his behavior toward you."

"Ok." I was instantly spellbound.

"Well, William's mother desperately wanted a normal life for him. She and her husband were very successful in their business and were able to blend in effortlessly among the humans. They enrolled William into a normal first grade class where he was well liked among the children but was careful to keep a safe distance. There was a young girl in his class by the name of Emily. She followed him everywhere. She sat next to him and continued to peruse a friendship with him despite the fact that he continuously pushed her away. Over time William started to care about the girl as well, and they became good friends. William knew to be very careful around the human children, but on Valentine's Day sweet Emily brought William a Valentine's Day card. When he turned around on the playground, she planted a big kiss upon William's lips. All that he had tried to guard her from, all that he had feared came to light that day, as young Emily's life energy was transferred to William. Poor Emily's lifeless body fell to the ground, as William stared on in horror as his only friend died. Of course no one could find William at fault, and the girl's death was ruled an undiagnosed fatal medical condition, but poor young William knew the truth, and was forced to live with the guilt that comes with taking a life. It was at that time that his parents found me, and relocated from Charleston to the area. He was immediately pulled from school and hidden away here by his parents out of fear that if Sironian officials found out about the incident, then they would all be killed. You see, it is against our laws to mingle with humans in such a way as to expose ourselves in this manner. It was then that we started our training, far sooner that most protectors begin to train. His training first began for his own safety, but his talents far surpassed my wildest expectations. When I first heard of the incident with his parents, I had hoped that I had trained him well enough for his own survival. When he was discovered three days later adrift in the ocean, I cannot tell you how overjoyed I was. For he did not only survive the explosion that killed his parents, but also had been strong enough to ward off whatever forces Theron had sent after him. No telling what the boy encountered over those three days. After he was returned, he was in pretty bad shape, both physically and emotionally. I was named his legal guardian and worked out a deal with Theron for his safety.

"What was the deal?" I asked, now so in shock, I was barely able to utter a sound.

"That I would train his granddaughter, and agree to a betrothal between William and the girl, Theron's first born granddaughter. You see, William is extraordinarily powerful, even for a Sironian. Theron wants to use that power to secure his own reign and that of his family."

"Who is his granddaughter?"

"Isn't it obvious?" He looked over at the beautiful brunette perched on a piece of driftwood."

"Aria." I whispered.

"Yes. William is aware of the arrangement and hates her for it. Oh, she has tried many times to capture his affection, but he will have none of it. I think it has made her *own* heart quite bitter in the process." I thought back to just a few days earlier and how they seemed to be in some type of argument on the beach. He seemed to carry no affection for the girl; in fact, it seemed quite the opposite.

"Can he get out of it?"

"No, we are bound in such arrangements as these, though William profusely refuses. Our word is final. William is to one day marry Theron's granddaughter, as one day she will take over the leadership of our people."

"But wouldn't her father be in line for the title?"

"Her father was killed many years ago in combat with the African sects. He was trained as a warrior. Aria is next in line, but she was only recently made aware of this."

"How could she not know her own lineage?"

"As all Sironian children are taken from their parents at the age of ten to train, Aria is aware that she is born of privilege but not of royalty. She became aware of the betrothal only after overhearing a very heated conversation between William and me a few years ago. She has not seen her mother or grandfather since she was a child."

"But William doesn't love her!" I felt a tear fall down my cheek and for the first time acknowledged to myself what I had known for quite a while now. I was in love with William.

"Marguerite, I had no choice. They would not have stopped until they killed him."

And then it hit me. They would never stop pursuing me either. Silas knew this. William knew this. I would be killed or an arrangement would have to be made on my behalf as well. What would be my ultimate sacrifice, would I have to give up love, my freedom, or my life.

"Silas, I am feeling a bit unwell. Do you mind if I head back to the Inlet Joy for the day?"

"Of course not Marguerite. I know this is a lot for you to process in one day. Let me have Kirby take you home."

"No, I'm fine. Just a bit tired. I am certain I remember the way back. I began to make my way down the beach and stopped to watch the nest of baby sea turtles making their way to the ocean. How strange to see this at this time of the year. *This place is truly magical!* I did not try to hide the tears streaming down my face at this sign of hope. If these tiny creatures could make it, be brought to life far earlier in the year than possible—if they could find their own way to the water's edge, then, I would find my way as well.

"Uh—nice to see you again Margo." Tobie said as I passed by the crew on my way back to the embankment.

"Had enough?" Shot Aria with a smirk on her beautiful face.

"Not a chance." I replied. "I will see you tomorrow." All eyes looked up at me with these words. But even as I spoke them, they hardly sounded like my own. They almost sounded confident.

"Let me take you home." Kirby sprung to his feet, but William was already there.

"Not happening." He growled at Kirby.

"Hey princess, I'll catch up to you later—when your guard dog isn't around." William shot a piercing look at him.

It was just then, that I sensed something—panic. My eyes scanned the crowd but no one among our group seemed in distress. And then as if in slow motion, I saw it, a large gull circling overhead just where the baby turtles had been. It swooped down, catching the lone baby straggler in his beak before soaring high over the ocean. I did not think, I did not aim, but my bow was instantly lifted high into the air as two arrows instantaneously flew by my own hands. Both arrows pierced the body of the gull, causing it to drop the baby turtle safely into the ocean below.

I was amazed at my own reaction and even more so by my own skill. Apparently, I was not the only one as the look of shock was shared on the faces of all who had witnessed it.

"Dude! Did you just see that? She killed a sea gull...*Cool!*" The mortification hit as I saw the lifeless body of the seagull bobbing in the waves. Tobie's words broke the tension, but couldn't save me from my awkward words that would follow.

"I like turtles."

I dropped my bow and made my way back to the boat. William didn't hesitate to help me down the steep embankment. I didn't reject his help. Each time his hand touched mine, my skin burned from the electricity between us. I fought to ignore it. I finally understood why William so adamantly refused my friendship. Who could blame him after he had accidently taken the life of his only childhood friend. I also didn't object as he slipped into the driver's position. I took the seat in the bow of the boat. If I were to move past the feeling that I had developed for William, it would be best to stay as far from him as possible.

As we approached the Inlet Joy he slowed to an idle. "It would probably be best if you avoided the waterway for the remainder of the day."

"Why is that?"

"Well, I am not picking up a sense of danger close by, but all of the protectors in the area have been at the embankment all morning. No one has had an opportunity to sweep the inlet."

"I have a broom."

"Very funny." Was that a smirk in William's face? It looked good on him. "When the Obyascon doesn't return, they will send others to look for it?"

"You shouldn't be in any danger during daylight hours, but you need to be aware none the less."

"So is that why you didn't let Kirby take me home?"

"No. I didn't let Kirby take you home because—I don't like you with him." His brow furrowed.

"Oh."

William stood and removed his shirt, obviously to keep it from getting wet.

"Wait. Look, I know from what you've just told me that you haven't gotten very much sleep. I am assuming since it hasn't been since you were in my room last."

"That would be accurate. Don't worry about me."

"Well, if something does come looking for the Obyascon, I would feel better if I knew you were well rested." He briefly contemplated this.

"Fine. I will meet you in your room."

"When?"

"Soon." I crossed towards the driver's seat to take the reins, and he was gone, leaving only his shirt behind. *Great! My own Cinderella.* I quickly folded his shirt and put it in my satchel.

I found my grandmother in the house reading. She closed her book when I entered the room and placed it in her lap. "How was your morning?"

"Good. Did you get lots of studying done?" I looked down at my satchel that still contained my unopened books.

"I learned a lot today actually. It was very productive." At least it wasn't a total lie. "Oh, and I saw a nest of sea turtles hatching. It was very cool."

"Baby sea turtles? At this time of year? Huh? Very rare."

"Yeah I know."

"Must be due to the unseasonably warm weather this year."

"Yeah. Probably something like that."

"I was glad that you were inspired to begin painting again. Do you mind showing me some of your artwork when you have time?" I had forgotten about my paintings and sketches! I blushed at the massive number of sketches of William's face that were stacked upon the dresser in my room. I knew that my grandmother had not seen them. She wasn't the type to invade my privacy, but I knew William would arrive soon.

"Oh yeah. Sure. I was going to go take a nap, but I could show them to you later this afternoon. Also, I thought we could go for a walk this evening after dinner." I had more questions I hoped she could answer.

"Sounds like a nice idea." I nervously headed out of the main house to my room. Surely William wouldn't already be there. I was mistaken.

When I opened my door, I found William still shirtless already laying widthwise across my bed. Nothing could prepare me for the sight of him. He was stunning. I opened my satchel and pulled out his shirt. "I think this belongs to you." He smiled and slipped it on. "I could have been my grandmother coming in." I eyed the sketches on my dresser. They appeared to be untouched. I luckily had left a landscape at the top of the pile and not one of him. The portrait of William remained covered in the corner of the room. If he had taken a peek, I couldn't tell it from his expression.

"No. I knew you weren't your grandmother. I know the sound of your footsteps."

"Oh." Of course he knew the sound of my footsteps—he knew everything.

"Silas told me that you are able to sense things before they happen. Is that true?"

"Sometimes. If I am really concentrating, or sometimes things just come to me. It isn't like I can see the future or anything; I can just sense when something is going to happen."

"So you knew that James was about to walk through the door before he did it?"

"Yes, but that is not how I knew it was him. I only sense danger."

"How did you know?"

"I have learned the sound of his footsteps as well, and I know his scent."

"He smells?" William roared with laughter at the comment. His face shone like the sun when he laughed. I had never seen him more beautiful.

"Everyone has a scent. It is my duty to know the scents of those you surround yourself with."

"But if you knew he was coming, why didn't you warn me?" He didn't respond. "You *wanted* him to see us didn't you? You knew he would make the wrong assumption about us."

"Yes."

"But why?"

"He complicates things." My face began to flush. I wanted to snap at him, *Well, you complicate things! You complicate things by making me think of you every second of the day. You complicate things because you are betrothed to Sironian royalty! You complicate things because you watch over me like I am the most important person on earth, and yet still refuse to allow me your friendship.* I refrained.

"James is my *only* friend." I felt the anger well up inside of me. He would refuse to be my friend, and yet, would rob me of the only friend that I had! The room fell silent. I put the key in my door and turned the lock. I didn't want any more surprises this time. I lay on the other end of the bed and looked up at the ceiling.

"He will come back you know." William whispered, breaking the silence.

"I know."

"He will come back because he is in love with you." After a short pause, I responded.

"I know." I admitted, feeling the blood rush into my cheeks.

"Are you in love with him?" He asked, his eyes narrowing as he waited for an answer.

"I love him—if that is what you mean."

"No. If you were in love with him, you would know it."

"Maybe I am in love with him and I just don't know it yet." He propped his face in his hand as if to contemplate this. Then leaned back and closed his eyes.

"You have been painting. I can smell the fresh paint."

"Yes, I have—yesterday."

"Can I see your work?"

"No."

"And why is that?"

"Because…I am mad at you."

"That's fair." A smile crept across his face.

"Can I see them one day?" His words were almost playful. He was quite charming when he wanted to be. He turned his face towards mine and cracked one eye to look over at me.

"Maybe. Better watch yourself; it almost sounds like you are trying to become friends with me." He laughed.

"I'm not."

"Well then—no! You can't see my artwork." He laughed again. At least he was laughing now. My eyes began to drift. I crossed my arms over my chest. For some reason I was able to sleep more easily when he was near. With as nervous as he made me, I would have thought the opposite true.

"You know. You did pretty well out there today."

"I missed every single target." I said embarrassedly.

"But when it really counted you hit the target."

"I shot a sea gull." I said flatly. He laughed again. I really liked the sound of his laughter. I was still pretty angry about the situation with James, and now here he was out of the blue paying me a compliment! I stuffed my face into the bed pillow. He laughed again.

"And for the record—I like turtles too."

17

———

"Life isn't about finding yourself. Life is about creating yourself."

George Bernard Shaw

When **I** **awoke** there was a note on the pillow beside me.

I will meet you on the dock tomorrow —7am. William

I checked the time—four o'clock in the afternoon, and leaned back against the pillow. My body was still adjusting to the difference in sleep patterns, and to me it felt like 6 a.m. I checked my appearance in the mirror. My hair was a bit disheveled, but my face looked quite rested. I looked—well, pretty. I could not get used to the change in my appearance. I had never pictured myself as beautiful, and with each glace in the mirror, I couldn't help seeing a striking stranger staring back at me.

I found my grandmother on the front porch reading. She smiled when she saw me.

"I was wondering if you were going to sleep the day away."

"Yeah. It's kind of a Sironian thing."

"I know dear." A subtle smile crept across her face. She folded her hands across her lap and looked across the road towards the ocean. The waves could just barely be seen past the dunes through the sea oats. She seemed deep in thought.

"You're thinking about *him* aren't you?"

"Who?"

"Silas." She closed her eyes briefly and nodded.

"Yes. I always think of him. Oh, don't get me wrong; the man that you called Grandfather was the love of my life. I cherished every second that I shared with him on this earth, but there was always a part of my heart that belonged to Silas. He was more than my first love. What we shared could not be measured in words. We had youth. We had history." The creases in her face seemed more visible. She looked like a woman with much weighing heavily on her mind.

"Sounds like you still miss him." A gentle smile crept across her face.

"When you share what we shared, one could not help but carry that with them. I could never wash from my memory those afternoons when we were so young. There was a time when my memories were so painful that I wanted to, but not anymore." She leaned back into the rocking chair and closed her eyes. "He would patrol at night and be so tired in the afternoons that he would often fall asleep on the bow of the boat—I would watch him sleep for hours. He didn't want to leave my side for a second." Her brow furrowed as if she were in pain, and she took my hand. "One doesn't choose love, Marguerite; it chooses you. And when it does, not space, nor time, and not even death can take it away from you. I can still recall the way his hand stroked across my face, the salty smell of his skin, and how my heart ached for him when his duties called him away. I still agonize over the time when I thought he had rejected me and blame myself for being so easily swayed into believing that he no longer cared for me."

"But you couldn't have known!"

"I should have believed in him—believed in what we shared. I knew the truth in my heart—I always did, and yet, still allowed my head to be swayed by another."

"It isn't too late you know. He is still here. Just over the creek."

I know. The protectors take their job very seriously. Silas took a vow as my protector, and as long as I am here, I know he is close by. I moved back here after your grandfather died just to be near him. But the letter that I sent to him when you were sick in the hospital was the first time I had contacted him since we parted all of those years ago. I am old now, and he would have remained youthful. It is the Sironian way."

"But he's not young. He has aged. Whatever keeps Sironians young, he has not done it." She looked at me in disbelief.

"I know Silas' beliefs, and I know that he would not take the life force of an innocent human, but there are other ways. Some take the life force of the evil, others take it from those who are dying, and it is even possible to rejuvenate through some aquatic mammal species."

"But Silas has not. Or at least this doesn't appear to be the case."

"I can think of no reason why he would not extend his life!"

"Can you not? Isn't it obvious?" It was for her. After all of the years that had passed, Silas still loved my grandmother as much as she loved him. He would not stay youthful in a world in which she aged.

"It doesn't matter." She shook her head as if to try to erase thoughts of him from her mind. "It's too late. Too much time has passed."

"I don't believe that! Why won't you see him?" Emotion churned inside of her until it exploded.

"Because we would once again become discovered and the relations could lead Aaron to your father—to your family."

"But the Sironians know of me! They already know that I am here—that I am a half breed."

"Aaron never knew that I lived. He never knew that I was pregnant with your father. Even if they suspect that there is someone like you in the world, there is nothing linking you to Aaron. He would be infuriated and once again try to kill us all. If I were to reunite with Silas, they could discover the truth, putting everyone in our family in danger."

"But what if I were already with him?"

"You have been with Silas?"

"Yes. He has agreed to train me. I want to know what I am. I want to figure out what I can do, so that if the time comes, I can protect myself and my family."

"So that is where you were earlier."

"Yes. But I promise to keep up my studies."

"I—I don't know how I feel about this? What if you get hurt?"

"That's why I am doing this. To protect myself. I have been clumsy my entire life. I have never really felt I like fit into the world—I still don't. But at least now I know why. I know what I am. I want this. Besides, I'm not alone. I have a protector. He was assigned to me years ago when the Sironians first got wind of my existence."

"Who is he?"

"William Avery."

"Of course. Now it makes sense to me why you would be asking about him. I am also guessing that it is his features that you were painting the other day."

"Yes," my face blushed with embarrassment. My feelings for William would be obvious from my paintings. She knew.

"I must admit that I am relieved to know that Silas has provided a protector for you. It would make sense that he chose the boy. I had suspected that his family was Sironian when they were killed years ago, but I was unsure as to why the boy was allowed to live."

"Silas bargained for him. Because he was so gifted, he was allowed to remain under Silas' care."

"That could only mean that Theron wants to use him for his own bidding in the future."

"Yes. Theron wants him to marry his granddaughter." My grandmother looked ill. I continued. "Her name is Aria. She is being trained by Silas as well."

"I see—William must be skilled indeed to be betrothed to Theron's granddaughter."

"Her importance to the regime must be great as she will one day rule when Theron steps aside, as her father was killed in combat years ago."

'My, you do seem to know quite a bit more about Sironians than I was made aware. All that I have wanted to keep you from—protect you from, you are already entangled in this world." I nodded. "What does William think of this betrothal?"

"I have not spoken with him on the subject, as he is quite guarded, but he seems to have no affections for the girl that I have seen in the short time I have witnessed them together."

"Interesting, just be careful Marguerite! Always keep in mind that they may appear to be human, but they are quite different."

"Yeah, I am finding that one out."

"They are from another world, another way of life that somehow has merged with our own. These worlds are kept separate for the safety of everyone."

"And yet, I connect them."

"You do. My wish was that you would be able to remain solely part of the human world and could forget all of this, but at this point, I cannot deny that I am unable to shield you any further. My prayers will be for your safety as you discover all that you were born to be."

Caleb called just after dinner. He was all in a fluster that I had gone several days without calling. I quietly gave him the rundown of all that had been happening. I suppressed the details as much as possible but did tell him that I was training and learning new skills. I could tell he was very impressed and eager to know more. He said the family was planning a trip to come down for a weekend soon, and I urged him to put them off as long as possible, despite the ache in my stomach to see them all— especially Lucy. I delayed in telling him about my physical changes. I wasn't sure exactly how I would explain that one to my family, but the longer I went without them seeing them, the easier I would be able to credit the change to just getting older and maturing. I spoke to everyone before getting off the phone. My father was as encouraging as ever, my mother as talkative, and Lucy's giggle brightened my entire day. I adored my family. I would protect them no matter what.

Next, I called James. It was the eighth time this week. *Once again,* I got his mother, Dolly, and *once again* I left a message for him to call me. I sighed as I hung up the phone. Surely he wouldn't keep continuing to ignore my calls.

****

Just before dawn, I grabbed a pair of slender dark jeans from my bottom drawer and a long sleeved dark blue knit shirt from my closet and hurried downstairs to shower. I didn't want to wake my grandmother, so I used the wooden shower stall under the house. The warm water seemed to revive me from a long night of studying and painting. I quickly dried my hair and braided it into a low side ponytail. I slipped on my tan flats and grey windbreaker before heading to the dock. The air was still crisp, and April held true to its reputation of fierce winds.

The low morning fog was beginning to lift as I headed out to the waterway, and I was a bit surprised to see both William and Kirby waiting for me upon the dock. They appeared to be arguing, but as I neared, Kirby at last seemed to resign and dove into the fog covered inlet. His exit was so graceful that had I not seen it with my own eyes, it would have been doubtful that I would have heard it at all.

"Good morning," I said as I made it down to the floating pier. He held out his hand to help me into the boat, but he did not look at me. I could tell he was still a bit angry over the altercation with Kirby.

"Good morning," William said, as he quickly untied the boat. I sighed to myself. I had hoped that after yesterday, we had made some progress in the friend department, but nothing appeared to have changed.

"Um—so what was *that* all about?"

"Kirby came to take you again this morning, and I had to inform him that you had alternate transportation."

"Oh. I didn't mind riding with him. It could have given you a break from babysitting." I threw my knapsack in the boat.

"I don't trust that guy."

"He seems perfectly safe and amicable to me. Besides, his so called 'powers of persuasion' doesn't seem to have very much effect on me."

"He seemed to be able to persuade you to go to the beach that night."

"No, I wanted to go. I would think that if I were to have friends, other protectors would be the safest choice."

"I still don't like him. He thinks he is some sort of 'gift to women'— uses being a Sironian to his advantage in that department. He is all about the conquest."

"I think I can handle myself." I shrugged tossing my bag into the boat.

"I don't like it. He seems interested in you because of what you are. You are a one of a kind. Of course, he would show an extra interest in you." He swiftly started the motor. But just before we headed out, we both noticed my grandmother watching us from the screened porch.

"She knows you are with me?"

"Yes. She also knows I am training with Silas."

"So she also knows I am your protector?"

"Yes."

"Well then, tomorrow there will be no need to take your boat. We can take mine." I rolled my eyes as he picked up speed.

"I like my boat. It has a certain charm—wouldn't you say?"

"No."

I giggled. He took off so fast that I had to grab hold of my knapsack so that it wouldn't blow out.

We arrived at the embankment after taking the same route that Kirby had taken just the day earlier. The crew all were standing around talking but seemed to grow quite as William and I broke through the trees. Kirby had arrived just before us, and it was obvious that I was the topic of conversation. *Great.* Silas was across the fields pulling out different weapons from the large black bags. This weapon, I recognized. It was a gun with a spear attached to the top—a spear gun. *Lovely, I get to embarrass myself with a bow and now with a spear gun.* Silas pulled out one of the weapons as an example and began to school us on the features of the weapon. I had seen something similar on TV before, but I was quite certain that like the crossbow, this weapon was unique only to us. It appeared much like a traditional spear gun, not that I had actually ever laid my hands upon one, but unlike those I had seen before, this one had a mechanism that reloaded automatically from a cartridge of four extra spears. We all took a seat on a few logs that had been rounded up at some point for this very purpose. William stood off to the side as he had done the day before. He only looked up from time to time to glare at Kirby who didn't seem to hide his interest in me. I would often catch his glances at me throughout Silas' demonstration.

Mace took his mark first. It was easy to see why he was the leader of this crew, as his skills seemed to be far superior then the others—the others that is, except for William. The two of them completely ignored each other all together, making it quite clear that there was no love lost between them. Mace punched the trigger sending the spear towards the target. Both the spear and an attached cable sprang from the gun at lightning speed plunging into the target just shy of the bull's eye. With a flip of a mechanism on the gun, the cable retracted propelling the target towards Mace. He caught it easily with the opposite hand and extracted the spear before returning the target to its original position. The others took their turns, all making contact with the target very close to the bull's-eye. And then it was my turn. The weapon would have been extremely heavy for an ordinary human, but I lifted the gun with ease. I swallowed hard as I took aim.

"Quick, someone save the sea gulls; Margo is armed and dangerous!" Tobie teased.

I didn't let it break my concentration, but I could feel the nerves welling up inside of me. I shot, but the first spear dropped just shy to the target, plummeting violently into the ground. They snickered behind me—all but William, whose expression continued to be emotionless. The gun automatically reloaded, and I took aim, closing my eyes. I channeled the target across the field with my senses and plunged the trigger over and over until all of the remaining spears had been fired. I opened my eyes to find the very center of the target decorated with the spears from my gun.

The crew look dumbfounded, but Silas nodded in affirmation. I turned to look at William. The corners of his mouth briefly turned up for what almost appeared to be a smile. He winked at me.

After several turns on the target, Silas ushered us down to the waterline to teach us about the maneuverability of the weapon in oceanic combat. I listened intently, but all the while my heart pounded louder and louder in my chest as I knew what was coming next—something that I knew that I was not ready for. The concerned look on William's face only added to the worry. I wondered if he could hear how my heart was racing or if he too knew what was to come.

The crew began removing their blue jeans and shirts. It was freezing, and I was shocked that no one seemed at all fazed by the extra low temperatures. Apparently, I didn't get the memo that swimwear was required for the day's exercises. The guys all wore board shorts, and Aria was once again absolutely stunning, this time in a simple brown one-piece bathing suit. Her figure was stunning. She was every guys dream, and every girl's worst nightmare. But I was the only one in the group who seemed to notice. "And now the real training begins!" Aria said, taking hold of her spear gun and heading towards the water.

"Time to separate the men from the boys!" Mace exclaimed as he retracted and reloaded another of his spears.

"Margo, are you coming with us?" Kirby said, crossing to hand me my gun.

"I wasn't aware we were swimming today. I didn't bring my suit." My chest pounded harder.

"Well, I am sure that won't be a problem. Aria will let you borrow one of hers, won't you Aria." She grunted but pulled out yesterday's skimpy bikini from her bag.

"You can change here Margo. We promise not to look." Kirby said. William growled at him. Even more embarrassed at the thought of my less curvy body in Aria's tiny swimwear, was the revelation that I knew had to be spoken. I might as well go ahead and say it, as they would all know soon enough.

"Um—I don't swim." I muttered.

"Yeah, we know that doll." Kirby responded with a cocky smile. We patrol these waters every day, but you are completely safe out here with us. No one would even dare touch you with this many protectors around. We can round up a wetsuit if the temperature is too…."

"It isn't that. I…I don't swim at all."

"You don't swim? That is pretty funny," Tobie sniggered with his dimpled grin.

"She's not joking." Mace's eyes narrowed as he looked directly at me. I could feel the blood rushing to my cheeks.

"What kind of Sironian are you if you can't swim?" Aria smirked.

For the first time all day, William spoke. "Marguerite is perfectly capable of swimming; I have witnessed it. But it would be a bad idea for her to spend any length of time in the water this time of year. She is warm-blooded and cannot adjust her body temperature the same as we do." I listened dumbfounded as Will explained to them details of my anatomy in which I was completely unaware. So far I had only noticed the traits that seemed to link me to this Sironian race, I had not also thought to note the differences. There was so much to learn.

Silas spoke, "William is correct; with the water temperature this time of year, Marguerite could only withstand a short while in these waters before becoming quite unwell. That is, if her temperature runs a standard ninety-eight degrees, which I am quite certain it no longer does." *Great, as if I needed one more thing to make me a freak.*

"Come on!" Mace said impatiently. "We are wasting time on this." Aria glided to the waterline and swiftly dove into the icy waters. The other's followed. I waited for several minutes believing that each would return with an array of large game fish, but no one appeared.

"What are they doing?" I finally asked William and Silas who had remained on the beach nearby.

"Hunting," Silas said with a smile.

"But what are they hunting for?"

"Each other," William said flatly. My knees felt week, and my stomach felt sick.

"Surely, you are joking," I managed to get out. I was sure that my face was green.

Silas responded. "The most affective training is authentic physical combat. This prepares the mind and body for actual battle. How else can one actually know how they will respond in life or death situations? Don't worry, this group is skilled enough to know what wounds are fatal." William motioned to the water's edge where Tobie was emerging with a spear jutting straight through his shoulder. He appeared barely shaken, but I felt weak in the knees at the sight of him.

"Hey Silas, ya think you can pull this out?" He crossed over to us. It looked even worse up close. My knees began to buckle. Silas screwed the tip of the spear off. He gripped the injured shoulder tightly in his left hand and grasped the shaft with the other. With one hard, quick pull the bloody spear was removed. He let out one a blood-curling roar of pain, but quickly seemed to recover. "Thanks," he replied. He winked at me teasingly, as I was quite sure he could read the horror on my face. Tobie turned on his heels, retrieved his gun, and hurried back off into the water.

"But, shouldn't he wait until it is healed?" I managed to get out, still feeling a bit queasy.

William spoke first. "Our bodies heal quicker in the salt water— yours does too." I thought back to the oyster wound. Of course I knew this. Then I thought back to the massive amount of blood that had come off William's hand the day in my room. They still bleed.

"But won't the blood attract sharks?" They both smiled. Silas answered.

"Sharks are not a problem for us. They are no match for a Sironian in the water. They fear us and avoid us in most situations."

"Oh." I responded, feeling even more ignorant.

It was then that Aria came out of the water. She was pale and collapsed onto the sand with a spear through her abdomen. The cream colored sands became red with blood. Both Silas and William rushed to her side. Kirby sprang from the water, spear gun in hand. He looked beyond distraught.

"Oh my gosh!" I exclaimed.

"I am so sorry Aria! I thought for sure you would be able to catch that one before it hit you." Kirby pleaded with her. William shot him a look that could kill. It was the first time that I realized that William may actually care for her after all. A sharp pain was felt in my lower abdomen. I wondered if I had been shot too, but it was just a strange ache inside—the ache of heartbreak. She screamed in pain. I winced at the sight of her. The sight was more than I could take. I stumbled to the dunes and got sick. I watched from afar as they removed the spear and bandaged her up. She looked pretty bad.

"Kirby—you take Marguerite home. I need William to keep pressure on the wound until we can get her back." William didn't look at me but kept pressing tight to her abdomen.

"Sure," he said still really distraught. He crossed to me and took my hand. "Are you okay?" I nodded. And with that, he began to lead me back across the field. Mace and Tobie emerged from the water, and I could barely make out the four of them gently lifting her just before we reached the tall marsh reeds that concealed my boat.

We were both silent for the ride home. Kirby was still visibly shaken. He easily slipped the boat against the dock and tying it before I could even turn to help. He leapt to the pier and swiftly took my hand to help me out. I accepted as my knees were still a bit weak. But he kept hold of my hand a bit too long, and before he left, his eyes met mine. "You know she is going to be alright. It was just an accident. I mean, I know you were trying to shoot her—you were supposed to try to shoot her, but we all know that you weren't actually tying to…."

"I know. It was odd out there. She saw it coming, had plenty of time to react but let it hit her anyway. We've done that drill a hundred times. She should have caught it. Anyway, I hope you will be feeling better by tomorrow." I gently pulled my hand from his.

"I'll be alright. Just worried about Aria." *And William.*

"Well, I will keep watch over you until William returns and chases me off."

"Oh no. Kirby, I will be fine. You go check on Aria."

"I'll be around. Just know you are still safe."

"I know," I faintly smiled realizing that I not only had William keeping watch over me, I had this motley crew of Sironians all on the lookout. Kirby dove into the waters.

My grandmother was on the back porch when I walked back up to the house. I realized she had seen Kirby dropping me off. "My my—looks as if you have yourself yet another admirer."

"Oh no…it is nothing like that. He was just dropping me home from training."

"Alright dear. You keep telling yourself that. Just don't want you to find yourself in even deeper water—pardon the pun," she smiled. It was nice to see her smile for a change.

"Ha—you are hilarious," I said sarcastically.

The warm shower water helped to soothe my tired body but did little to calm my nerves. I couldn't erase the look of concern on William's face as he tended to Aria. Maybe he did love her—after all, he was betrothed to marry her. Maybe he didn't resent the marriage contract and part of the resentment he felt toward me was because my presence here kept him away from her. My entire inside ached. So this was heartache. Well, I could definitely live without this feeling. I would have to find a way to get past this if I were ever to be trained well enough to challenge William for my own guardianship. At this point that really did seem impossible. I felt more dedicated than ever to do whatever it takes to challenge him. I would win. I would be my own protector so he was free to search for his sister, be with Aria, or whatever else he wanted to do.

I thought back over the day. Was it even possible? I thought of the spear through Tobie's shoulder, and the blood dripping onto the sand from Aria's wound. I had no idea when I asked to train what would be expected of me. I got sick again, this time falling to my knees in tears. I remained there, with the hot water falling against my back. I would have to do this. I would prove to them that I could take care of myself, and whatever force was out there waiting for me—I would find a way to take them on as well. I may not know exactly what I am capable of doing, but I knew that I would have to die trying if need be.

I crawled into my soft powder blue sheets and snuggled the white blanket around me. I shouldn't still be chilled from earlier, not after the hot shower, but I felt cold inside. It was dark. I tried to read my favorite books, but I couldn't concentrate. I tried to paint, but I couldn't. At last I slept. It was the first time I had slept at night in almost a week, and yet, that human part of me was still so strong, that sleep eventually found me. It was a dark dreamless sleep. I did not dare to move or wake until the sun was well overhead the next day.

There were two people at the breakfast table when I finally rejoined the world. The smell of bacon and syrup permeated the house, and their loud conversation filled the air. To my surprise, Kirby sat just across from my grandmother, and they both looked up at me as I entered the room. "Well, look who decided to join us!" My grandmother's wide grin was evidence that she had been falling victim to Kirby's charms for quite some time.

"We thought you were going to sleep the day away!" He said with a grin was just as wide as my grandmother's. He winked at me as my grandmother turned to grab another plate. I rolled my eyes at him, and grabbed a piece of cantaloupe from a large bowl in the center of the table.

"So I take it the two of you have met." They both nodded.

"Kirby here has been filling me in on how your training is going. I must say, I am very proud of you." I shot Kirby a stern look. He smiled and shrugged.

"Thanks," I said, with little enthusiasm. "What time is it?" I asked, anxious to get to the landing.

"8:45—I peaked in there after you several times to make sure you were still alive. You must have been extra tired dear, as I can't ever remember you sleeping so late."

"Oh my gosh! Kirby! We are late for training! Let's go."

"Not until I finish this marvelous breakfast prepared by your beautiful grandmother."

"Seriously! Let's go now!" I jumped up and was heading for the door.

"I'm just teasing you princess. Silas canceled training today."

I was about to ask "why," but I already knew the answer. He was tending to Aria. I wanted to ask Kirby how she was doing but decided it would probably be best not to let my grandmother know the dangers of our training. "Oh," I mumbled. Kirby continued.

"I came this morning to tell you, but I didn't realize that I would find a sleeping beauty. Then your lovely grandmother invited me inside for breakfast. She has so graciously been entertaining me with stories about you growing up." I shot her a disapproving look. She smiled and shrugged. Kirby continued. "And I was just about to ask her permission to take you sightseeing for the day." I gulped.

"Oh Kirby, of course you have my permission to take Marguerite. That sounds like so much fun." If I would have had a book, I would have thrown it at her.

"Um—actually, I have a lot of studying to complete this week and I...."

"Oh, that's just nonsense! Go and have fun dear! You can't do any better with your classwork than straight As. Did I tell you Kirby that Marguerite has had straight As since kindergarten? Well, except for PE, but we don't count that."

"Has she now?"

"Kirby, I will meet you *downstairs* in ten minutes." I put extra emphasis on the downstairs part, and grabbed his hand to pull him out of there before my grandmother made another excuse to keep him longer. I slipped on my favorite pair of jeans, a thin tan sweater, and my sneakers. I quickly brushed my teeth and ran a brush through my hair. I crammed a couple of ten dollar bills and a tube of lip gloss into my back pocket and hurried downstairs.

Kirby's car was waiting in the drive. Of course he would drive a tiny silver sports car—anything to call attention to himself, as if he would need anything more than his supernatural good looks and over the top charm. "Ready to go princess?" I pointed to the car.

"In that?" Kirby was both a tall and muscular guy. I studied the vehicle trying to decide if we could both fit.

"Sure! It's a beauty! Besides, this car wasn't really what I had in mind for transportation for today's sight-seeing anyway." He opened the door to the car, and I slipped into the passenger's seat. I wanted to ask if he knew of William's whereabouts. Had so much changed in a day, that my protector was nowhere in sight. I didn't even have to ask—he was with Aria. I ached. Why did I have a sudden sense of loss over someone who had never been within my reach?

Kirby jumped into the driver's seat and slid on a pair of aviator sunglasses. He looked over at me with a big grin. "You are much too serious all the time princess. You know, there are some advantages of being Sironian."

"I was just thinking of Aria. How is she doing?"

"Better I think. William and Silas were still working on her last night. The abdomen is a much bigger deal than say, an arm or leg. The main thing is that it didn't kill her, if an injury doesn't kill us immediately, we will usually heal up pretty quickly. I kept watch on the inlet for William so he could be there."

"Oh." I wanted to ask more questions, but I wasn't sure if I would like the answers.

"Let's go. Can't wait to show you what we are going to do today!"

"I thought we were going sightseeing?"

"Oh, we are—sort of, just by a different means of transportation."

"Why do I have a feeling that I am not going to like this?"

"Oh! This one is right up your ally! No swimming involved. I promise! You will love it—once you get the hang of it."

"I am afraid." Kirby chuckled.

"Fear is a good thing. Be afraid. Be very, very afraid." He raced away from the house at a speed that even my grandmother would disapprove. I turned back to look at the house, but she was nowhere in sight—neither was William.

"So where are we going?" I asked as the car raced towards a small town called Socastee, about fifteen minutes from the coast.

"You'll see." His grin stretched clear across his deeply chiseled features. The car pulled off the main road through the countryside and down a pine tree lined lane. *Great.* I thought to myself. *I may never be seen again!* Several minutes later we arrived at an old abandoned parking lot. It housed a large dilapidated building, and on the sign in front of it, I could barely make out the words Socastee High School. There was also a large, shiny, black truck waiting—a truck I recognized. It was Mace's truck. *They are going to kill me for sure.*

"What are we doing here?" I nervously asked.

"Come on. I'll show you. Since we weren't in training today, I thought I would show you what we do for fun," he said, jumping out of the car and making it around to open my door in a flash. He grabbed my hand and quickly led me through a covered awning that wrapped around to the back of the school.

"So, I take it, you all don't go to school here?" Several windows were boarded up, and the lawn had not been up kept in quite a long time.

"Nah, they built a new school about ten years back. It is about ten miles inland from here, closer to Conway." The mention of Conway made me think of James. How strange to have both my new world, and my old world, so close together—two lives, neither of which I seemed to fit into? When we rounded the last turn, it became quite obvious why be had brought me here. Two extremely large skateboarding ramps prominently stood where a series of connected tennis courts once resided. There were also a series of smaller ramps and wedges around the facility.

"Wow! You really did bring me here to kill me." I exclaimed, unprepared to see such an amazing set up hidden back here.

"Cool huh?" I nodded just in time to see Mace drop into the largest ramp on a small skateboard. He seemed to fly as the board went from one peak to the next. At the top of the other side, his body rotated spinning into the air before smoothly landing back onto the top of the ramp and soaring back to the other side. I was sure my mouth hung completely open.

"That was amazing! Can *you* do that?" I asked. He laughed at my enthusiasm.

"Sure princess, we all can. Aria, too, but she isn't here today for obvious reasons."

Tobie spotted us from atop the other ramp and issued a friendly wave as we approached. Then he dropped in as well, finishing with a series of aerial skateboarding maneuvers in which I didn't even know the names. The boards looked like tiny toys in relation to the size of the large Sironians.

"How did you guys learn to do this stuff?"

"Honestly? One day we saw some guys doing it and decided to give it a try. It's pretty neat being a Sironian when it comes to this type of stuff. It is like, you can see someone do something or watch something on television, and it's like "boom" you can see yourself doing it—and you do it! Cool stuff! Anything like that happen to you since the switch?"

"The switch?"

"You know, from being human to Sironian?"

"Oh, I've not thought of it like that before." Sure, I knew that I was part Sironian, but I had not thought about that equating to not being considered human. I swallowed hard and tried to put it out of my mind.

"Well, you are one of us—at least sort of." I didn't like the "sort of" part either. How strange that I wanted it both ways. I wanted to be considered human and Sironian. But the question was, was I really either one now?

"Oh yeah. That did happen to me once, just before I moved here. This cheerleader from school made me really mad by making fun of the fact that I wasn't athletic. She made me so mad actually, that I flipped clear across the gym floor."

"Bet that was pretty cool—put that girl in her place."

"It actually put me in the hospital."

"Oh, yeah—right. I bet it did. Yeah, whenever we do extra strenuous stuff. You know, land stuff, we have to be sure to revive immediately afterwards."

"Revive?"

"You know, head straight for the salt water. Land activities like this really take a toll on us, as our bodies were designed to do this type of stuff in water—makes us dehydrated, salt and mineral dehydration." It was all making sense. The bath salts my grandmother had given me had been like a super powered energy drink. The crash my body received after it was depleted put me in the hospital and almost killed me.

Mace finished another amazing round of stunts and left the half-pipe for some smaller ramps down below. It was then that he first saw me standing there with Kirby. "What is she doing here?" He scolded.

"I brought her."

"So now you are babysitting William's girl? You trying to piss him off or something?"

"Na, I just volunteered to keep an eye on her. William had some other stuff he had to take care of."

"You are crazy to keep that girl around with Theron putting a target on her back."

"We are protectors aren't we?"

"Sure, from the feeders, but I didn't sign up to go head to head with the Theron's Guard. No one stands up against Theron and lives to tell about it. You know the Guard is willing to go to any extreme for Theron, and they won't think twice about taking out a few protectors in the process."

"William did—when his parents died."

"Don't be naïve, girl. If they wanted him dead, he would have already been dead. It's all about power. They will use him for their own agenda when the time is right."

"But I thought Silas reached an agreement."

"Theron's Guard doesn't make agreements unless they are the ones that come out ahead. Trust me—being around William is about as much of a death wish as being around you."

"Well, I think I'll take my chances. At least with the blonde anyway." Kirby winked at me trying to ease the tension in the air.

"Suit yourself, but don't say I didn't warn you." He tossed his helmet into the grass and skated off to some of the smaller ramps and rails. I watched him from a distance as Kirby retrieved two boards that were being stored away under the largest half-pipe. His board foot work was as accomplished and meticulous as his ramp skills. Kirby handed me a board and a helmet.

"Um—you don't actually think I am participating. Look, I agreed to go sightseeing."

"Yeah—there are some pretty awesome sights when you are doing a 360 flip in midair," he laughed. I had to admit that though Kirby was not my type at all, he was extremely charming.

"You are insane if you think I am going up there."

"Oh you will—and you will do it today. I am very persuasive." He flashed his wide-mouthed grin that I was certain he was famous for.

"See if I ever go sightseeing with you again!" I said as I latched the helmet under my neck. If I survived this, it would be a miracle. I had a feeling I would need an extra dose of their supernatural healing power to get through the day.

After showing off quite a bit with an impressive display of skateboarding that even a professional would marvel, Kirby patiently taught me the basics. After learning how to stand and pedal the darn thing, we started in the center of the largest ramp slowly and gradually picking up speed and height. I was surprised how quickly I picked up the difference between a half-pipe and quarter-pipe, ollie, and kick-flip. Then we moved on to more advanced moves. Kirby threw out names such as Indy and McTwist. I tried to pay attention and learn the best I could. I fell—quite a bit actually, but I eagerly got back up. I wasn't sure if it was so much a desire to learn as it was a yearning to prove to them that I could do it. And impressed they were. I became quite competent with the board early on. The clumsiness of my earlier days had now become a distant past.

Tobie became my cheerleader early on. He seemed to support me every bit as much as Kirby and was encouraging every step of the way. Mace ignored me almost completely. I would occasionally see him checking the progress out of the corner of his eye, but he was careful not to let us catch him watching. I knew that he wasn't going to let me into his circle of friends easily. By the end of the day, he had at least learned to tolerate my presence in the group and didn't object when Kirby suggested we all grab a bite to eat and shoot some pool.

Each of the guys devoured almost an entire pizza each. I was quite hungry as well. Kirby filled the air by continuously bragging on my accomplishments of the day, leaving me in a surprisingly good mood. The fun of the day had help distract me from the fact that my best friend was ignoring my call, the guy that I thought about constantly was nursing his betrothed, and I was still coming to grips that I was no longer classified as "human." How crazy my life had become.

We were just about to rack for our second game of pool when the pool hall door opened. A guy stood there staring at us—a guy that looked surprising like James—in fact, it *was* James. Surely my eyes were playing tricks on me for James to appear here. But they were not. My heart leapt in my chest at the sight of him. How strange that it would act in such a way, as he looked every bit the mortal—and I stood among the gods. Before I even had a chance to react, he quickly strode towards us.

"Come on, Marguerite. Let's go." He gently took hold of my arm. In shock, I leaned my pool stick against the table and followed. Kirby began to object, but a look from Mace silenced him immediately. I didn't look back as James led me out of the pool hall. He opened the door of his Cherokee, and I speechlessly climbed in. We pulled away before he spoke again.

"Do you mind if we just drive a while." I shook my head. We were both silent as the car took off into the night.

"What are you doing here?" I finally asked.

"I don't know exactly. I have been doing everything that I could think of to not think of you. I was so angry when I left last time, that I swore I would never look at you again. But, I didn't believe it. I could never stay away from you very long. So, I was in my car, and a song came on the radio that reminded me of you. The next thing I knew, I was racing down here to find you."

"James, please let me explain about last week. You totally misunderstood what you saw." He winced at the memory.

"I don't know what is going on with you. I don't know what is between you and William Avery. I have no idea why on earth he would be lying across your bed next to you, and I have no clue why you would be here with those Socastee boys—but the truth is—I don't care. All I really care about is you. I don't want to lose you in my life." He pulled over onto the shoulder of the road and took my hand. For a second I thought he was going to kiss me. I slowly leaned away to prevent something we would both someday regret.

"I want you in my life too, but not like this. I don't want things to change between us, and if we go down that road, things would never be the same."

"Or it could be better." He added softly under his breath.

"James...please don't!" I slowly pulled my hand from his.

"Is it *him?*"

"No. William is the grandson of an old friend of my grandmother. We just fell asleep the other day. He has been kind of looking out for me since I've come to town. "

"Looking after you?" I nodded. "Since when do you need looking after?"

"I don't!" I snapped, "I guess we have become friends."

"It's a bit odd if you ask me. From what I have seen and heard about the guy, he is pretty antisocial. Seems a bit out of character for him to be pursuing the new girl."

"I can assure you that the very last thing he is doing is pursuing me."

"Are you in love with him?"

"It's not like that."

"You didn't answer the question."

"Like I said before, it's not like that."

"And the Socastee guys?"

"All just sort of new friends...."

"Friends?"

"Yes, friends—but none like you. No one could ever compare to you in my eyes. James, you are my best friend—always will be. I need you in my life." He sighed.

"Friends, eh?"

"The best!"

I could tell it wasn't the words that he wanted to hear, but he seemed as relieved as I was that our relationship was healed.

"Well, you have that. Looks like I will just have to take what I can get of you."

I smiled. "That's fair."

"So does this mean you will agree to be my prom date?"

"Your prom date?" I laughed aloud.

"Yes, I know it is stupid, but I have to go to take pictures for the annual, and it would really stink if I had to go stag." He batted his eyes dramatically.

"You know I wouldn't make you go to something as dreadful as prom without me."

"Seriously?" His face beamed. "So that is a "yes.""

"Yes! I will go with you. But no limos or prom-type stuff."

"I can deal with that." A sudden relief spread over me; I had my James back.

"So do you have to go back to Conway tonight?"

"Na. We're on break this week."

"Oh, I should have guessed that." Especially since the crew were off this week. With the schools so close, it would make sense that they would be on the same break schedule.

"So how did you meet up with those Socastee guys anyway?"

"Well, my BFF dropped me, so I had to go looking for fresh meat."

"Very funny. No really?"

"I just met them out at the corner. They figured out I was new in town and thought I might enjoy hanging out sometimes." It wasn't a total lie, but my story sounded awkward. It would be best to keep all explanations to a minimum.

"Sounds like that makes *you* the fresh meat."

"Not a chance! I can assure you they are not interested in me like that."

"You don't seem to know guys very well if you truly believe that."

"Most of them are pretty nice. There is usually a girl with them too—Aria."

"They seem like freaks to me. Come on! You must have seen them surfing out there the last time we were here. I mean, who surfs without a wetsuit in this weather! And the tricks that they were able to do, you don't see that kind of stuff around here. Heck, we usually don't even have the waves for stuff like that. What'd they do, bring the surf with them."

"Yeah. Probably something like that. They must surf a good bit to be able to do all of that stuff."

"They don't seem odd to you? Like too perfect or something?"

"Honestly, I don't know them very well. Today was really the first time we have hung out as friends, so I don't know very much about any of them—except I am pretty sure the big one doesn't like me very much."

"I wouldn't take it personal. He doesn't appear to like anyone very much if you ask me. Just promise me one thing."

"What is that?"

"Just be careful okay. I mean, they just seem like trouble to me."

"I am a big girl. I can take care of myself."

"Just promise, okay? Don't want you to wind up like that guy in *Lost Boys.*"

"Ok. I watched all three of them wolf down a pizza a piece tonight, so I can assure you they are not vampires. Besides, look at their tans!"

"Alright! Alright! Maybe the whole vampire thing is stretching it a bit. Just be careful what you get involved with. There are some pretty rough characters out there, and I would hate for you to get mixed up with the wrong crowd." I couldn't help thinking, "*You have no idea about what all is out there—out there after ME!*" How funny that the ones he is trying to warn me about are the ones keeping me alive.

"Deal, but you have to promise that next time you get angry, you won't storm off until we have talked."

"That's fair."

I hoped that if the truth ever came out that James would understand—understand the lies and half-truths that seemed to slip out more easily each day, were only for his safety. Maybe just maybe, I was *his* protector. But I couldn't shake the feeling that the one thing needing protection the most was his heart. Who would protect him from me?

18

*"Every man has his secret sorrows which the world knows not;
and often times we call a man cold when he is only sad."*

Henry Wadsworth Longfellow

The air had warmed, a sure sign that spring was just around the corner. The warmer temperatures came with mixed reservations, as tourists had steadily begun to show up on the beaches during the weekends. The area that had seemed almost completely isolated began to stir to life. It had once seemed so odd to me to not have the constant stir of vacationers, and yet now, their presence seemed out of place.

James stayed for the remainder of the week. It was great having him around, and much to my relief, he no longer seemed insistent on pushing our friendship into a romance. We would meet in the early morning for our walks along the shoreline and alternate our afternoons between boat rides in the inlet and reading in the hammock. Late at night we would just sit for hours and talk. We talked about our families—our past experiences—our dreams. It was like old times. There were no signs of anything unusual or supernatural at all. It was as if that entire part of my life had temporarily vanished. Vanished, but not forgotten.

The entire Leighton family came to town for the weekend. It was a fun change of pace to be surrounded by them all. Dolly doted on me exceedingly and could not stop talking of how much I had "blossomed" since she saw me last. I had not seen them in almost a year, so the lapse in time helped to conceal my physical changes that were more obvious to James. His sisters Rebecca and Kitty seemed a bit intimidated by my improvement in appearance. They were as warm as ever, but I couldn't help but notice the way that they stared at me. Rebecca brought her friend Amy down for the weekend. She seemed more than impressed by James and constantly seemed to try to draw his attention. The blonde girl was silly and a bit immature, but quit attractive. James seemed to pay her very little attention, which only seemed to feed her growing obsession with him. I thought it hilarious and teased him excessively about the girl.

I spent as much time with the Leightons as possible, as it kept my mind off of William. In the evenings sometimes, he would turn on the radio, and they all would head to the porch of the Merri Mac to shag. The party would dance for hours. Against my objection James would pull me to my feet to dance with him, but it usually wasn't long before Amy would steal my partner. Her persistence amused me greatly, and so I usually passed him over without objection. James always seemed quite unhappy to lose me as a partner; however, this was in no way a reflection of my abilities on the dance floor. Becoming Sironian had greatly improved my coordination, but I tried to disguise this as much as possible.

With James' company, it was easy to be my old self, but when he left for the evenings, it was sheer agony. I wondered how long it would be without William's protection until they would come for me. Could I protect myself well enough to survive? With only two days of formal training, it was doubtful that I would be able to resist the forces that were out there should they come for me.

There was no sign at all of William. It had been days since I had last seen him on the beach at Aria's side. Had he abandoned me altogether? I continued to go out to the dock each morning before sunrise in hopes that he would be there to meet me for training, but still no one came for me.

On the third morning, I decided I could wait no longer and took the boat to the unknown embankment myself. It was isolated. There was no sign of Sironian or human. If there was no one to train me, I would train myself. I remembered seeing Mace pulling our bags of weaponries out from a hidden underground bunker in the brush. I found the bunker and pulled out my bag of weapons, as well as a few targets. I worked relentlessly through the dark morning hours trying to perfect the use of the equipment, combining the skills Silas had showed me, with the acrobatics that now seemed to come natural to this new body. I trained until I had little energy left. I worked until each target became shredded from the accuracy of my arrows and until my arms were so tired I could barely find the energy to lift them. I returned to train alone each morning despite my sore tired body.

Nightfall was difficult for me. All seemed quiet at night—too quiet actually. I waited for any sign of Kirby or the crew, but it was if they had all disappeared. Two of the evenings while James and I were walking on the Garden City Pier, I half expected to see the crew out in the moonlight on surfboards. But once again, there was no sign of any them. By Saturday, I wondered if it had all been a dream after all. As if both William and the Socastee crew were all just an entire figment of my imagination? Maybe their presence in my life had just been a mirage— they were Sironians after all so anything was possible.

The Leighton's all packed up and left on Sunday. James promised to return the following Sunday for the day. He had several school events booked to photograph on Friday and Saturday that would keep him away for the early part of the weekend. It was with mixed feeling that I watched them drive away that evening. They were like a second family to me, but I needed to find out what was going on with William and the crew.

I didn't have to wait very long. I was just walking back upstairs when I heard a car pull into the drive. I could tell by the sound the tiny silver sports car made as the tires screeched to a halt exactly who was the driver. Kirby was at my side in less than the time that it would take me to blink. I thought it careless that he would act so utterly nonhuman with so many tourists around. He spoke before I could even process that he was standing in front of me. "So, I must admit—I took quite a blow to my ego when you left me in the pool hall." I smiled. The look on his face let me know that he was about to milk this one for everything it was worth.

"Oh really? And why was that?" I thought I would play along.

"I have never actually had someone cut out on a date with me for another guy—and a human guy no less!"

"A date! I would hardly call flying through the air on four wheels a date."

"Alright. Maybe that was just wishful thinking on my part, but I'm not accustomed to being ditched none the less. I've been in fear that this whole siren thing is wearing off a bit—I mean, you are part human too. I thought my charms were designed to render humans at my mercy." I giggled.

"Ah! But maybe I've been given just enough of the gene to resist you entirely."

"I'm not liking that hypothesis one bit! That's it! I agree! You must be destroyed!"

"Very funny! You forgot that I am learning to protect myself. I may be able to take you."

"I believe it! You sure did down that sea gull! I think it was a particular aggressive breed at that—maybe even rabid! One should always be on the lookout for rabid gulls!" He flapped his arms mockingly.

"Shut up! Don't make me pull out that bow and take you out!"

"You already shot me through the heart leaving like that!"

"Ok. That has to be the cheesiest line ever! And you call yourself a siren!" He scowled. "But you're right. That was extremely rude of me. I apologize for just walking out like that. I just didn't know exactly how to handle the situation with James."

"I understand. He is lucky we didn't take him out. But we knew he was a friend of yours."

"How did you know that?"

"We saw you with him on the pier that day while we were surfing."

"Oh. That's right. I remember."

"Princess, you should know by now that we see everything."

"So what have y'all been up to for the past few days? And how is Aria?" I could take this small talk no longer. I had been dying to know if he had any information on William.

"She is completely healed and back to her charming self." I was relieved but still anxious on any word about William.

"I'm glad she's well. So, what else did I miss?"

Well, after you left, we were reassigned to the mouth of the inlet on guard detail." My ears perked.

"Reassigned? Let me get this straight? So the other day when you asked me to go skateboarding, you were actually babysitting me?"

"Na—I wouldn't put it like that. I was just asked to keep you occupied for the afternoon while William swept the inlet. It seems that he was picking up on a new scent—something that he didn't recognize. He just wanted to be sure nothing was out there that we needed to worry about."

"And the skateboarding?"

"Totally my idea." He said proudly. "Will was actually really pissed. I thought he was going to take my head off. Gosh! If I didn't know better I would think that guy was in love with you. Jeez! He takes things a bit too seriously if you ask me." My heart skipped a beat.

"And Aria? I thought he was with her."

"William? With Aria? No, I don't think he stayed with her very long. Technically, he lives with Silas, so with Aria there on the mend, I guess he would have to run into her. But he's been preoccupied lately, and I don't think it has to do with her. I do feel sorry for Aria though?"

"Why is that?"

"It must suck to be betrothed to a guy who hates your family that bad. I mean, it isn't her fault that her grandfather is Theron. It's not like she is personally responsible for what happened to his family, but you would think it were so by the way he treats her. Don't get me wrong, it isn't that he's hateful, he just ignores her completely—not really something a girl dreams about from the guy they are supposed to one day marry."

"No, I guess that is why she hates me too…because William is stuck watching over me?"

"Oh, I am sure she hates you, but I am not sure that's the whole of it. She doesn't like outsiders very much. She'll come around."

"I'm not so sure about that."

"Well, let's give it a go shall we. We are all going to hang out at the pier tonight, and I want you to come with me."

"As your date?"

"Preferably!" I cut him a look of apprehension. "But we can just go as friends if you would rather." I looked at him skeptically. He flashed his wide grin in my direction.

"Alright, I'll go…as long as it's just as friends."

"Deal, but I am not promising that you won't fall in love with me anyway. I can be quite charming you know."

"I know. You won't seem to let me forget that part."

"I will pick you up at eleven o'clock."

"Eleven? Who goes out that late?"

"We do!" He said with a smile and was once again back in his car in a flash.

I decided not to tell my grandmother I was going out, but once again told her I was going to bed early. I wasn't sure how late this crew stayed out, especially since they didn't sleep at night, but I was quite certain that it was later than she would approve. I dressed in jeans and a grey tank, with a white long sleeved knit, and low top sneakers. Just before eleven, I crept downstairs quietly to find Kirby's car just two houses down with the engine off. He met me in the drive dressed in black jeans and a grey knit. I might have missed him if it wasn't for his gleaming smile.

"Are we going to rob someone?"

"You're precious! Na princess, just after I left I realized that if you were headed out with us this late, than you would probably have to sneak out."

"Yeah, I wasn't sure how well that one would go over, but even if she did let me go, I didn't want her staying up half the night worrying." He opened his door for me.

"I must admit that I'm a bit envious. I haven't seen my parents since I was a kid. They take us away to train pretty early—it is our law. We were all shifted around a lot as children, to different sects. Theron's Legion does this to prevent strong attachments from forming, but Tobie and I have been together since we were eleven so we are as close as brothers. We were sent to train with Silas two years ago. Mace trained in several sects before getting moved here last year. He has a bit of an authority problem. I think Silas is the only Sironian elder he has shown any kind of respect towards. And Aria...well, she arrived with Mace, but they weren't stationed together before they arrived. Aria was sent here by Theron to train as a protector, but we aren't fooled by Theron's premise on that end. As William's betrothed, she was sent here to remind Silas of the treaty as she is close to marrying age, Theron will expect that deal to be carried out soon.

"Seventeen hardly seems like an appropriate marrying age?"

"No...that is pretty standard in our world. Gotta remember, it is pretty old school down there where we come from."

"So you all live with Silas?"

"No, we did the first year, but last year when Mace joined our group we relocated to a house just a ways down creek from Silas. Anyway, guess they are really the closest thing I have to actual family."

"You all bought a house?"

"Yeah. Money isn't really an issue for us." A wide grin swept across his face.

"And how is that?"

He chuckled. "Gosh Margo, I would guess you would be able to figure some of this stuff out. I'll just have to show you one day when you finally decide to take the plunge. Let's just say, the sea is full of what humans value as treasure."

The pier was dark, but Mace's large black truck was pulled into an adjacent lot. Kirby carefully pulled in with his sports car, careful to keep the tires on the asphalt. The others were already on the dark pier cutting up, drinking the same strange beverage that I had seen on the beach before. "What's up Margo!" echoed Tobie as we sprang over the locked gate at the top of the pier. "Thought you decided to go back all human on us after we got ditched for coppertop."

"Yeah. Sorry about that."

"It's all good." Tobie turned to the chestnut beauty glaring at me. "Aria, you missed it! Believe it or not, this hybrid girl can shred on a skateboard!" Everyone turned to Aria, for the first time I got the courage to look at her. She was as beautiful as ever. Her dark curls blew around her, and her skin seemed to glisten in the moonlight. There was no present indication that she had been so close to death just a few days earlier. I thought back on the painting I had always been drawn to, Knut Ekwall's *The Fisherman and the Siren*. There was no way to duplicate these magical creatures, the painting of the siren paled in comparison to her.

"Sorry I missed that." Aria responded sarcastically.

"I hope you are feeling better Aria." I muttered, still afraid to meet her gaze.

"I am. Thank you. Better than fine actually. William and Silas were very attentive during the course of my recovery. Both have hardly left my side for the past four days." Her words stung like a dagger in my side. Kirby must have been mistaken; William had stayed with Aria after all.

"Here, this is for you." Mace said, throwing me the drink, this time at a non-life-threatening pace. He laughed, as if he too was remembering the last time he threw a drink in my direction. I wasn't sure what was in the drink, however, and with four pairs of eyes upon me, I took sip of the substance. It tasted just as the sip I had had before, but this time it burned slightly going down, as if it were spiked with alcohol.

"You still haven't told me what is in this stuff." I took another drink as it was starting to grow on me, much more than the last time I had tasted it.

"I told you, it's our version of an energy drink. Be careful though, I'm not sure how it could affect you." Kirby said a bit concerned. I took another sip—no, I took a gulp.

"Margo can handle anything, can't you Margo?" Tobie's dimpled grin glimmered in the night. "Bet you can do this, can't you Margo?" Tobie stood on the pier railing and did a backflip onto the deck.

"I have never tried this on a rail, but I think I can. I boasted, desperately wanting to impress them. I climbed onto the barrier and duplicated Tobie's acrobatics. I landed the stunt effortlessly."

"Awesome!" shouted Kirby. Tobie gave me a high five. The guys seemed impressed.

"So, you want to be Sironian, eh?" Aria asked eyeing me through the darkness.

"I didn't choose this, if that is what you are implying. I am what I am." I said flatly.

"Well, let's see what you can do, shall we?" Aria stood on top of the rail at the edge of the pier and starched her arms out into the night sky before diving off of the end. Her body tightly wrapped into a graceful front flip before extending once again as she plunged into the water.

"Is she alright?" I gasped as the other's laughed at the expression on my face.

"Why should Aria have all the fun!" shouted Tobie as he lunged towards the edge, vaulting effortlessly over the railing and into the water below.

"How did I know you guys were going to make me ruin my best sweater?" Kirby said, he slid off his sweater exposing his muscular bare chest, before gliding onto the railing and back flipping over and over through the air before slipping into the waves.

"Sure, you don't want to join us?" Tobie called from the dark water below. You know, it's better down where it's wetter!" chortled Mace as he jumped atop the pier railing. He smirked before gliding high into the sky like a bird, then swooping into the water. Before I even had a chance to look for the group in the surf, they had already climbed the pilings and were back on the railing for another round. I watched in amazement as they all performed different stunts off the side of the pier, each time gliding into the surf and returning for another unbelievable feat. I stood there drinking the strange beverage until every last drop was gone.

Aria approached me again; the water seemed to slide off of her. Despite coming out of the surf, she barely looked wet at all. "So, you don't swim, and yet, you are rumored to have these amazing skills. What exactly can you do?" She asked teasingly.

"I don't know exactly."

"Can you do this? She climbed onto the rail and did several back handsprings before smoothly landing once again atop the rail." I wasn't sure I could come close to her agility, but my drink seemed to have given me all the courage I was lacking.

"I think so." I said taking a deep breath and climbed onto the railing. Confidence replaced all fear as I not only duplicated her moves but added two more back handsprings before landing smoothly once again.

"Impressive Margo!" complemented Mace. It was the first positive thing he had ever said to me.

"That was cool, Margo!" Tobie hooted.

"Very good," Aria said with a devious twinkle in her eye. "Well, what about this?" She burst back onto the rail into a complicated and virtually impossible series combination of front flips, back handsprings, and back tucks, all flawlessly transitioned together as if it were a dance.

"I don't think this is a good idea," said Kirby as I fearlessly leapt back onto the railing, accepting her challenge. I replicated each step, each flip as graceful and as accurately as Aria adding a full twist at the end, but just as I landed the routine, my pants leg got caught on a protruding nail causing me to lose my balance, and I began falling backward. Four pairs of arms reached forward to catch me, but it was too late as I tumbled backwards off the side of the pier.

The icy water took my breath away. For a moment I wondered if I were still alive, but I could feel the goose bumps rising on my skin, so I determined that I was still alive. I opened my eyes, but all was black. Panic spread through me as I realized that I no longer knew the direction of the surface. The pressure was building in my lungs—they began to burn. I needed air. I closed my eyes again remembering Silas' training. I could hear his voice in my head, *focus—channel what is inside of you, what you were born to be.*" What I couldn't see, I could feel. I drove my body through the water with all of my strength until I could see the flickering lights of the pier glowing atop the surface. I emerged to see four faces looking down at me from the pier.

"Are you okay?" Kirby shouted down to me.

"Yeah. I think so."

"Thought you said you don't swim—showoff!" Tobie said jovial.

"I'm coming down to get you!" Kirby shouted with a serious look of concern on his face. He jumped back onto the railing.

"No, I think I remember how to swim well enough to make it back to shore." I said brushing my wet hair out of my face and starting to paddle in the direction of the distant shoreline.

I had not gone but a few yards when I felt something brush my side. Before I could gasp, something had a hold on me. My sides were burning as if they were on fire. One's first instinct would be to think shark, but not mine. I knew this was no shark—*they* had found me. Long claws dug into my sides, and with one quick swoop, it pulled me under into a deep breathless abyss. I struggled in vain to look at my attacker, thick red hair circled around me, with skin as white as snow. I only caught a glimpse of her face—so beautiful that it was blinding. Her legs moved so fast that the waters streamed from her long white feet giving them the impression of fins. And then I saw the others—three males on one side and two female on the other. They had me completely surrounded. Even through the dark water, I could see that each was more beautiful than the next. I fought to free myself, and as I did, their beautiful faces became twisted into the creatures of my sleep. Their beauty vanished—replaced by a monstrous facade. Their eyes glowed fierce crimson shades, and their skin as clear and cold as ice. I was too frozen to acknowledge my fear. Would William be able to save me this time? Did he even know I was out here? Surely even his skills could not combat such a force!

Four rockets shot through the water in all directions around me. Their bodies moved with lightning speed as they engaged the forces that had taken me. A mix of jubilation and fear took hold of me as I realized that the crew had come to save me. They were fighting for *me*! Through the darkness, I realized that their faces were no longer the faces of my memory. Their faces had also been transformed and twisted like the monstrous creatures that surrounded me.

Mace took on the largest of the males. Their two large bodies intertwined together in combat. The male pressed his legs against Mace's midriff and kicked him so hard that his body soared from the water high into the air before falling once again into the deep. Despite the impact, Mace attacked again this time with greater force. He snarled violently, and his teeth gnashed like an animal. He was unstoppable as he delivered blow after blow; his hands were a blur of motion with the speed of his furious attack. With one final thunderous blow, the creature dropped deep into the dark, crimson water.

Fearlessly Aria had simultaneously taken on both of the female Sironians. She grabbed the first around the neck, gripping tightly to her raven black hair and sending her spiraling far from me and the others. The second white-haired female grabbed Aria by the ankles digging her teeth deep into her leg. She let out a cry of outrage that pierced through the underwater battlefield. Aria grabbed ahold of her face with such force that I thought she would rip her mouth in two. The white-haired creature let out a low pitched moan and went for Aria's throat, but Aria was too quick. She darted in the opposite direction at the last possible second. The creature hissed and sprung again and both Aria and the creature tumbled through the dark surf out of sight.

The other slender blonde male was the fastest of the group. He was careful to remain close to the tails of the red haired Sironian who held me tighter and tighter in her clutches. Kirby saw me struggling and tried to bypass the blonde one to get to me. It was useless as the creature snarled and hissed blocking each approach. Kirby went in for the attack, but the slender opponent was too quick and intercepted each of his blows. Though this male was slender, he was excellent at countering each attack and seemed to be one step ahead of everything that Kirby would attempt. I grimaced in pain as my sides burned hotter and hotter under her vice-like grip. The altercation escalated as they tumbled end over end through the dark surf. I screamed as Kirby took a blow to the face that knocked him unconscious, falling deep into the depths. Mace had just delivered the final blow to his opponent and turned to help me. I frantically motioned toward Kirby seeing his opponent readying for a fatal strike. Mace sprang to Kirby's defense but clearly was reluctant to leave me in the clutches of the red haired monster that was dragging me further and further out to sea. Torn between his friend and his duty, Mace ignored my frantic movements insisting that he save Kirby. I would not be responsible for Kirby's death, not even if it meant my own. But the red haired creature was too smart and plunged me deeper into the black surf far from the others.

The pressure in my lungs was intense—I was suffocating. I needed air. The red-haired creature strangely seem to acknowledge this as she pulled me out to sea, lifting my body toward the surface only long enough for a quick gasp of air before pulling me back downward. I frantically looked around me, we were traveling out to sea at such a rapid pace, that my eyes could barely focus. But through the swift current and sea mist I was certain of only one thing—they were all gone. She had successfully managed to separate me from the crew. If I were to escape, it would have to be at my own hands. Determination and anger swept through me. *They would not take me like this!* Had I been able to see my face, I would have seen the same twisted monstrous features come over my face as the one belonging to my captor—but this face was my own. I was Sironian after all. I ripped her arm from around me with such force, that I was surprised it still remained in its socket. She dug her nails deeper into my side, I roared—tearing her hand from my side and grabbing hold of her only long enough to throw her from my body. She flew far through the water and into the air with a force I never dreamed myself capable of delivering. I surfaced gasping for air, expecting for her to pull me under at any second. I braced for her to return and attack, but all was still.

The lights of the coastline flickered dimly no less than a mile away. All was dark, except for the moon that beamed across the water casting a purplish haze to the water around me. Could I make it? My face softened and emotions took over. The tears streamed down my already wet face as I treaded water. My worst nightmare paled in comparison to the current situation. I was alone—alone in the dark churning waters of the sea.

And then she was there—like a mirage appearing out of the night. It was Maris. Her dark hair glistened in the light of the moon, just a few yards away. She watched me as a snake would watch its prey, and I felt the hope inside of me begin to fade. It would never stop. She was once again not alone. There appeared to be several shadows behind her, but I could not make out their faces. She spoke. Her voice with a soft, sultry high pitch that floated to my ears like a song.

"How long do you intend to run? You need water, and we *are* the water." And then without warning, all beauty was gone. The being that she became was far scarier than anything I had seen thus far. Her flame raven hair stood off of her head like snakes preparing to attack, and her clear white skin now as dark as soot. She sprang toward me with teeth gnashing like nails, and her eyes bulging red spheres. I braced for her attack, but something distracted her attention from me.

William appeared like a white knight coming into battle. My heart swelled in my chest at the sight of him. His eyes only briefly met mine, as if to check to see if I were alright, before engaging the monster. His skill in battle became obvious as he attacked. His blows swift—more direct upon his target than the others. His speed and accuracy was unbelievable. She retaliated, but it was to no avail. She ripped at him—sprang at him, but with each pass, she couldn't even land a single blow, as he was able to anticipate her every move. She refocused her attention on me and came after me as I struggled to tread water in the rolling surf. He was there again, between us like a shield, blocking her from me. But the monster was relentlessly fixed upon her target. She disappeared into the dark waters, and grabbed hold of me from below. I plunged deep into the water, struggling to free myself. Suddenly William was everywhere at once as he ripped her arms from me and knocking her far into the depths below. He desperately pulled me to the surface.

"I have got to get you out of here before the others return."

"Do you think there are more?"

"Yes. We haven't much time. Climb onto my back."

"I think I am well enough to swim."

"Not like this," and with one swift motion, he flung me onto his back, and his body took off like a rocket through the water. I tightened my arms around his neck and closed my eyes, pressing my face against his back. His body was like the beach on a warm summer day, as my fingers and toes were frozen to the bone. I clung to him trying to press as much of my body against his as possible, as I was so cold by this point that I imagined hypothermia would soon set in. I thought he was swimming straight to shore, but when I finally opened my eyes, we had traveled diagonally quite a distance down the beach—two miles actually. I knew where we were instantly—Knoxx Point. As he transitioned from the depths to the shallow, he shifted me from his back into his arms, as we traveled through what appeared to be an underwater tunnel. We emerged into the wading pool that I had just seen weeks earlier in the solarium. Even through the darkness, I would recognize this place. The moonlight beamed through the glass panes that encased the entire room. *So the pool was bottomless after all—a passageway to the sea.*

"Wait! William, we have to go back for the others! Kirby and Aria an..."

"They are all fine. I am sure of it—but I will call Silas to be sure that everyone has checked in. They are most likely more worried about you."

"But this is all my fault. They put themselves at risk for me! If I hadn't..."

"Marguerite, this is what we do. This is what we train for."

"But…" He put his warm finger over my lips to silence me and looked at me tenderly. It was the first time he had ever looked at me this way.

"How badly are you hurt?" he asked as he gently placed me against the rocks that circled the edges of the pool. He flipped a switch on the wall, and the entire solarium became beautifully lit with an array of electric lantern and accent lights that adorned the place.

"Not very badly, I think." I lifted up the edges of my soaking wet knit shirt to take a look at the damage. My shirt was torn on both sides from her claws. The wound on my right side was pretty deep. There were lacerations on both ankles as well, but I was so cold that I was in no pain.

"These should be mostly healed by morning, but we need to get the wounds cleaned up and get you into some dry clothes."

We both looked up to see Sadie and Henry in the entrance way.

"You almost gave us a heart attack William! We heard something and had no idea what was in here." I was shivering uncontrollably.

"It's just us. I apologize for arriving at such an hour unannounced. Sadie, Marguerite is injured and close to hypothermia. Could you help her into some dry clothes and help her back here, so I can dress the wounds."

"Of course! Marguerite honey, let me help you get into some dry clothes. Henry, you go light a fire and start some hot tea for this girl. We better warm her up quick before she catches her death."

"Actually, I think death would have already caught me tonight if William hadn't found me." Sadie took off her white cotton robe and wrapped it around my quivering body.

"Sweet girl, you do seem to get yourself in a heap of trouble." She brought me to the same room that I had slept in during my last visit to Knoxx Point and helped me out of my wet clothes and wrapped me in a thick wool blanket. The clothes that had been placed in the armoire before still hung there as if they were waiting on me. She flipped through the dresses but came up empty handed.

"These won't do. You need something warmer. She rushed from the room and returned with a long light grey cashmere sweater and a fresh dark pair of jeans. The sweater had long sleeves and the plush, luxurious fabric came up high around the neckline.

"You're a size four, right?" I nodded accepting the clothes. "Well, these should fit you perfectly. But first let me turn the shower on for you. Some warm water is just what you need to warm up those cold bones."

"Thank you, Sadie."

I watched as the blood still trickled from my side and mixed with the steamy water before running into the drain. Even after a hot shower, I was still shaking. Maybe my body temperature had just not returned to normal, maybe I was still in shock over the night's events, or maybe I had really taken a glimpse into what I actually was. They were not just beautiful sea dwellers, they were monsters—and I was one of them. I had not truly understood this until tonight.

As soon as I turned the water off, the smell hit me—oak logs burning in the fireplace. I slipped on the clothes Sadie had provided and quickly ran a brush through my hair before descending the grand staircase to find William. He wasn't in the solarium so I crept through the dimly lit house in search of him. I found Henry in the living room adding another log to the fireplace.

"Come warm yourself by the fire, Marguerite."

"Thank you, Henry. I don't mean to cause so much trouble."

"It's no trouble at all. Sadie and I are just glad you are both safe."

"Do you know where William has gone?"

"He's in the kitchen. I think he went to go call Silas to tell him you are alright. William was seriously worried about you when he couldn't find you."

"William came here tonight looking for me?"

"Yes ma'am. He came here earlier. He was all worried about you because he said you weren't any place to be found."

"Oh. I guess I am pretty lucky he found me." Lucky wasn't the half of it. Had William not found me, I was unsure what my fate would have been.

"Yes ma'am. William is a fine young man—fine indeed. Is there anything else I can get you?"

"No—no. You and Sadie have both shown me such kindness. Thank you." Henry poked the fire a few more times sending the dry wood into a fiery blaze, then gave me one final smile before leaving for the night. I moved to the hearth and began warming my hands by the glowing embers. Out of the corner of my eye, I saw William there watching me. He had changed clothes too. He now wore a dark pair of jeans and a grey shirt. I was certain he had to be the most beautiful creature on earth. Not "unnaturally pretty" like Kirby, but fiercely stunning. He crossed to me carrying a tray of supplies. After setting the tray down on an end table, he pulled a plush throw off of one of the chairs in the corner of the room and spread it out at my feet. I watched as he once again regained the tray and took a seat on the throw.

"Will you join me?" This was the first time I had ever seen him look visibly unsteady. He almost looked, well—nervous. I sat down next to him. He reached back and took several large throw pillows off of the couch behind him. "Do you mind lying back, so I can get a better look at your injuries?" I nodded and reclined back among the pillows next to him. He carefully lifted the cashmere sweater just above the wound. I trembled as his fingers brushed against my skin.

"This may sting a little he said as he squeezed a cotton ball full of something into the wound." My fists tightened as the pain reached me. He instinctively leaned his lips close to the wound and began to blow. My body trembled. His breath was cool and instantly began to relieve the stinging. He looked up at me, his face just inches from my skin.

"I remember my mother doing this when I was a child," he said as his fingers continued to move across my skin as he bandaged my wound. I could think of no pain, only the exhilaration I felt each time his fingertips touched my skin.

"You miss her," I whispered, unable to pull my eyes from his. He gazed into mine as well, giving me some faint hope that he felt something for me. He briefly looked away to cover the wound with a large bandage.

"Every second of every day," he said as his fingers reached up to touch the side of my face. His fingers tenderly ran the length of my jawbone down to my chin. He finished and gently took hold of the cashmere sweater and slowly slide it back over my side. "It fits you well," he said brushing his hand over the soft fabric. "I remember the feel of this very sweater against my face from when she held me."

"This sweater was your mother's?"

"Yes," he said. And suddenly it all made sense—the clothes, Knoxx Point, William's connection to Sadie and Henry. This had been his family home. I felt foolish for not figuring it all out sooner.

"I am sorry. Sadie brought it to me, but had I known it was your...." He smiled.

"No, it suits you. You look lovely actually." He gently slid my pants leg up just above the ankles. His fingers traced the slashes, but I was in no pain when his skin touched mine. He cleaned each wound before bandaging them. I could not hide the fact that my body shivered each time he touched me. We both lie there in silence next to each other. He seemed so tormented to be next to me, and yet, he didn't move away. By some miracle he seemed drawn to me. I kept expecting to wake but my dream continued. "I thought you were gone—that they had taken you."

"I am very much alive, once again thanks to you."

"The others were able to fight them off until I found you. Do you know how lucky you are to be alive?" He exhaled moving closer to me.

"Yes." I whispered. He leaned back and closed his eyes. I looked around the room. It was so eccentric, so beautiful, so unlike anything I had ever seen before—just like William.

"This house was your home wasn't it?" He paused to look at me. I could see the pain in his eyes, and how very hard it was to answer my question.

"Yes—it still is I suppose. I haven't spent one night here since their death—too many memories. Sadie and Henry have worked here for my family since I was a boy. They are more like family actually. They remain to keep up the place. I live with Silas, but I could never sell Knoxx Point."

"It's so beautiful here."

"My parents designed all of it. My mother traveled the world bringing back books, art, and literature—right down to each and every shell. They are in every inch of this place. I still feel them here. That is why it is so painful for me to come, but it is also the same reason I return." He seemed overcome with emotion. I knew without asking that he had never shared this emotion with anyone else. "And one day, my sister will return, and all of this will be here so she can know them, and see them here as I still see them in this place." I touched his hand, but his eyes remained fixed upon the flames of the fire.

"What makes you so certain that she's still out there somewhere?" My words were as soft as a whisper.

"Because I can still feel her out there. She was only five when they came for us, but we had this kind of connection. I know it is crazy, but I think she could hear me speaking to her even when I wouldn't say a word. It was like she could hear me through my mind. If she were dead, I don't think I would still have that feeling, but I do."

"No, that doesn't sound crazy to me anymore. I don't think anything would surprise me after everything I have witnessed lately."

"Did I scare you?" His face grimaced.

"What do you mean?"

"When you saw me like that out in the water—fighting."

"No, no more than I scared myself with my own reflection just before you arrived. You weren't kidding when you said we are monsters."

"You turn like that as well?" He seemed surprised.

"Yes, somewhat at least. But I don't know how to control it. She could have killed me if she wanted to."

"I know. I almost didn't find you in time. Theron must want you alive. If he had given orders for you to be killed, I don't think you would still be alive. Honestly, what were you thinking?" he scolded.

"I slipped," I said embarrassedly.

"That's not what I meant. Why would you ever sneak out with Kirby in the first place?" *Was that jealousy in his voice?* "I didn't anticipate that one at all! Just doesn't seem very much like you."

"I know."

"I warned you about them. I almost didn't find you. I got worried when there was no movement from your room for several hours. You sleep very poorly you know."

"I know," I confessed. "I wasn't sneaking away from you because, honestly, I didn't even know you were still watching me. I haven't seen you in a week," I protested.

"I thought it best not to cause any more trouble between you and your friend. It wasn't easy staying away from you, I assure you." My heart raced inside of me. I knew that he could hear it despite my calm exterior.

"Everything is fine now between James and me."

"I am glad. I don't want to cause trouble in your life, Marguerite. It was wrong of me to allow him to assume the wrong thing. What did you tell him concerning me?"

"As little as possible—that you are the grandson of one of grandmother's friends, and that you have been kind of looking out for me since I arrived."

"I suppose that explanation it as good as any. But the less you tell him the better."

"I know. I'm careful with my words." I looked away, knowing that I needed to address the inevitable. "I feel the same way. I don't want to cause a problem between you and Aria." My voice cracked at the mention of her name.

"Aria? Why would you think that?"

"I saw the two of you fighting on the beach one day, and I guess I assumed it was over me."

"It was. But things aren't like that between Aria and I. They never have been—at least not on my part."

"But you've been taking care of her all week." He looked confused.

"She led you to believe that tonight, didn't she? Marguerite, I haven't seen Aria since Wednesday."

"Wednesday?" I did not even try to conceal the shock on my face. "But that was four days ago? I assumed you were still with her since I have not seen you."

"Just because you haven't seen me, doesn't mean that I haven't seen you."

"You've been nearby?"

"Yes. I am surprised that you would still even question that."

"I just thought with Aria…"

"They told you about the arrangement?" His brow furrowed.

"Yes."

"I will not marry Aria," he said flatly.

"But the arrangement?"

"It was made when I was a boy. I never agreed to it."

"I suppose I just thought…well, I see how committed you are to your vows as a protector, so I guess that I just thought you were committed to that as well."

"I will not allow Theron to use me to keep his family in power. I want to fight for what is good in the world. His laws keep the Sironian people slaves under his leadership. I have nothing against Aria, but I do not love her. Nor do I feel any more loyalty to her as I would have if any of the others would have been shot in such a manner. I won't allow stunts like what she pulled the other day keep me from my duties, including my duty to you."

"What do you mean by 'stunts', I thought Kirby shot her?"

"He did, but she *let* that spear hit her." I was baffled!

"How do you know that?"

"Because I know Aria's abilities. There is no way that spear would have struck her unless she ultimately allowed it to do so. Her abilities make her senses so keen that a mistake like that one should have been nearly impossible."

"But surely she wouldn't do that on purpose."

"She did."

"Why would she possibly do that?"

"To try to gain both my attention and my affection. She knows I have no real affection towards her."

"So she is in love with you?"

"No. I don't think so. Aria wants what her family wants—power. If I don't follow through with the betrothal, she is afraid her cousin Larifus will be next to take the throne. But there isn't anything that will not derail me from trying to find my sister one day. I refuse to become entwined in her families' politics, nor could I ever wed into the family that destroyed mine." It was the most candid he had ever been with me. I realized that he was finally beginning to open up.

"Why do they want you to join them so bad?"

"Because of my gifts. You have seen how I can anticipate an attack. I would be the ultimate defense. And yet, I must be losing my touch because I had no idea the type of danger Kirby would put you in. For some reason, I can't sense when someone is coming for you."

"Skateboarding? That hardly compares to the monsters waiting to snatch me up at a moment's notice."

"He had no business taking you to Socastee! It wasn't safe for you to be that far from me. I mean, if something would have happened, I wouldn't have been able to find you in time."

"It was—nice."

"It is unwise for you to spend time with them. Sure, I had asked for them to keep watch over you for the day while I double checked the inlet perimeter, but taking you away was out of the question. I almost lost my mind when I realized you were missing."

"But I wasn't missing. If you trusted them enough to watch after me, then you knew I was safe no matter where we were."

"But I didn't know where you were. I didn't know that day, and I didn't know tonight. I don't trust Kirby's intentions."

"He's a good friend. He truly is." I could see the muscles tighten in his neck when he spoke of Kirby.

"I—I don't like it. You, who never seemed interested in making friendships before, are suddenly sneaking off with a bunch of monsters." It was my turn to open up to him. I had the overwhelming need for William to really *know* me, to understand what I had been feeling for the past few months.

"I don't know how to explain it really. Imagine the feeling of going through life completely out of step, and suddenly a whole world opens up, a world you never dared to dream existed, and by some miracle or nightmare, you realize that you are entwined in that world. I suppose I want to be with them because when I am with them, I am discovering *me*." I now felt the tears begin to well up in *my* eyes. "I am still discovering what *I* am, William." He stared into my eyes, and for the first time, I felt William truly understood. His hand brushed against my cheek, and I realized he was brushing away a tear that had escaped.

"All of this time, I have been pushing you from that world because it is my job to protect you. But it would be pushing you away from finding who you are. I don't want to do that anymore. If you are so determined to do this, I want to be the one to teach you." When he returned his hand, he placed it so near my own that our fingertips were touching.

"You will teach me?" This time I wanted to cry out tears of joy.

"Yes."

"Can we start tonight?" I asked eagerly.

"I think you have learned enough for one night. We start tomorrow." He brushed back a strand of my hair that had fallen in my face.

"So does this mean we're friends?" I said with a teasing air.

"Yes. I suppose so. But, no more sneaking off. I would hate to ruin all of Silas' hard work by taking out his entire little group of protectors."

"You would do that?" I asked still teasing.

"For you?" He nodded curtly. "I would. I am a monster you know."

19

"We were together, I have forgotten the rest."

Walt Whitman

William drove me back to the Inlet Joy just before sunup. I was afraid my grandmother would discover my room empty and think that I had been kidnapped. He left me with the promise to return by late morning. I took extra care as I dressed, trying on at least a dozen shirts before deciding on a pale green button up with a white tank underneath. But remembering my last day of training when everyone had worn swimwear under their clothes but me, I slipped on a black one-piece beneath the ensemble. What was wrong with me! My clothes had never mattered to me in the past—but there was no William before.

I assumed he would be waiting for me on the dock but instead his blue pick-up was waiting for me in the drive. It was an older model, built for work, hardly the vehicle one would expect the owner of Knoxx Point to drive, but it was clean and kept in good working condition.

"Are you ready?" he asked as I approached.

"Sure, I assumed we would be traveling by sea today?" He opened the truck door for me and took my hand to help me in. Maris could have killed me at this moment, and I probably wouldn't have noticed anything other than the magical feeling of his hand against mine.

"We aren't going to the embankment today. I have some place else in mind." I would have gone anywhere with him. Yes, I knew he had that natural Sironian pull over my human side, but it was more than that, more than he was the most magnificent creature I had ever laid eyes upon. There was so much more to him.

"Are the others coming?" I said trying to pull my eyes off of the strong lines of his cheekbones.

"No, they have school today. Kirby, Aria, and Tobie are juniors and Mace graduated last year, so he keeps watch while the others are away." He started the truck and quickly pulled out of the drive.

"Oh, I guess I already knew that. You aren't in school?" I asked blankly. It never ceased to amaze me how easily and continuously I put my foot in my mouth.

"I was, a senior, but I decided to take some time off when a certain blonde came to town."

"You dropped out of school because of *me*?"

"I didn't drop out per say; I prefer the term "time off." It suddenly occurred to me that it would physically be impossible for him to continuously stand guard over me and attend classes.

"I can't have you do that for me!" If I couldn't beat him in the challenge for my protectorship, and I was quite certain that I could train for a thousand year and never match his skills, then I would have to find another way to release him of this duty.

"Marguerite, school is just a technicality for us. Ever wonder why you seem smarter than everyone else in your class? Our brains work more efficiently; we learn and retain information far better than humans. Besides, your safety is the most important thing right now. I could ace any of those year-end high school exams when I was ten." I knew his words were truth, but I would not allow him to continuously put his life on hold for me. I couldn't do it; I cared too much at this point. I let it go for the time being, but it weighed heavy on my heart that William had sacrificed so much once again for me.

"So where are we going?"

"It's a secret. I would rather just show you. Hope you brought a swimsuit."

"I did." I thought back to the vision of Aria in her black swimsuit, wishing I had picked another color. I could never compete with someone with the figure of a goddess.

"Good."

"I'm not so sure that's a good idea. Water seems to be pretty unlucky for me lately."

"You won't have those kinds of dangers where we are going, and well, you *are* Sironian. We can't have you unable to swim, now can we?" His words were playful; I liked this side of him, I liked it too much actually.

"I technically know how to swim." I said, hoping he could not see how nervous I was—not just about whatever he had planned, but from his nearness.

"Oh I know. You would have drowned last night if you hadn't been a very good swimmer actually, but it is time you learn to swim—swim like us." William headed south towards Pawley's Island, but turned east off of the main road just past Huntington Beach. The truck meandered through side road after side road for about ten miles before turning onto a dirt road. The dirt road itself was quite overgrown, as no one had traveled down it in quite some time. The entire area was sheer southern splendor with a vast array of timeless magnolia trees and large, moss-covered white oaks that stood like soldiers along the roadway.

William mainly concentrated on the road, and I mainly concentrated on William. I couldn't help but secretly study every perfect feature, from the shape of his fingers, to the narrow crease above his forehead.

"So how are you at hiking?" He asked, as he turned to me in the seat.

"Um—pretty terrible. It has been quite some time since I hiked anywhere." He pulled off to the side of the road near a dense forest of trees and underbrush.

"Well, let's just hope that your skills have improved in this area as well, shall we?" He was at my door before I could even make the move to open it.

"So how far is this hike anyway?" I asked.

"Just a few miles, but I promise you, it will be worth it."

"Is there a trail?" I asked looking for some type of pathway; there wasn't one.

"No, but don't worry, I have an excellent memory." He took my hand as we entered the dense brush. I didn't object. There was a growing desire inside of me to be close to him. When his hand touched mine, I never wanted to let it go. He seemed to sense this as well, and only held tighter to me as we made our way through the forest.

"Won't someone be angry that we are out here?" He laughed. He seemed to be in a surprisingly good mood today. I wanted to explore more of this person that was slowly beginning to peek around the walls he had spent so long building.

"This is my family's land. My father would take me here when I was a boy. He taught me to swim out here." He seemed amused.

"But all I see are—trees!" He laughed as I stumbled along the fallen logs and unsmoothed terrain.

"Be patient. I promise you will like this place." He would occasionally turn to me to help me over a fallen tree or around a deep gully. I couldn't have asked for a more attentive guide—or a more handsome one.

About an hour into our hike he turned to me with a smile, "Not much further now. Look there, just ahead!"

The sunlight beamed through the trees just ahead, alerting me that we had indeed arrived, but nothing could have prepared me for the sight. As we broke through the trees we stood atop a high rocky embankment. Approximately fifteen feet below, a circular, natural pool filled with crystal blue water was surrounded on three sides by the steep rocky landscape. On the fourth side, the rocks were smooth and level, coming right up to the water line. The entire area wasn't very large, just an acre or two, but the magic of the place could not be denied. Water trickled from the sides of the rocks, running into the pool below. A soft mist rose into the cool air from the clear aqua blue water; wildflowers grew between the rocks, and the birds and wildlife seemed completely unfazed by our presence. I gasped at the site that I never dreamt existed other than in story books.

"What is this place?" I cried looking at William who had been studying my reaction the entire time.

"The quarry. It is an old mine that was once used to harvest oceanic rock, limestone and shale."

"It's breathtaking!"

"I agree. There aren't very many of these in the area because it is so close to sea level here. Apparently, whoever built this one was fairly ambitious, and as they dug the limestone collapsed causing this cenote. It is surprisingly pretty deep considering its location and the effort it would have taken to mine here.

"How are we going to get down there?"

"Jump." He said flatly, but his eyes sparkled with the excitement.

"You must be joking." He laughed. "Alright, there *is* another way down, but you must hold on tight." I nodded, and he led me around to an area with a steep slope that ended just off of the flat rocks below. He stepped in front of me.

"Now grab tightly around my waist." I did as he said. "When I step, you step."

"But what if *you* fall." The corners of his mouth turned upward, and he turned around and looked deep into my eyes; his emerald eyes sparkled in the sunlight.

"I won't fall. You should know by now, that I will never let anything hurt you." Maybe it was the way he looked into my eyes or maybe it was the utter closeness of our bodies together, but in that moment, I knew that it was too late for me. My heart had already fallen—fallen for the beautiful Sironian whose body fit perfectly against mine. I pressed tighter against him.

"Ready?" he asked. I nodded and we took that first step together. William made the steep climb appear easy. He never faltered, never slipped, never let go of my arms that were wound tightly around his waist. I just followed each of his steps cautiously, and within just a few minutes, we reached the smooth rocks at the bottom. The quarry was even more magical from down below. This place was more than a limestone sinkhole. It was like we had stepped into another country; it reminded me of the cenotes I had seen pictures of in Mexico, combined with the blue waters of the Caribbean—but more enchanting.

I turned to say something to William, but lost any train of thought at the sight of him. He stood there upon the rocks shirtless, now wearing only a pair of cut off khaki shorts. I had been so consumed with the splendor around me, that I had missed the most breathtaking view of all. Luckily he was too busy removing his hiking boots to notice me appreciating his physical perfection. Each muscle on his lean body was chiseled, as if Michelangelo had carved him out of marble. I wanted to pinch myself; I should know better than to fall in love with someone nothing less than perfect.

"What do you think?" he asked. He seemed to breathe in the splendor as much as I. Despite the beauty around me, I couldn't take my eyes off of him.

"It's breathtaking." I said, forcing myself to look away from the emerald eyes that flickered brighter than the sun. William dove off one of the rocks into the quarry. His body soared through the air much higher than humanly possible before smoothly gliding into the crystal water with no more than a ripple. For a moment he was lost in the mist, but quickly returned to the rock nearest to me.

"Alright, your turn." he said with a smile that beamed from ear to ear. The butterflies that had made their home in my stomach all day became hummingbirds, as my nerves battled to get the best of me. I swallowed hard—putting all thoughts aside. I slipped off my sneakers, then my jeans slid from my narrow waist, and finally I removed my shirt and tank; only my black swimsuit remained. The chilled air spread goose bumps across my body. I paused and all of my previous fears began to swell up inside of me again. It was if he could read my thoughts as I stared across the water. "It's alright, Marguerite. You are safe with me—there is nothing here that would harm you."

I stared cautiously at William. There would always be the fear of getting hurt, but living wasn't really living at all until I learned to take that leap—and so, I closed my eyes, and jumped. Exhilaration! I expected the water to be frigid, but it was actually quite warm. As soon as I hit the water, William's arms were around my waist guiding me back to the rocks.

"It's warm! How is it warm?" I gasped.

"I remember the first time my father brought me here I was dumbfounded by the same revelation. I have several scientific theories: the surrounding rocks heated by the sun or possibly an underground hot spring. But in all honesty, I still believe the one that I came up with as a child—it's just magical." You could see both the joy and pain sweep across his face with each childhood memory that he shared.

"I believe that one too." I said, my words so tender that they were almost a whisper. He took both of my hands in his and pulled me to him. There was air all around me, and yet his nearness made it virtually impossible to breathe.

"I've got you—just relax." I obeyed trying to steady my breathing. "Now, cast aside everything you learned about swimming in the human world. Forget about your arms and upper body completely for the moment, and let's just concentrate on your legs and feet." I nodded trying to not think about the nearness of his body to mine or the sweet cool scent of his breath against my face. "Alright, humans tend to swim like—like cranes, with long fluid strokes. Their legs fluidly paddle through the water as a crane would flap its wings. Their feet are basically used just as an extension of the leg. In contrast, the Sironians are the hummingbirds of the swimming world. Both our feet and legs flutter rapidly against the water creating a churning motion that both propels and supports the body. Think quick rapid strokes, as oppose to long fluid ones—watch!" he said, looking downward into the clear water at his own legs and feet that were moving too fast for my eyes to focus on them. Tiny bubbles swirled around them creating the appearance of a tail.

"You are a mermaid." I said sheepishly. He laughed—a deep laugh from inside of him. I had never heard him laugh like that.

"I would prefer the more politically correct term "merman," if you are getting all technical." His face beamed as he laughed. "Yes, I suppose that is how the legends started centuries ago. Think the humans would be disappointed to find that we really don't have tails?"

"I do actually! In fact, there would be some pretty angry children to find out that all their storybooks are incorrect."

"Maybe we should just keep this one our little secret. What do you think?"

"Most definitely! Who are we to shatter the fairytales of children everywhere?"

"Precisely! Alright, it is your turn to try. Start with just your legs, begin with your basic paddle motion, then refine it tighter and quicker, again and again as fast as you are able." I began my first attempt with a slow paddle, then following his instructions built up speed until my legs were moving almost as fast as his." William seemed pleased.

"Excellent! Now think about the power you were using running on the beach that day; channel that same power, that motion into your leg strokes. I obeyed my excellent teacher and was surprised how easy the strokes came to me. William seemed surprised as well. My slow smooth strokes became quicker, tighter, and with the speed came power. "Ok, good! Now add the feet again." My feet begin to move independently of my legs; after a minute or so, both my legs and feet began to work together in unison—separate, but complementing each other like the parts of a well-oiled machine. "That's it!" William exclaimed as he dropped my hands. As my legs began to pick up more speed, my body began to rise up out of the water to my waist. I could not hide the excitement on my face. William was a mermaid—and I was now one too.

The motion created such power that my body raised higher and higher out of the water—up to my knees, and then I lost control and fell backward into the water. William laughed as I returned to the surface with a flapping motion that resembled a dog paddle. He roared again with laughter. "Easy there! I think we need to work on control before we get too ahead of ourselves."

"Sorry. That was pretty amazing." I said, a bit out of breath.

"You're pretty amazing—actually." He said casually, but the look on my face said it all. It was the first direct complement he had ever given me. He continued, "I mean, I didn't expect you would pick up on this so quickly."

"Thank you." I said sheepishly, suddenly afraid to look at him, not wanting him to see through the feelings I was trying so hard to suppress.

"I think we should add some control to that power before you hurt yourself. It is time to add the arms now." He said as switching back to teacher mode. I nodded. "Your arms direct the movement. Think of the rudder of a sailboat. Your arms focus the direction of your movement. When humans swim, the arms are used for extra force, but in our case, our feet and legs provide all of the power needed. However, our bodies are moving so fast that there is little time for direction."

"I see. So the legs are moving too fast to change direction."

"Exactly, the arms handle that part—the torso as well, but even the slightest bend of the torso can create a substantial change in direction. "Alright," he said picking me up out of the water and gently hoisting me onto a large rock at the edge of the water. He was so strong that I felt weightless in his arms. "Now, place your arms above your head as if you were going to dive." I immediately raised my hands above my head, pressing my palms together as a small child would pray. "No silly," he said pressing his body towards mine to adjust my palms. In his hands, he turned my palms downward, adjusting my fingers to overlap slightly. I looked down from inspecting my palms to find our faces just inches apart. His eyes met mine. My pulse raced, and my heart pounded so loudly in my chest that I was certain it would break. But my heart did not break; it swelled larger and larger in my chest as my feelings for this boy grew more intense. I thought for a moment he was going to kiss me, but he slowly moved backwards."

"Now, that's better." He said softly, looking up at my arms that remained above my head. "Do you know how to dive?" He finally asked. I nodded—still afraid to speak. "Give it a try. Close your eyes and think of a bird soaring through the sky. Push off of your toes as hard as you can and plunge outward towards me." I moved my feet to the very edge of the rock. My knees began to shake a bit as I thought about what I was about to do. But *he* was watching—and I could not allow myself to fail. I closed my eyes and pushed off as hard as I possibly could placing my arms in the same position that William had placed them. My body soared upward, but I kept my eyes closed out of fear. At last, my body plunged smoothly into the water. I opened my eyes under the water and rose to find William quite a distance across the quarry. "Excellent!" He said with a gentle smile. "Now, swim to me using the techniques I showed you earlier. I placed my arms back over my head for direction, and swiftly moved my legs and feet as fast as possible. I was at his side within seconds." He wrapped his arm around my waist for support. I tried not to melt beneath his touch.

"Not so bad." He said, but in a fraction of a second, he released me. "Race ya!" He took off under the water. I instinctively took off after him. He reached the rocks on the other side of the quarry in only a few seconds, but much to his surprise, he turned to find me right upon his heels. I smiled pleased that I had accomplished so much in such a short period of time.

"Very good! See, you are a natural." His face beamed. "I think it is time for some fun!"

"Fun? Did you say fun?"

"I did."

"No offense, but I didn't know that you had *fun*?"

"Well, believe it or not, Kirby and the crew are not the only ones who like to have a good time. I am quite a fan of extreme sports myself,"

"Are you sure you are not just saying that so I won't be tempted to put my life in danger again?" He laughed.

"Well, possibly. But as long as we are here, I thought it would be amusing to show you something. He disappeared into the woods and seconds later appeared at the top of a large rock at the top of the quarry. His body edged to the very tip of the ledge. He smiled at me before soaring off the top like an eagle in flight. His body glided into the water, the water folding in around him with barely the tiniest ripple. I was amazed. He was instantly at my side again, the beads of water rolling off of his glorious body. "Your turn," he said grabbing my hand and leading me through the woods towards the top. But he stopped about midway to the top and led me to a ledge. "Thought you might want to start from a bit lower for your first jump?" Despite the lower level, the height of the ledge was still twice that of the pier. I trembled.

"We call this jump white rock and the higher jump red rock."

"Very creative I teased."

"I was only four when I named them." He stepped forward with me to the edge. The distance to the bottom was as frightening as it was beautiful. "Alright, you're up!"

"I'm afraid," I said honestly.

"I promise you will love this. Just be sure to jump out away from the rocks."

"But what if...."

"I will be right there," he said gently lifting my chin before doing a back dive off the edge of white rock. I watched as he swam just far enough from the rocks to give me room to jump. "Come on," he called to me from down below. I took a few steps backwards, then took off running and jumped as high and as far as I possibly could. My body plummeted towards the shimmering water—the experience was exhilarating. I hit the water feet first, and the impact sent my body quite a distance into the depths of the quarry. William appeared under the water to help guide me back to the top.

"What did you think?" he asked as we surfaced.

"Unbelievable. Can I go again?" He smiled, quite pleased that I had enjoyed the experience.

"Sure." He said helping me out of the water again. "We have all morning."

With each jump my confidence grew, and soon I was flipping and diving off of red rock as well. Anything seemed possible with William at my side. He taught me stunt after stunt, and seemed impressed at how quickly I picked up on his instruction. How exhilarating the feeling of flying through the air! For the first time, I truly felt greater than ordinary...supernatural even. I had spent seventeen years feeling clumsy and awkward, but with this magnificent Sironian next to me—I could fly.

My stomach begin to growl as the midday sun set high into the sky. "You're hungry! We better head back. I brought lunch, but it is still quite a hike back to the truck."

"Only if you promise to take me back here very soon." I smiled at him softly as he handed my clothes to slip back on over my swimsuit.

"I promise," he said sincerely, as he pulled on his soft tan knit shirt.

Despite the fact that my legs now felt like jello, we completed the return trip in a fraction of the time. When we arrived at the truck, William pulled out a blue plaid flannel blanket from the back and spread it on the ground underneath a large poplar tree close by. He pulled out a basket containing two turkey and Swiss sandwiches, a container of mixed fruit, and some homemade cookies.

"My, you came prepared!" I said, very impressed, and thankful for his thoughtfulness.

"I had a feeling we might work up an appetite." He sat upon the blanket, pulling out the basket's contents and spreading them out before me.

"This looks delicious. Did you make them yourself?" I said accepting the sandwich and sitting on the blanket across from him. He nodded. "So you cook too? Tell me William, is there anything you cannot do?" I said taking a bite of my sandwich. It was delicious. He smiled.

"Yes," he replied, but was quick to change the subject. "Are you cold?" He asked, noticing the goose bumps that had risen on my arms. Despite the warm sun, the air was still cool in the shade.

"No, I'm fine," but William had already leapt to his feet retrieving a blue button up from the truck. I slipped it on as he handed it to me, as I knew any objections were futile.

"I forget that your body temperature doesn't adjust the same as ours. Kind of makes swimming a challenge this time of the year."

"Except here. This place was perfect."

"I've never brought anyone here before. I often come here by myself. I have so many fond memories of my father here."

"Thank you for bringing me," I said tenderly, realizing what a big step it was for him to share such a magical place with me.

"You are welcome," he said looking up at me under his thick lashes. He leaned over to hand a strawberry to me, and his hand brushed against mine. I thought for a moment my heart may just leap completely out of my chest. The connection between us grew stronger each time we were together, and yet, he was still so hard to read. He had spent a lifetime building up walls to protect him from the hurt he had endured as a child, but could my inexperienced heart ever be enough to heal him. I had changed over the last few months for sure, but I was still the same awkward girl on the inside, and he was unlike anyone who had ever been created.

Several minutes passed in silence. He was so near to me that it was hard not to stare at the perfection of his face. I could read that he had something on his mind as every so often his expression changed—as if he were fighting a battle within him. At last he spoke. "I've wanted to tell you something, but I haven't been able to find the right words."

"Alright," I said feeling more nervous than I have ever felt before. He took a deep breath. I was quite certain that I had stopped breathing all together entirely.

"I am sorry that I wasn't there the other night." My head tilted curiously, confused by his statement. I exhaled relieved at his words.

"But you *were* there. William, you saved my life."

"The truth is—I didn't stay away from you last week because of James. I was trying to stay away from you because I don't want to put you in any further danger." His face was full of distress, as if he were searching for the right words to say.

"You're the reason I am alive right now." I pleaded, trying to put him at ease.

"No, that's not what I mean," he leaned closer to me. My heart stopped. "Being with me would only cause more trouble for you Marguerite. That is why I have continuously been against a friendship between us."

"I don't understand," I muttered under my breath.

"My parents were killed because of me—because they loved me. I swore that I would never put anyone at risk ever again. I had fully made up my mind to stay as far away from you as possible while still securing your safety, but the truth is—that I couldn't do it. Even if you hadn't needed my help last night, I would have come to you. I wasn't going to be able to stay away from you much longer. I may have been Sironian from birth, but you are the true siren. The more that I am with you, the harder it is for me to leave you." His eyes broke free of mine casting downward, as if he were too afraid of my response.

"Then don't leave," I said unable to hide the emotion in my trembling voice. He was silent again, but upon hearing my words, his face turned upward towards mine again. His words were slow and calculated.

"I don't know what this is—I have never felt this way before. All I know is that my every thought is of you. I stay near to you not because I have to, but because I can't help myself. I watch you so closely not because it is my duty, but because I don't know what I would do if anything ever happened to you." I felt a tear run down the side of my face. He brushed it softly with his fingertips and brought it to his lips."

"I am sure it is no mystery that I have feelings for you as well. I know enough of your abilities to know that you must hear my heart race when you are near." He smiled.

"I am a siren. We were created to have that effect on humans—that is all."

"But that's *not* all. If that were the case then Kirby and the others should have the same effect on me, but they don't. It's you—it's only you."

"It's only because…"

"What I feel has nothing to do with you being Sironian." He sighed and ran his fingers through his tousled hair.

"If you really feel this way—even a fraction of the way I feel about you, then I am sorry. I should have never added this conflict into your life." He buried his face in his hands.

"I want you in my life. Whatever the conflicts may be, I would not erase them if it were to erase you." He looked at me quite puzzled.

"I don't think you fully understand what you are getting into.…"

"No, I don't, but it's too late now. I can't go back to just human—I don't want to. And I can't image a world without you in it." The depth of my feelings surprised me. I had laid it all out there before him. Just as he had placed his trust in me, I had placed mine with him. I was too far gone to protect myself from a broken heart, too far gone to turn back now. It was sink or swim at this point.

"So where do we go from here?" he asked. His body was now only inches from mine. Surely I was dreaming; this could not really be happening. He reached out and cupped my face into his hands. His fingers gently rubbed against my cheekbone, his thumb traced the edges of my jawline. My body quivered. He seemed unfazed by my reaction to his touch.

"I don't know," I whispered. My eyes closed involuntary when he tilted my chin upward. But his lips did not meet mine but instead rested softly on my forehead. They moved to my temple—then softly brushed against my cheeks, as his hands caressed the back of my head. The nearness of him made me feel intoxicated, as he gently kissed every part of my face, carefully avoiding my lips. I remained frozen, afraid that if I moved at all, I would lose all control.

He exhaled slowly pulling his face from mine, and gently leaned back against the blanket, pulling my body against his side. His free hand guided my head against his chest, and he buried his face into my sundried hair. My cheek rested perfectly in the hollow of his chest just below his shoulder blade. I could hear his heart pounding. Was it possible that he could truly feel this way about me? His nearness made me feel befuddled, and yet, I never wanted to leave his side. The smell of his skin left me breathless, and the feeling of his hand gently caressing my face was unlike anything I had ever experienced.

"Do you mind if we stay here for a while?" He asked softly.

"I would like that," I replied. "Let's stay forever." His hand slid from my face to the back of my head still nestled against his chest; and his other hand slid into mine. He closed his eyes and stroked my hair gently. I reluctantly closed my eyes too, hoping that if I were dreaming—I would never awaken.

The late afternoon sun had begun to descend when my eyes opened. The sound of cicadas and crickets serenaded us from the forest around us. I slowly rose from William's chest to find him already awake and staring softly at me.

"What time is it?" I asked. William sat up as well. His expression was hard to read.

"It is almost four o'clock. You were sleeping so well that I didn't want to disturb you." I smoothed down my hair with my hands, hoping that the damage wasn't too bad.

"Thank you." I said. "I had no idea it was so late in the day." I had spent the majority of the afternoon in the arms of someone who was still such a mystery to me. He was my own beautiful mystery. I watched him carefully, trying to read his expression. It was impossible.

"Your body seems to not be able to make up its mind whether it should sleep in the afternoon like a Sironian or night like a human."

"I have never slept very well at night, and it seems to only get worse the older I've become."

"Sleep is essential with the transformation your body is going through."

"Transformation? Do you think I am still changing?"

"I don't know. It's still too soon to tell. But it seems like your abilities grow stronger by the day. I'll have to make sure you are getting enough sleep." He said with a crooked smile.

"I am not sure that falls under your duties."

"I wasn't thinking about my duties." He said softly helping me up from the blanket and folding it neatly over his arm. His words were just the reassurance that I needed to know that he did not regret his earlier words. I had not been dreaming after all. His eyes narrowed, and he stepped toward me intently. My eyes closed as his face stopped just inches from mine. His hand cupped my chin, and I felt his thumb stroke across my lips. He chuckled.

"Open your eyes. I am not going to kiss you." He reached behind my head and pulled out a long piece of straw that was stuck in my hair.

"Oh," I said embarrassingly. It was the second time today that I thought he was going to kiss me but did not. I sighed to myself. His words earlier were so heartfelt, that I was certain that he had feelings for me. No words could have ever been more perfect or eloquent as his had been to me, and yet, still he did not kiss me.

He opened my door for me and loaded the blanket and basket in the back. He easily slid into the seat next to me and started the engine. I was sure that my face was still flushed, and I tried to avoid looking at him, but I could not help but to sneak peeks at him through my lashes. As he pulled away back through the countryside, I reached over to put on my seatbelt. As I fumbled with the buckle, I felt his hand on mine gently slip it in place. He didn't look over at me, but his hand remained on mine and every so often, his thumb would gently stroke the back of my hand. The feel of his hand against mine made my pulse quicken. I hoped his senses were not keen enough to notice, but his thumb once rested on the inside of my wrist, and a big sly grin spread across his face indicating that he most certainly did know his effect on me. He snickered under his breath.

"Shut up." I playfully bawled at him, trying to mask my total embarrassment. He roared with laughter, still keeping a firm grip on my hand.

I stared out of the window for the most part, trying to pinpoint the location of the quarry for future reference. I wanted to remember every detail about the glorious day, but after several turns, I had forgotten the way completely. "So, since today seems so full of admissions, I ask that you show mercy on me and give me the answers to so many questions I have about you." He turned and winked at me. His presence filled the entire cab of the truck.

"*You* have questions about *me*? You're the one of mystery. I am just a girl from…." I paused trying to figure out how to fill in the blank. I moved so many times throughout my childhood, that it was hard to claim anyplace as home—until now.

"See that will be a good place to start." He grinned. "Where were you born Marguerite?"

"I was born in Charleston actually. My parents attended college there—got married their senior year; I arrived just a few months after graduation. My mother and father had only been married for six month before my mother surprisingly became pregnant with me."

"See. That wasn't so hard. I was born near there too, so we have that one in common." He said, smiling at me. He spent the entire trip back asking me question after question about my life, my family, and my feelings on a variety of different topics from literature to politics. I tried to answer them all as truthfully as possible. He seemed intrigued with each answer. It was extremely flattering to have someone so interested in the smallest details about my life. I had questions for him as well, but I knew his situation was a bit more difficult to talk about, so I rambled on about my own, saving most of my questions.

When we pulled into my drive, he turned to me, his eyes staring deep into mine, "Can I see you tonight?" he asked tenderly. I nodded.

"What time?" I asked, reaching for the door handle.

"Late. I have a few things to take care of. I'll come to you."

"Ok. See you tonight." I said, slowly pulling my hand from his and pulled myself out of the truck. I never wanted to leave him. He winked at me once again as if he could read my thoughts. I tried not to watch as he pulled out of the drive but couldn't help but sneak a peek just as he was pulling away.

His eyes met mine through his rear view mirror. He was watching—always watching.

20

"A kiss makes the heart young again and wipes out the years. "

Rupert Brooke

I t was just after 3 AM when I turned to find William standing in my doorway. I stopped to take a mental picture of him, as I was certain that there had never been a more stunning creature born. He wore dark faded jeans and a deep blue thin sweater; clearly swimming had not been his evening mode of transportation. His eyes flickered in the dim lamplight of my room. He was here—and yet, he carried with him the same tortured look upon his face that he had had earlier this afternoon when I first awoke.

"You decided to come." I said putting down my paintbrush and brushing back a piece of hair that had escaped my ponytail.

"Yes. I couldn't help but notice that your light was still on," he said, his eyes narrowing as he looked at me so intensely that I could scarcely move. I nodded. "I distinctively remember telling you that I would have to take a more active part in assuring you received enough sleep."

"I'm Sironian now. We are like vampires you know, we don't sleep very much at night." I smirked, reciting back his earlier comment. He smiled.

"Ah, but you are human too. You need to sleep at least a few hours."

"I didn't sleep because I thought you were coming."

"I know," he said apologetically.

"I was waiting for you—well, for the first seven hours, then I decided that you weren't coming.'

"I almost didn't come. It is wrong for me to be here like this." His brow furrowed and he looked away.

"But you have been here before, quite a few times actually."

"I've been here—but not like this. I shouldn't be here."

"I don't understand," I said trying to mask the confusion and hurt that I was feeling.

"Before, I was here as your protector; I was here to watch over you. But I realize now that I was just telling myself that to justify wanting to be near you. There is no reason that I cannot guard you just as effectively from the inlet waters. I've been out on the water all evening trying to stop myself from coming here."

"But you came. You're here. I am glad you're here." I crossed to him and took his hand in mine. I was afraid that he would pull it away, but he did not. He laced his fingers into mine and gently rubbed the back of my hand with his thumb.

"I'm here, like a fool. I'm a fool to disregard my duties in such a way; the one that is your protector now puts your life further at risk because he selfishly can't stay away from you." He ran his free hand up the back of my neck, lacing his fingers into my hair.

"If you haven't noticed, I kind of already have a pretty large target on my back. It isn't much consolation to know that there is only a small strip of sand and a few houses between me and the army that is out there waiting for me."

"They can't get to you. Only the protectors have the gift to exist on both land and water."

"I think Maris disproved that one."

His hand slipped from the back of my head, and he began to gently stroke the side of my face with his fingertips. "Maris is no threat to you. The evening we saw Maris, you were along the waterline; she is completely powerless without the strength she receives from the ocean water. You are stronger on land, stronger than all of them." I felt my mouth drop open. They wouldn't come for me on land because of my own strength? It seemed impossible, but the look on William's face assured me he spoke the truth. I felt empowered. I couldn't help the smile that spread across my face with the knowledge of this revelation.

"Surely that's not possible."

"It is true. I watched you training this week, from a distance of course, but I saw your determination and your skill improving each day despite having no one there to train you. Silas was watching too."

"You and Silas were there?"

"Of course."

"But why didn't you come help train me?"

"We have a theory about your talent. We think that once you observe someone do something, if you focus and have the right motivation, you can *will* yourself to do it." I paused to let his theory sink in.

"But my first day of training, I missed the target almost every time!"

"True. But you were distracted by the others. When you were focused you nailed the target...and seagull if I am remembering correctly." He laughed. I blushed and buried my face in my hands.

"Don't remind me."

"The point is—you needed that time to see what *you* could do. If you were really determined to do this, then we knew you wouldn't give up your training, even without Silas and the others. You proved your commitment, and what a strong asset you could be, especially on the ground." He beamed at me as if he was proud of me. But more significantly, he looked at me as if I belonged to him.

"Am I stronger on land than you?" I teased, taking his other hand in mine. He smiled, playfully twisting my arm behind my back with his arm wrapping around my waist—our fingers still interlaced.

"That one, I am still unsure of. A protector's strength on land is about equal to that of a human, but unlike the others you encountered last night, many of our skills carry over into this world. The Feeders are powerless on land. You, however, have an unnatural strength on land due to the Sironian gene. I guess one could say you have the best of both worlds...and then some." He eyed me in a way that made me blush. I had never been looked at that way before. "You just haven't learned how to use your abilities yet."

"But you're stronger than the others. Is this why you are so valuable to Theron?"

"Yes, this is also why he wants you Marguerite. Even if he doesn't know your exact strengths, he can speculate on what they would be—what *you* could possibly do. His options would be to use your talents for his own use or destroy you all together. As you were not killed yesterday, I can only assume the orders are to take you alive—for now anyway." He continued to remain with his arms around me, but his eyes dropped to the floor.

"This is also why we shouldn't be together. If he knows we are together, he wouldn't rest until he separates us. You see, the abilities that we possess may be a slight risk separate, but together, we would cause too much of a threat. Especially since I am a bit of a wild card, and your abilities are a complete mystery."

"Don't you see, if Theron fears us together, then maybe that is the exact reason that we should give this a chance!" I was surprised at how easily my emotions overflowed. He placed both of his hands behind my head and pulled me so that the sweet fragrant smell of his skin permeated my lungs leaving me listless.

"It is too late for me. I've tried to stay away from you. I've tried to push you away, to rid my world of you for your own safety and my own sanity, but it is no use. If you were to leave at this point, then I know that I would eventually come to find you. I struggle now in those short hours that I cannot see your face. You are a siren in every sense of the word, as I am completely entrapped by every part of you." I felt lightheaded, as if I were dreaming—dreaming a dream in which I never wanted to wake. Once again, I thought he would kiss me but he did not, he just stared at me ardently for several magical minutes.

He abruptly released his hold on me, his eyes dancing excitedly. "Come on! We have to go. It's almost time!" He laughed as he began to pull me from the bedroom.

"Where are we going?" I asked still feeling unsteady from his closeness.

"It's a surprise. Since I messed up our evening, it is the very least I can do."

"Should I change clothes first? You know, I was dressed quite nicely earlier this evening."

"You are perfect just the way you are, though you may want to grab your jacket."

I convinced him to at least let me change into a pair of jeans; I grabbed my jacket, and we quietly crept downstairs together. I thought we were headed for his truck, but he surprised me by leading me out to the dock where his beautiful little wooden boat was waiting.

"We are going out on the water—at night? Are you completely forgetting what happened with the Obyascon?"

"The inlet is secured. Don't you trust me?" he said with a solemn gaze. His eyes met mine. "You will always be safe as long as I am with you. Besides, I've told you that the Feeders don't usually come into the inlet."

"But that 'thing' was out there."

"Sure, but there has been no sign of them since. I am quite certain that when the last one didn't return, the Obyascon learned their lesson about following the orders of Theron. It is perfectly safe; I checked it myself earlier this evening, and the crew is standing watch over the mouth tonight to make certain nothing enters." He easily lifted me into the boat holding me closely before gently setting me into the hull.

"You know, I could've gotten in by myself."

"Oh, I know." he said, as he took the seat behind me.

It was a clear night. The dark twinkling sky couldn't have been a more perfect backdrop for the shimmering waters of the inlet. The majesty of the setting completely calmed any fears that I may have had. I was with William, and at his side, there was nothing to fear.

William swiftly paddled quite a distance from the Inlet Joy before starting the tiny boat engine. I couldn't help but admire the way the moonlight highlighted the thick lines of his muscular forearms. Surely it was a dream that this marvelous creature had developed feelings for me.

The trip ended far too soon; I was a bit confused as we pulled up to a small beach cottage on the far side of the inlet. The whitewashed wooden cottage was rather small and tucked away among ancient oak trees. There was a large screened porch that encompassed the entire back of the cottage, laden with vines of wisteria and confederate jasmine, and a small garden off to the side. But its most prominent feature was a large grey barn tucked just off to the side, nestled between several very large, Spanish moss encrusted white oaks. It hardly held the same sort of grandeur that so many of the houses on this side of the inlet possessed but held a timeless charm that surpassed any of the newer properties.

"It's magical! Where are we?" He took my hand and helped me out of the boat. I was both relieved and disappointed that he did not scoop me into his arms again.

"Technically, we are at Silas' house, but I've lived with him since my parents' death." The house was dark except for a dim light in one of the corner rooms. I could faintly make out the outline of a figure that briefly came to the window before disappearing again.

"Silas?" I asked motioning toward the window. "He knows we're here?"

"He does now."

"Won't he be surprised that we're together?"

"I don't think so."

"Do you think he suspects there is something between us?"

"Silas is a very smart man. I am sure he could guess that something was developing." William touched the back of my forearm and gently led me towards a large barn just off the side of the house.

"But with the treaty, surely he would be opposed to anything that would interfere with your safety."

"...And yours. Absolutely. I am sure he has concerns—all completely justified, but Silas just wants me to be happy." I knew that Silas had seen William experience a lifetime of pain. Would he see my presence in William's life as a blessing or as a curse?"

William swung open the large door to the barn and pulled a long string that was attached to a light bulb that dimly lit the large space. The smell of sawdust filled the air. In the center of the room was a large boat that was partially covered by a tarp. William pulled back the dust-covered tarp to reveal a glorious sailboat. "It's stunning!" I replied, quite at a loss for words.

"It was just like my father's, or at least what I can remember about my father's boat. I began building it about five years ago."

"You built this?" I exclaimed astonished. He nodded. "Like from scratch?" He nodded again.

"It's built for both speed and protection. I equipped it especially for long trips at sea."

"It's magnificent. Have you finished?"

"No—not yet. There is still a lot of work that needs to be done before..."

"Before what?"

"Before I go after my sister. She is out there somewhere, and I have to find her."

Any thought of him going away, now pained my heart. Would I lose what I had only just been given? "Oh."

His mind seemed to be transported to another place, and I knew he was thinking of her. "You see, I know for certain that she is alive. Silas assures me that it's not possible, but I know she is still out there."

"If you believe, then I believe..." my words were as soft as a whisper.

"When I was a boy, I would dream of building a boat that would sail across the waters to find her, and one day, I just started building. The irony, huh, a siren building a boat, but it is the safest way to travel unnoticed."

"Do you sleep here too?" I asked noticing a small loft that had been added to one of the corners of the barn. He nodded. A patchwork of mismatched antique windows encompassed the loft area and served to protect his sleeping quarters from the construction and sawdust below. Narrowly built steps led to the small space. I began to climb the narrow steps leading to the loft, half expecting William to stop me, but he did not. When I reached the door at the top, I turned to find William right behind me. He reached out and turned the rustic knob that led to his room.

"Silas has insisted many times that I join him in the main house, but ever since the day I started building my boat, I have preferred to stay here."

I could relate as my grandmother had insisted many times that I take one of the rooms in the main house, and yet, I still preferred my tiny room off of the porch. "I understand. My grandmother insisted the same for me, but I prefer my own space."

"Guess you and I aren't worlds apart after all."

"Only a half a world." I smiled. The usually cool and collected William seemed nervous to have me in his room. It was humorous to watch his cool demeanor slip ever so slightly as he fidgeted.

The space was clean, surprisingly clean to be in the middle of a barn. The floors were a dark rich mixture of wide heart of pine planks and scrap hardwood, all stained to match. In one corner was several large stacks of books, and in the other stood a small bookshelf filled with records. The record player rested on the top shelf along with three small pictures of his family. I took a step closer to take a look at the pictures. William sat upon the blue patchwork quilt on the foot of his bed. There were no family pictures displayed at Knoxx Point, and so this was my first glimpse at his family.

The first one was of William and his mother—her arms were wound around the boy who appeared to be about ten. William simply looked like a miniature version of himself. His mother was stunningly gorgeous with dark copper hair that fell just below her shoulders; her eyes were a mirror image of William's. The next picture was of his father and mother. She looked even younger and if possible, more beautiful than she did in the first photograph. They looked as if it were taken when they were dating and appeared very much in love. The final picture was of the family standing along the dock. His father looked remarkably like William, except with much lighter hair, dark blonde or light brown maybe. It was hard to tell from the age of the photograph. His smile seemed to be as infectious as William's. His baby sister about the age of four hung on his mother's leg, her hair the same sun-kissed color as her father's, but the picture was far too small to make out the fine details of her face. A large sailboat, remarkably similar to the one William is building, could be seen in the background.

"Your family is beautiful," I said softly. He nodded. I could sense his eyes completely focused on me from across the room. "It means a lot to me that you brought me here."

"You're the first...ever."

"I know." I whispered back to him with a gentle expression that matched his own.

I began to flip through his albums. The vast collection seemed to touch on a wide verity of genres.

"Wow. This collection is unbelievable."

"They belonged to my parents—well, most of them anyway. I have picked up a few of my own here and there."

"Which is your favorite?" He smiled and crossed to the player, slipping a record from the shelf and sliding it from its case. He placed the old vinyl on the turntable and carefully dropped the needle along the spinning edge of the record. The sounds of Ella Fitzgerald filled the room. "Fitzgerald is wonderful." I said as the melody instantly drew me in.

"One of my favorites as well—but I like most genres of music." He was so near to me that I could feel his sweet breath on the back of my neck. Each time he was near, my heart would race so fast that I was afraid it would leap from my chest. I moved toward the books, partly to see his literary interests, but mostly in an attempt to slow my racing heart before he noticed the effect he had on me.

"You have quite a collection." I eyed so many of the classics that I harbored on my own shelf. He moved next to me again, this time even closer. The smirk on his face led me to believe that he knew exactly the effect he had on me. "You know you really have to stop doing...." My words caught on the tip of my tongue.

"I have no idea what you are talking about," he teased as a sly smile spread clear across his flawless face.

"Oh, I think you know exactly what I am talking about." I continued scanning the book titles. I was quite surprised to find several in his collection, and I suddenly felt quite inferior in comparison to his studies. Mixed with the familiar novels were political and world history books as well: Machiavelli's *The Prince*, Thomas More's *Utopia*, and a few titles I wasn't familiar with. I held up a worn copy of Plato's *The Republic*, with a puzzled look on my face. "For a class?"

"No. I like political philosophy and political histories."

"You always seem to surprise me. I wouldn't have thought that about you. Planning to run for president one day?" I smirked.

"Most definitely not, but there are many policies in our world that need revision." He said quite seriously. "You forget, in the world I live in, there is no democracy. Our leaders are through lineage only, and somehow the laws that were designed to protect my people and humans have been twisted and manipulated over the past few thousand years solely for the purpose of power."

"And you want to change that?" He didn't respond for several seconds as he pondered his response.

"I don't want anyone to experience the loss I've felt at the hands of Theron. One day, there will be someone powerful enough to challenge him and the laws that have become tainted with the blood of destroyed lives." I had never heard such passion in this voice. He suddenly noticed the alarm clock by the bedside. "We have to go." He abruptly grabbed hold of my hand, and before I could speak, we were once again dockside.

I couldn't help but feel a bit disappointed as the boat meandered through the inlet canals toward my house. I didn't want my time with William to end. But much to my surprise, before we made the final turn toward the Inlet Joy, the boat turned heading back toward the mouth of the inlet. Even through the darkness, William easily maneuvered the vessel past the embankment far to the north of the waterway. There, large oak trees lined the waterline. William pulled the boat just under one of these magnificent trees and tied the boat off on one of the overhanging branches. "What are we doing?" I asked curiously, trying to mask both my excitement and nervousness. I inhaled the crisp salt air into my lungs. With each breath, my body became more alive.

"You'll see." He opened the front hatch of the boat and pulled out the blue patchwork quilt he brought to the quarry earlier and spread it out along the bottom of the boat. Next he pulled out a large throw pillow and leaned it against the seat. "You've thought of everything." I said as he lay across the hull of the boat, and confidently pulled me down to his side in one swoop. My body melted against his. I closed my eyes and soaked in his marvelous scent.

"Marguerite, what are you doing you silly girl? Open your eyes or you will completely miss it." I opened my eyes to find his mouth only inches away from mine. His eyes seemed to be studying the lines of my face. "It's almost time," he said with a smile.

The dark night sky had begun to lighten toward the east, casting a purplish haze across the sky. And then, like a painting, the sun began to peak just above the horizon sending shades of pinks and reds, yellows and golds across the sky. There were other colors as well, some that I could identify, and others shades so perfectly blended together that they had no name. I gasp as the first rays met the inlet waters and shone upon us in the tiny boat. I had experienced many beautiful sunrises with James, but nothing like what was before me.

"It's like a dream!" I exclaimed. His arm that was wrapped firmly around my waist pulled me tighter to him.

"I am glad you like it." He whispered into my ear. The sweetness of his breath against my skin sent shivers through my body. He wrapped his arms around me pulling me tighter. William was no longer watching the sunrise but was completely focused on my reaction to his surprise. I could sense he was pleased. As the sun inched higher into the sky, the colors only intensified filling the entire sky in vibrant hues that I had not dreamed imaginable.

"I've never seen a sunrise so beautiful!" The boat gently rocked back and forth in the smooth inlet waters.

"Nor have I." But his eyes no longer were on the sunrise, as they were now focused solely on my lips. My face blushed under his stare, and my heart pounded loudly in my chest. His face moved closer until his nose brushed against mine. His hands twisted into my hair as he pulled my face even closer to his. My eyes closed in anticipation, but his lips did not meet mine and instead rested gently against my forehead. Then he moved slowly across each cheek pressing his warm lips against my tender skin. I shuttered under his touch. Next he moved to softly kiss my eyelids, which remained tightly closed, afraid that I would wake from my dream. I melted into his kisses wishing that his lips would meet my own.

"It is a crime to want to kiss you so badly." His cheek rested against my own.

"Then kiss me," I breathlessly murmured. "I have been waiting for you to kiss me since we first met. I didn't know it then, but I know now." I leaned closer to him.

"I can't...I can't ever kiss you." he groaned. I stroked the lines of his face.

"I know about what happened William...when you were a boy. Silas told me." I said tenderly. "It wasn't your fault; you were just a child."

"But the same thing could happen to you. You are human too Marguerite! What if I couldn't control myself and I took your life energy? I have spent my life trying to forgive myself for taking the life of that little girl. She, who innocently, was the one person who wanted my friendship, and her life ended because of me. I can't help but feel like I am making the same mistake again by allowing you into my life. It is wrong for me to act on my feeling, and yet I selfishly can't seem to stay away from you."

"The difference is that I'm Sironian too. You won't take away my life energy because of this gene inside of me. I *am* like you William—I am. I am like you in more ways than genetics too. I have spent a life time trying to find my way—to discover my place in this world. And now I finally know why, because I was created to feel this way for you. I understand you because I am an outcast from this world too." He tenderly wiped back the tear that rolled down my cheek.

"Could it really be true that you were put here for *me*?" He asked himself as he gently stroked the sides of my cheeks."

"All I know is how I feel about you. I would risk my own life for a single kiss." I muttered, pressing my lips against the hollow of his neck. The smell of his skin consumed my senses, and I could think of nothing except a desire in which I had never felt before.

"That is only because I am a siren. I'm making the human side of you feel things that aren't real."

"I think you underestimate me, and I think you underestimate you. I feel this way because of my heart and only my heart. I want you because of *who* you are, not *what* you are." His fingers traced the lines of my lips. "As appealing as your qualities may be, I am fully capable of seeing right through the exterior." I looked into his deep emerald eyes, and I could no longer see the majestic sunrise behind us. I could only see him. "*I see you.*"

"And I *see* you," he said as his lips suddenly pressed against mine—at first very softly and then with an intensity that caused me to whimper under his passionate kiss. His lips were soft, almost dreamlike. His arms around me grew tighter as his hand moved from my chin unto the back of my head. My mouth responded as his lips suddenly pressed hard onto mine. My lips parted, and the kiss only intensified until my knees became weak, then my legs. My hands began to tingle, and then I couldn't feel my body at all…all that I could feel was his lips against mine and my heart pounding faster and faster, and then suddenly slower and slower.

I couldn't think straight. I began to feel listless, and yet, I could not dream of pulling his lips from mine, my heart beat became faint and a small voice inside of me realized what was happening. I was dying—and yet, I could not pull away from him. I didn't want to—there was no fight in me, nothing that I could muster up to separate him from me. He had already taken my heart—and now, he was taking my life as well. I couldn't move—I didn't want to. I had not fallen under a siren's spell, but into the arms of the boy I had fallen in love with. I tried to open my eyes, but I couldn't. The crimson marbled sky had completely faded to a new blackness—a silence that I knew was only a step away from death.

****

"Marguerite! Marguerite, please answer me!" The words were dreamlike as I drifted in and out of consciousness. Sometimes I could make out the features of William's guilt-stricken face—others I could see only darkness. I could feel the soft familiar fabric of my bed quilt and the soft scent of my pillow so I knew I was in my room. I could detect the sweet smell of William's skin, so I knew he was close.

Little by little, hour by hour, the world started to come into focus. I could hear the buzz of the air conditioner and see the soft white window sheers streaming with sunlight. There were text books scattered on the bed around me. My head was pounding, I rubbed my temple trying to relieve the shooting pain—and then, I remembered. I remembered the barn, and the loft, and the sunrise—and the kiss. Had it all been a dream? I was still pondering this when I first spied William across the room slumped in the chair next to my closet. The look on his face told me that the events of last night had not been a dream. His face was twisted with guilt and painted with remorse. He didn't speak. He didn't move actually. He just sat there frozen as he watched me awaken.

"I'm okay," I said faintly. He buried his face into his hands, sinking further into the chair. My grandmother's footsteps could be heard crossing the wooden porch planks outside of my bedroom. I turned in a panic toward William, but he had already silently disappeared. I assumed he was in my closet, but he was supernatural after all, so he could have disappeared into thin air. The door creaked open, and her round face appeared around the corner. She smiled as she saw me awake.

"Well, I'm not sure it is such a good idea to study half of the night dear—you have slept half of the day away." Instantly the text books sprawled around me made sense. William had provided my cover. It always amazed me how he always thought of everything.

"Oh, is it that late?" I asked, checking the clock next to my bed. It was almost noon. "Wow, I guess I *did* stay up too late."

"I have been checking on you through the morning. Was about to get worried that you might be sick or something. You must be famished! Why don't you dress and come grab some lunch?" The mere mention of food made me feel sick. I was anything but hungry—thirsty for sure, but there was no way I would be able to keep down a solid meal. I moved my leg under the covers, then my arm. I wiggled my toes and fingers; everything appeared to be working, but I was still unsure that my legs could support my body weight."

"Actually, I think I may have the flu or something," I said realizing that I would have to provide another cover for my clearly altered physical state.

"Oh dear! I knew you didn't look like yourself." She moved to the bedside and felt my forehead. "You do feel a bit warm. Let me go get you something to drink and some medicine. The last thing you need is to get weak and dehydrated." *Too late.* I thought, as she pulled the covers more tightly under my chin and left the room. She had no sooner closed the door before William was standing there in front of me.

"I almost killed you." His face was guilt stricken.

"I will be fine."

"How can you say that? You are anything but fine! I am a monster for doing this to you!" He buried his face into the covers next to me.

"I'm alright. I knew what I was doing William. I wanted you to kiss me despite the risk."

"It is too dangerous for you to be near to me. I should have never dreamed of putting your life at risk in such a way. I am not safe for you, especially with me feeling the way I do when I am with you." He took a step towards the door and panic spread through me.

"Pease don't go. Look, I expected there were going to be complications."

"Complications! I nearly sucked the life right out of you!"

"I'm alive aren't I?"

"So, I should rejoice in the fact that I didn't kill you!"

"Yes."

"I can't resist you, and I can't put you in further danger." Once again he moved for the door, and I stood up to stop him. My legs weren't yet strong enough to support the weight of my body. I felt myself falling. He caught me, scooping me up back into the bed just as my grandmother was turning the knob to my bedroom. I pulled the covers back under my chin and turned to find him vanished once again. I was aware that he was both designed and trained to move in silence, with speed, and without notice, but to watch the ease at which he went undetected was still astonishing.

I closed my eyes and listlessly opened them again as she entered the room, to give the appearance that I was sleepy. I needed to be alone again with William, to try again to mend the emotional damage that his unbelievable kiss had caused. "You look flushed. Here, take this." My grandmother handed me several medications that I am sure would have very little benefit. I was Sironian. I would heal, and heal quickly. Sure, there was no precedent for a half Sironian, half human who had almost had the life sucked out of her by the Sironian boy she was in love with. But I had witnessed how quickly this race rejuvenates, and I knew that it would be only a short while before I was back on my feet and as good as new.

William was less convinced. When my grandmother finally left the room again, he slid effortlessly out from under my bed to continue our heart wrenching debate. He took over where my grandmother left off, sitting on the edge of the bed with the glass of water. "Drink!" He insisted. I leaned forward and took a sip from the glass he held out for me. "We need to get as many fluids in you as possible. How bad do you feel?"

"I have a headache and I'm still a bit weak, but I'll survive." I smiled trying to relieve the pain that was deep set into his emerald eyes."

"Survive! I am standing here physically stronger than I have ever been, because I was born a thief, designed to feed off of a life force that is not my own. But don't you see, you are a thief as well, not because you are part Sironian, but because you have torn my heart right from my chest. It belongs to you." He turned away from me and abruptly crossed the room.

"Don't leave." I felt a single tear roll down my cheek. He turned back in anguish. I could see how difficult it was on him to see me like this, feeling as he was the cause.

"I couldn't even if I wanted to." He turned back.

"Don't stay because you *have* to. Stay because you want to." He looked into my eyes, his expression more sincere than I had ever seen it.

"I never want to leave you." I didn't respond—not because I couldn't find the words, but because there wasn't any words in the entire world that could have sounded more perfect.

William did not leave. He was by my side for the remainder of the day. We both tried to talk of everything other than our present situation. I was eager for any conversation that would relieve the wretched expression that still encompassed his face. He asked me more detailed questions about my life growing up, about my family and interests, and for the first time began to share with me the intimate details of his own life. I savored every morsel that he provided, from his favorite dishes that his mother would make, and the trips he took with his father, to the first words of his baby sister. On occasion my grandmother would appear to check on me, and he would vanish before the door would open.

By late afternoon, my condition had slightly improved, as I was able to get up for short periods of time, but William was still quite displeased with the time it was taking my body to rejuvenate. "I need to go talk to Silas. He can give me a better idea of what needs to be done."

"What are you going to tell him?" I cringed at the knowledge that Silas was to know.

"I am going to tell him the truth. Maybe he will have something that will help to get your energy back."

"Maybe I can just kiss you again and suck it back myself." I teased.

"I don't think it works that way, nor do I think you are capable of such."

"You can't be sure of that. It isn't like I've been making out with any human guys since the gene took effect, especially with you watching over me like a hawk."

"No, only a Sironian one, and look where that got you."

"Funny, I don't remember you complaining at the time."

"You are a comedian, Marguerite. Can we save the jokes at least until you are back on your feet?" He lifted my wrist and kissed the palm. Even in my debilitate state, his touch sent shivers down my spine. He laughed. "You are impossible. I will be back in an hour."

William returned as promised, bringing with him some type of herbal drink. The taste was awful, but my strength increased dramatically. He had also dressed, showered, and carried two bouquets were daisies. He wore a casual pair of khaki slacks and a white shirt with small pale blue pin stripes.

"Wow, you look amazing."

"I hope so; I have to make a good impression."

"But I always think you look amazing."

"Your impression of me is usually the highest on my list but not this evening." I felt a twinge of jealousy travel through my body. I despised the feeling.

"So, the flowers aren't for me?" He laughed.

"Of course they are—well, one set of them anyway. The other set is for your grandmother." My jealousy shifted to another emotion—fear.

"For my grandmother?"

"Yes, I suppose it is time to tell her about me."

"She already knows about you. She even knows that Silas appointed you as my protector."

"That's not what I mean...I meant about *us*." I can't go on forever hiding in closets and under beds. I was thinking that I would call and ask to speak to you, and then when she told me you were ill, I would ask to come see you. Once she has officially met me, you can take it from there." Once again, he'd thought of everything.

"What should I say?" I asked.

"I guess I will have to leave that part up to you, but I guess you should tell her that I am your boyfriend." I couldn't help but to smile at his words. The word "boyfriend" seemed almost a comical way to describe my relationship with William, like calling a "Ferrari" a "car."

"I suppose I could say that." I blushed.

"Only if I am so lucky as to be granted the title."

"Is that what you told Silas?"

"Something like that—just before I told him about what happened last night in the boat."

"How did he react?"

"He shockingly didn't seem too surprised. He actually apologized to me for not warning me ahead of time. He said it was unlikely that it would have actually killed you, but he couldn't be certain of this. He says he thinks you have too much Sironian in you to kill you in this manner. But he was unsure what the effects may have been if I hadn't stopped."

"I guess it's lucky for me that you can control yourself."

"Control myself? Marguerite, you give me far too much credit. If I would have been able to control myself, then you wouldn't be in this situation in the first place. Maybe your grandmother will hate me and banish me as far away from you as possible. It would be the best thing possible for you, you know."

"First of all, that is highly unlikely, and second of all, I think we both know I'm much safer with you around."

"That is still debatable."

"What will the others say about us? The crew? Aria?"

"James?" He asked raising one eyebrow anxious for my response.

"Yes, I suppose I will have to tell him too," I sighed at the thought of hurting him.

"If we are really doing this...you and I, then it is probably best just to put it out there. But I must warn you—I am afraid there will be consequences."

"Like not being able to kiss my own boyfriend?" I asked tilting my chin at him.

"Are you asking for a death wish?" He seemed quite unamused by my flirtations. "Seriously, Marguerite. I shouldn't be putting you in this situation. I am asking too much of you."

"You aren't asking for anything that I don't already want." I said solemnly. "Besides, I hear you're pretty strong now—I bet you can take on the entire world by yourself." To my surprise he laughed.

"Not very likely, but I think I would have a better chance with you at my side." He leaned over and gently kissed my forehead.

"Better be careful with those lips. I hear they are a pretty dangerous weapon."

"Only for you," he smiled pressing his lips against my forehead again.

21

"What lies behind us, and what lies before us are tiny matters compared to what lies within us."

Ralph Waldo Emerson

"**M**arguerite?" My grandmother opened the door to my room. I was relieved. I had been waiting for nearly a half hour for William to call, and the anticipation was killing me. "William Avery is on the phone for you, dear. I told him you weren't feeling well, and he is asking if he could come see you. What should I tell him?"

"Tell him to come," I said, more quickly than I intended. She seemed surprised with my response.

"But dear, you still look quite unwell. Are you sure you are up for company?" I swallowed hard and decided the best thing to do was just say it.

"William isn't company exactly. He's *different*." She stared at me with an odd expression trying to process what I was trying to tell her. "He's pretty special to me." It took several seconds before the actual meaning behind my words took effect. The pleasant look on her face began to vanish.

"Oh…well, I knew that he was helping with your training and that Silas had assigned him to look over you, but I didn't realize that things had gone further than that."

"It's kind of a new development," I said quickly, praying that this conversation would be over soon.

"So you *like* this boy?"

"Very much," I said nervously fumbling with the covers, secretly wanting to pull them over my head to hide.

"And does he have feeling for you as well?" I nodded. She sighed, much louder than she intended I would guess.

"Well, that changes things now, doesn't it?" I shrugged. "I mean, from what I have seen of the boy, he is handsome for sure, but he has had quite a rough life dear. I am just not sure that…."

"I know. He's been through a lot, but he *gets me*, and I understand him too." I may have been the sick one, but my grandmother was the one who suddenly looked ill.

"Sounds like things are more serious than I thought."

"No." I lied. I was getting better at it. "Like I said, it is a new development."

"I must admit, I had hoped you wouldn't become romantically involved with a Sironian boy. There are just so many complications where that is concerned, and you are awfully young, dear."

"Seriously, it's no big deal. It's isn't like we are going to get married or anything." I was careful not to meet her eyes as I tried to back pedal the situation a bit. The last thing I needed was for her to know how I really felt about William. Then she would be sure to overreact.

"Alright. I will tell him that he can come if you are sure you are up to it. If he will be spending time with you, then I need to at least meet the boy."

As she closed the door, I slowly made my way to the closet and pulled out a thin pale blue cable knit sweater and a pair of grey jeans. I had to sit on the edge of my bed to dress, but at least I was able to stand without falling over. I looked into the mirror, expecting the worst, but aside from the purplish circles under my eyes, the physical damage wasn't so bad. *Of course not—it was the human aura that was pulled from me, not the Sironian beauty.* Was it bad that I was relieved that I was at least still pretty? I use to never worry about my looks! It was William Avery's fault!

My grandmother re-entered just as I was brushing my hair. I could tell she was surprised with my appearance. I blushed—embarrassed that she knew I was primping for a boy. "Well, I suppose it was only a matter of time when this was going to happen."

"What?" I asked, scared of her response.

"Boys have been interested in you for years now, but you've never seemed to notice. I guess it was bound to happen that someone would eventually come along to grab your attention."

"Like I said, William is different." She set down a tray filled with a bowl of chicken noodle soup. I wasn't hungry, but decided to humor her by eating a bit.

"You know, I kind of liked that Kirby fella. Now, he is a real charmer!"

"Yeah! Too much of a charmer! Promise me you'll give William a chance. You will like him." I gulped down a few more spoons of soup under her watchful eye before finally pushing the tray away.

"If you like him, I am sure I will too."

The front door bell rang. *He came to the front door.* I giggled.

"Why don't you bring him out to the back porch?" I suggested. "It is a beautiful evening, and I could use the fresh air."

"Alright," she agreed as she took my arm to help me onto the porch. She helped me into one of the rockers and retrieved the bed quilt from my room, before walking through the house to answer the door.

A big smile swept across my face as William entered the porch carrying one of the bouquets of flowers I had seen just an hour earlier. The sun was just going down over the inlet casting an array of layered colors into the evening sky—it failed in comparison to the splendor of his face.

"Marguerite, your grandmother told me you were not feeling well. These are for you." He leaned in to hand me the flowers whispering, "You look beautiful," into my ear. I winked at him.

"Thank you so much for coming William. It is good to see you." Despite him only being away for a short period of time, I always waited impatiently until we were reunited. My grandmother entered the room, carrying two vases half filled with water.

"William these are so beautiful. How did you know that daisies were my favorite?"

"Silas ma'am." Her expression changed instantly, and she quickly turned away. I was hoping William did not realize the impact of his comment.

"How thoughtful." Her words got stuck in her throat. After all of these years, he still remembered her favorite flower. I ached for her. It went without saying the memory was not overlooked by her heart.

"He and I go way back," she finally responded.

"Yes ma'am."

"How kind of him to remember after so many years."

"Yes ma'am, he has an excellent memory." William said eloquently.

The next hour went by flawlessly. My grandmother politely drilled William on numerous topics; his answers were always delivered with eloquence far beyond his years. She was polite enough not to say very much about his parents and stayed on neutral subjects. He talked with her quite extensively about growing up along the inlet, and the pair compared stories and memories of the coast. I mainly listened, injecting a question or comment from time to time. When she went into the kitchen to bring us out some tea and cake, William turned to me, "How am I doing?" he asked with a smile as he reached over and took my hand.

"Perfectly." I squeezed his warm soft hand still nestled against mine. It was easy to be impressed by William. I had not seen him interact very much with others, and I must admit that it was quite a relief to know he was capable of being social. The visit was quite different from the one she had shared with Kirby, as William's energy radiated from inside, while Kirby's spilled outward covering everything in its path. I couldn't help but admit that it was William's quiet inner radiance that had completely captured my heart.

My grandmother studied the two of us together closely. I could see her eyes moving back and forth between William and me as we talked. When she would ask William a question, many times she would look at me during his response as if to see my reaction to his words. He left an hour later, asking for permission to come again tomorrow. My grandmother returned from walking him out with a quite serious expression. "So, what did you think?" I asked referring to the beautiful creature she had just sent out into the cool night air."

"I think things are about to change for you, and it scares me. This Sironian boy has serious feelings for you, greater than I think you even realize.

"Do you really think so?" I asked a bit too eagerly.

"One would have to be blind not to see it from the way he looks at you. And you were being a bit coy with me about your feelings with him as well. You are in love with this boy."

"I have never been in love before, so even if I were, my heart is far too inexperienced to judge such a thing at this point."

"Oh, you are young for sure, but a girl knows her own heart, and I fear yours resides wherever this young man may be." She sighed, shaking her head. "Love is a wonderful thing, but the circumstance under which it has come to you frightens me immensely. I just don't want to see you hurt."

"I'm afraid that it's too late for my heart either way." I mumbled under my breath.

"Yes. I believe you are right...."

I expected William to return to my room after my grandmother had gone down for the night, but he didn't come. After several hours of waiting, I pulled out the copy of the book he had given me and crawled up in bed. Sleep did find me, and through my dreams, my subconscious replayed the events of the past few months—breathtaking sunsets, dark churning waters, beautiful faces, and mystical monsters that all climaxed with one life altering kiss.

The silent morning hours arrived bringing with it strength, as my body finally felt as if it were fully on the mend. I dressed without feeling winded or sick, and after breakfast was surprised as my first visitor arrived. It was Kirby. Kirby got out of his sports car holding a large bouquet of red roses. He held them up to me from below, as if he were Romeo from a Shakespearian play. I laughed. My grandmother appeared impressed.

"Wow! These are beautiful. Thank you."

"You are very welcome. I thought they may make you feel better." My grandmother and I were having coffee on the front porch when he arrived, and after jovial greetings between the pair, she took the flowers in for water and left us for some privacy.

"So, didn't your momma ever tell you not to go around kissing Sironian boys? It is bad for your health." he teased, flashing a deep dimpled smile in my direction.

"I know, right. I must have missed that part in the Sironian/human relations handbook."

"I will have to get them to boldface that part in the next edition."

"So you all know about that? Huh?" He noddle and raised his eyebrows with a tight smile. I felt my cheeks turning fifty shades of pink.

"Word travels quickly on the water. Plus, we were fairly close when it happened. The crew has put off training and have been assigned to guard the mouth of the inlet until things settle down a bit."

"Oh, why is that?"

"Silas is a bit nervous since the pier incident. The Feeders aren't supposed to come into Murrells Inlet, but I bet you have Theron a bit miffed right now. It's one thing to speculate on a hybrid's existence, but another to be sure of one." My stomach felt like it twisted into a knot. "But don't be alarmed, princess. Things have been completely quiet, too quiet actually. I'm not sure what Theron may have up his sleeve or even if he knows how to proceed where you are concerned."

"How do you mean?"

"Well, you aren't full Sironian, now are you? So you don't exactly fall under Sironian law, and yet, you are aware of our existence and mingle freely with us. No one is quite sure 'how' the Sironian gene could have leaked into the human race. If anyone has broken a law, it would be the Sironian who originally sired a child with a human thus producing your linage."

"But we don't even know who that could be?" I didn't want to tell him the name my grandmother had given me. Despite what Aaron had done, I had not been given permission by my grandmother to circulate her story. Nor did I expect to ever do so. There are some family secrets that were meant to remain secrets.

"The crew assumed it was Silas, as he is so protective over you."

"It's not. Both Silas and my grandmother have both assured me that he is not my grandfather."

"At least we can rule out William as your grandfather." He teased. "Whoever it is must have had extreme control not to have taken her life. I am the only Sironian I am aware of that has this kind of control around humans. That is why I was originally chosen as a protector. If you would have kissed me for example, you would have walked away as good as new, better actually as I am a fabulous kisser." I rolled my eyes. "Huh, on second thought, maybe you should try it out and see for yourself. You know, strictly for educational purposes of course."

"Very funny." I said flatly. "But whoever sired my father didn't care about saving my grandmother's life. It wasn't about control. He left her for dead; it was the Sironian spark of life growing inside of her that kept her alive."

"Interesting theory, but there must be more to it than that. Theron must be interested in answers as well."

"They could have killed me the other night. I haven't had a chance to thank you for trying to save me." He smiled and nodded.

"It is what we do princess. Theron now knows you are under our protection, which has to be a factor. Theron likes to do things quietly, without human detection. I think he knows that he will have a pretty big fight on his hands if he wants to take you out."

"Why would you all risk your lives on my behalf?"

"Well, William may be your specific protector, but we are all protectors. It is what we do, what we are all trained to do."

"But Aria is his own granddaughter. Surely she wouldn't fight against his army."

"Aria's never met Theron. She has no known loyalties to him. She is from the line of his first wife. Theron's son, Alexander, died, but Aria's mother, Maris, is a leader in his regime."

"But Maris is pure evil!" I gasped.

"You know her?"

"You could say that. Theron sent her after me, not long after I arrived, but William saved me. She is also the one responsible for this." I pointed to the scar that had adorned my ankle since I was a child. "Guess you could say that we go way back."

"Well, Aria was supposed to be a royal, but Maris gave her to be trained as a protector instead. Didn't even wait until she turned ten, gave her up to be raised by others not long after birth. Pretty sad story actually, Aria doesn't really even know her mother." My grandmother came back onto the porch with a cup of coffee for Kirby. He graciously accepted. She smiled at the pair of us before returning back into the house. "You know, she likes me."

"Yes, I'm quite aware of that. What's not to like? You have charmed her completely, just as you seem to charm every female that comes into your path."

"And yet, I can't seem to charm you." His deep blue eyes stared into mine, I quickly looked away.

"Oh, you charm me as well, it's just that, I can see through it."

"Ouch! That was kind of painful to hear."

"I didn't mean it like that..." I objected, angry with myself for hurting his feelings.

"I am pretty amazing on the inside too, if you would only take the chance to get to know me." He dazzled me again with his smile. But despite his charms, I could only see William's face.

"I am sure you are. It's just that..."

"It's just that it's too late—huh?" I smiled and slowly nodded. "So I guess this means the two of you are a couple?"

"I think so," I said.

"So he's ignoring the marriage contract with Aria?"

My stomach knotted again. "I guess. We haven't really talked about it."

"Theron will be furious as soon as he discovers this. Do both of you have a death wish or something?" I was searching for a response when a Cherokee pulled into the drive. Logically, I knew it was James' car, but it took him actually getting out of the car before I could process that he was actually here. It was Saturday. With the changing events of the week, I had completely forgotten what day it was! Of course he would come. James looked great as usual. His copper hair was complemented by a brown t-shirt.

"Looks like our visit is about to be interrupted; we will have to finish this discussion later." We both stood. Kirby wrapped his right arm around my waist in a tight embrace before making his grand exit. The look that passed between James and Kirby was anything but friendly as the pair passed on the stairwell leading to the porch. I buried my face in my hands realizing my dilemma. I had two amazing guys vying for my affections, but I had already given my heart away.

"Hey Darlin'! I've missed you!" He said loudly enough for Kirby to hear as he was climbing into his sports car. "I heard you were a bit under the weather. These are for you." He said, holding out a handful of daffodils he had picked somewhere.

"You know daffodils are my favorite. Thanks! How did you know I was sick?"

"I called yesterday when you were sleeping, and your grandmother told me."

"Oh yeah—the flu or something. Better not get too close."

"I'm not about to let a little something like the flu keep me from coming to see my favorite girl!" Kirby's sports car spun a wheel as it pulled out of the drive catching both of our attention. "Really, Margo? Kirby Winslet? What is that joker doing here? Please tell me you aren't dating that guy!" James' face started turning red. His face would always turn red when he was even the slightest bit nervous or angry.

"Of course not! Like I told you before, we are just friends. He heard I was sick and just wanted to stop by."

"I'm sorry, but I seriously don't like that guy at all. He always seems to be around school starting trouble."

"But I thought he goes to Socastee High?"

"He does, but that doesn't stop him from messing with some of the girls at Conway High. Walks around thinking he is God's gift to women. They always seem to fall for that *look at me...I am handsome, rich, and constantly flatter you* act!" I laughed aloud so hard that my sides hurt.

"Well, I promise you that I don't fall for that stuff. Come on James, you know me better than that." My grandmother appeared again this time bringing a large tray of sweets; she did a double take when she realized that my company had changed.

"Oh, James! I didn't realize you were in town this weekend. Did your family come down with you?"

"No ma'am. Not this weekend. I'm only down for the night. I wanted to see how Margo was feeling. The family will be down next weekend, and probably most weekends here on out now that the weather is finally warming up."

"Well, that will be just wonderful. I'm always excited to see this place come back to life in the spring. The winter month can be so quiet around here!" She held out the tray for James, and he accepted a colossal brownie. "Thank you," he replied as he stood to get the door for her. The expression on his face instantly changed as she walked through the door. I didn't have to guess the cause as the two large bouquets of flowers from Kirby and William were just inside the door on the kitchen table. James looked down at the flowers he had given me. "Well, it looks like you have had quite a few visitors lately." He tried to remain in good spirits, but I could see that he was bothered.

"I know. Maybe I should milk this whole flu thing for a while longer."

"So, how are you feeling, anyway? It is still a bit cool out here, and I don't want to keep you outside too long." The outdoors seemed to revive me, and I felt my strength increasing with each passing hour.

"I'm feeling much better actually. I'm quite sure the worst has passed."

"That's great news. I would like to get you out of the house tomorrow for a bit if you are up for it."

"Yeah. That sounds pretty great actually." I knew I needed to find a way to tell him that the situation had changed between William and me, but I couldn't find the words to tell him that we were now sort of a couple. I could scarcely believe it myself. I was quite excited for James' company, and yet I couldn't help but wonder what William was doing. I consistently tried to keep myself from thinking of him, but I continuously failed.

James stayed through lunch but headed over to the Merri Mac in the early afternoon with a promise to return after I rested a few hours. I wasn't sleepy at all but went along with his suggestion in hopes that William would return. I was momentarily disappointed to find my bedroom empty, but as I closed the door behind me, William was waiting. His right hand firmly closed the door behind me, and his left arm wrapped securely around my waist pulling me tightly against his chest. I could barely catch my breath. "I thought your friend was never going to leave," he said as he pressed his lips against the top of my head. "I've missed you."

"Well, don't leave." My hand stroked the lines of his muscular back. My heart leapt in my chest at the sight of him.

"I wish I didn't have to, but I have a job to do. It isn't easy keeping you safe, especially when I know there is a line of suitors outside the door trying to steal the heart that I just won."

"Oh really?" I laughed. "I don't think you have anything to worry about." He brushed back a piece of hair that had fallen against my forehead.

"Yeah? I thought if Kirby didn't leave soon, I was going to have to cram those flowers down his throat." He winked at me, and a narrow smile spread across his beautiful face.

"If possible, you are even more handsome when you are jealous." He smiled again, this time softer, his eyes locked onto mine and he began to softly stroke the back of his hand across my cheek.

"I was more than a bit jealous, actually." His thumb stroked my spine leaving me breathless.

"You were watching?" I asked curiously, but my words barely left my mouth. It was impossible to concentrate on anything other than his gentle touch.

"No, but I knew he was here. Man! That guy loves a challenge."

"What do you mean?"

"Well, he's never had much competition as far as females are concerned. Most protectors know to avoid that type of contact with humans. It would be quite conspicuous to have women falling dead around us, but Kirby seems to have a knack for that sort of thing. I am not sure how he does it, but call it a talent or learned skill, he hasn't taken a life yet."

"And how would that make me the 'challenge'?"

"Because you are the first girl that I have ever shown any interest in..."

"Oh...." The emotions that swelled in my chest were overwhelming. I was the first—his first. His only.

I didn't sleep but spent the next three hours in his arms. I knew that it was crazy, but I couldn't stop thinking of his lips against mine again. How could one crave so badly the thing that only days earlier had almost killed them. The world seemed complete as long as his arms were around me. I would risk whatever it would take to be with him—to feel his body next to mine. I couldn't help but love him, despite all risk and obstacles, and by some miracle he seemed to be in love with me too. He had not said the words, but I knew.

Soft footsteps could be heard across the wooden porch planks, and in an instant, William silently disappeared. "Marguerite? Are you awake dear?"

"Oh yeah. Just resting."

"James has been waiting for you out on the dock for nearly an hour now. He is pretending to be fishing, but I know he is waiting to see you. Do you think you are feeling well enough to go out for a while and put the poor boy out of his misery?" I walked to the window pulling the sheers back far enough to see James casting a line into the creek. I smiled. James wasn't a very good fisherman. Oh, he adored fishing, but it was rare that he brought back much of anything.

"I am actually feeling much stronger this afternoon. I'll go down and meet him."

"Alright, but be careful not to overdo it.

"I promise," I said as she quietly closed the door behind her. William reappeared just behind me.

"How do you do that?" I asked staring into his deep emerald eyes.

"Do what?"

"Disappear like that?" He smiled.

"It comes with the job. I am right here actually, just very good at moving undetected."

"Will you teach me sometime?" I flirtatiously tilted my chin upward towards his face.

"Now how am I supposed to ever tell you 'no' when you are looking at me like that?"

"That's the whole idea."

"Alright, I promise to teach you, but you better not keep Romeo out there waiting any longer. I would hate for him to diminish the entire fish population of the inlet waiting for you."

"I think there is little chance of that." I said with a grin. "I don't think we've ever caught anything out there." William swiftly glanced out the window at James, carefully not to be seen.

"What is he fishing for?"

"Redfish I suppose."

"Ah, see the lure he is using." I peeked out of the window. The distance between the window and the rod would have been far too great for the human eye to catch the details of the lure, but I could see even the smallest details—one of the new perks of the Sironian gene. I nodded.

"Have him pull the feathers off of the top and shorten the tail by a quarter inch."

"Think that will help?" I was intrigued. He nodded.

"Or, if you are really hungry, I could just swim down there and catch you one? It would only take a few minutes."

"Showoff!" I said teasingly. He caught me around the waist and pulled me close to him tenderly kissing my forehead. My body shivered under his touch.

"Just come back to me, okay?" I nodded, secretly wondering if my knees could still support me. My strength had almost completely returned, but I still melted each time his skin touched mine. He released me and crossed to the chair to retrieve my jacket. He held it out for me, and I slipped my arms through, but just as I turned around again, he was gone.

"Hey there!" I called to James as I stepped out onto the dock.

"Good afternoon, darlin'! You look rested." James leaned over to grab a fishing rod for me.

"I am actually. I think my strength is returning." With the salty fresh air filling my lungs and my best friend at my side, I was in excellent health.

"Ah! That's probably because I'm here. A healthy dose of me is better than any medicine."

"I agree! I'm so glad you're here this weekend. Everything feels complete with you here." I said enthusiastically.

"I know the feeling. I remember counting the days each spring waiting for you to arrive. Even though I knew you weren't here, I would continuously look over my shoulder hoping to see you out here on the dock."

"And now the situation is reversed." I watched him as he pulled back on his rod, reeling the line in a bit closer to the dock. He was family to me, a part of me. We had shared so many summers out here together. My world was changing. I was changing, but he was the one thing that I didn't want to change. I would do whatever it took to keep him in my life.

"It's funny how life changes," he said casting his line again.

"What? You can read my mind now? I was just thinking that or something like that."

"Great minds think alike you know." I took the lure from the rod he had set aside for me, tearing off the feathered head, and shortening the tail as William had suggested.

"Lordy girl! What are you doing to that lure?"

"Just wanted to try something. Someone told me to try this."

"Someone as in ..."

"William Avery." I could see the muscles in his neck begin to tense up.

"There is that name again. So he's been around, has he?" I nodded.

"I had a feeling that third set of flowers was from him."

"Oh, you saw that, huh?"

"Hard to miss—quite an impressive bouquet of roses. Clearly he doesn't know you very well. Daffodils have always been your favorite. "

"Actually the roses were from Kirby, William brought the daisies. But you are correct in that daffodils are still my favorite."

"So the two of you have been spending a lot of time together?" His brow furrowed.

"Yes." James was going to have to find out about William and me at some point, and I wanted it to be from my own mouth. *Best to pull the*

Band-Aid off quickly. "He has actually been around quite a bit lately." I pulled back my rod and cast the line far into the creek.

"Oh." He reeled in his line, recasting it to a further spot down creek. "So what does that mean exactly?"

"I don't know."

"So you guys are like "best friends" now?" I shook my head.

"I already have a best friend." I was a coward. I couldn't find the right words to say all that I needed to say. I needed to tell James that I loved him, but not in the way that I was in love with William. I wanted to tell him that I didn't want to lose him in my life, but that my heart belonged to another. I wanted to tell him that my heart sang when I was with him, but it soared with William at my side. But I said none of it.

"You are more than friends now aren't you?" I hesitated to respond, but James already knew the answer. I could see the agony all over my face mirrored through James' expression.

"Yes. I think so." I said meekly. He sighed.

"I knew last time I was here. I could see it in your eyes. I wanted to tell myself that it wasn't true, but I knew then." I shook my head.

"Well then you saw something that I didn't know existed. This only happened a few days ago."

"Maybe technically, but I've known since the first time I saw him looking at you that there was something between the two of you."

"James, I don't want things to change between us. He knows how I feel about you. He knows you are my best friend and that no one else could ever take that spot in my heart." He bowed his head. My heart ached to hurt him this way.

"But it sounds like he was able to fill the *one* spot in your heart that I couldn't." I didn't know how to respond to his heartfelt honesty.

"Please promise me you won't let this change things between us. You mean far too much for me to lose you over this."

He looked up at me before shifting his gaze out over the inlet. The silence was sheer torture. He finally responded. "I am not going anywhere." He bravely smiled at me and a huge wave of relief traveled through my body. Could I possibly be so blessed to have them both in my life—both my best friend and William? I knew that it was an unfair thing to ask given his feelings had grown for me over the years, but I couldn't give him up. The somber mood was broken when my rod suddenly surged forward with such a force that I barely caught hold of it before it toppled into the water.

"Got it?" he asked as I scrambled to grab hold of the reel. "Looks like something big hit your line." The end of my rod was bowed nearly in half. I began to reel in the line a little at a time, keeping tension on the rod in an effort not to let my catch get away.

"What do you think it could be?" I asked excitedly.

"I have no idea, but this is one pretty large fish! Give it some slack. I am afraid it will pop your line." I let the fish take some line and then slowly began to reel in the line again. Remarkably, the line held as the fish inched closer and closer to the dock. After quite some time, we got our first glimpse of the fish. It was a large redfish, appearing to be no less than eight pounds, a record for us. James looked stunned and hurried to get a dip net from the storage room. Neither of us had ever caught a redfish so big.

"It's huge!" I exclaimed giddily as he dipped the net into the rising tide to retrieve our trophy.

"Looks like we will be having redfish tonight."

James and I spent the remainder of the afternoon cleaning and filleting the massive fish. My grandmother was also thrilled with the catch and quickly whipped up some slaw and hushpuppies while James started the grill. The fish was delicious. The light and flaky fillet was by far the best meal I had had in several days. After cleaning up from dinner, James and I played a few rounds of cards with my grandmother before she excused herself to bed. We moved outside to the porch to avoid disturbing her.

The moonlight bounced off of the dark water. James brought out the vintage portable radio my grandmother kept on the kitchen counter and fumbled through the stations before finding one with beach music. "Dance with me." He asked. I tentatively accepted his outstretched hand. We had danced together a multitude of times over the years, but why did this time feel so different. James' hand felt different in my palm, and each time his body brushed against mine, I felt as if I were doing something wrong. Something was different. As much as I tried to pretend that nothing changed between us, I couldn't deny that something had changed. It was William.

When James finally left for the evening, I returned to my room feeling quite a sense of remorse for enjoying my day. I had spent a lovely afternoon and evening with James. I waited nervously for William to come, afraid that he would sense my guilt. I was reading when I heard a soft knock at my door. I knew that it was him. "Hi. I'm glad you're here." I said as he slowly entered my bedroom.

"I didn't know if you were too tired to see me after such a long day."

"I always want to see you." I said softly. He didn't say anything but came over and lay across the bed next to me. I eased my hand across to his until our fingers intertwined.

"Well, that was a bit hard to watch today." He said gently pulling me towards him.

"You were watching me?" I felt the blood rush into my cheeks. He smiled, tenderly running his thumb across them.

"I tried not to, but I find it nearly impossible not to watch you. I tell myself that it is just because of your safety, but the truth is that I can't help but watch you."

"Was it the dancing tonight? I won't dance with him again if it bothers you."

"Don't be silly. Of course you have every right to dance with your friend. I just have never known this feeling, this jealousy, before. It wasn't just the dancing; it was every look, every glance, and every conversation that I didn't get to share with you."

"I missed you too." I stroked the back of his hand with my thumb. He closed his eyes and inhaled deeply.

"I was worried about you, that you were getting too tired, doing too much too quickly. And I was angry that he stayed so late when he knew you were coming off of an illness."

"But I am feeling perfectly fine. I think my strength has almost completely returned."

"I can see that. Nothing could make me happier than to know that you have recovered."

"Does that mean I can begin training again?" He smiled.

"I suppose so. I see no reason for a delay. We can start tomorrow if you would like." I was ecstatic, but then remembered that I had promised to meet James to go fishing in morning. He wanted to take our newfound luck out on the water.

"Oh. James and I are taking the boat out in the morning—just in the inlet. It should be safe shouldn't it?"

"Of course. I will ensure it. Will you be spending the entire day together?"

"I think he's leaving after lunch."

"We could go to the quarry after he leaves if you would like?" I beamed with excitement.

"I would love that!"

"I'm glad." He wrapped his arms tightly around me. I pressed my face against the nape of his neck. The intoxicating fragrance of his skin filled my lungs. I sighed. "What is it?" He asked.

"You smell so good."

"Imagine that feeling and multiply it by twenty; that is the way I feel when I am next to you. How I managed not to take your life the other day is a miracle. I crave you—your scent, your fragrance, your essence. Being this close to you drives me mad, and yet, the moment I part from you, I can't think of anything other than being with you again."

"Really?" I said tilting my chin towards his face. "That must make me pretty special," I teased.

"A one of a kind actually—you are definitely one of a kind."

I laid my head against his firm chest. Yes, I may be the only half-human, half-Sironian girl around, but he was equally as unique. He was the strongest, fastest, smartest, and most beautiful of all of the protectors. And he was with me. Yes, that would make me a "one of a kind" indeed.

22

"Everything you can imagine is real."

Pablo Picasso

I **awoke to a tapping sound.** I rolled over and William was gone. I sighed. The realization was that his absence now made me feel incomplete. A beautiful, completely unique seashell rested on the pillow beside me—a gift no doubt from William. It was very small, disk shaped, white in color with small creamy, acute lines spiraling down its perfectly defined shape. The back shimmered with a multitude of colors like an opal but with more depth. It was one of the most beautiful things I have ever seen. I picked it up and ran my fingers across the smooth lines of the shell. I was in awe that such a shell even existed, as I had never seen anything like it before. A thin silver setting encompassed the edges with a thin silver chain attached to the bale. I was speechless. It was by far the most treasured gift I had ever received. I would have to thank him later. How could I even come close to letting him know how much it meant to me! I slid the treasure around my neck, the keepsake sliding deep into my shirt resting close to my heart—of course it would rest near my heart, where it should be.

I leaned back and was suddenly reminded of why I had awoken in the first place. There it was again! The tapping did not appear to be coming from the door but my window. I got up, and sleepily pulled back the sheer curtains. It was still dark outside. Through the darkness I could make out Kirby's muscular frame down below tossing pebbles against my windowpane. I shook my head in disbelief and raised the window.

"What are you doing here? Are you crazy?"

"Come on! Get dressed princess! We've got training today."

"Training?"

"At the landing. Don't worry. We warned all of the sea gulls ahead of time that you were coming."

"Ha ha—very funny." I called down below. "I can't. I am supposed to meet James at nine o'clock."

"Don't worry. We will have you back in plenty of time."

"What time is it?"

"Five a.m. You have four hours—plenty of time to terrorize the aviation population of the area."

"You really aren't that funny, you know. That joke is getting pretty old actually."

"What? I think my humor is part of my charm."

"Yeah. That is what you get for thinking."

"Come on. Everyone is waiting. I'm sure you will give me plenty of new material before the morning is over."

"Is William coming?" He rolled his eyes and groaned.

"Sure. He'll be there."

"Okay. I will be down in five minutes." I slipped on some jeans and a soft cream knit long sleeved shirt and some sneakers. I quickly ran a brush through my hair and darted downstairs to brush my teeth before finding Kirby with my boat running."

"You know. You should really invest in a newer boat. This one is on its last leg." He suggested this as I made it out onto the dock. "I will get you one if you would like." I had no doubt of his sincerity. Kirby tossed around money like he did compliments—to an excess.

"Thank you, but I prefer this one actually. It suits me. Besides, I don't think William would like that very much."

"If you haven't noticed, I don't seem to really care what William likes and doesn't like."

"Well I do. If we are going to stay friends you need to respect that he and I are together." I said firmly. He sighed and offered me a hand into the boat.

"Aright! I'll try, but old habits die hard, especially when you look so beautiful in the early morning."

"Kirby!"

"Alright! Alright!" He snickered. I shook my head, and took my place at the front of the boat leaving no doubt in his mind of my intentions.

The crew was all at the landing taking target practice when we arrived. The arsenal of weapons, all that we had used before with a few others mixed in, were scattered about the landing. Silas and Tobie came over to greet us. Mace looked up at me and nodded. It wasn't much of a greeting, but it was a start. Aria ignored my presence altogether, but the scowl on her face said it all. She knew about William and me. If she didn't like me before, she absolutely hated me now.

"So glad you are feeling better, Marguerite," Silas said with a gentle smile. Tobie busted out a goofy grin, settling any doubt that they *all* knew about the kiss.

"Thank you," I said, but our conversation was instantly cut short.

An arrow shot through the air in my direction directly level with my head. I darted out of the way as the arrow narrowly passed only inches from me. I turned to see where the arrow had gone finding it in William's outstretched hand. He'd caught the arrow in midair. I stared at him in shock, but his eyes did not meet mine, instead glared past me.

"I think this belongs to you Aria," he said holding the arrow out to her.

"It slipped," she said flatly, leaving no doubt of her true intentions.

"Aria, you are excused from training for the remainder of the day. It appears you are distracted from your targets," Silas said firmly. She grabbed her bag of weapons and glared at me as she exited the field.

"What were you thinking, Kirby! Bringing her here today!" he roared over my shoulder. I had only once ever seen William so angry, the night on the beach with Maris. He appeared as if he was ready to rip Kirby's head from his neck.

"You should have told her we were training today," Kirby scolded William.

"She only just regained her strength! It wasn't your place to interfere!"

"I am a protector too. Come on William. You know she's safe with me. Besides, I am not required to follow your orders."

"Safe? She nearly just got shot in the head!"

"Aria may be a bit angry right now, but she wasn't going to hit her. She is a better shot than that and you know it. If she wanted to shoot her, she wouldn't have missed." William turned to me in anger.

"Why would you come here with him—without me?'

"He said you were going to be here." William let out a snarl and instantaneously his face was inches away from Kirby's."

"How dare you lie to her! I should rip your head off!"

"I didn't lie to her. You're here aren't you?" He roared again; this time with such force that Mace and Silas came to intervene.

"I am here only because I discovered her missing. If you ever...." Mace was across the field in a fraction of a second.

"Don't make this a problem, Will. The girl has been nothing but trouble since she first arrived." William turned and pounced at Mace, all traces of a human façade diminished.

"If you *ever* speak of her like that...." Silas stepped between them.

"That's enough William." He said. William stormed out of the landing. I went after him, but as he reached the edge of the water, he leapt off of the embankment into the air at an incredible height and disappeared into the dark water below. I stood there staring into the water. I knew why he had left; Kirby had drawn out of him a side that he didn't want me to see. Silas came up behind me and put his arm on my shoulder. "Why don't you rejoin us dear?"

"Do you think he will come back when he cools off?" I said looking into the tender eyes of the older man.

"To you? Yes. He will have no choice."

I scowled. "Because he's my protector?"

"No, because you hold his heart. I have spent a lifetime training him for every possible situation, but this one is one that I am afraid he will have to learn on his own."

"What lesson is that?"

"Love."

Mace was right. I *had* been nothing but trouble for William since I arrived. He had given up too much of himself as my protector. If only I could free him of the obligation, maybe then he could feel free—free of this burden, free to find his sister, free to love me. "Silas, can you continue to train me?"

"Of course. Anything to help secure your safety."

"Yes, but I still want to go ahead with my original plan to challenge William for my protectorship. I wish to free him of his greatest burden—me." His brow furrowed.

"By law I cannot prevent you from challenging him, but let me advise you of the complications this could cause. Just think about this...."

"I have, and my mind is made up."

Silas resumed my training for the reminder of the morning with the rest of the group. I joined with a determination I never knew possible—a determination driven by love. With each exercise I grew in strength, speed, and accuracy. My arrows were swift and on target, my spears shot with precision, and my harpoons delivered with unparalleled force. With each skill mastered came a growing earned respect from the crew. Within a few hours even Mace had complimented me several times on my growing skill. Time slipped away from me. I winced when I realized it was almost nine o'clock and took off towards my boat. They all looked at me as if I had gone mad. "Sorry...I'm supposed to meet someone. I'm running late." I took off running across the field at a pace that was quite inhuman.

"Wait Margo!" Mace startled me as he called after me. I stopped at the edge of the landing just a few feet from where William had exited earlier. "Are you coming again in the morning?" I nodded. "Good." It was his form of an apology; his way of welcoming me into a group that I never knew I wanted to be a part of so badly. I beamed.

"Want me to drive you back Margo?" Kirby called after me.

"Let her go Kirby," said Silas. "The girl is perfectly capable of driving herself back. Marguerite, we will see you here in the morning at five o'clock." I nodded and off went my tiny boat.

James was standing on the dock looking puzzled as I pulled up along the side.

"I was beginning to think you'd left without me."

"Oh, no. I couldn't sleep, so I thought I would get a jump on the morning." I knew I looked as frazzled as I felt.

"I never pegged you as a morning person. If I remember correctly, I would practically have to pull you out of bed to meet me at sunrise to go walking." He loaded the boat with several fishing rods, a dip net, and a tackle box and climbed in the bow.

"Mornings are growing on me." I was anxious to change the conversation. "So I get to drive today?"

"Sure. It's your boat."

"Alright. Well, you better hold on. I am a maniac on the open water."

"I think I will risk it, darlin'." He winked at me as I restarted the motor. I took off towards the other side of the creek, half expecting William to come leaping out of the water at any moment, but there was no sign of him. I found a spot that was close to a half sunken shrimp boat and hurled out the boat anchor. The heavy anchor soared through the air until the rope snapped taunt sending it plummeting into the waters. James looked impressed. "Wow! That was pretty impressive. Have you been lifting weights?" I had a flashback of ninth-grade gym class, the very last time I ever touched a weight. It was a disaster. But I could think of no other possible explanation for my increased strength and so I lied.

"Yeah. I have a couple of dumbbells stashed under my bed." James raised an eyebrow, but ultimately let it go. Maybe I wasn't getting any better at lying after all. "I am learning all sorts of new things about you today—and to think I thought I had you figured out!" I shrugged and threw out a line. I couldn't help but notice that James had changed all of the lures as William had recommended me do. I giggled a bit on the inside.

"You do know me! Better than anyone, but I guess people are always changing. Life would be dull if nothing ever changed." James cast his line out just a few feet from the wreck and began reeling it in slowly.

"I guess you're right, as long as they didn't lose who they were on the inside." His words made me think. *Was I the same person on the inside that I was a few months ago?* My physical changes were obvious, but there were other changes as well—so many of them. Would James find the changes in me on the inside to be a good thing, or was he trying to tell me something?

We had only been there a few minutes before James pulled in the first fish, a medium sized flounder. He was ecstatic! I was the next to catch a fish, a large striped trout, and over the course of the next hour, our stringer was full, and we had reached our limit for the day. We headed back to the dock by late morning to clean our daily catch. James did most of the work, but I did the scaling after James gutted the fish. My grandmother brought us out some sandwiches and chips for lunch. I was starving. She was quite impressed that we were able to stock her freezer with fresh fish.

"So, what time do you want me to come pick you up next Saturday?"

"What? Do we have plans I have forgotten about?"

"Seriously? Marguerite, are you backing out on going to the prom with me?"

"Oh, prom…no, of course not." I had completely forgotten my promise to be his prom date. "I just hadn't realized that the date was so close."

"So, you don't think your boyfriend will mind if I steal you away for the night?" It was the first time he had mentioned William all morning.

"Oh, it really won't be a big deal. He knows we are best friends, so…." I couldn't help but notice the way he grimaced at the word "friends."

"Not a big deal huh?" I could see on his face that I had hurt him.

"I didn't mean it like that. You know what I mean…we will have a great time together." It suddenly occurred to me that I didn't own a prom dress. I would have to go get something. That was more of my mom's department. I would have to give her a call to see if she would like to go dress shopping. The whole shopping thing sounded like a nightmare to me, but I knew my mother would love the idea. She would be thrilled that I was going to the prom—any prom.

"I'll come to pick you up at six o'clock. My family is coming next Friday, so everyone will be here. I will try to keep my sisters in check, but they have already started scheming—everything from your make-up to your shoes. I am not sure I will be able to keep them from knocking your door down to help you get ready." I adored his family, but the idea of the Leighton girls fussing over the event made me feel a bit nauseous.

"It will be fun." I somehow managed to get the words out. He wasn't fooled. My friend knew me far too well.

"Thank you for trying to sound convincing. I will have to get you an extra-large corsage for being a good sport."

"Oh please don't." I pleaded, feeling quite sick to my stomach. He chuckled.

"On second thought, I may have to let that one slide after all. Looks like you have the flower thing covered." He shrugged. I rolled my eyes with a smile. "How could I ever possibly compete with all of those roses?"

James left after lunch. I was quite exhausted from the day. My body ached from the training exercises. *Maybe I had done too much too quickly after all. I was only human—well, sort of.* I tried not to think about William, but it was futile—the feeling of his fingers brushing against my lips, the intoxicating smell of his skin, and the soft sound of his voice. I wondered if he would keep our afternoon plans to go to the quarry after such a morning. I feared he wouldn't come. My heart ached at the possibility that he was angry with me for going with Kirby to the embankment, but I also swelled with pride over the progress I was making with my training. I wished so much that he had been there to share my accomplishments. I hoped to find him waiting in my room for me, but it proved to be empty. I sighed. *He must be angry.*

I flung myself across my bed picking up my Biology II book from the table. I flipped through chapter after chapter, realizing that I already knew most of its contents. It began to rain as was common during the early spring months along the coast. The raindrops rapped gently against the thin window panes like music, and I felt my eyes beginning to close. I fought them back open. I would wait for William to come for me; but raindrop by raindrop, the music calmed my anxious heart. I was soon fast asleep.

I was having the sweetest dream and didn't want to wake. In my slumber William's arms were coiled around me tightly, and his lip delivered warm kisses against my lips. His lips stirred against mine slowly, and then with a stronger intensity, my lips parted but instead of my essence being abstracted, his own energy intertwined with mine as if we were one person. We became fervent together—as one. I nestled tighter against his chest, feeling the length of his body pressed firmly against mine. His hands moved down my sides pulling me tighter against him. I wrapped my fingers around the back of his neck pulling him even closer to me as our bodies ...

A loud roll of thunder shook the room, robbing me of my slumber. I instantly sat upright both startled and still under the trance of my dream world. I gasp. "It's alright, Marguerite. It's just a bit of thunder." I rubbed my eyes open completely to see the brilliant creature across the room moving toward me. He was sitting in the chair near my closet.

"You're here." I said tenderly. He moved next to me and wiped away a tear that was sliding down my cheek. He nodded, staring deep into my eyes.

"Were you having a nightmare?" I blushed still disoriented from my dream.

"It was a good dream actually—about you." I said a bit embarrassed. He didn't smile, but looked at me intently. He was so close that I could barely breathe.

"When I dream it is about you too—it's always about you." Another rumble of thunder shook the room. I wanted badly to kiss him, to feel him against me as in my dream, but I tried to push all thoughts of that from my mind. We could never be together in that way. I ached.

"I didn't know if you would come. I thought you were angry."

"I was angry, but not with you. As much as I would like to keep you held hostage from the world, you're not my prisoner. You are free to go with whomever you chose." He gently rubbed his thumb across my lips and down to the corners of my mouth, before running his fingers along my jawline. I trembled at his touch. "My responsibility is to keep you safe but not to keep you from living. I was angry because Kirby lied to you to get you into the boat this morning, nothing more. You are always free to make your own decisions." He brushed back a bit of my hair that had become disheveled while sleeping. His touch, as brief as it was, was even better than in my dream. "I left because I didn't want for you to see me like that."

"I know." I drew closer to him, pulling the shell out from my shirt and gently holding it in my fingers. "I didn't get the chance today to tell you thank you for this. I can't tell you how much it...." He nodded.

"It's rare—an exceptional species, just like you." He cupped my face in both of my hands and brought my face forward towards his lips. His eyes locked on mine as he pulled me closer. I shivered.

"Don't be afraid of me." He pleaded softly. "I promise to never put your life at risk like I did before." His lips brushed against my cheeks, then gently each temple before resting against my forehead.

"I'm not afraid of you—I am more afraid of myself when I'm with you." My voice sounded childlike. He smiled tenderly.

"You say that like it is a bad thing. Don't worry I'll be strong enough for the both of us. You have no idea how I felt seeing you lying there in the bottom of my boat limp and virtually lifeless. I thought I had killed you." The pain and guilt re-emerged on his face.

"But you didn't." He encompassed my frame in his arms and leaned back slowly against the headboard. The rain outside my window began coming down harder, and the gently tapping escalated into a downpour.

"It looks like the quarry will have to wait." The room shook again—the lightning now right upon us.

"Oh come on. It is just a bit of rain. Where is your sense of adventure?" I teased. "Besides, it is supposed to rain tomorrow as well."

"Rain, I can handle, but there is no way I am taking you out there in weather like this."

"Well, how else would you like to spend the afternoon?" I said very disappointed that I wouldn't get to spend the afternoon at the quarry with William.

"With you—anything with you."

****

The afternoon turned out to be magical after all. William talked me into showing him my artwork. I was extremely embarrassed at first—especially with so many of the pictures of him, but he seemed genuinely impressed and the only teasing between us was in complete gest. There was a small self-portrait in the mix that he was quite taken with. It wasn't one of my best pieces, mainly because *I* was the subject, but William asked me if he could have it, so I gave it to him.

He talked me into painting a picture together, pulling me to sit upon his knee. Our brushes battled for canvas space as we talked, laughed, and painted through the rainy late afternoon. The completed picture was of a sunset with dark, golden water below. I thought it quite beautiful despite the playful manner in which it was created.

"Do you want to come for dinner?" I asked, as we were putting away the paints.

"I would love to, as long as your grandmother wouldn't mind." The rain had finally started to ease up a bit, and the only thunder that could still be heard was far in the distance.

"Are you kidding? She would be ecstatic to have another mouth to feed. " He genuinely seemed pleased with the invitation.

"What time should I arrive?"

"Stop by to check on me in an hour, and she will insist on you staying for dinner."

"I can do that." He said with a smile. "I must admit that I am a bit jealous that she likes Kirby so much. I am going to make it my quest to win her over."

"That won't be very hard to do. She already likes you very much."

"But she prefers Kirby for you."

356

"No, I wouldn't say that. She thinks I am much too serious. And you are serious too. Kirby doesn't take anything seriously. She has mistakenly taken his irresponsibility for fun."

"And she worries about that I may be scarred, huh?"

"Understandably. Not many people have had to experience all that you have had to endure. But mostly I think her concern is that you are Sironian. She has her own history there you know."

"She has every cause for concern, but we will just take this a day at a time."

"Together."

"Together. Oh, and I guess I will just have to prove to her that I can be fun too."

"Just be yourself. She will love you just as you are."

Just as expected, an hour later when William arrived at the front door, he was issued a dinner invitation. In his absence I had slipped on a feminine simple white blouse and tan skirt. As he now stood in front of me, I was glad that I decided to dress for dinner, as he looked amazing in a pale blue button down shirt and khaki pants.

I was beaming on the inside. Dinner could not have gone more perfectly. William was attentive, charming, and funny, entertaining us with a variety of stories and was careful not to touch on any heavy subjects such as Silas or his parents. I had never seen him smile so much, laugh so much—eat so much. He graciously accepted everything my grandmother offered to him, which was as usual in excess, and even though I knew he was full, he asked for seconds. Food may be considered the way to a man's heart, but he knew that accepting it was also the way to my grandmother's. I was increasingly pleased with his efforts as not only did it speak volumes as to his character, it also clearly expressed the depth of his affections for me.

After dinner he played all of my grandmother's card games, letting her win of course, and also introduced us to several new ones he enjoyed playing. After completely winning her over, he excused himself for the evening. Upon my grandmother's insistence, he promised to return again for dinner the following evening.

Just as he was leaving he secretly winked to me and whispered. "I will see you in a few hours—miss me, okay?" I nodded as he pulled away in his truck.

"Well, that boy certainly has a way about him." My grandmother said as she closed the door behind me. "It is just a miracle that he has turned out so well despite of his circumstances."

"Yeah—he is pretty special." I said, helping her put away the dishes that were already drying from our exceptional meal.

"He's Silas. Silas made that boy, that makes him more than special— that makes him sound. I'm no fool, that boy was here tonight for my blessing." I nodded, impressed with her insightfulness. She leaned forward cupping the shell necklace that I hadn't realized had escaped onto the front of my blouse. I blushed and tucked it back in. Her smile broadened as no explanation of its origin was needed. "Despite any past reservations I may have had towards him, I wholeheartedly give my blessings to you." I felt myself welling with tears; I had not realized her approval was so important to me until this very second. She laughed, "Besides, any young man who would stomach three helpings of creamed potatoes and two slices of pecan pie after that meal is worthy of my approval."

Late that night he returned, this time much more casually dressed. He had just finished a sweep of the inlet and had barely dried off and changed before appearing at my door.

"So, how did I do?" he asked, taking my hand in his.

"Are you kidding?" I teased. "You let her feed you for an hour straight! She loves you."

"That's a relief. I was afraid I may explode if I had to eat another helping of creamed potatoes."

I laughed. "You aren't the only one! She and I both thought that too!"

"Ah! So she guessed I was seeking her approval."

"She did."

"So what is the verdict?"

"Granted." I said playfully. "One down, four to go."

"Four?"

"The remainder of my family is coming in town for the prom this weekend, and I was hoping you would meet them. I know you met Caleb briefly, but I wanted you all to get to know each other."

"Of course! I would like very much to meet your family. Will Caleb and I have much time together or will he be too busy with prom activities."

"Prom activities? Oh, no, Caleb isn't going to the prom—I am."

William took the news that I was going to the prom quite well. He commended me on being such a devoted friend as to endure an event that was so contrary to my personality. He was right. The whole concept of prom was silly to me; overly made up girls wearing extravagant dresses, guys puking in rented tuxedos, twinkling Christmas lights sloppily wrapped around artificial houseplants. Prom was ridiculous, but I would do virtually anything for James, and it seemed a small penance after all he had endured over the last month.

The next morning I dressed earlier than usual for training and left a note for my grandmother. The sun had not broken above the horizon, and I was already headed out toward the dock. The early morning was just beautiful. The air was crisp but unseasonably warm for early spring. Much to my surprise, none of my suitors were waiting for me. I was relieved. The boat motor started easily—too easily, and once again the small red fuel tank was filled with gas. I didn't have to guess who was responsible. As I started out on the water, I noted how the wildlife had begun to return with the warmer temperatures. The entire inlet seemed to be coming to life. We were one in the same, both coming to life—growing, changing every day.

The entire crew was at the embankment, and one perfect face I should have expected. William was off to the side intently talking to Silas. He looked up and smiled faintly as he saw me join the group. The guys greeted me as I joined them. Aria nodded. *It was more than I expected.* There were no weapons or targets on the field, and it didn't take me long to figure out why. "Where are the weapons?" I asked Kirby as I scanned the embankment for our black duffels.

"Right here," Tobie said flexing his arms. Everyone laughed and the teasing remarks exploded. I cringed at the knowledge that we were working on combat training. When I turned around, William was gone. My heart sank.

"Where did he go?" I asked Silas quietly.

"To go keep watch over the mouth. He already did a thorough scan this morning, but he is trying to be cautious. He feels it is unsafe to have us all here and no one on watch.

"Oh." I said as I watched Mace hurl Tobie across the field, and Aria fiercely engaged Kirby in combat. I couldn't help but think that it may be safer out on the open water. Silas rounded up the crew and spent the morning reviewing basic fighting techniques. They were all familiar with combat training—it was of course all totally new to me. I started off slowly learning a few blocks and the different types of jabs and punches, but we quickly moved on to harder techniques such as throws and grappling techniques. Luckily, once again I seemed to catch on quickly. It wasn't long before I could hold my own with the others. Silas, please with my progress, introduced us to a combination of moves that combined various forms of martial arts.

Silas and I continued training after the crew left for school. He insightfully began integrating my tumbling abilities into some of the fighting combinations. Much to my surprise, I found that I enjoyed the combat training immensely. After a particularly long and complex sequence was mastered, I heard applause from the edge of the underbrush—it was William. He crossed and began talking to Silas again. I couldn't hear their conversation, but I was quite sure it pertained to my progress. They both seemed very pleased. I swelled with pride.

"Are you ready for lunch?" he asked. I turned to Silas.

"Is it alright if I call it a day?"

"Absolutely. You made incredible progress today. We will begin again in the morning." I thanked him for his help and followed William to my boat. I climbed into the bow to take my seat. He looked at me puzzled, his eyes narrowed, and he patted the seat next to him. I smiled and moved back to be next to him. My heart beat faster at his nearness. He started the boat and put his free hand in mine as he pulled out into the canal. He didn't head back to the Inlet Joy but instead pulled up to Silas' dock.

"I have to pick up something." He took my hand, and I followed him into the dusty barn. It appeared that he had made even greater progress in finishing his boat, as one of the masts now protruded high into the rafters of the structure.

"It's amazing!" I said motioning towards his sailboat.

"Thank you," he said as he led me up the staircase that led to his tiny bedroom loft. The idea of going to his room sent the butterflies in my stomach into overdrive. I tried to hide the feeling of nervousness that should have subsided by now, but as my feeling for him had intensified, so had my nerves. I glanced around his bedroom, everything residing just as it had been in my memory except for one new article that I knew quite well. My cheeks reddened. There next to the pictures of his family was the self-portrait that I had given him. I was so touched that I could barely speak.

"Your picture belongs here, don't you think?" His words were cool and as fluid as ever. I nodded. William took the familiar blue blanket and a couple of towels out of the old cedar chest at the foot of his bed, and retrieved the pick-nick basket next to the door. "I thought we would take advantage of this warm weather; up for a trip to the quarry?"

"Absolutely! But I thought it was going to rain again this afternoon."

"I thought you were up for anything?" he teased.

"Only if I have my bodyguard with me."

"With the rate you are advancing, I am a bit concerned that I may need you to protect me." I sat on the edge of his bed as he retrieved the remainder of our supplies. He observed me there. The way he looked at me was in a way that he had not looked at me before. My heart stopped altogether.

"I promised to be strong enough for the both of us, but you are tempting fate sitting there like that."

"But you are on my bed all of the time." I mumbled teasingly.

"True. But your grandmother is near. There is no one here to rescue you." His tone was teasing, but his eyes narrowed in a way, that let me know there was some truth to his words. He slowly crossed over to me, so closely that his legs were pressed against my knees. I couldn't breathe— but I no longer wanted to if it would make this feeling go away. In once scoop he swept me up from around my waist and pulled me to his chest. My hands rapped around the back of his head pulling it towards me. "We have to go." He slowly pulled away and scooped up everything we'd come for. "We have to go now, before I decide to tempt fate further."

"Do we need to stop by and grab your swimsuit?" he asked as he led me down the steps. Not knowing what to expect with training, I had worn one under my clothes. After Aria's skimpy bikini was offered up to me—I had vowed to never be unprepared again.

"No, I have one under my clothes."

"Then we are good to go." He led me to his truck. William flipped through a wide variety of music on the radio before settling on a classic rock station. We both lightheartedly sang along to an old Bon Jovi song. I tried to pay closer attention to the route to the quarry. I wanted to remember every detail, but it was impossible to think straight with William next to me.

We pulled to spot in which we had parked before and began the hike through the woods. The hike was much easier this time, partially because I knew what to expect, but mostly because William had my hand the entire time. We moved easily together through the gullies and underbrush quickly making the hike to the quarry. This time, we didn't head down to the rocky landing below, but instead headed straight to the highest point. I slipped off my outerwear, and William abandoned his shirt, hanging our clothes on a low branch, the red rocks of the cliff protruded out over the crystal blue quarry below.

"Are you ready?" He asked as he led me out to the edge. I was more than ready—I was elated. "Just wanted to be sure you still remembered how to swim." I dropped his hand and took off towards the ledge, soaring off the cliff.

"Swim better than you!" I called out teasingly through the air before I hit the warm water below. I plunged through the evaporating mist and into the sparkling deep, but instead of coming up right away, took a minute to look and explore. The water was magical, like an entirely new world was hidden just below the surface. I could see perfectly. Light blue-green vegetation adorned the rocks along the sides, with a variety of translucent fish that swam in and out of the crevices. William plunged just a few yards away from me—I could tell he was a bit concerned that I had not surfaced. He found me mesmerized by the tiny fish swimming about and plucking at my fingertips. He smiled, taking hold of my hand and guiding me underwater to the different unique areas of the quarry, introducing me to the vast array of aquatic life that made its home here. I was quite surprised at how little I needed to come up to the surface for air. In the water, it truly became evident that I was different. I was human for sure, but as my body moved swiftly and effortlessly using the skills that William had shown me, the Sironian inside flourished.

We spent the afternoon swimming and exploring. William showed me an underwater cavern he had discovered through a narrow opening in the rocks deep below. Long stalactites hung from the ceilings, and tiny pools of water adorned the cavern containing both colorful crystals and rare, aquatic life. My eyes were opened to yet another entirely different world that I would have only dreamed existed in storybooks.

Just after one o'clock, we began the hike back to the truck. When we arrived, William opened our picnic lunch and laid out the contents on the blanket just below the same large poplar tree. *Some couples shared a song, it appeared that William and I shared a tree.* The two delicious cold cut sandwiches on rye bread were accompanied by an array of fresh sliced fruits and veggies.

"Are you tired?" he asked after lunch. I felt amazing. The brackish salty water had revived my body, strengthening me. But it was afternoon—and Sironians slept in the afternoon. I sighed, not wanting to miss a minute of our day together.

"Tired, but not sleepy." No sooner had my words left my mouth than he scooped me up against his chest. My head fit perfectly just below his muscular shoulder. The branches of the old popular spread a fresh layer of springtime foliage as our canopy.

"Do you mind if I ask you some more questions? I often wonder things about you, small things that I wish that I had the answers to."

"Alright. That is fair, as long as I can ask you questions as well," I replied cutting my eyes over at him.

"What is your favorite ice cream flavor?" I laughed softly.

"You had me worried, but that one I can handle."

"I am just warming up." He smirked with his crooked smile.

"Well, I am a southern girl, so butter pecan all the way!"

"Good choice." He grinned and fired again. "Alright, if you could travel anywhere in the world, where would you go?" he asked this time a bit more serious.

"Um, well that one would be a hard one. I would probably say Paris."

"Eiffel Tower?"

"Sure, but the main reason would be the museums. I dream of the Louvre."

"I've been—once. The summer before my parents were killed. My mother wanted to go, and so my father planned this big family vacation to Paris and Italy. She was like you in that she loved art, and so we spent the entire two weeks staring at walls and ceilings. Even as a boy, I thought it wonderful. We will go one day." I put my hand over his. "One more question?"

"Okay." I said gently.

"How do you feel about me?" I swallowed hard. I did not expect this question. I froze, contemplating how to respond.

"Well ..." I began softly, "I think of you most every second of the day. I dream of you when I close my eyes, and when you leave I wait impatiently for you to return. I admire you more than anyone else that I have ever known—I owe my life to you."

"Are you in love with me?" he asked tenderly. I paused for another moment to absorb his question.

"I have never been in love—but I couldn't imagine a feeling stronger than this." I looked down unable to meet his eyes.

"I ask this because…I am in love with you." He took my chin in his hands tilting my head upward so that our eyes met. I felt my eyes swell with tears. "I don't know the exact moment that I knew, probably much sooner than I care to admit, but my heart belongs to you. My whole heart belongs to you, Marguerite."

Sleep came easily for William. His breaths were slow and rhythmic, and his chest barely moved with each inhalation. There were no longer walls between us. There was no longer the need to fight emotions. His body relaxed at my side, and he slept like he hadn't slept in many months. I closed my eyes, wanting nothing more than to freeze this moment in time. My future was so uncertain—and yet, the one thing in which I was completely sure was that I was desperately in love with William. In his arms all obstacles were erased, as with his words anything seemed possible.

He was in love with me.

23

"And though she be little, she is fierce."

William Shakespeare

William kept his promise and stayed for dinner. Everyone seemed more at ease than the evening before. I thought it impossible that someone like William, someone so far removed from a normal teen-aged boy, could fit so easily into my world. After dinner William helped to dry the dishes as I washed. Every so often I would look up and grin at him. It wasn't every day that one had a siren—the most skilled and valued of all of the young protectors, to help with the dishes.

"The sun has not quite set for the evening, would you like to walk out on the beach with me?" he asked as we stepped out on the back porch.

"Yes, that sounds nice actually." I knew without saying that William wouldn't risk taking me out on the beach after nightfall, but the sun was just beginning to set, and there was still time before dark. As we crossed over the narrow walkway that led to the shore, everything had changed. I had changed. I looked out over the horizon and no longer saw a body of water, but a new world.

The evening sky was magnificent! The cascading array of colors shone so beautiful that it seemed impossible to be true. I tried to memorize each shade of yellow, and pink, lavender and orange to duplicate them into a painting, all the while realizing that I would never be able to capture the feeling and majesty of such a wonder. How could any sort of darkness or danger mingle with such majesty? I knew the answer. It was all the call of the siren. "Do you think there is an army of Sironians out there watching us right now, ready to pounce if I so much as get close to the water?"

He laughed softly. "No. It doesn't work like that. They can only sense you by scent, scent carried through the water, similar to a shark alerted when there is blood present."

"Oh. But they know I'm close by?"

"Yes, but no one knows how far the gene has progressed. They don't realize that you are now unable to sustain life apart from the coast. I am sure they have this area monitored, but they probably aren't sure if you are still in the area."

"But they're still out there."

"With the warmer temperatures, the beaches are more populated, which makes things more difficult for them. They won't appear when there is a possibility that they could be detected. Just stay out of the surf and off of the beaches at night, or better yet, just stay close to me for safety."

"I think I like the second option." His fingers brushed against mine as we walked, the electricity between us was undeniable—our hands twined together.

"Can I take you somewhere tomorrow, after training? There is something else that I want to show you."

"I wish I could, but I can't tomorrow." He looked up at me curious as to why I had rejected his offer. "I have to get a prom dress."

"You don't have a dress?" I shook my head. "But the prom is in three days."

"Yeah, I know. I kind of forgot that I had promised to go."

He laughed. "Do you have an idea of what style dress you would like?"

"No. I haven't looked. Shopping isn't high on my "to do" list."

"Would you like for me to go with you?" he asked sincerely. I looked up at him unsure if I had heard him correctly. The idea of William going with me somehow made the ordeal bearable.

"You want to go dress shopping?"

"Sure—as long as it is alright with you." It was more than alright with me. I was thrilled! It saved me from having to ask my mother to come down to help, as I knew she was already swamped with Caleb's ballgames, Lucy's activities, and packing for the weekend.

"That would be pretty great, actually."

"Good. Then it's decided. I will meet you again tomorrow at the embankment around noon. Silas should be finishing up your morning training by then. I will make lunch plans for us—then we will find just the right dress for you."

"If you're sure it's no trouble?"

"None what so ever—I want to. I think I should at least have *some* say so in the dress my girl wears when going to prom with another guy."

****

Morning training was nothing short of exhilarating—well, at least the first half. William once again didn't attend so he could keep watch while we worked. Silas expanded our hand-to-hand combat exercises, reintroducing our weapons and introducing an obstacle course. Obstacles were designed to be completed as teams for each challenge. He timed us as we repeated each exercise. Mace had the fastest time in the first go round, Aria in the second, and much to everyone's surprise I took the leading spot in the third and fourth go round. All were extremely impressed by my progress and shocked that I was capable of beating them after such a short amount of time in training. Next, Silas divided us up into groups to complete the obstacle course. Each one of us carried a different weapon, and the targets were moved. Aria was far from happy about being selected as my partner but at least refrained from using my head for target practice. We were quite a distance in the lead until the last turn. There was a large rock wall at the finish-line. William had taught me how to climb the rocks at the quarry, so the ascent was easy, but Aria's boot slipped between the rocks midclimb. I turned back to help her, but she refused my offered hand, and the other team quickly went ahead of us. Silas was quite displeased when she finally freed herself and arrived several seconds after Tobie and Mace.

"You would choose to lose rather than accept help from your teammate?" Silas asked looking at her with a stern look of disapproval.

"The half-breed is no teammate of mine!" she scoffed shooting a fuming look in my direction. "Her existence is a complete abomination of who we are. Do you not see what a danger she is? She nearly killed us all last week! Would we die protecting someone who should've never been created in the first place?" I was stunned. Tears began to swell up in my eyes, but I refused to blink, scared that they would see the impact her words were having on me.

Silas face turned severe. I had never seen him angry, but his gentle demeanor had slipped. For the first time I could see the warrior under his kind façade. "Her safety is our utmost concern right now, not simply because she is human, but because she could be used by those who devalue humanity, those who work against our fundamental beliefs."

"I didn't sign up for this!" she hissed.

"No, none of you signed up for this life. You were all born into this, born Sironian, chosen as a protector. I have treated you all as my own children, and in many ways, we *are* a real family. I have cared for you, trained you, and loved you, asking very little in return—but I ask that you stand with me now. Marguerite is a strong asset to our cause—possibly stronger than all of you. I currently do not know what she is capable of or the extent of her abilities, but they *want* her, and we cannot risk the outcome of that scenario." I stood as a statue, scared to move, barely able to even breathe. In shock and awe of his words, and yet frightened at the response his words would cause. Aria began again—I braced for the worse.

"You all rally around her—as if she is your trophy, and yet no one seems to acknowledge what she has taken from me!" A knot arose in my throat as the truth finally came out. She hated me because of William.

"William did not agree to the marriage treaty; I arranged that agreement for him when he was a child only to spare his life. Would you expect him to be bound by an agreement that he had no part in making?"

"But it is the law!" She protested. Her expression was a mixture of guilt and anger.

"Don't you see? Those are the very laws which need to be abolished! Do you honestly want to force a union with someone who does not love you? You are better than that Aria—as a protector and as a young woman." His words had little effect on her and only seemed to fuel her hurt and anger. She turned to the others.

"Who do you stand with?" She challenged each of the males in front of her, all that obviously loved her dearly as a sister. Kirby spoke first. Silas allowed the confrontation.

"Aria, my dear sister, I understand your situation, but we have been trained for this very day, the day when we could possibly make a difference. Marguerite is far more special than we've given her credit for. I will not turn away from what I feel is right simply because you carry a broken heart." I was moved by Kirby's words. He was of far greater character than I had previously thought. Tobie was next.

"I have to agree with Kirby on this one, Aria. I mean she is pretty cool if you would only give her a chance. We're supposed to stick together—she is one of us now too." I didn't expect this from Tobie; my heart beamed with his affirmation. Aria grew very emotional, and I questioned for a moment if she would physically attack me. The others sensed this too, and they each took a few steps closer to me for support.

"Mace, surely you do not continue to stand behind this girl—this *human* girl!"

"I stand for truth Aria. What Silas speaks is true. I have lost my brother to Theron's army. I do not want to lose my sister as well. You must put these feelings aside for a greater cause. Stand with us—all of us." She looked hard into the faces of those around her, carefully avoiding my existence completely. At last she turned to me, staring directly into my eyes. They were the same eyes that had pierced into mine many years ago in those churning waters. Jealousy had almost completely overtaken her.

"I can't do that! I won't!" She spat as she retrieved her bow and strode quickly out of the embankment. No one went after her, but clearly training was over for the day, and the others soon left as well for school.

I was quite emotional from the incident, but Silas continued with my training as if nothing had happened. What I discovered was that I was able to focus my emotions into my skills. My strength, speed, and accuracy increased trifold. I could see myself through Silas' eyes, assessing my progress through his expressions. "You are advancing more quickly than I could have ever expected. I fear that Theron will discover how strong you have actually become. You must be extra careful not to let them take you. The inlet is continuously guarded, but there is no way to keep them from you in the ocean waters. I am sure Theron has the area monitored, and with one splash, they would surely be alerted to your presence."

"I'll be careful," I said with the same concern in my voice that Silas carried.

"I can teach you many things, but *courage* is the one thing that I cannot teach you. You will know when the time is right to show your new skills. But you will have to learn that lesson yourself, and I can only pray that you will be prepared when that time comes."

William returned to the embankment at precisely the time we had agreed upon. Silas quickly met him, undoubtedly to fill him in on our eventful morning. I could see his expression change from concern to anger, so I was sure Silas told him about Aria. "I should not have left you! Are you alright?" He asked as he took my hand and led me back to the boat. In a million years I knew that I would never tire of the feeling of his skin against mine.

"I'm a bit shaken, that's all." I replied. There was more to say, much more, but neither of us discussed the subject any further, possibly because there was just too much to say.

"Let's get you out of here." He wrapped both of his arms around my waist and hoisted me into the boat.

"Where are we going?" I asked as he did not make the turn towards the Inlet Joy but instead traveled toward the mouth of the inlet.

"Lunch," he replied with a narrow smile. He was clearly up to something.

"But I have to go get a dress," I pleaded.

"I know. We will get to that," he responded with the same sly grin. I was delighted when he pulled the boat up to Knoxx Point, anxious to see Sadie, Henry, and Olivia again. He helped me out of the boat and led me down the narrow stone pathway that meandered through the dunes to the main house. "I love it out here," he said slowly. I could see across his face that he was reminiscing about his life here. "My sister and I use to stay out here for hours playing, pretending, collecting shells at the water's edge. She was very small at the time but very smart; at two she was speaking almost as fluently as an adult. She had not yet turned five when…."

"I can see how much you miss her, how much you miss all of them," he nodded.

"I rarely come to Knoxx Point since they have been gone. It's too painful. I would only come when there was business to attend to with Henry and Sadie, and even then I was quick to leave. But since you have come, it is like everything has awakened. When you walk into this place, it is like the life returns. I see it…Sadie sees it—you make everything feel alive. You make me feel again, not only about you, but about everything. I have so many emotions, so many memories that I was able to suppress— and now those emotions are real again."

"I am sorry—I had no idea. I would never have…."

"Don't apologize. You haven't done anything that requires an apology."

"Even still...."

"I was so angry when you first arrived, and now I know you have come for a reason—to show me how to feel again." I was speechless. His words were more than I could have dreamed.

They were waiting for my arrival. Olivia scampered through the door squealing with excitement. I caught her in my arms with a big hug as I would do with Lucy when I would return home from school. Suddenly I ached for my little sister—only two days until they would arrive!

"We are so happy to see you again Marguerite!" Her glance immediately turned to William as she gave him an obvious look of pleasure.

"Thank you for having me. It is so good to see you all again too!" Her eyes excitedly danced between us as she was unable to hide her delight to see the two of us hand in hand. The estate was even more beautiful than I remembered. William's hand gently guided me into the dining room. Sadie had prepared a marvelous spread of pastas and salads, adorned with a variety of homemade breads and cheeses. The meal was topped off with a decadent caramel cake for dessert. I convinced them to share the meal with us and was pleased when the family agreed. Olivia entertained us with an array of stories; Sadie and Henry mainly watched and listened as William and I energetically commented and asked questions of the lovely child. I was enjoying myself so much that I began to lose track of time. The very last thing that I wanted to do was to break from the lovely party of friends to go shopping for a gown, but with the prom only three days away, I knew procrastinating any further was out of the question.

"Thank you so much for the lovely lunch, but I really must be going. I promised a good friend of mine that I would escort him to prom on Saturday, and I am afraid I haven't even shopped for a dress. I really must go before another day slips by." I rose and tucked the fine mahogany chair back under the table.

"Oh—William, you didn't tell her." He smiled and shook his head.

"Why dear, you are specifically here today for that very purpose." I was confused.

I knew that William had volunteered to help me find a dress, but I couldn't imagine how that could tie into our visit to Knoxx Point. Sadie smiled and led me towards the back of the house. William followed several steps behind. In the rear of the house was a large set of heavy double doors, undoubtedly imported from a castle or monastery far from our southern shoreline. I had no time to more closely examine the doors before they were flung open to reveal a large bedroom. The sight took my breath away. A large dark colored bed of finely carved aged wood adorned the center of the room. There were two distinctively unique bedside tables that could have been centuries apart in age, and yet seemed to belong together, on either side of the bed, several other large timeless wardrobe chests, and dressing table that accented the room with a worldly eclectic style that seemed impossible to fit. A collection of artwork, both contemporary and traditional in style, all obviously originals, and all undoubtedly could have been hanging in a fine museum somewhere, hung from the walls. There was a small leather chair across the room.

Sadie opened another set of double doors, these equally as ornate as the others, but completely unique as everything else in the room, which lead to a large closet and dressing area. "Wow! This is unbelievable!" I exclaimed. There was a long wide walk-in closet. On one side appeared to be casual dresses such as I had worn last time I was a guest here, and on the other side, it was lined with formal and semi-formal gowns with tags of expensive designers. There were no less than forty of the most beautiful gowns before me, some appeared to be fine vintage, while others looked as they could have just stepped off of the latest runway.

"Pick one," William said in a soft voice behind me. I didn't realize he was there. It was the first time that I had ever been distracted from his presence.

"These were your mother's?" I asked sheepishly. He nodded.

"One of the many perks of building magnificent ships for important people. My mother was loved by many. Most of these were gifts straight from the designers themselves."

"But William, I could never...."

He scowled. "If you don't see anything you like, I will be happy to...."

"Are you kidding! These dresses are unbelievably beautiful—too beautiful!"

"There isn't anything that could be too beautiful for you," he said. This time it was Sadie's face that blushed, as if she had interrupted an intimate moment between us.

"But they were your mother's," I protested.

"And she would like nothing more than for you wear one," he said tenderly. A smirk arose on his face. "Even if you *are* going to a formal with a guy that isn't me," he teased.

"I think you are a bit thinner since I saw you last. If one needs to be taken up a bit, I can do it up for you in a jiff," Sadie said ushering me into the dressing area. "Now you go sit, William!" She pointed to the leather chair across the room and closed the large doors to the dressing area behind us. Not knowing where to start, I pulled out the first dress hanging on the bar in front of me. I slipped out of my clothes as Sadie began unfastening the tiny covered button that traveled down the back of the cream chiffon covered gown. The top was a fitted strapless sweetheart neckline before plunging into yards of flowing fabric. I had never come even close to putting on anything like this in my life, and I felt naked under the layers of sheer fabric. The dress fit me remarkably well.

"Oh, Miss Marguerite! You look stunning!" Sadie exclaimed ushering me out of the closet and into the room where William was waiting.

"You're—beautiful," he said softly. I felt the color flush into my cheeks.

"Not sure how all of that chiffon would work for a prom," Sadie injected some much needed motherly advice. "We can't just settle on the first dress!" She exclaimed, still wanting to play dress-up. She ushered me back into the dressing room.

The next dress was a sleek black gown with a high slit up the side. I giggled as William's mouth almost hit the floor when I stepped out.

"Stunning!" He replied, eyeing me with a look that made me blush. "Turn around," he said, and for the first time, I caught my first glimpse of the dress from behind. The dress was backless plunging the entire length of my torso stopping just beneath the small of my back.

"Oh, my! I most certainly can't wear this!" I replied, my face turning every possible shade of crimson. His sly smile deepened.

"I think I may be rethinking this whole prom thing," he chuckled. "I may not be strong enough to fight them off of you."

"Next dress Sadie," I responded, heading quickly into the safety of the dressing room.

She went to work slipping dress after dress on my small frame. Each dress seemed more beautiful than the next—some were far too formal, others too sexy, some too flowing, others so tight that I could hardly move. William was complimentary on each gown and didn't seem to tire of our fashion show. I was deciding between a pale blue silk gown and a buttercream yellow organza frock when Olivia emerged in the closet from behind the gowns.

"I was wondering where you scampered off to!" Sadie said to the small girl who had remained hidden except for her face that peered through several brightly colored dresses.

"What about this one Momma?" She asked holding out the bottom of a straight, red one-shouldered gown that had somehow managed to miss both of our attention. The fabric was simple but sleek. Sadie unzipped the gown and held it out for me to step into it. It fit me like a glove.

"What do you think?" I said as I turned around to await the response from my audience.

"You look like a princess!" Olivia squealed!

"Let's go show William," Sadie replied as she pulled me through the dressing room doors. William's eyes slowly lifted as I entered the room, but he didn't speak. I stood before him, slowly turning around as I had seen models do in fashion shows. I was by no means a model, but I had to admit, I felt spectacular in this dress. He didn't speak at first he just stared at me with an unreadable expression.

"What's wrong?" I asked. His eyes smoldered in a way that it was hard for me to catch my breath. I barely noticed as Sadie ushered Olivia from the room gently closing the door behind them.

"You are a siren."

I was confused. "Yes. I think we have covered this point adequately over the last few weeks." He crossed to me leading me into his arms with one hand and stroking my face with the other.

"You have never looked as bewitching as you do at this very moment." He pulled my face so close to his own that our mouths were mere centimeters apart. I wasn't afraid that he would kiss me, I wanted it. If death would come of it, I could think of no better way to die. He held me there, us both yearning for each other, before gently brushing my hair to one side, and his lips tenderly caressing my neck just below my ear. His hands stroked the small of my back, pulling me tighter and tighter against him. I shivered under his touch and clung tighter to him hoping that he would never stop. But he did stop, his lips hovering just above my neck. He exhaled frustrated, but still his lips remained. I could feel his warm sweet breath with each exhale.

"Do you see what you do to me? I am completely under your spell," he murmured, his body still pressed tightly against mine. It was impossible to ignore the massive ornately carved bed behind us. With one swoop, he could have me between the billowing fabrics that covered its canopy.

Would I even protest if he pulled me back into it? Would I even want to? Was such a thing even possible between us? He had bewitched me as equally as I had bewitched him—siren lured by siren. Physically, I wanted him more than I ever dreamed it possible to want anyone. But I couldn't help but want more—love lured by love.

He gently pulled away, slowly giving me time to steady myself. His eyes swiftly glanced past me to the bed behind us. It was if he were able to read my thought. "It's pretty hot in here," he managed to get the words out. I doubted I would be able to speak anything coherently. "Maybe we should go for a walk?" I nodded. We stared at each other one more time, each of us being able to read each other's thoughts as we looked back at the bed. He finally took the first step away from me towards the door.

"Oh, and by the way, that is definitely your dress—if I can bear to let you go looking like that." He closed the door behind him, and I stood there in the mirror for several minutes before I was composed enough to return to the dressing room to change.

The late afternoon sun beamed across the waterway; its rays were so bright bouncing off of the water that I could hardly see. I found William out on the rear veranda terrace looking out across the water. He didn't turn to greet me as I made my way down the rocky steps towards him. "I almost couldn't find you," I said as I finally made my way to him. Of course he could hear me coming—he could hear everything. I was still waiting to develop this talent, but doubtful that I would ever be as skilled as the handsome mirage standing before me.

"I'm sorry." He turned to me at last, the beauty of his face as blinding as the sunlight against the water. No mirage—he was real. "I had to get some air. It was getting a bit hot in there." He winked at me, and a narrow smile spread across his face.

"Thank you for today, for the dress, for everything actually. You took a day that was turning for the worse, and somehow made it pretty wonderful." He reached out and caught a strand of hair that was blowing in the breeze and tucked it behind my ear.

"You're welcome. It is going to take every ounce of effort I have not to follow you Saturday night," he chuckled. "It isn't every day that one sends their girl off to the prom with another guy." His words made my heart flutter.

"Your girl—huh?" I teased.

"Yes. But only if you want to be…." My eyes looking up into his.

"I think I have been 'your girl' longer than I care to admit."

"Is that so? He asked, wrapping his arms around my waist.

"Yes."

"How long would that be?"

"Probably before you even noticed me."

"Oh, I have always noticed you. I have been drawn to you from the beginning. I thought at first that it was solely because I was your protector, but I couldn't deny for long that I was drawn to you for other reasons as well. How could anyone not be drawn to you, Marguerite? You are a siren, remember?"

"True. But you have seen quite your fair share of siren."

"Yes, but no one like you. There has never been anyone like you. I am not immune to you; in fact, it is quite the opposite. I have never wanted anyone the way that I want you. Do you have any idea how bad I want to kiss you right now?"

"Well—kiss me. I didn't die the first time."

"Nearly."

"Now that you know what to expect, it should be easier. You said that it is controllable, right? Kirby does it with the human girls?"

"Yes."

"Well, you are supposed to be the most skilled protector around, aren't you?" I teased.

"Aside from Silas, I am, but Kirby's the one who is skilled with the ladies. Besides, it isn't possible for anyone who wants someone the way that I want you. You can hardly compare the two." He sighed. "Maybe one day—when the change has fully taken effect." His words took me by surprise.

"You think I am still changing?" I was puzzled. Sure, I seemed to be having better hair days than usual. It was growing quite rapidly and now shone like the sunlight.

"Oh, I know you are. You don't see the changes?" Now he was the one who looked puzzled. "You become more skilled and more beautiful each day. I am surprised you don't notice when you look in the mirror."

"I have never paid much attention to mirrors," I admitted.

"Why does that not surprise me?" He chuckled. "But it isn't just your outward appearance. You grow stronger and stronger by the day. Silas keeps me well posted on your accomplishments. Surely you've noticed the drastic improvement in your abilities."

"Silas is a very good teacher."

"He is, but do you not see how quickly you caught up and even surpassed the rest of the crew?"

"I am a quick learner," I shrugged.

"Do you always have an explanation for everything?" I nodded. He laughed. "Alright, well then, tell me how this is going to turn out between us?" His thumb stroked my jaw bone. If it was still cool outside, I wouldn't have noticed as my body surged with heat each time he touched me.

"Well, Sironians can live to be thousands of years old, right?"

"They can."

"Well, then we should have enough time to figure that one out, now shouldn't we."

"That's the plan." He leaned forward and gently pulled out the thin silver chain that I had worn since he had first laid it upon my pillow. The shell fell softly against my blouse. He fumbled the shell between his fingers.

"It's so beautiful," I said looking down at the treasured gift.

"This type of shiva shell is very rare—it is used by our people to show intention."

"Intention? Of what?"

"The simplest way to explain it would be—it says that you are "spoken for" and that you are with me." His words were so serious that I couldn't help but smile. "I know it's a bit archaic."

"Just a bit, but I love it." He scooped me into his arms, effortlessly spinning me into the air. I giggled, wrapping my arms tightly around his neck.

It was then that we simultaneously saw her, high upon the rocks along the "point." She looked more like a statue of a Greek goddess that a girl. But her heart was not of stone—it was poisoned with jealousy. Aria's chestnut curls could not mask the imminent pain that was plainly etched across her face as she watched the two of us together. Even from across the waterway, it was obvious that she had seen the symbol that hung around my neck, signifying the bond between William and me. The symbol that she felt rightfully belonged to her. She stared at us for several seconds before plunging away from the inlet into the icy ocean waters far below.

We both stared into the foaming whitecaps as if she would reappear, knowing all the while that she would not. William smoothed his finger across my wrinkled furrowed brow, as if to try to calm my fears, but we both felt the danger that went along with her scornful glare. He returned me to my feet, suddenly pulling away from me. I crumpled inside.

"I am supposed to be your protector, and now I have put you in imminent danger."

"What do you mean? What does *this* mean?" I exclaimed motioning to the empty rocks where my adversary once stood.

"I don't know?" He said, suddenly resembling the cold stone being that I had encountered when I first arrived this winter.

"She's going to Theron, isn't she?" I could hear my voice shaking.

"I'm not sure, but it is a possibility. A month ago, I wouldn't have thought her capable of doing such a thing, but I've never seen her like this."

"I don't understand? That night, in the water, she fought for me?"

"Did she? I am quite familiar with her strength and was surprised that she didn't more easily defeat the creature. I have my doubts about that evening, especially the crew's defense of you."

"I watched them fight! I truly believe they were trying to defend me!"

"These protectors are trained to be the best in the world. It should have been no contest. I am not saying that they weren't defending you, I am just saying, be careful who you trust. My biggest question is why there was such a high concentration of Sironians there in the first place? How did they know you would fall into the water? Surely Theron doesn't keep those kind of numbers on constant patrol just in case you were to enter the water. He should know we are guarding you better than that." I remembered the events of that night. I remembered Aria's challenge. Had she intentionally set me up to fall with the knowledge of what was waiting for me?

"She will tell Theron that we are together. That you refuse to honor the marriage contract."

"I know."

"They'll come after us."

"Yes, but not solely over the marriage contract. Theron will try to separate us because she will tell him of your abilities. He knows that our sect doesn't agree with his laws; he will try to keep us apart because of the strength we have together."

"But maybe all of this worry is in vain? Maybe we aren't giving Aria enough credit. Maybe she just needs a bit of time to cool off."

"It's possible," he said, his eyes narrowing as he looked out over the massive ocean. "But at this point, it isn't very likely." In an instant everything had changed. The walls between us were resurrected. William took me home in silence. It wasn't as much that he was avoiding conversation with me, as it was that he was on high alert. The inlet suddenly seemed unsafe to him, as his eyes did not rest from scanning the waterway as he drove my ancient boat back to the dock.

"Everything will be fine." I pleaded with him, trying to ease the tension that suddenly filled the space between us.

"I have to go," he said flatly as we reached the Inlet Joy. "I don't want you out on the water alone until we know what Aria has up her sleeve." I nodded. "I will have Kirby pick you up in the morning for training."

"You aren't staying?" I asked sheepishly, feeling as my heart was being shattered one piece at a time. He shook his head, but his eyes only met mine briefly before turning away again. "I thought you didn't trust the crew?"

"Kirby is the only one I do trust actually. He may be a lot of things that I don't agree with, but he's not disloyal to Silas, or to you. He will make sure you reach the embankment safely. I need to complete an extra sweep of the area tonight and be extra vigilant tomorrow."

"When will I see you again?" I asked as I laid the crumbling pieces of my heart at his feet.

"I will always be close by, but I won't rest until I know you are safe. I won't allow my presence in your life to place you in even more jeopardy."

If only he weren't my protector. If only we had met and fallen in love like normal teenagers do. I wouldn't be the cause of this pressure on him—I wouldn't be the weight holding him down. He would have the freedom to go after his sister, have the freedom to live his life—have the freedom to love me. I knew his feelings for me were strong, but as my protector, there would always be this wall dividing us. His first responsibility was to keep me safe, and if he felt that us being together would put my life at risk, then it was only a matter of time that he would step aside altogether for my security. My feeling for him had reached the point that I knew that any life without him seemed dark and lifeless. I wanted more than anything in the world for him to be free to choose me.

Through tears I watched as the sun sank behind the clouds, but with the rising sun the next morning came a determination to fight for what I wanted, even if it meant fighting the one that I loved to obtain it.

I tore through my closet and drawers, looking for something. What, I wasn't really sure, but if I was going to be a warrior, it was time that I dressed the part. I found a pair of tight black pants that fit like leggings. My mother purchased them the previous winter to go underneath a long sweater-dress that I'd never worn. I paired it with a tight white long sleeved knit shirt and a black jacket. The puffed jacket seemed too bulky, so I cut the sleeves off of it. Perfect! Except for my shoes, a pair of black boots would have completed my "tomb raider" inspired ensemble, but the best I could come up with was a pair of black canvas sneakers. They would have to do.

As promised, Kirby was waiting for me the next morning. "You look different. Like Laura Croft meets Supergirl!" He said eyeing my attire, his eyes nearly popping out of their sockets. In truth, I was expecting this response from him as I knew my attire was more action hero and less of the girl I was only the day before. I ignored the comment.

"Thanks for coming," I tried to sound as appreciative as possible. I didn't need a babysitter. I was fully capable of finding my way to the embankment myself.

"You're welcome. I was surprised when Will asked me to meet you. I don't think he likes me very much." I wasn't in the mood for his chit chat. "You guys have a fight or something?"

"Or something," I snapped ignoring his out stretched hand and jumping effortlessly into the hull of the boat as swift and quietly as a cheetah. He thankfully picked up on my mood and didn't ask any further questions. Kirby watched me carefully. A week ago I would have blushed from the way his eyes moved over my curves, but now I completely ignored it. My mind was far too heavy to enjoy the morning on the water. Would I see William this morning? Would Aria show for training? I hoped for both and that we could just put all of this behind us, but as we approached, my hopes began to crumble. Mace and Tobie huddled around Silas with a very concerned look on both of their faces. As Silas turned to greet me, he was obviously concerned as well. The tension in the morning air was so thick I could hardly breathe.

"It appears Aria has left our sect," Silas explained. "When we awoke this morning, her belongings were removed, and there has been no sign of her since late yesterday afternoon. I spoke with William, and he is concerned that Aria may be going to Theron."

"But he's already aware of my existence. He knows you are all protecting me."

"Yes. But he isn't aware of how strong you have become. Aria's jealousy will make it easy for Theron to extract the information he wants from her. Couple that with your relationship with William, and he will have more than enough cause to attack."

"Attack? Here?" The tears began welling in the corners of my eyes. "I can't ask all of you to keep putting your lives at risk for me. Maybe I should go away? Up the coast to hide."

"Theron would be able to find you within weeks—days even," Silas replied.

"But at least you would all be safe."

"We won't be safe, nor will the humans along this coast until Theron is defeated," Mace growled his reply.

Tobie stepped forward passionately—it was the most I had ever heard him say. "Our whole purpose is to protect human life from the feeders. Theron may not value human life, but Maris and her army are the ones consuming it. Is she not next in line for the crown? I could only imagine how things would become if she came to power."

Mace's low voice echoed through the embankment. "Maris is not related by blood to Theron, so she does not have the authority to take the crown. It must pass by next of blood kin only. As Aria's father was killed in battle, and there are no other blood relations, Aria is next for the crown. But I've never understood why she would be sent here, to train under a sect of protectors that are clearly adverse to Theron's policies."

Silas smiled. "For several reasons. The first was for her own protection. As the only known successor to the crown, any rogue sects could come after her. What better place to keep a princess safe than to add her to a group of protectors. Secondly, though Theron has never admitted this, he was trying to build alliances between our sect and the princess. So that when she one day takes the crown, our allegiance would be to her. It is the same with the marriage treaty with William. He wants the most powerful aligned to him."

"And our sect is the most powerful. If you are going to train to rule the oceans—you better train with the best!" Kirby proudly boasted.

"Well, then we better get started," I said

I pulled out my dousie bow. "Looks like we might just have a pretty big fight on our hands," I said this trying to hide the quiver of my bottom lip.

The hand-to-hand combat came much easier to me this time, possibly because the gene had almost fully awakened inside of me, but most likely because I had more to fight for. If there was to be a battle, I couldn't have William's primary focus as my protector. I needed to be able to fully protect myself. There was no time to waste. I would have to be strong enough to challenge him, and it would have to be soon.

I sparred with Tobie first, using the techniques Silas had taught us. He was the strongest but also the least strategic. As he primarily relied on brute strength, I had to use my wit and speed to outsmart him. He came at me full force, and I managed to escape by propelling myself into the air using his left shoulder as my vault. He immediately charged me again. I easily dodged his first few blows before landing a sharp kick to his chin. The force of the kick sent him momentarily stumbling backwards giving me time to sweep his legs out from underneath his large frame and drawing my bow against his chest. Silas was pleased.

"Very nice. Tobie is the strongest Sironian I have ever trained. How smart to avoid your opponent's strengths."

Cool! I thought as I watched the largest Sironian I had ever seen stumbling to get up. For the first time, I was finally able to grasp my abilities. Was I seriously able to defeat Silas' strongest protector?

"Let's see how she would do against multiple attackers. Kirby, Mace, you are up!"

"You can't be serious," Mace replied.

"That's absurd," Kirby protested. "You can't expect us to gang up on her. That is hardly a fair fight!"

"They won't just come after Marguerite alone. They will attack as a group. She needs to be prepared for every situation."

"I don't play with girls," Mace smirked under his breath.

Both my blood and my nerves began to boil over. Before they had time to further protest, I attacked them both. I knocked Kirby clear across the embankment with a hard kick to the center of his chest with one foot and spun around knocking Mace in the face with the other. I flipped backwards a good twenty yards to safety before landing in a defensive crouched position ready for their retaliation.

"You don't play with girls—huh?" I mocked as Mace realigned his jaw from the impact.

"I may have to re-evaluate that policy," Mace sprung at me, but Kirby was faster. He caught me from behind, but I fought his grasp flipping backwards over his head just in time for Kirby to catch the force

Mace's blow that was intended for me. Kirby was knocked to the ground as Mace continued with his charge towards me. He flew at me with a kick, but I instantly fell to the ground sending him end over end into the brush behind me. He immediately came at me again. As he came at me from one side and Kirby from the other, I leapt high into the air into a split kicking both attackers in the face simultaneously. I landed between the two drawing my crossbow in one hand and my harpoon in the other. Kirby's hands flew up in surrender as the harpoon was pointed just between his legs.

"Easy there. I surrender," he replied in shock. I nodded, keeping the harpoon pointed at him with the crossbow pointed in a similar position at Mace.

"Do you yield?" I said curtly to Mace whose eyes stared at me as if they could kill.

"I never yield," he snarled.

"Wrong answer," I coolly replied sending the arrow from my cross bow between his legs purposely missing him by only a few millimeters. Startled he sprung backwards.

"Geez! You could have dismembered me!" He roared.

"Guess you better be glad that I'm a pretty good shot," I smirked.

Silas roared with laughter. It was the first time I had ever heard him laugh. "Marguerite proved some very good points with this exercise. A good fight isn't about numbers; it is about smart calculation. Your opponent will not play fair. He will also not take prisoners." Silas looked disapprovingly at Kirby. A ping of guilt swept through me as I saw Kirby blush from embarrassment. "You are responsible for your choices in battle. Don't underestimate your opponent. Poor choices can cost you your life—or other parts," he chuckled again looking at Mace who was removing the arrow that had pinned his pants to the ground.

"Clearly Marguerite's human side heightened by the Sironian gene has given her advantages in combat on the ground. I think there is no one here who can dispute that, but most Sironians are not even capable of sustaining life out of the water."

"She can't even swim! Let's put the girl in some actual water and see who will win!" Mace exclaimed.

"It isn't safe for…," Silas words barely made it from his mouth before I took off towards the edge of the inlet. I would prove myself no matter the cost. I could hear the words of protest as I leapt off of the side of the embankment into the chilly waters. The inlet water was much different from the water of the quarry. The high salt concentration made it more buoyant. I felt as if my body was completely weightless. It took a moment for my eyes to adjust to the murky green water that was barely lit by the rising sun. But they did adjust, rather quickly, and within a few seconds, I could see the muddy creek bottom perfectly. There was an entirely different world under the water's surface. It was breathtaking! But there would be time for sightseeing later. I was in these icy waters for a purpose. I would prove my skills in the water to the others! Drawing my harpoon I speared three large trout that were schooling in one swift shot. I instantly pulled out my crossbow spearing through the body of an extremely large flounder that was blending in with a sandy area just below a fallen log.

I had just taken hold of my catch and was returning to the surface for air, when something swooped upon me grabbing me through the water with such force, that I barely had time to fight back, but fight I did and with a fierce kick, sent my attacker plunging through the waters. I scrambled to the top before my attacker struck again grabbing hold of me from around the waist. I thrashed as my attacker flung me onto the embankment. I continued fighting before realizing the face of my attacker was the face that haunted both my dreams and every second of my waking hours. William's perfect features looked upon me through the rising sunlight. I blushed suddenly realizing I had been fighting the person whose only crime was that he had stolen my heart.

"What are you doing out there Marguerite! You know it isn't safe for you! Not now! What were you doing you silly girl?"

"Fishing?" I replied noticing my catch was still attached to the lines that dragged behind me.

"Why am I out here fighting for you if you continuously are putting yourself in danger? I told you! They can smell your scent from miles away!"

"Don't be cross with her, William. It was our fault actually." I suddenly realized that the others had joined us along the embankment. The looks on their faces proved that they had seen the entire altercation. Kirby's words were sincere. William was unmoved, as he shot Kirby a frightening look reminding me again that underneath their beautiful exteriors my dear friends were indeed vicious.

"She did well today, William," Silas injected. "She took out Mace, then outwitted both Kirby and Tobie simultaneously."

"Unbelievable!" William responded. "She has only been training for a short time. How is she skilled enough to do that?"

"It's the gene—its properties are far more powerful that we could have speculated. The combination of the Sironian gene mixed with her human properties, seem to have created an exceptional effect on both parts—a type of "super" effect."

"So what are you saying Silas?" He asked, his face twisted as if he were in pain.

"I am saying that she is unparalleled," Silas exclaimed flatly. Suddenly it became clear to me why they were all protecting me—why Theron would stop at nothing to either obtain me…or kill me. Everything began to make sense.

My grandmother had brought me here from the very beginning specifically for this group to take me in. She'd known since the change first began that I would have to live near the water to survive. I would die without it, and thus eventually Theron would find me. But what she didn't account for was that William and I would fall in love, creating an even bigger obstacle. I couldn't allow William to give his life for me! The others were not bound to me, so surely they would be spared, but not William. He had already defied Theron by refusing Aria. Theron would see his alliance with me as another slap in the face. I felt a shiver run down my spine. He would find a way to get to me! I wouldn't be fighting a few Sironian warriors; he would send his army after me. He wouldn't stop. Everyone that surrounded me would be destroyed. If I had defeated my new friends, a Sironian army could do it as well. I ached inside suddenly realizing that I was putting them in danger by being here. I would release William as my protector, not just for his freedom, but for his safety, and then find some way to keep them safe.

William insisted on taking me back to the Inlet Joy. I waited until he had started the motor, so that he couldn't hear our conversation, before making an excuse to go back for a moment.

"Silas. Can I talk to you?" The others had already left.

"You did very well today, my dear." He smiled at me warmly, but I could see the worry behind his kind eyes.

"Thank you. I don't have but a second because William is waiting, but I want Saturday to be the day." His smile faded as he knew exactly what I was talking about.

"I cannot object to your request, but I wish that you would reconsider. William was chosen as your protector because he was the best. You need him right now more than ever."

"As long as he is my protector, his life is at risk. I can't live with that. I may not be able to defeat him, but I have to try. I couldn't live with myself if anything happened to him because of me."

"You love him?" He asked tenderly.

"I do," I said, unable to meet his eyes.

"Then I understand your request." His hand touched my chin lifting it to meet his tender eyes. His eyes told his age, his wisdom—his life experiences. "Are you fully aware of the consequences of this? How William will feel tomorrow when you are the one to challenge him?" I had thought of this, but could not predict what his reaction would be. Each time it crossed my mind, I had to push it away. Would he be relieved to be free of me? Or would he feel rejected and never want to see me again?

"No. Not exactly, but I don't have a choice. I have to do this Silas," I pleaded.

"Then I will tell him tonight. But he won't know that it is you he will be up against until the actual challenge."

"Thank you."

"Best of luck dear. William is the most skilled Sironian I know."

"I have to try." He gently stroked my cheek before tuning to leave.

"I know what it is like to sacrifice for love. I will wish you luck and safety in both."

William pulled me tightly against him for the boat ride home. I had not been cold in the water, but my lips were now blue and I couldn't stop my teeth from chattering. I still was unable to sustain a warm body temperature outside of the water in the way that the others Sironians were able to do. "You are freezing!" he said, pulling me tightly against his chest. I didn't object. His body was so warm and smelled so sweet that I couldn't have resisted his closeness if I had wanted to.

"I have missed you," he whispered into my ear, putting to rest all of the doubts that had been running through my head since he had last dropped me off.

"I have missed you too," I said pressing my lips against his warm neck. "I was afraid you had changed your feelings about me."

"Don't you see, I have already fought against my feeling for you, and I have lost—lost miserably. I know the consequences and yet, I can't help myself. The minutes I am away from you pass like hours and the hours linger like days. Each time I tell myself I have to stay away from you, to protect you only from a distance, it is torturous. Sometimes I wonder if you've cast a spell on me, if you're not more of a siren than I am."

"I would beg to differ on that point." I pressed my lips against his neck again, "As I cannot seem to keep my lips off of you."

"That's only because they're frozen, and I'm warm."

"No, it's only because you are you." We pulled up to the Inlet Joy, and I heard him sigh. I knew he wasn't going to stay.

"Come tonight," I whispered.

"I cannot."

"Please come tonight," I whispered again, my lips hovering just above his skin. He shivered.

"I really can't." I smiled at him and moved to get out of the boat. He caught hold of my hand. "It is my job to keep you safe. The night is the most critical time. I won't let them near you," he said looking out along the water.

"I know," I said.

His fingers slipped from mine and he was gone.

24

———

"The very essence of romance is uncertainty."

Oscar Wilde

"**D**o you have these in a size seven?" I held up a neutral pair of dress flats that would go adequately with the red dress that my grandmother had spent the entire afternoon hemming. Sadie had offered to hem it for me, but she had done so much already that I refused.

The sales lady was a rather portly woman in her mid-forties with unnaturally colored red hair. She seemed almost as thrilled to be there as me. "Um. Let me go check in the back." She made little effort to hide her lack of enthusiasm. It was then that I saw the boots from the corner of my eye—black and sleek—that were light weight enough for combat but sturdy enough to clomp through oyster beds.

"Will you also check to see if you have these in my size?" She smiled and nodded, but I was pretty sure that she rolled her eyes as she turned to go into the stockroom. I loathed shopping. After what seemed an eternity, she re-emerged with two shoeboxes in hand.

"Let me know if these work out for you." I slipped on the flats first. They seemed adequate and would at least be comfortable for the prom. The idea of a room full of hormone-charged teens in poorly fitted tuxedos and overdone dresses seemed absurd with so much hanging in the balance.

But James was the one bit of normalcy that I had managed to retain since I had been thrust into this crazy new existence, and I would do whatever was required to keep him.

The boots fit perfectly. The sales lady was waiting impatiently for my final verdict from behind the counter. "I will take both pairs." I looked down at the shoes—two very different shoes representing two very different lives—both mine. I thanked the lady as she handed the bag to me. As I was walking away another employee was walking to the counter, a pale thin woman with blonde stringy hair. She turned to the red-haired casher.

"Well, they are crazy if they think I am going to come into work if that hurricane hits around here! Did you see the size of that thing? Looks like it is barreling straight for us." My ears perked up. I had been so preoccupied that I hadn't turned on the television or looked at a weather report in days.

"Excuse me?" I asked quite dumbfounded. "Did you say there is a hurricane coming?"

"Yeah. It has been all over the television this morning. Don't you watch the news?" She added with a bit of a sarcastic tone. My mind was spinning too rapidly to allow her tone to get to me.

"I don't watch much television actually."

She unwrapped a piece of gum and popped it into her mouth. "Figures." She eyed me curiously. "You *are* somebody aren't you?"

"Excuse me?" I was confused by her comment, and suddenly very uncomfortable at the way she was looking at me. I was aware that I stood apart physically from most humans, but surely I could still blend in.

"You know *somebody*…an actress or model or something? I don't mean to pry, but you just have that look about you."

"No," I replied flatly trying to make my escape.

"Huh? That's funny. I could have sworn you were on one of those soap operas or something." I ducked my head and high-tailed it to the door as the two women stared after me. "Yeah, told you she was somebody! Did you see how fast she ran out of here when you called her out on it?" My hearing wasn't as strong as William's, but I could still hear them talking as I left the building.

I hopped into my Jeep and flipped through several fuzzy radio stations before turning to the local news and weather broadcast. I listened intently as the announcer described the category two hurricane that was headed toward the East Coast. Landfall wasn't expected until Sunday night, but they were already asking residents to begin taking precautions and to begin preparing for an evacuation if needed. Category two didn't sound so bad to me, but they were expecting the storm to pick up speed as it neared the coast.

When I opened the door to the Inlet Joy, my grandmother was pacing anxiously in front of the television, as the local weather hack was reporting the hurricane's path projection.

"Why didn't you say something—about the storm?" She flipped the channel to another broadcast.

"Well, I have hardly had the opportunity dear. You seem to be away now more than you are here." I swallowed hard. I could not deny that statement. "Besides, it just made a turn for the coast and is still several days away from landfall."

"What do we need to do?" I was unable to hide the concern in my voice.

"Well, your father is coming today to help me board up the windows, but aside from that, there really isn't much that we *can* do. We will just have to wait it out until we figure out if it is headed here or if it will follow the projections and turn north."

About that time the phone rang. I hurried to answer it. "Hey darlin'." It was James.

"Hey you! Looks like we have a storm coming." His voice always brought a smile to my face, even at a time like this.

"I heard something like that," he said teasingly. "I'm heading there in a few hours to help Dad board up some windows on the Merri Mac—just a precaution. You ladies need any help getting things ready over there?"

"Nah. I think we got it. My parents are coming later, so my father can get things boarded up over here as well."

"Cool. Tell him I will be around if he needs an extra hand." His words flowed with sincerity. I was lucky to have him.

"So what's happening with the prom?" I asked trying to change the subject. I felt a bit guilty hoping that the storm would cancel the evening.

"Don't you worry! I'll have my dancing shoes with me. The storm isn't supposed to arrive until late Sunday, so it shouldn't interfere with the prom. I think the prom committee is even incorporating it into the 'Sea of Love' theme." I grimaced as my mind filled with thoughts of gaudy prom decorations. I was glad that James couldn't see the angst on my face. I would have to work on my acting abilities.

"Sounds fun. I am looking forward to it."

"I think I know you a bit better than that," he laughed into the phone. "But I do appreciate you going with me. I promise it will not be as awful as you think, and who knows, we may even have a good time."

"We always have a good time together."

"My sisters are still hoping you will let them help you get ready. They have been bugging me nonstop to ask you."

"Sure. That will be fine. Just send them over about four or five."

"Will that give you enough time to get ready? I need to be there about six-thirty to start taking pictures."

"Yeah. You know I'm not big on primping. An hour is plenty of time." I loved his sisters dearly, but I was not looking forward to the added attention.

"Someone who looks like you doesn't need much time in front of the mirror anyway." James' voice always got a bit higher when he paid me a compliment. I smiled.

"Flattery will get you nowhere young man!"

"I am hoping it will at least keep my prom date from canceling on me before tomorrow night."

"As long as this storm doesn't blow me away before you get here."

"Nah—the winds are supposed to be picking up a bit on the big night, but aside from that, the weather should hold out."

"I will be the one in red."

"Then red is my new favorite color."

"I am hanging up now before all of this flattery goes to my head." He was still laughing as I hung the receiver up.

I was sure that I had worn a path into the carpet of my bedroom waiting for my family to arrive. I needed the afternoon to sleep, but my family would be arriving just after lunch, and it was not going to be possible. I would have to put off sleep until nightfall—if sleep would be possible knowing the two events that were coming so soon.

I dressed down as much as possible, tying my long hair back into a low ponytail and slipping on some old jeans and a worn sweater, with no make-up. It didn't help much. My transformation would immediately be evident to my family. I couldn't deny that I was still strikingly different in appearance—my hair longer and more golden, my skin as creamy and clear as the airbrushed pictures of the models in the magazine, and my eyes sparkled an emerald-green, luckily not as bright as William's and the other Sironians, but quite a change from the hazel color they had been just a few months earlier.

What would they say when they saw me? I would play dumb as I had done with James and hope that after a few minutes they would just accept the new look as blossoming and move on. Caleb knew the truth, but I worried about how the others would see me—especially Lucy. I pulled out my old pair of reading glasses from the drawer and tried them on to see if it would help. I felt silly, like superman trying to turn into Clark Kent. The strong prescription muddied my now perfect vision. I removed the glasses with a huff and flung them into the garbage can. This was me now. For better or worse, those that I love would have to adjust.

My heart raced in my chest as I heard the car doors closing downstairs, and Lucy's small footsteps clomping up the back steps. I ran to her, hoping for the best! She leapt into my arms smothering me with wet kisses. "Margo! I missed you!" She cried as I spun her around through the air. I embraced her in a giant bear hug and then hurried to greet the rest of my family.

"Is that you, Marguerite?" My mother exclaimed, as I flung my arms around her.

"Sure mom. It's me. I've just grown up a bit that's all." Not surprisingly, she seemed a bit startled, but passed me over to my father and then to Caleb, both of which obviously could detect the change as well, but refrained from saying anything immediately. I had not realized how much I had missed them all until my arms were wrapped around each of them. I almost felt all human again—almost.

"You look different Margo!" Lucy exclaimed grabbing me around the waist.

"You look different too Lucy-bug! I think you are a half a foot taller than when I saw you last, and you hair is longer too." It was true. Her face had slimmed a bit, and she looked like she had aged several years in the weeks it had been since I last saw her.

"But you look really different!" She exclaimed. "Like one of my Barbie dolls." I laughed, trying hard to play along. I had never been good at lying, but I was realizing that it was a part of this new world I had entered. I would have to get better at it.

"Nope. It's still the same ol' me. You just haven't seen me in a while." It felt wrong to lie, especially to Lucy, but there was no way I could possibly explain—not now." My father and Caleb were carrying small suitcases so I quickly ushered them into the house, but neither seemed to be able to break their stare from me. Crap! This wasn't going well.

"Jeez Margo! I wish the soccer team could get a look at you know. I'd be the most popular guy on the team."

"Very funny Caleb! I'm the same as always, you guys just haven't seen me in a few weeks." He smirked giving me a private knowing look, before grabbing another bag to bring into the house.

My mother took me by the arm and stared at me dead in the face studying my features, then eyeing me from head to toe. "Lucy is right dear, you do look different. Don't get me wrong, you look beautiful—stunning even. I just hadn't expected you to blossom like this in such a short amount of time. You almost don't even look like yourself." She pulled back one of the arms of my sweater revealing creamy perfect skin.

"It's all gone," I said flatly. I could see the tears in her eyes as she realized the ailment that I had suffered through since childhood had completely vanished.

"Unbelievable!" She gasped putting her hands over her mouth.

"Grandmother was right. I think it was the salt air. I think it's good for me." At least it wasn't a lie. I nervously fidgeted trying to come up with a better story, some type of explanation, but there was nothing that could explain this away but the truth, a truth that I could not reveal, even to those that I loved.

"Forgive me dear, it's just that—you're just so lovely," she gasped again before breaking into nervous laughter. I could hear my father talking to my grandmother from inside the house. I wished one of them would come rescue me, and then without warning, my knight in shining amour arrived.

The small boat engine caught the attention of everyone as William pulled up in his small, wooden boat up to the dock, quickly tying it off to the floating pier. "Who is that?" My mother asked, her attention diverted to the beautiful creature along the dock.

"William," I replied. "William Avery. My boyfriend." It was the first time I had said the words aloud; they sounded silly coming from my lips. She shot me a stunned look but didn't have time to respond. He looked gorgeous as he strode towards us in a pair of dark colored jeans and a pale blue button down. His unnaturally stunning looks would clearly offset any noticeable improvements in my own appearance, as anyone would pale in comparison to him. I didn't notice that my father and Caleb had walked up beside us until William reached out his arm to shake my father's hand.

"Hello sir—ma'am. It is a pleasure to meet you all. I am William Avery, Marguerite's boyfriend." The words slid off of his tongue so easily, as if he had introduced himself that way a hundred times. My father accepted William's firm handshake. My mother stared at him, mesmerized by the stunning creature in front of her. I was afraid that the combination of my new appearance and the entrance of my new godlike boyfriend may be too much for her to take. I knew she felt as if she had stepped into some type of parallel universe. It was a feeling I now knew all too well.

"Hello William. I wasn't aware that Marguerite had made any new friends here." My father looked at me with a raised eyebrow. William was the first boy that had ever been introduced to my parents—and never had anyone ever called themselves my boyfriend except for Rupert Brooks for three days in the second grade.

"Yes sir, she has made quite a few actually."

"That's good to hear," my mother replied looking over at me as if she had never seen me before. I should have prepared them more for my life here—but how? How could I ever have explained William to them—and the crew? My parents now felt as if I were a stranger to them. There would be much explaining to do, and yet, I had very little explanations in which I could give.

"Hello Caleb. Nice to finally meet you," William said turning to Caleb with an outstretched hand. Caleb curtly accepted. Though they had shared a brief meeting before, my parents were not aware, and the formal introduction was a necessity. Caleb had no idea how much I appreciated his discretion in keeping my secret.

"Hey William." Caleb was indebted to William for saving my life when they last saw each other, and William grateful that Caleb had trusted him enough to deliver me to him in the first place. They had already equally earned the respect of the other. My heart leapt in my chest, as I felt instantly that they would be good friends.

"And this must be Lucy." She took a step towards William and held her hand out to him. We all smiled.

"Hello William," She replied both sweetly and curiously.

"Your sister has told me so very much about you! I am very happy to finally meet you." His charming smile made my fluttering heart melt in my chest—not because he was a siren, but because he was William.

"But she hasn't told me *anything* about you." Chagrin swept through me, as I was certain my cheeks were now flushed from both being dazzled and embarrassed all in a matter of seconds.

William looked over at me and playfully raised an eyebrow. Everyone laughed, even William, and I instantly felt a bit more at ease. "Well, that's probably because she wanted to keep me a surprise."

"I like surprises." Lucy clapped her hands together.

"Well, then I hope you like this." William pulled out a shiny pink whelk from his pocket and presented it to my sister—once again a very rare shell that I had never seen before. It was then that I notice a small hole towards the end of the shell. "Now blow into it right here." William pointed to the end of the shell, and my delighted sister immediately obeyed. A gentle high pitched whistling sound came from the shell. Lucy clapped again, this time with even greater excitement.

"Can I blow it again?" He nodded just as she blew another puff of air into the shell sending out another loud ringing sound; it pierced through the air almost like a song.

"Now, if you ever get lost or need anyone, all you have to do is blow into this and they will be able to find you."

"I love it!" She squealed wrapping her harms around his shoulders.

"How very kind of you William!" Exclaimed my mother as her eyes shifted between the two of us. I was weary at the knowledge of my mother trying to analyze circumstances that were so far outside of anything she could have ever imagined.

My grandmother came out to invite William to dinner, an invitation that he readily accepted. My mother, Lucy, and I helped her get her fabulous meal underway, then she hurried us out of the house so that she could put the finishing touches on it. Lucy was anxious to go down to the dock, so we walked her down while my father and Caleb, along with William's help, began boarding up the house. At some point, James and his family must have arrived. From the dock, I had a view of him and his father boarding up the Merri Mac. He looked over at me from two houses down and delivered a friendly wave, but didn't come over. I could only presume it was because he saw William. If James still harbored ill feelings about William, at least he was trying not to let it affect our friendship. It was as much as I could ask of him.

I watched Lucy scooping tiny brine shrimp from around the edges of the floating pier and filling a small yellow bucket with the sea life. My family was here! I felt complete! But their presence here made me nervous as well. If I was in danger, then surely my entire family would be if they were discovered. My mother surveyed me as I observed Lucy. With William here, I knew that one of the crew must be keeping watch over the inlet, but it still made me nervous to have Lucy so close to the water's edge.

"You're different," she said when we were finally alone. "Physically you hardly resemble the daughter that left me just a few months ago." We watched from across the lot as my brother and father passed a large piece of plywood to William who was standing atop of an extremely high ladder. I could barely focus on my mother's conversation. It was easy to get distracted by William's well-defined arms so effortlessly holding up the large piece of lumber. I giggled to think how hard it must be for him to have to pretend that it was heavy. He could easily board up the entire house himself within a matter for minutes.

"Don't get me wrong, you really do look amazing dear, but I wish you could offer up some explanation for this *transformation*."

"I wish I could too, Mom. I guess it is just magical here. Magic enough to turn a frog into a princess." She rolled her eyes. I sighed, "Ok, I admit that was a poor analogy, but you get the idea."

"You have never been a frog, Marguerite, but no one can deny the change that has come over you, and I don't just mean physical changes. You seem more self-assured than I've ever seen. You seemed to have developed a confidence about you that I've always wanted you to have."

"Oh, no! I still have my insecurities, but things are different now." William looked across the lot. I knew that even at such a distance, and despite the hammering, that he could hear our conversation perfectly. I regretted again that I hadn't developed that ability. Oh, how I wished I could hear the conversations passing between them up there, but try as I may, I could only hear hammering, and the wind that had begun to pick up ever so slightly from the approaching storm system.

"Would that reason possibly be that Greek god-like young man over there on the ladder?"

"Probably," I said looking up at William from across the lot. My mother caught him looking back over his shoulder at me.

"He seems to watch you quite a bit."

"Does he? I hadn't noticed." I was getting better at the whole lying thing. If she knew that I was lying, she didn't let on.

"He does. He must like you a lot."

"I hope so. I mean, I feel that way about him."

"I can see that," she said, her expression turning quite serious.

"What? You don't like him?"

"Oh, no. It's just that, well he is very handsome, almost too handsome—and the boy has had quite a rough life. Your grandmother reminded me of the boy. I remember when his parents passed away. It was in the news all over the state—very tragic." I shifted my weight, suddenly very uncomfortable. Especially since I knew William was listening. "Just be careful. I don't want you to get hurt." I nodded, anxious to move to another conversation. My safety seemed to be a running theme quite a bit lately. The more I heard it, the more I wanted to prove that I could take care of myself. Besides, it was too late for my heart at this point.

I was relieved when my grandmother came onto the porch and motioned for my mother to come to the house. "Keep an eye on Lucy. I'll be right back." She sighed, "Your grandmother must need help with something in the kitchen."

"Margo, look! My bucket is full!" Lucy exclaimed as I stepped onto the floating pier. Lucy took the small whelk blowing it again.

"Wow! It is!" I said peering down at the collection of small shrimp and minnows that she had somehow managed to scoop into her bucket. But what caught my attention was that all of the sea life seemed to be facing in the same direction—towards Lucy. As she moved her tiny finger along the top of the bucket, the creatures seemed to follow. She giggled. I watched, trying to mask my amazement, and then, I noticed the water around her. Just off of the sides of the dock schooled a multitude of tiny fish and sea life, that all seemed to move as she moved, as if they were drawn to her. With each step she took, the ocean life shifted with her, like they were waiting for her. I gasp, but tried to hide my astonishment and sudden worry for Lucy. I would have to talk to William about this as soon as we were alone. It seemed that the gene was active within her, though I had thought it would be years before we would know if it would develop or remain dormant like my father. All indications were pointing to the first option as there was obviously some type of connection between her and the creatures here—a connection that even I did not have. I became nervous as I realized more and more fish began to congregate around the floating pier.

"Come on Lucy. I think it is almost time for dinner."

"Alright." She looked down at her bucket. "Goodbye friends," she said easing the bucket into the water. A fish remained in the bucket. "Go on little fella," she said, pointing her tiny finger out towards the murky inlet waters. The fish swam from the bucket, as I stood speechless. I thought that there was nothing that would surprise me by now, but I was wrong. Lucy could apparently communicate with, and possibly control, sea animals. I had been training for many weeks, and could not yet come close to doing anything as amazing as what I had just witnessed.

Back at the house, William seemed to blend in with my family quite effortlessly. My parents were both excessively polite to him, and the conversation over dinner flowed smoothly. Caleb seemed skeptical at first, but eventually started to warm up to him. He was the only one in the family who had any idea that William wasn't human, so a bit of concern from my little brother was expected. But over the course of the evening it seemed that William was slowly accepted into the family, as if he had always belonged. As the hour started to get late, William excused himself with a promise to see everyone soon. I walked him out onto the back porch so proud of the effort he made to spend time with my family.

"I love you," he whispered to me as the sun was setting behind the clouds. I closed my eyes as he kissed me softly behind the ear.

"And I love you," I replied softly.

"I will see you tomorrow?" He asked slowly pulling his hand from mine. I would have to wait to tell him about Lucy. I nodded, as William slipped into the night, realizing that the next time I saw him…I would be his competitor.

25

———

"There is always some madness in love. But there is also always some reason in madness."

Friedrich Nietzsche

I **quietly pulled the screen door** shut just before 5 a.m. I was hoping to get to the landing before William even knew I had left. He hadn't specified if he would be picking me up for training, so I was relieved to find the dock void of life. Much to my relief, Kirby wasn't waiting either. I needed the time to focus. My insides were a jumbled ball of nerves, and I felt as though I could get sick at any moment. Not exactly the way one would want to feel just before challenging the most revered of all of the young protectors.

I restlessly spent the entire night questioning my decision but ultimately could not reverse what I knew in my heart was right. Would he understand the reasoning behind my decision to challenge him for my protectorship? Would he feel relieved to finally be free to go look for his sister or hate me forever? Sure, it was doubtful that I could come close to William's skills, but maybe, just maybe I could find a way to release him of his burden of me. I loved William too deeply to keep him bound to me—I had to fight to let him go.

My clothes were the same as the day before except I had swapped the white shirt for a grey one, and added my new black combat boots. I pulled back my unnaturally golden locks and wound them tightly against the top of my head. Today, I needed to completely forget the girl I had once been and become the warrior that I knew was inside of me.

When I climbed through the reeds and shrub brush that hid the embankment from the waterway, I found the clearing empty minus one. Silas stood in the center of the lot carrying a serious expression. My heart was pounding so loudly in my chest that I was sure that the entire population of the coastline could hear it.

"I was hoping you had changed your mind."

"No, I have to do this Silas. I have to try. It's the only way."

"You are perfectly in your rights to challenge him, but let me advise you. I am unsure what his reaction will be when he discovers it is you waiting here. He was quite upset last night when I told him he was being challenged today."

"What did he say?"

"He was of course shocked. He demanded to know which of the protectors dared to try to take over his position. He considers it Kirby and wanted to confront him last night. I, of course, could not give him that information until the challenge, and he immediately stormed off. Just after, he launched the sailboat he's been building. I also noticed that he had removed most of his books and clothes out of his sleeping quarters. His boat was anchored in a cove on the south side of the inlet early this morning." I wanted to cry.

"Do you think he'll come?"

"Of course. It is his duty."

I waited impatiently for the next thirty minutes. The rest of the crew arrived before William. Their presence only added to my nervousness and anxiety. It made sense for them to be there and yet, for some reason I had not anticipated an audience. Tobie carried a smirk on his face, as if he were excited to see the fireworks. Kirby looked confused and eyed his two friends wondering who the challenger could be, and Mace stared at me with a labored expression. It was obvious that he had figured out that I was William's challenger.

The boy that stepped foot on the clearing carried all of the features of William, but his faces was twisted so fiercely that I could barely recognize him. He didn't acknowledge my presence at all but immediately faced the crew. His eyes blazed so intensely that my nervousness had completely been replaced by fear.

"Thank you for coming William." Evidently his resentment carried to Silas as well, as William glowered at the man that he both respected and loved.

"Let's just cut to why we are here. Who is it that dares to challenge me?" He growled leaping towards them fiercely. All traces of his human facade were gone. He was every bit a Sironian warrior—every bit as fierce as the monsters that had so often crept into my dreams, and yet, seeing this side of William only made me love him more. "Who has called me here?" His words were barely audible.

No one spoke. No one even dared to move.

"I do," I somehow found the courage to say. His beautiful body turned still in its crouched position to face me. "It's me William. I'm the one who has come to challenge you." He stared at me half in disbelief, but his face did not soften—his expression twisted from anger to hurt.

"It's you?" He cried as his eyes pierced through mine. I nodded, barely able to unlock my frozen state. If I had shot an arrow through his chest, his expression could not have shown any more pain as it did at that very second. "You wish so severely to be free of me?" He asked with no attempt to disguise the pain in his voice.

"It's not like that. I only want to…."

"I thought there was no one here that could defeat me, and yet, with your very words, I am proved wrong. Don't you see, you have already won?"

"Let me explain…," I pleaded.

"I understand perfectly. All of your training, all of perseverance was just to be rid of me." Tears swelled in the corners of his perfect eyes. "You have your wish." Before I could even respond, he had disappeared across the landing and into the icy waters. We all stared after him. And then there was nothing but silence.

"I don't understand?" I muttered to Silas, my body still visibly shanking.

"My dear, you see, you've won merely by challenging him. You are the only person who could have beaten him, because you're the one person he could never harm. Even if he didn't have feelings for you, he still couldn't have accepted your challenge. He has vowed to protect you, Marguerite. How could he fight what he has sworn to protect?"

"But I didn't know!"

"Marguerite Westly, you are hereby granted your own protectorship," Silas painfully uttered. Suddenly everything in the world felt wrong. I felt the tears welling up in my eyes. I had gotten what I had wanted, but at what price. I buried my hands in my face. The others looked away as it to spare me any more pain and embarrassment. I wept, and turned to leave, but Silas stopped me.

"Marguerite, I know this is a difficult time to bring this up, but I am extremely concerned about the storm front moving towards the coast. The size and speed is uncommon for this time of the year, and I can't help but wonder if this is one of Theron's ploys to get to you. We will be closely monitoring things on our end, but you need to be on high alert as the situation could turn critical for the entire area."

"You think Theron has *created* this hurricane? To come after me?"

"No, not even Theron could create such a storm, but he and his Legion could use their powers to strengthen and redirect it here if he so choses."

"But I am just one girl."

"No, you are officially a protector now, a protector who will soon be quite coveted by Theron. Just be prepared." I was visibly shaken.

"Do you want me to take you home?" Kirby asked compassionately. "Silas, I think Margo needs some time to process some of this." I began to object, but the tears began to flow so swiftly down my face that I was pretty sure that I wouldn't even be able to see to make it home. I nodded and he gently put his hand on my shoulder and began to lead me back towards the boat.

Kirby slowed the boat just up the creek from the Inlet Joy. "Do you think you are able to take it the rest of the way?" I was confused. "Someone is waiting on your dock, a scent that I am unfamiliar with, but similar to your own—it must be a family member of yours." It was still very early for any of my family to be awake, but the last thing I needed to have to do was to explain Kirby to any of my family, especially as they had just been introduced to William the day before as my boyfriend.

"I've got it from here," I responded wiping away the tears that were still streaming uncontrollably down my face. Kirby leaned forward and gently cupped my face.

"For the record, I think it was quite admirable and brave what you did today. Give it some time. William will think about it and realize why you chose to do this today. It is actually the most selfless thing I have ever seen. You truly are one of us now."

"But what have I done? I feel as if I've signed my own death warrant. I'm scared that they'll come for me, and I won't be strong enough to protect myself."

"We all stand together. We all stand with you. You don't have to fight alone. There is no need to be afraid."

"But I am even more afraid that William won't forgive me."

"He's an odd bird for sure, but not unreasonable. He'll forgive you." He stood at the stern of the tiny boat. "Gotta go. We have an inlet to protect," and with one sweeping leap, the boy soared high into the air before gliding into the water with almost no splash at all.

Caleb was waiting for me along the dock when I pulled up. He caught hold of the front of the boat as I idled in and began to tie up the bow. "So, where have you been off to so early this morning?" He asked as he double looped the rope around the rusty cleat tie-down.

"Don't ask," I responded trying to hide my tear stained face beneath my hair. He took my hand to help me out of the boat and caught sight of my expression.

"You've been crying." I have never been a crier so Caleb was alarmed.

"It's nothing," I protested. He became angry.

"You know, we never use to keep secrets from each other, but now it seems like I don't even know you at all. Margo, you need to tell me what is going on with you."

"I already have explained to you more than I should have Caleb."

"Well, I think that is B. S.! Let me just say what everyone else is thinking, you aren't acting like yourself, you don't sound like yourself. Hell, you don't even look like *you* anymore."

"I'm the same person—just different," I sobbed. "I didn't ask for this, I'm just the first one of us that it has happened to. You could have it too you know. Lucy does. I am pretty sure."

"Lucy? Heck, I don't really even know what *it* is?" he shouted. "You need to tell me what you know."

"Now isn't the time."

"No, now is exactly the time! Start from the beginning and tell me everything." I started to protest again before realizing that Caleb wasn't going to let this go. I sat on the edge of the floating pier and Caleb sat next to me. He deserved to know the truth, as this may affect his future as well, and so I began from the beginning. I started from the moment I dropped the bath salts and tossed his stopwatch many months ago. I concluded with the events of this morning and how I had given up William as my protector to give him his freedom. He sat in disbelief at first, then he slowly opened and closed his own hands, studying them as if he were looking for something.

"Well, at least I can see why you have been too busy to call or write very much. You think that I'm Sironian too?" He responded when my story had reached its conclusion. I nodded.

"You are, but if the gene will affect you as it did me, I think it is just too early to tell."

"And you're in danger now?"

"I am. That's why you need to get the family and leave as soon as possible, especially with the possibility of this storm coming."

"But what would the storm have to do with you? Heck, the reports all are expecting it to go north of here, even if it does make landfall."

"A hurricane this time of the year, this close to the coast, it isn't natural, especially one this size. I won't put my family at risk! The longer you're here, the more danger you're all in. I was discovered, but they still don't know anything about the rest of you. I can't leave, but you can!"

"I'm not about to leave you here without protection."

"I'm not unprotected Caleb. William isn't the only protector. I have friends that will stand with me, and fight—if it comes to that."

"And William?"

"I don't know what he thinks of me right now."

"You are in love with him, aren't you?"

"Very much so." I fought to hold in the tears that were welling up again in my eyes.

"Well then, he must be a pretty amazing guy for you to feel this way about him."

"He is." One tear escaped. I brushed it away quickly so that Caleb wouldn't see it. I had never been a crier but the past few months had changed that. I finally had something that I cared about enough to cry over.

"Then he will forgive you. And if he doesn't, I will kick his merman ass!" I giggled as Caleb tucked a stray golden lock behind my ear. Only Caleb could make me laugh when my entire world was falling apart. "Oh, and by the way—nice boots!" He brushed back the tears that flowed freely from my suddenly not-so-tough exterior.

Caleb and I spent the remainder of the early morning talking. I told him about all of my new Sironian friends, about Silas and Maris. Lucy scampered onto the porch just after nine and called us in for breakfast. I couldn't eat. I felt as though my heart had been ripped from my body. I had to find William and explain, but my family's presence made that virtually impossible.

My Mother had promised to take Lucy to the mall to get a new pair of ballet shoes. I saw this as my opportunity to find William. Luckily my mother insisted I rest up for the prom tonight, suggesting I lay down for a bit before James' sisters came over to begin their doting. Poor Caleb was not so lucky and was dragged along for the shopping despite his relentless protesting. I cringed at the thought of going anywhere tonight—especially prom! It was the first time the impending event had crossed my mind all day. All I could think of was William. I had to see him.

It was just after noon when I grabbed an extra gas can from the storage room, and I headed down to the dock. This time, I was surprised to find someone waiting for me. It was my father. The look he carried was a mixture of solace and worry. "I can't let you go." He said solemnly.

"I was just going out for some fresh air," I mumbled fairly unconvincingly. He shook his head as he began slowly.

"You were only partial right when you told Caleb that the Sironian gene lies dormant within me." I gasped.

"You know?" I whispered barely able to make a sound.

"Yes, I know what I am—what we are. I always have. I've been able to provide you a relatively normal life up until this point because it is true that so many Sironian traits lie dormant within me. Unlike the others, I can successfully live apart from the water. I seem to be no stronger or faster than the average man. I am able to swim with speed as the Sironians, but I can't breathe under water as they can or even hold my breath for the extended periods like you can."

"You know of my abilities?" He smiled faintly.

"I have always known. Even when you were a small child you were able to swim long distances without coming for air. I'd hoped you could live a healthy life inland, but I knew when you became ill that you were changing. There was no choice in you coming; despite the risks, I knew you belonged here. How else could I bear to part from you?"

"Grandmother thinks the gene is completely dormant within you."

"It is, for the most part. I never experienced the kind of change you have over the past few months. The one other trait that seemed to awaken within me is that I can hear from long distances. I have been able to hear conversations from up to a hundred yards away with crystal clear accuracy since I was your age."

"You have?" Nothing should be able to shock me anymore, but I had gone an entire life without knowledge that my father had any special abilities.

"Yes." He put his hand on mine. "I've always hidden this ability from others because I was afraid. I didn't know what was happening to me, so I remained silent out of fear. When my father passed away, I became aware of the truth by accident. I happened across one of his medical charts that contained his blood type. As my blood type was different from his or my mother's, it only made sense that the man that I had known and loved wasn't my biological father. I was confused, but my mother was grieving so, that I waited to speak with her about the situation. I assumed I was adopted, but it always seemed that I was something other than normal. Silas called her not long after my father's death; I was outside and so she assumed that I couldn't hear their conversation. It was the first time they had spoken since I was born. This is how I discovered I was part Sironian. I overheard a telephone conversation my mother shared with Silas. He asked if any of the Sironian traits had been passed to me and seemed relieved when she told him they had not. I wanted to speak with my biological father, to learn what I was but had no idea how to find him. I decided not to let my mother know that I had learned of what I was and have devoted much of my adult life searching for answers. The more I researched the Sironians, the more it became imperative that I keep all of you away from them. I wanted to keep our family's entire existence a secret. I took a job that would allow me to travel a bit, and as I traveled along the coast on these trips, I listened. It took almost five years before I was able to discover my first group of Sironians. They live just south of Charleston near Folly Beach. I studied their conversations for months while working on the beach renourishment project that I had been hired to oversee. In fact, all of my knowledge of Sironian life has been gleamed from conversations that I have overheard over the years, as most of the written accounts of the siren life is nothing more than folklore. During the summer months, the times that I brought you here, I had always hoped of learning more about my biological father, Silas, but I have learned nothing of him.

"Silas isn't your biological father." He seemed startled by my information.

"How do you know this?"

"I asked him. He wouldn't lie to me. I know him well enough to know that he wasn't lying when he said he was not my grandfather. Plus, he didn't have any reason to lie to me." It was my father's turn to be surprised.

"Well, who could it be?" He sighed and closed his eyes.

"I don't know. He wouldn't say."

"I just presumed it was him. He clearly had a very close connection to Mother."

"True, but something happened. There was someone else who came between them—your biological father. Aaron, I believe she called him." He shrugged and slowly shook his head. I studied the features of the man that I had adored my entire life. It was impossible to deny that he was beautiful—far more handsome and youthful than the other fathers with daughters my age.

"She isn't aware that I know any of this. She has clearly gone to great lengths to keep me away from this world and spent a lifetime sheltering me from the truth. I love her and the man I called "Father" for my entire life too much to churn up things for my own benefit. I was given the most wonderful father a boy could ask for, and I thank God every day that he allowed me to be his son." The wind picked up again swirling my hair around me. A large flock of pelicans flew overhead traveling inland from the coast. We both looked out into the sky. The storm was beginning to move closer to the coast with little sign that it would follow the northern projected path. We both knew it was coming.

"The storm is coming here isn't it?"

"Yes. It appears to be heading this way despite the weather reports—it's not large now, but I fear it is growing larger by the hour."

"How much time do we have?" I asked solemnly as if it were a death sentence.

"You should be fine tonight for the prom, but the first waves of rain should start swirling in tomorrow afternoon. I am going to take your mother, grandmother, and Lucy back inland with us tonight. Caleb has asked to stay and drive back with you tomorrow morning."

"Grandmother is going back to Florence with you?"

"Oh, of course she protested, but I was afraid that if she didn't travel inland with us, she may give you a hard time about evacuating tomorrow. She wants to stay and ride out the storm, but that is ridiculous! If she comes back with us then I know she won't be here to aggravate you and Caleb tomorrow when you go to leave."

"Smart idea," I said as another band of wind swirled across the inlet. I needed to go find William before the water became too unsafe to travel. "I won't be gone very long dad, but I need to go see if I can find him," I said motioning to the boat that he seemed to be blocking. My father knew exactly of whom I was speaking.

"It isn't a good idea, Margo. The wind and current has already begun to make the water choppy."

"It is very important Dad! You are just going to have to trust me on this." He looked skeptical. "I will wear a lifejacket!" He shot me a funny luck—a Sironian in a lifejacket was ridiculous. "Look, just give me an hour. If I am not back, you can send a search party after me."

"It isn't just the storm. What if *they* find you? You are unprotected."

"They won't."

"One hour. If this boat isn't parked here by then, I will send the entire Navy to find you."

"Thanks Dad!" I gave him a big kiss on the cheek and jumped into the boat before he could have the opportunity to change his mind.

One could not deny the eerie feeling that had swept through the inlet with the impending storm. The water was beyond choppy; it was fierce, especially when I made it out past the marina. The current pulled against the small boat engine, and I could hardly see from my hair blowing into my face. Huh? I thought there was a quite peacefulness before a storm. Maybe that time had already passed while I was chasing away the only boy that I had ever loved. I had to find him! The boat could not carry me quick enough. I thought briefly about ditching the boat and swimming. What was the use of being Sironian if my legs were of no use to me? But the uncertainty of what was waiting out in the inlet kept me in the little boat.

I checked Silas' house and the barn first to be sure he had not returned. There was no sign of either of them. I ached at the sight of his empty room, void of all of his personal treasures. Next I searched the coves in the northern part of the inlet where Kirby had seen William's sailboat last night. I found nothing. Lastly, I circled the "point." Flocks of birds were leaving the sanctuary to head further inland. Even they knew instinctually what was heading in our direction.

My heart sank as I saw the boarded up Knoxx Point just over the waterway. All was covered except for the large domed glass roof and beacon that was impossible to safeguard. I ran the boat clear up onto the sand, before running across the dunes to the large wooded double doors. Henry met me at the door and ushered me inside where Sadie and Olivia greeted me. They were obviously happy to see me, but a look of concern cast a shadow over Sadie's beautiful features.

"He's not here, Marguerite." He came by to help Henry board up the place early this morning. He hardly said a word. I have never seen him like this—not since his parents passed. We saw him heading out past the mouth in that sailboat just a short time later."

"Which way did he head?"

"South towards Pawley's Island, but, Miss Marguerite, there is no way I am going to let you head out there in this weather in that little boat!" Henry added in a quite firm tone.

"I just need to talk to him. I need to clear up a few things."

"Just say, 'I'm sorry.' That is what I always say when I hurt someone's feelings," replied Olivia. The dark skinned young girl's Sironian beauty was growing by the day. How long would Sadie and Henry be able to hide the girl from the world? Would we be able to hide our Lucy's beauty and abilities as she grew? Fear swept through me.

"You are right sweet Olivia. I do need to apologize to him."

"He will forgive you. He loves you," the girl said, her perfect smile reaching from ear to ear. I smiled and patted her head trying to fight back a tear.

"Do you know where he is going?" I asked Sadie and Henry.

Sadie shook her head, but added, "Well, I did happen to see the Sironian boy that goes by the name Kirby talking to him briefly on the jetties just before he left. The boy was out by the rocks when Mr. William passed through, and he seemed to stop a moment to have words with the boy."

Of course Kirby would be out on the jetties. I had to find Kirby to see what William had said to him. He would be around here—somewhere! The crew wouldn't abandon the inlet. Three protectors wouldn't be able to withstand a force of any great magnitude, but at least there was some protection. And I would stand with them if the time should ever come.

But I didn't find Kirby and barely made it back to the Inlet Joy before my hour was up. I wanted to keep searching, but I would keep my promise to my father. The last thing I needed was to have him out searching for me. I couldn't help but wonder if he would take to the water like a true Sironian if required. What a sight it would be to see my father gliding through the water as William and the others!

I barely had time to shower when another set of forces descended on me, forces even I could not withstand—James' sisters. My mother and Lucy returned from shopping, and Lucy was showing off her new pair of shiny slippers when the tornado hit. The two girls took over my tiny bedroom, replacing shelves of books with trays of hair and beauty products. Kitty took the blow-dryer to my hair, while Rebecca began with my make-up. My mind was too consumed with William to put up much of a fight. My heart was gone.

Rebecca brought her friend Amy with her, who made her displeasure quite clear that I was going to the prom with James. The girl had clearly been jockeying for an invite from him for quite some time. I almost felt guilty as my mind could think of nothing but William, and here this young girl wished so much to take my place tonight. I knew that it wasn't James that she wanted as much as the "idea" of James—the handsome older brother of her best friend. He was her unobtainable. I wondered if she ever captured the heart of my best friend how long she would be happy. Her type was easy to read; it wouldn't be long before she would move on to another conquest. My mother and Lucy just sat on the edge of the bed watching. My mother would occasionally add her input on a shade of eye shadow or lip liner and seemed to be enjoying herself. Lucy just giggled each time they pulled out another torture device. Our time ran out before they did; I whispered a silent thank you to the clock as it finally read the time James had said he was coming to pick me up.

"Where is the dress?" Kitty squealed opening my closet and pulling out the zipped bag hanging in the corner. She slid the zipper down revealing the simple red gown. My face reddened at the gasps from around the room as she help up the elegant gown.

"Where did you find this vintage, couture Channel? Marguerite! This dress must cost a fortune!" Kitty exclaimed.

"You have been holding out on us! I have seen what is hanging in your closet! You don't know one designer from the next!" boasted Rebecca. Amy pouted at the sight of the dress.

"True. It's a loner. I borrowed it from a friend," I mumbled under my breath as the girls stripped off my old bathrobe. The dress slid onto my frame as if it had been molded just for me. Much to everyone's dismay, I pulled the simple flats I had purchased out of the box and slid them onto my feet.

"You look beautiful! My mother exclaimed as her eyes welled up with tears. At least she could check this one off her list—*oldest daughter goes to prom!* She eyed me carefully. She may have not known the exact details of how I had acquired the dress, but she didn't need to guess—William.

"You aren't going to wear flats to the prom are you?" Amy scolded brushing back one of her platinum curls from her face.

"I most certainly am," I replied, just as there was a gentle knock on the door.

"Margo, James is here to pick you up." Caleb took a double take at me as he opened the door. "Geez, Margo! You look like a movie star or something!"

"I am hoping for the 'or something,'" I responded as the girls drug me from the bedroom to where James was waiting. James was beaming from ear to ear as I stepped out onto the front steps. It was still early, just after five, as James had to arrive at the prom early to take pictures.

"You look beautiful, darlin'," he said as the camera flashes began going off in all directions. James looked remarkably handsome. It was the first time I had ever seen him in a tuxedo—a deep grey that went well with his eyes.

"Thank you. You look very handsome as well," I said, not having to pretend a smile.

"Ready to go?" I nodded as he took my arm and led me down the steps. I saw my father loading down the car out of the corner of my eye.

"Can I have a minute?" I asked.

"Sure," he responded.

My father saw me coming and shook his head. "My, my, it crushes a father's heart to see his baby girl looking all grown up like that. Almost as beautiful as the day you were born!"

"Awww Dad!" I exclaimed, giving him a big hug. "Don't make me cry and smear the five tubes of mascara those girls slathered on me." He laughed.

"We will be heading back to Florence before you get back. Caleb will be here, so you guys be sure to finish locking up and head out by late morning. The weather reports are still predicting any landfall to be a good bit north of here, but I don't believe it. Be sure to take anything you want to keep and hit the road before the traffic gets bad. I am predicting they will figure this thing out before long and order an evacuation sometime late morning, so you guys clear out before that happens."

"Got it! Love you dad! Take care of Lucy, Mom and Grandmother."

"And you look out for Caleb. We will expect you guys in Florence just after lunch, okay?"

"Alright! We will be there." I thought of telling my father about how far the gene had progressed inside of me, and that I would be lucky to be away from the coast for a night before getting gravely ill, but that would have to wait. There was no need to further worry him, and odds are, if we did have to evacuate, I would be able to return to the Inlet Joy as soon as the storm passed.

Or that was the plan, anyway.

26

"Seldom, very seldom, does complete truth belong to any human disclosure; seldom can it happen that something is not a little disguised or a little mistaken."

Jane Austen

James brought me to a quiet Italian bistro for dinner. I was unfamiliar with the restaurant, which was both elegant and casual. We were the only formally dressed patrons, but the place was upscale enough that I didn't feel awkward. *Well, any more awkward than I would have felt anywhere dressed like this.* I wasn't very hungry but politely ordered the evening's special—some type of chicken and pasta dish, and picked at it as my excited date rambled on about all of the classmates I would meet over the course of the evening. I was too preoccupied to pay very close attention, but tried to play it off with a general question or comment here or there. A bit of guilt swept through me as I realized that my handsome date deserved much more of my attention. James deserved someone who could give him more than what I was able to offer. He deserved better than to have his honest and true affections wasted on someone who couldn't stop thinking about someone else.

After dinner, I was surprised when James didn't take the turn to Conway but began driving north. "We aren't going to the high school?" I was confused.

"Come on, Margo, you didn't expect us to hold our prom in the school gymnasium?" I shrugged. I did actually. "We rented out one of the dance clubs along the strip, just down from the Myrtle Beach Pavilion."

"Oh. Guess that would make more sense," I said, swallowing hard and wishing that I had developed a severe case of the flu. James laughed.

"Don't worry; I promise not to make you dance the entire night, but I did put in a requests for a few shag songs for old time sake—that is, since your boyfriend doesn't seem to mind you dancing with me." The mere mention of William was enough to bring me to tears.

"Do you mind if we not talk of him tonight." I asked sincerely. It was going to be hard enough to get through the evening without crushing my heart into pieces each time he was mentioned.

"You guys have a fight or something?" James said with a peaked curiosity.

"Something like that," I mumbled. It was as if all of the butterflies in my stomach had died. I ached at the mere mention of his name. "But like I said, I really just don't want to talk about it tonight."

"Done! Not a word!" He said reaching over and taking my hand across the seat. I knew I should have pulled it away, but he securely laced his fingers into mine. This was James' night, and I was determined not to ruin it for him.

At least that was the plan, anyway.

We weren't the first to arrive at the prom, but not far from it as there were only a handful of students and chaperones throughout the place. The club was two stories with a large dance floor in the center of the downstairs and several smaller rooms that opened off to the sides. There was a small upstairs loft and balconies with tables that encompassed all sides, each with a view of the dance floor below. In an effort to be cute and run with the unfortunate timing of the event, the theme of "Under the Sea" had been modified to "Through the Storms of Love." Each table was appropriately adorned with hurricane drinking glasses and within the room was decorated with cut palm branches, lifejackets, and a hodgepodge of misplaced street signs, signal lights, and even a working siren light spinning around the room. The mood was urban and far less cheesy than the previous theme.

James began snapping pictures of the décor as I wandered about the place. A DJ, who appeared to be in his late thirties with overly tanned skin and slicked back raven dyed hair, was setting up his equipment alongside the dance-floor. I couldn't help but notice that he kept ogling me from the corner of his eye. I was glad that I hadn't inherited laser vision as a Sironian trait or I would have probably fried him to a pulp for being so openly rude.

James brought over some type of blue punch in a hurricane glass as the guests began to flock into the club. The girls were in a state of agitation as the strong storm winds had disheveled their newly manicured hair styles. I giggled as each of their dresses seemed bigger and more sparkly than the next. My red vintage gown hardly fit in with the latest prom fashion. It stood as a fine wine in a room full of cheap champagne. James began introducing me to friends who seemed only lukewarm to the new interloper amongst them. Most of the guys were friendly enough, some overfriendly, which only seemed to heighten the cool reception I received from their dates.

My date was suddenly at the mercy of his classmates who kept him busy for the next forty-five minutes as he snapped photo after photo of the partygoers. I mainly stayed off to the side and watched as he completed the couple photos. The DJ jumped right into the top forty dance hits. Between shots, James glanced over at me and motioned to the dance floor suggesting I join the fun. I shook my head, trying to smile. There is no way I would get out there to dance and definitely not alone.

A group of guys made their way into the club—all without dates. Several were quite handsome, leading me to believe that they had chosen to come together. I knew the type well—the guys that existed to be the life of the party, though usually more than a bit intoxicated. The types of guys that are well liked by everyone but with a bit of alcohol become loud and obnoxious. They were clearly pretty good friends with James as they pulled him to the side. I wished I could have heard their conversation, but even with my heightened senses, it was impossible to hear what they were saying over the deafening music. James pointed towards me, and four pairs of eyes looked me up and down before giving James a high five of approval. Strangely out of character, he appeared to be enjoying the attention of having me as his date, a revelation that began to strike a chord with me as the night continued on. The usually attentive James seemed to be feeding off of the attention of having me as his date more than actually enjoying the evening with me. In fact, during the entire first hour, he had only been able to break free once to come over to me before being swept away again. I knew coming into the evening that he had to take photographs, but clearly neither of us had thought the evening through.

A slender attractive guy in a tuxedo and black converse high-tops maneuvered through the crowds over to me. He had that surfer look about him—bronzed skin and shoulder length hair that was the exact color of golden sand. He could have been Sironian except for a slight crook in his nose and his eyes that were brown and not emerald green. "I was a bit concerned seeing you over here all evening by yourself." He said confidently approaching me. "I *am* Justin."

"Nice to meet you, Justin. I *am* Marguerite." I mimicked, trying not to roll my eyes. James looked over and saw Justin talking to me. He smiled, but I couldn't help but think his expression had changed a bit. He looked a tiny bit jealous.

"You go by Margo, right?" Justin asked as he tossed back his blonde hair. I nodded.

"Yes. How did you know that?' I replied as disinterested as I felt.

"James and I are buds. He talks about you all the time."

"We weren't sure if James was just making you up or if you were a real person."

"I'm real—well, at least the last time I checked." My words were not intended to be funny, but Justin laughed anyway. I scanned the room trying to find an exit from this conversation. I wasn't good at small talk and definitely not with someone I didn't know.

"You are pretty funny. Somehow this doesn't seem like your type of place."

I looked over at James who was taking some candid photos in the front of the club. My face began to feel warm. "It's not. I have to admit, I would much prefer a quiet evening with a good book." His eyes looked over me, but I was pretty sure he hadn't even heard my response.

"Is that so? Why don't you and I get out of here? I was wondering if you might maybe want to go out with me on the beach." I was momentarily stunned. Seriously! Was one of James' friends actually hitting on me! I suppose I couldn't completely fault the boy, as it was true that I had been by myself for most of the night. It was rude nonetheless. My insides began to boil, but I tried to keep it in check.

"Thank you for the offer, but I think I'll just wait for James to finish up."

"Are you sure? I am a pretty nice guy you know, and from what James has told me about you, I think we would get along pretty well." If there was any doubt that the boy had been propositioning me, it was completely affirmed. He was now openly hitting on me with my date just across the room.

"I don't think James would like that very much." I replied, slightly more firm than I had intended.

"Actually, he already gave me the go ahead to ask you. He said you guys weren't a couple, so I asked him if he would mind me asking you for some alone time." I was about to explode!

"We aren't a couple—but James is my date. Will you excuse me? I need to go to the ladies room. It was a pleasure to meet you Justin," I somehow managed to politely say before hastily making my exit. I was fuming mad at James! He was right; we were not a couple, but the thought that he would give one of his friends permission to approach me like that, was out of character and distasteful. I was beyond angry.

I hid out in one of the bathroom stalls for longer than I care to admit. However I expected this evening to go, I by no means expected to feel like this. I was hurt, angry, and more than a little confused. I wanted to leave. Heck, James probably wouldn't even notice I was gone until he went to show me off to one of his friends and couldn't find me. I closed my eyes amongst the stall graffiti and tried to imagine myself in the most wonderful place I could think of—the quarry. If I only closed my eyes then maybe I could see the sun glistening off of William's beautifully bronzed skin. A twinge of pain swept through me once again. He was gone. Who knows if I would even see him again? I would somehow find him and explain everything—no matter how long it took, I would find him. I didn't belong in this world; I wasn't sure if I had ever belonged here, but I had found the place that I belonged, and somehow managed to lose it. I belonged with William.

I had just mustered up enough courage to make my exit when two girls came into the restroom. One was a brunette with a poorly cut bob, the other a girl with unnaturally red permed hair. They did not see me hiding out in the stall. "Did you see Justin falling all over himself trying to talk to that girl James brought."

"Wish he would fall over me like that! Wonder where James picked her up?"

"Who knows? Maybe she is an alien or something, I guess she is pretty, but something seems a bit odd about her." I chose this moment to make my exit, dropping my appearance of normalcy just a bit. Both girls looked mortified as I made my way to one of the sinks and washed my hands very slowly—careful not to make eye contact with them. I turned just before leaving the restroom, lowering my head just a bit and glaring my emerald-green eyes at them. Through the mirror I could see them glowering unnaturally through the dim bathroom lights.

"I would go with the alien theory." I added with a smile as both girls sprung back startled and shaking. I buried my face in my hands as I headed for the exit. I knew that I shouldn't have done that. None of the other Sironians I had known had ever dropped their façade even for a moment. Maybe I was dangerous for everyone.

I didn't even look for James as I pushed my way through the crowded room towards the patio, but he caught my arm just as I was leaving through the double doors that led down to the beach. "Where are you going, Margo? I have been looking for you for the past half hour!" I looked up and glared at him, trying not to glower as I had done in the bathroom. "What is going on with you? You don't seem like yourself tonight?"

"Oh, I don't seem like *myself!* I'm not the only one!" I shot at him angrily. "Why did you even bring me here if you were just going to try to pass me off to one of your friends?" James closed his eyes and threw his head back, his hand rubbing his temples in frustration.

"I guess I understand why you are angry," he groaned under his breath. "Look, I wasn't prepared for questions about us. He asked if we were a couple, of which I had to respond "no" and when he asked if he could have a shot at you, I really didn't know *what* to say."

"How about NO!" I growled, my human façade slipping again ever so slightly.

"Justin is the type of guy who doesn't really know the meaning of the word "no," guess he doesn't hear it a lot."

"Well he did tonight!" I snapped at him again. A sly smile that I had never seen before swept across James' face, as if he could not help it.

"I know you will be mad at me for saying this, but I am proud of you. I guess I have been wondering where I stand with you. I don't know… call it a test or something." My blood boiled again.

"A test! Really?" I had never been so angry with him! I shot past him across the stone bar patio and onto the beach below. The fierce wind swept through my hair and along the light colored sand sweeping it up as it blew across the beach. The moonlight could not break through the cloud cover that was swiftly moving across the night sky. Large choppy waves plowed into the shoreline as if to devour it.

I had barely stepped onto the sand when James had hold of my arm again. I had to keep my anger in check as I could easily snap his arm in two if I wasn't careful.

"Please Margo!" I pulled my arm away and hastily walked down the beach. I wanted to run, but even without my shoes, which I had discarded Cinderella style, it was impossible in this dress without tearing it into shreds. James running full speed in his tuxedo could barely keep pace. "Just give me a minute!" He pleaded at my heels. There was a different tone in his voice, one that I had never heard from him—one that I had played over and over in my head since I had challenged William. I stopped and turned to face him. "Look, I wanted to punch him. To tell him you were *my* girl, but I couldn't rightly *do* that now *could* I!" He said tenderly as his hand moved to stroke my face. I pulled away.

"James, it isn't like that between us. It can't be like that! You're ruining everything!"

"But why? Why can't it be? You clearly want it to be that way with that William guy."

"You promised you wouldn't bring him up tonight!"

"Jeez! I feel like he is between us even when he is not here. You aren't yourself anymore!"

"Well, you weren't yourself tonight either! I expected you to have to take pictures, but what I didn't expect was that I was brought here tonight to be some kind of trophy that you could pass around to your friends!"

"I was just being stupid okay. I know it was a mistake. I am sorry. Please don't be angry with me. I am going to make mistakes, I am only human, but if you care about me at all, you have to forgive me. I am asking you to forgive me!"

I heard all of the words that I wanted so desperately to say to William flowing sincerely out of James. My mind raced and my heart suddenly softened. If I couldn't forgive James, how could I ever expect William to forgive me? I turned to face my friend's pleading blue eyes that shimmered faintly in the dark night. He took off his jacket and wrapped it around my shoulders, but his arms did not retreat from around me. He held me as the wind churned the lose sand around us. James moved one of his hands to my chin. I knew what was coming.

"James—don't!" I protested, but it was too late, his cool lips were on mine, pressing hard against my mouth. It felt wrong, all wrong. My instant response was to pull away, but before I could do so, his sweet aura crept between my lips. I began to panic as I didn't know what was happening. The moment it swept inside of me, something primal took over. It was an emotion I had not felt before, one that I wanted to control, but instantly knew that I could not. I craved not his kiss, but his essence. The overwhelming feeling of strength began to come over me—it intoxicated me as if it were a drug. There was nothing in the world that I craved more than the sensation that filled me as his very soul was sucked from its core. All trace of humanity had vanished from my body and the siren within me fed on his life-force filling me from limb to limb. The more it filled me the more vicious I became. I could not control the thirsty lust that took over as it devoured the strength within him. The body in front of me became limp, and for a brief second as he fell to the ground the flow of essence was broken. I sought to follow him, to finish off every drop of life left within his flesh, but in that brief second, I saw my best friend's drained face. I had robbed him of all of his strength, and now I was seeking to take his life, to finish him off.

I threw myself backwards as far away as I could possible manage, trying to break the connection. Even at a distance, my body once again surged towards the human lying limp in the sand. My body was so consumed with this unstoppable craving that I did not notice the rising water that now rolled over my feet. And then before I could finish off my prey—she was there.

Maris appeared out of the water like a dark goddess rising out of the surf. Whatever hold James had held over me was broken as I was snapped back to reality. I sprang back upon the beach startled. "My, my. What do we have here? It appears that you are more Sironian than I have given you credit for." Her words cackled through the choppy surf. "Mind if I share your meal?" She asked slyly as she descended on James who lay there only barely alive. My body leapt into the air as a lion protecting its prey—but James was not my prey, above everything, every urge, he was my dearest friend. The impact of our bodies colliding sent us both a good twenty yards into the surf.

I reached down and within a fraction of a second, tore the bottom of my gown free. The fresh essence that ran through my veins made me stronger than I ever imagined—stronger than Maris, stronger than anyone I had ever known. Maris knew it too and fought to get to James to retrieve what was left of him, only then could she become strong enough to defeat me. Our bodies were sent tumbling together into the surf. She broke free, and for a brief second, I thought she was looking for an escape. But Maris caught sight of my necklace, and attacked again, tearing it from my body and throwing it far into the dark surf. I let out a bloodcurdling yell, as the pain of losing this treasure was by far more painful than any blow. I became the monster.

With the break of a large incoming wave I hurled myself through the air catching her by the head. She flipped me through the surf, but I kept hold of her as she thrashed and snarled. She growled a deafening roar that echoed above the bursting waves.

Her monstrous mouth opened so wide it appeared her face split in two. There was no human façade left, no beauty; she was a demon from the sea, a creature I could not even create in my darkest of dreams. The teeth that rose from her mouth were as long and sharp as daggers that tore deep into my right shoulder. I roared with a pain unlike any that I had ever felt. I felt as if my bone and flesh was being torn from my body.

I hissed. My right fist slammed into her face despite the dagger like teeth that remained deep in my flesh, and I grasped hold of her lower jaw. My left arm snaked out and grabbed her upper jaw. If only I could pry her jaws from my shoulder, I could make it back to the shore. My muscles bunched as my new found strength surged through my arms and body. One thought burned through my mind. *Get off of me!* The largest wave I had ever seen struck us from behind. My body twisted and turned over and over through the surf.

It was then that I saw the glowing green eyes that were coming toward me—from every direction it seemed. I had to get to the surface— to the beach quickly. I started to paddle, realizing that I still clutched something in my hands. The glowing eyes became brighter and seeing a faint glimmer of moonlight, I quickly fought to the surface. Then using the force of another oncoming large wave, I flew off of its crest through the air and rolled onto the shore just as a multitude of arms reached out for me. It wasn't until I reached the shore that I realized what I was clutching. Hanging from my cut and bloodied hands was the remains of Maris' severed head. I quickly cast it back into the dark current.

I grabbed the unconscious James under the arms and pulled him from the water's edge. I looked out over the water at the hundreds, maybe even thousands of glowing eyes that shone just below the water's surface, and then through the darkness made out the lifeless corpse of Maris rolling in the surf just before it slipped beneath the waves.

I instantly felt James' neck for a pulse. His pulse was weak, but his heart was still beating. *Thank God! I had not killed him.* I scooped my friend up and headed quickly towards the dunes. I had yet to make it over the dunes when I saw his face coming toward me. I closed my teary eyes and reopened them unsure if my mind was playing tricks on me. Could it really be William's concerned face coming towards me, or had Maris finished me off in the waves? His face would be my heaven. He was at my side in less than a second. I stood motionless. I was shaking from the adrenaline still pumping through me, shaking in fear at the possibility that I had cost my dearest friend his life, but mainly shaking with elation that William had returned to me.

"You're here." I muttered, barely audible through my tears.

"Protector or not—I couldn't leave you." He said in a low voice. "Are you alright?' He asked, his face twisted in what seemed like a combination of confusion, concern, and guilt.

"I think so, but I am a bit in shock right now. It was Maris." My voice cracked as I spoke her name. But through it all, I wanted to wrap my arms around him as the tears of joy streamed down my face.

"Let's get the two of you out of here quickly."

"I'm glad you came." My words seemed out of place as if he was arriving at a dinner party. He looked down at James in my arm and took him from me.

"Is he still alive?" He asked reaching to check his pulse.

"Just barely." I said suddenly realizing that I was going to have to tell William what happened.

"Looks like you saved him from Maris just in time."

"It wasn't Maris. It was me." The words that came from my mouth next were a complete jumbled mess. A hodge-podge of "he kissed me…I tried to stop him…then I couldn't stop…I almost killed him…but then Maris tried to kill him…and so I had to kill her." William somehow seemed to pick out enough of the pieces to understand. His incredulous look shone like a beacon through the darkness.

"You killed Maris? My god! How did you ever kill Maris?"

"I think I ripped her head off." I said with a sheepish expression, unsure if I should be proud or horrified from the brutality of the act. William was speechless.

"I'm pretty strong right now...I think." I said glancing over with a tremendous look of guilt towards the limp boy at my feet.

"The blood isn't his?" It was the first time I had noticed it. It was impossible to see the dark bloodstains on his suit, or my wet red dress, but James' white tuxedo shirt was glistening red with blood—my blood.

"Margo, this looks serious. You are hurt pretty badly! We have to get you out of here!" He looked over at my shoulder as we made our way over the dunes to his parked truck. Through the lamplights I could see my shoulder for the first time. Several jagged broken pieces of Maris' sharp dagger-like fangs still remained buried deep in my shoulder. "I need to get you to Knoxx Point and find the others." I had never heard him ask for the crew's help before, and so I knew something unprecedented was on the horizon.

"But James needs to get to a hospital!" I protested.

'You both need medical attention, but a hospital cannot help either of you. Could a hospital help when I did this to you?"

"No, but I didn't know this could happen with me. I didn't know I was capable of this."

"I didn't either." He admitted as he hoisted my bloodstained prom date into the passenger's seat of his truck. "I didn't either...."

27

———

"The fear of death follows from the fear of life. A man who lives fully is prepared to die at any time."

Mark Twain

I **insisted on stopping** to pick up Caleb on the way to Knoxx Point. James was still unconscious but appeared to be stable. The weather on the other hand was more of a cause for immediate concern. The hurricane now seemed to be blowing in at an alarming rate. It wasn't supposed to make landfall until late tomorrow night, but even from the truck window I could see that the aggressiveness of the waves had eaten away much of the dunes protecting the houses on the Garden City peninsula. It took Caleb only moments to lock the doors to the Inlet Joy and jump in the back of the truck. As William was starting the truck, Caleb held his head through the back window.

"So how was the prom?" He asked as he spied my ripped dress, unconscious prom date, and the blood stained makeshift bandages William had wrapped around my shoulder.

"Music was good," I replied returning his sarcasm, before shutting the glass.

William carried James inside, putting him in one of the downstairs bedrooms just off of the living room. Sadie supplied him with remedies similar as to what she had given to me but admitted that she was unsure of their effectiveness on a human. I quietly prayed for any signs of improvement, but no one really knew a definite outcome. It would take time for James to heal, much more time than it had taken for me to recover. My insides both reeled with guilt of what I had done to my best friend but also with joy each time I realized William was here—with me.

I slipped out of what was left of the beautiful dress and into some jeans, a black tank top, and my boots that Caleb had been thoughtful enough to grab from the Inlet Joy before he left. Thankful as I was to be back in my own clothes, I was mortified at the ruined condition of the gown that had once belonged to William's mother.

Henry managed to get a call to Silas just before the phone and power lines went down from the wind that was now howling out of control. He made the journey across the inlet to Knoxx Point in just a matter of minutes. "The storm is coming in too fast. It's unnatural. At this rate, it will make landfall in the early morning hours," Silas explained as he ushered me into the kitchen to stich up my bleeding shoulder. The concern was evident on Sadie's face. They were coming.

Little Olivia sat quietly crouched on the floor with her favorite doll for comfort. "Sadie, we will be fine here. You need to get Olivia out of here while the roads are still drivable. If Theron's Legion is coming, you need to get her as far away as possible." I exclaimed.

"Olivia is Sironian, Marguerite. She can't travel inland any longer than you can." Sadie said as she scurried around getting Silas the supplies he needs to dress my wound.

"What about the quarry? It's a bit further inland and the brackish water should be able to sustain Sironian life."

"There is no way they could get there." William interjected. "With all of this wind, it would be too dangerous to put them on the road out there. The place is surrounded by trees. Not to mention, there is no shelter on the premises." He watched Silas pull out a three-inch piece of tooth from my shoulder blade and begin to sew up the muscle and surrounding tissues. He had given me a shot to numb the pain, but it couldn't remove the discomfort altogether. I grimaced.

"But there has to be a way to get her to safety!" I protested.

"The worst of the storm is still expected a good bit north of here. Sure, we may get some damage, but she will be safe with all of us here."

Henry wiped his brow, unsure of his own words. Silas addressed his old friend.

"The hurricane has been upgraded to a category five, and I believe that it will strike near here. We truly don't have much time as the entire peninsula is now under a mandatory evacuation. I think if you leave now, you could at least get to a shelter in time. Henry, take your family. This is more than just a hurricane. We have kept your child hidden from Theron for many years now, and I don't want anything to risk her safety." The family quickly began to pack a small bag.

"Theron? What would the hurricane have to do with him?" Caleb asked.

"Theron is very powerful. He couldn't *create* a hurricane of this size but he, along with his Legion, could strengthen it and redirect it somewhat if they desired to do so."

"How is that even possible?" he asked dumbfounded. Another stich was put into place. This time the pain was so intense that I audibly groaned. William leapt to his feet, visibly upset at the pain I was enduring.

"So sorry my dear. You are such a brave girl." He said his soft hands rubbing my arm. William responded to my question this time.

"Theron surrounds himself with quite an arsenal of highly gifted Sironians—his Legion. Their linages, or abilities if you will, have developed over the course of millenniums. Just as some humans are especially gifted in athletics or art, there are Sironians that have developed gifts that to you would seem supernatural. To us, they are simply part of life. These lineages, or abilities, are passed on to the children of these individuals. In some cases, children have even developed new hybrid abilities that combine the abilities of the parents. Theron practically has an army of these Sironians, which our people call his Legion.

Some have the ability to control the wind. There is also a lineage that is able to create precipitation, rain, snow, even ice. There is a lineage that controls the currents, the pressure systems, tides, even the sea life." I thought of Lucy. She seemed to have this gift developing, but as we were of the same lineage and I did not seem to have such a gift, William's assessment seemed to be missing something.

"What of Theron? What gifts does he have?" Caleb asked, now very interested in everything Sironian.

"As his lineage goes back to Siron, the very first of our kind, most of the gifts of each sect are still alive within him. He is very powerful. But it takes his Legion, and many of his sects joined together, to create a storm this size and magnitude."

"Surely they couldn't have created this super storm just to come after me?" I asked sheepishly.

"I have been speculating for a few days that it was sent in our direction as a warning, as a way to try to scare us into turning you over to him. But I think it has become something more than that. You see, a hurricane could be the only possible cover they could use to hide an attack against a sect of our size. The area is too heavily populated with humans, so they would need a total evacuation to assure their presence would not be discovered. In the past few hours, as the storm has grown immensely and is moving towards us more rapidly, I believe they are coming…soon and with a tremendous force."

"I can't pose such a threat to him! I am just one girl! Why would he send an army after one girl?" I asked as a shiver went down my spine.

"Isn't it obvious, dear? Revenge," he said as he removed the last piece of Maris' tooth from my shoulder. "You killed Maris tonight."

Sadie, Henry, and Olivia took my Jeep and headed to a makeshift shelter at the new Socastee High School. Sadie promised she would call both my family and James' to let them know we were all safe and in a near-by shelter without phone access. I knew she would complete the task for me despite the obstacles, and at least it would provide our families with a small bit of comfort. Aside from William's truck, my Jeep was the sturdiest vehicle; it should be able to make it through most of the downed debris along the way.

The remainder of the crew joined us within the hour. They all huddled around a weather radio at the kitchen table for the latest updates on the storm, and Silas filled them in on what he now believed was the motivation behind the pending attack. They were all as shocked as I had been that I was able to kill Maris. Kirby and Tobie stood with the group ready to fight, but Mace stood off to himself deep in thought for much of the evening.

William and I had barely spoken. I was hopeful for forgiveness, as he had returned for me, but his eyes still refused to meet mine. He was hurt, angry, or both. I only hoped he would allow me a chance to explain. That is, if we made it out of this alive. As the evening wore on and the weather became unlike anything I could imagine, the gravity of the situation started to become real. My friends were all going to die because of me. I called everyone together in the living room. The rain pounded violently again the glass dome above us as we sat in silence, wondering what the early morning hours would hold.

"You are all risking everything for me simply by being here. I won't have you stay here and risk your lives for me. It doesn't have to end like this. Each of you still has a chance. I beg you head inland immediately. It is me that Theron wants. Let me face him! There is no need for you all to die for me." Caleb started to protest, but I silenced him with a disapproving look. William was the first to speak.

"I made a vow to protect you, to be your protector, when you and I were both only children. I've spent my entire life fulfilling that vow. I have lived a life preparing to meet whatever or whoever would seek to do you harm, and nothing will ever keep me from that promise." His eyes met mine for the first time all evening, but it was not the look of love I had been waiting for. His eyes burned with a fire I had never seen before, as if his very being was poised to wage war on anyone standing against him. A cold shiver ran down my spine. *May God have mercy on the soul of the man or creature that faces him tonight.*

"We stand together princess! Besides, if he takes away your pretty face, I will be stuck looking at Tobie for the rest of my life!" Tobie playfully punched Kirby hard in the arm.

"You know we aren't going to leave you to that bully Margo! We stand together!" Tobie leapt to his feet to emphasize his point. Mace remained silent for a while as we all waited nervously for his response. At last he spoke one sentence that left no doubt of where his loyalty lied.

"You are one of us. I stand with you till then end."

We all waited on edge through the night as the storm intensified. We learned that most of the area had been safely evacuated before the radio lost all reception. Both local and national stations couldn't attest to why the storm had intensified so rapidly, nor could they explain as to how the storm had shifted course so suddenly. The level five hurricanes was the largest storm to hit the southeast in over a decade. There was no denying now that it was barreling straight for us.

I sat by candlelight at James' bedside for most of the night. The rain and wind tore at the estate, threatening to rip it apart at any second, but still I couldn't leave his side. If something did happen, he would need me to take care of him, especially in this unconscious state. I buried my face in my hands. This was all my fault! Sure, he never should have tried to kiss me, but how was he to know that the girl he loved had turned into a monstrous siren that was going to try to suck the life out of him. I never should have put us in such a position in the first place! How could I ever live with myself if he died? I checked his pulse again. His seemed to be improving, though he remained unconscious. For the first time I felt the pain and guilt that William must have experienced when his lips fist touched mine, leaving me in similar state. But I had survived. All anger that I felt earlier towards him had completely vanished. Would James be angry with me if he awakens? Would he even remember? How could I ever explain?

A gently knock could barely be heard over the pounding storm. William entered the doorway, and his eyes met mine. "Can I talk to you?" The dead butterflies in my stomach began to flutter. Perhaps they were only asleep after all.

"Yes, I've wanted to talk to you as well. I joined him in the doorway, and he led me down the hallway and through the large antique doors I had so admired once before. The familiar room was lit by only a few candles, but the flicker of his eyes shown through the dimly lit flames.

"Marguerite, I…."

"Please, William, before you say another word, I want to explain about…." He tried to silence me, but I continued. "William, I only challenged you for my protectorship to give you your…."

"You don't need to justify this to me. I know why you did what you did today. Silas told me just after the challenge. I am not angry with you."

"But I looked for you. I even came *here* looking for you, but Henry said you were gone. I wondered if I would ever see you again." The memory of losing him welled inside of me and overflowed in my words. I would have cried, but there were just no tears left to fall.

"I *did* leave." He admitted softly. "I couldn't help but feel rejected. You're truly the first person I've let into my life since my parents died—the first one I've trusted enough with my heart. How could I not feel as if I were unneeded—unwanted? I thought you no longer wanted me as your protector. I thought you wanted to be free of me." I took his hand in mine. The feeling of his skin against mine brought me to life again. The water was his life force, but I knew that William was mine.

"Free of you? You may be the siren, but you've breathed the life into my soul. I would still be in the dark if you had not shown me how to paint the sun. Before I arrived the one thing you wanted most was to find your sister. How can I stand in the way of that! I don't want to be the thing holding you here."

"And I *want* you to be the thing holding me here." He brought his free hand to my face, cupping my chin into his fingers. "I realized today that I don't want happiness unless you are here to share it with me. I thought all feelings inside me had died; I thought there was nothing remaining that was capable of love, but you took the last tiny spark and turned it into a blaze. I will find my sister, but I won't leave you to do it. I can't leave you. I never had any intention of leaving you here alone to take on all of this without me."

"But you took the boat and headed south? Sadie watched you leave."

"Only to remove my boat and the most meaningful items that belonged to my family out of the path of the storm. I stopped to ask Kirby today to keep watch over you until I returned. I planned to return by the time you returned from the prom. Who would have ever imagined you would have run into so much trouble at a high school dance!"

"Trouble seems to follow me…and it looks like the worst is heading our way."

"Yes. I am not sure what the outcome will be in the morning, but I came here tonight to thank you for doing the one thing I had dreamt about since I was a boy. You killed Maris tonight."

"But I *killed* someone. I took a life—Aria's mother!"

"You killed the Sironian who took the life of my parents and maybe even the life of my sister. How could I ever repay you for what you have done?" I became silent as my thoughts swirled around me.

"I can't help but ask one thing, well two things actually. If you truly care for me, you have to do something for me."

"I love you more than love was meant to be. Don't you see, there is nothing that you could ask of me that could possibly begin to repay what you have done for me tonight!" His words were more than I could ever have dreamt, and yet, I could not be swayed from my cause. It was too important.

"You are a protector—the most skilled protector that ever existed." He inhaled as if he were preparing himself for whatever I may ask. "If there is an actual army coming tomorrow, we will undoubtedly be outnumbered. I need for you to protect Caleb and James."

"But if this comes to a fight, how could I ever leave your side?"

"I need for you to protect my family—the people I love. I can't have them die because of me. I could never live with myself."

"But I won't leave you! I can't do that!"

"Promise me!" He didn't respond. "You said *anything!*"

"Not that!"

"If you love me as you say you do, you will do this for me. Promise me that above all else you will protect Caleb and James."

"Then you are leaving me no choice." His brow furrowed and he stared into my eyes. "I will." He promised—and I knew he meant it, as William's word was his vow.

"Thank you," I replied solemnly as I put my hand on his. The closet of beautiful dresses loomed off to the side, reminding me of the gown that I had destroyed.

"I ruined your mother's dress," I said with a voice full of regret. William only smiled.

"I could think of no better use of it than to avenge her death. It somehow brings me comfort to know that part of her was out there in the surf with you."

"I think she was." I responded softly. William turned away and quickly wiped his eyes. He had been tough for so long that I was a little relieved that his eyes were still capable of tears.

"Well, you proved tonight that you were right. You no longer need me as your protector." I began to protest, but he pressed his finger to my lips. "It's true." He whispered.

"But I *want* you." It was the only thing I knew to say.

He slid his hand around my waist and pulled me to him tightly, so tightly I could hardly breathe. His free hand grasp the back of my neck pulling it to his face and all of us was pressed together except for our lips that trembled to meet. If I were to die tonight, I could ask for no better death than it to be in the arms of the one that I loved. He held me like this for several minutes. It was as if we knew this could be our last moments together. If we only held each other tight enough, we could close our eyes and pretend that the world wasn't literally crumbling in around us. If love was our sword, there could be nothing strong enough to take us.

But we knew what was coming, William more so than I, and yet, I'd heard enough to know that the chances of us surviving were bleak.

The storm continued to rage on, as if to signify they were coming—it was only a matter of time. William gently touched the blood soaked bandages on my shoulder. "I will get Silas to look after James. You need to soak that shoulder as much as possible in preparation for what could be to come. You'll need all the strength inside of you, and then some." His allusion wasn't lost to me. James' aura had made me stronger; it would be greatly needed for what was heading our way. It was a bizarre unbeknown gift from my friend, but at what cost had it been taken?

William stayed by my side for several hours as the indoor tidal pool worked its magic. The glass windows had all been boarded up, but the glass ceiling told the true story of what was creeping upon us. Debris and uprooted trees and shrubs were tossed through the night sky, and the rain no longer fell as droplets, but as sheets ripping and tearing at the beautiful home. I thought it only a matter of time before it crumbled in around us all.

The crew remained quiet throughout the night. Kirby and Tobie quietly played cards at the kitchen table as Mace anxiously paced around the room like a caged lion. Caleb immersed himself in the Sironian book, ironically in the same nook that I had read it in months earlier, and Silas and I took turns taking care of James. William sat in a chair in the corner of the room watching me. He eyes rarely left me. Perhaps it was just habit as my protector, perhaps he was afraid that this night would be our last night together, or maybe he could guess at the plans that were running through my mind.

What a short time I had been given to experience love. I felt as my life truly had only recently begun and now it would surely end at sunrise. I could not have those that I loved fight and be killed for me, and so to surrender was the only way I could protect them all. I spent the last few hours before sunrise planning my own demise. I would have to find a way to leave the house at just the right time. I would have to get away *before* they arrived, and yet, not as soon as for the others to find me missing and come after me. I was sure that after my death, there would be no reason for the army to advance on the others. I had killed Maris, I had enraged Aria, and I had broken the law by merely existing. If I were out of the way, Theron would certainly pardon William in hopes that he would go ahead with the treaty to marry Aria. With Maris' death, Theron would be anxious to increase his power, and the power available to his only heir. He would need William, and William had promised to look after Caleb and James so they would be safe.

The heartbreak in my plan would be the pain my death would cause my family. My death would be easy to cover due to the storm, but the pain it would cause to my sweet Lucy, my mother and father, tore my insides apart. I would only hope that Caleb could one day tell Lucy of my sacrifice, and she could be proud to call me her sister. Maybe knowledge could somehow lessen the pain of not having me as a part of the many events of her life.

"What are they waiting for?" Tobie shouted as bits of the roof became dislodged and pulled from the rafters. Water began to trickle down the walls, but enough of the roof remained as to provide shelter—at least for a bit longer.

"They are waiting for the tide to be at its peak," responded Silas. "With a high tide on a full moon, the water will surge clear over the peninsula giving their entire army access to not only the inlet but the entire area. The entire landmass will be underwater, including this house, at which time they will be at their greatest advantage. This is the point when they are sure to attack."

"How much time do we have?"

"It is impossible to say without someone going outside, and the storm is currently at its height. We can't risk anyone leaving."

"The crow's nest!" I pointed out the large light whose beam had not shown since William's parent's death."

"It is too dangerous for anyone to go up there at this point. The entire structure could come crashing in at any moment. It has already been compromised, and it appears the left side of it has been shattered completely. It isn't worth the risk, even to know their position. The entire structure is completely made of glass. With any piece of debris it could shatter." Silas was right. There could be no more dangerous place in a storm like this than the highest point along the strand. Anyone who would dare attempt it was suffering from a death wish. I only knew of one person at Knoxx Point who had already signed their death warrant. Me.

The water started to seep under the floorboards and through the cracks of the doors just after 5 a.m. Within a few minutes the entire downstairs was submersed in over a foot of water. I knew my time was up. The roof had somehow managed to hold, and only one section of glass had been broken out from debris, but I knew the estate only had a few minutes before it was completely swallowed up by the sea.

We had no choice but to move James to an upstairs bedroom. Silas and William began the task of moving him, while the others were busy moving furniture to block all access to the main house. I saw my point of escape as all hands and eyes were otherwise occupied. I quickly made my exit toward the spiral staircase in the back of the house that led to the crow's nest. The door was locked at the top but I easily crushed the locked door knob and pushed open the door. Through the darkness, a large lamp adorned the center of the small round glass room. But Silas was correct; the left side of the structure had been smashed in completely by debris, its remnants dangling over the swelling ocean below. I held on to the right handrail as I stepped out onto the structure, unsure if it were able to support my weight. I was suddenly exposed to the elements as the combination of insane wind and torrential rain began pelting me violently. I had no thoughts of turning back. So much of what I loved remained just below me. Their survival depended on my plan.

A lightning bolt lit up the sky and for a fraction of a second I had full view of the peninsula. The shoreline no longer existed, as the surf now rolled across where the sets of houses had once been, breaking straight into the inlet. Many of the houses seemed to be ripped from their pilings, churning against each other as the waves pushed then further back into the inlet. The entire area was devastated. Another lightning strike lit up the sky; I could not see if the Inlet Joy was still standing. But I saw *them*.

There, amongst the angry water was the glow of green eyes, hundreds of them encompassed the entire area. As I looked out in all directions, the evil glow shining just below the surface and spreading out across the water for what seemed like miles. We were completely and totally surrounded. They all hung just below the water waiting for a sign to attack. There was no hope. We would all perish....

Another lightning strike gave me just enough light to find what I was looking for. I fought through the elements and crawled across the floor to where the lamp switch should be. I squinted my eyes and flipped the switch—nothing. The lamp light did not work. My heart sank. This was the only hope that I had for Theron to see me—me alone. If I could only separate myself long enough from the others for them to kill me, then maybe they could survive this. The wind whipped through the glass enclosure so hard that I knew my life could end any second. A wooden piece of debris burst through the glass narrowly missing me. I flipped the switch again—William said that it hadn't been used since his parent's death, and it was possible that it did not work at all. I wrapped both arms around the bulb that was as larger as my head and firmly twisted it tighter in the socket.

The beam of light that beaconed from the tower momentarily blinded me, sending me stumbling backwards towards the tarnished broken handrail. The light cut through the storm and illuminated the dome. It would only take my friends seconds now to realize my plan. I hurled myself through the broken glass and onto the ledge. The bodies of the submerged Sironian began moving closer towards the light, a sure sign that they had indeed seen me. I roared through the darkness. My voice carried through the rain and over the wind.

"Theron! It is I—Marguerite Westly. I am the one you have come for." And as if by some miracle, the sky seemed to open up and the rain and winds began to cease. We were in the eye of the storm. The sun had yet to rise, but a gentle glow could be seen through the devastation just along the horizon. I wondered if this was the moment they had been waiting for—the eye of the storm.

They rose up from the water, each face more beautiful and evil than the next, but unlike my friends, their faces were as white as snow as these creatures lived deep within the water, far from the warming rays of the sun. A large wave arose and at its peak parted to reveal a man that needed no introduction.

Theron was like a fine work of art, but no more beautiful than William. He appeared ageless as if he could be twenty or fifty. It was impossible to tell, but I knew from the book that he could have been alive for a millennium. His bronze hair was cropped short, and he could have more easily been mistaken for some statute of a Greek god, rather than the ruler of an underwater empire. Aria rose up behind him, but in her face I did not see the anger and jealousy that she had possessed when she left. Her face appeared twisted with pain and regret. It was too late. Whatever she had done, whatever she had said, it was too late for all of us.

"You are the hybrid girl that killed Maris?"

"Yes." I responded as he moved closer, the wave that carried him rising higher towards the crow's nest. "She had come to kill me and my friend. I had no choice."

"And yet, you have chosen to face me." He seemed puzzled.

"I have." Through his anger he seemed amused by my presence.

"You are foolish to think that you can defeat me and my army—alone?"

"No. I cannot defeat you. Nor do I wish to try. I only ask that you take me and leave my friends and this area in peace." He appeared to be amused and impressed by my words.

"You are willing to give your life in this way?"

"I am." He seemed to contemplate my fate as one would contemplate what their next meal would be.

"You are an abomination of nature, and your existence violates our very laws. Who is the siren that is responsible for your existence?"

"I do not know." Theron turned to one of the Sironians in his army—a dark complexioned male with hair cropped very short.

"Darion?" He quickly responded.

"She tells the truth." He replied.

"And your father is Sironian?"

"The gene did not awaken within him. He lives solely as a human away from the coast." Theron turned back to his advisor who once again validated the truth of my statement.

"Such a situation is something that I never deemed possible."

I knew William and the crew had to be near, had to know what was going on, and yet they did not appear. Were they waiting to attack or would they let me follow through with my plan and let him take me in peace.

"And yet I exist."

"Yes, you do. When did your change occur?"

"Only a few months ago."

"And your abilities?"

"Fairly divided between both human and Sironian."

"I think you must downplay your talents, dear girl. Just yesterday you defeated one of the most powerful of sirens—my once daughter-in-law and one of the leaders of my Legion."

"I am sorry for your loss," I replied flatly.

"Are you? How could a single girl with mixed abilities defeat such strength?"

"I had just consumed a human." The shock on Theron's face was immense. He once again turned to his advisor for verification. He nodded. Theron burst out in low malevolent laughter that echoed through the night sky.

"How ever did your protector friends feel about you taking a human life?"

"I didn't take the life—the boy lives."

"Impossible."

"She tells the truth," responded his advisor Darion. Theron shot him a disapproving look for speaking.

"However did you do such a thing?"

"He was my friend. It was an accident. I did not wish to kill him."

"It should have been impossible for you to stop the transfer once it began."

"Maybe not if you truly care about the person."

"My, my; you do leave us with much to think about. How sad that your life must end here. But your kind is an abomination. The species cannot intertwine. I once thought it impossible, and yet, here you stand to prove me wrong. I might have even let you live—had you not killed Maris. He turned to another one of the Sironians that hovered near him.

"Zander." Theron said in a monotone voice motioning towards me. I had no time to realize this would be the end of me, as in an instant a bolt of lightning descended from the sky. I instinctively threw myself out of the way as the bolt struck the beacon crushing the structure on which I was standing. As I tumbled downward amongst the shattered glass and debris, I caught hold of the power supply line for the lamp that dangled flashing just below me. I held on tight waiting to die.

Mace appeared, leaping from what was left of the crow's nest toward the siren that produced the bolt. With a wave of Mace's hand, the siren was swallowed up by a swell that carried him swiftly out to sea. I had been told that Mace could direct the ocean's currents and movements but had never seen his talent in use. Another siren rose to take the place of the first. Raising his arm, a gust of wind swept across me so hard that the very beams of remains of the crow's nest began to rip apart. I dangled, and had I not the strength that I had stolen from James I would have been unable to withstand the force. Mace quickly pulled a dousie bow from his back and almost faster than my eye could follow fired an arrow that pierced the new siren's forehead.

The army seemed to swallow Mace as it attacked, but Tobie and Kirby were suddenly there diving through the surf to his aid. My friends, these young "protectors," stood as unmovable warriors as wave after wave of the Sironian army broke against their position. As I dangled, holding on for my very life, I watched as the ranks of Sironians tore themselves apart against the deadly wedge formed by Mace, Kirby, and Tobie. The Sironians attacked them from all sides, weapons raging, and surf churning, as the three stood back to back. But there was no end to the army Theron had brought to do his bidding. My friends stood doomed as there was no way to defeat them all. It was only a matter of time.

I knew their time was running out, and if I was to help them, I had to act now. I dropped from my perch, diving through the waves into the very midst of Theron's warriors. As I hovered at the surface, they surged toward me. The beautiful faces I had seen from afar were replaced by the faces of the monsters of my nightmares, but I was too strong for those who attacked. Still infused with James' essence I overpowered and battered the few foolish enough to come within my grasp. The remainder circled, as if they were waiting, content to hold me in place.

And then like some dark magic, they rose up around me—no less than a hundred of them in a circular formation. Their faces were that of mystic beauty, but there was no mistaking that I was staring at the faces of death. My legs, burning from the exertion, tiredly treaded water as those around me appeared to float along the top of the sea. They were submerged from the waist down, and yet their upper bodies did not move at all. Then all at once, they moved to attack.

"Dive Marguerite! Dive deep! As swiftly and as deep as you possibly can. Don't stop! Dive! Dive deep!" I could hear William's voice ringing through the air. I knew that once I made any movement, they would all be on me. I had to be so swift even those whose bodies were designed to be the fastest swimmers in the sea couldn't catch me. I knew that if I thought about it at all, I would fail. I had to rely on the creature inside of me....

Like a bolt of lightning I plunged as far and as fast as I could to the depths below, not realizing that William dove into the water, fighting off no less than twenty sirens, to make it to my side. He grabbed my hand, and we shot through the surf so far and so fast that we had traveled nearly a mile before we realized that the water behind us had become unnaturally still. We stopped and surfaced quickly to discover the reason

At a distance Mace stood on a tiny sandbar near what was left of Knoxx Point. In the battle he had somehow taken hold of Aria, the girl he once thought of as a sister, and now held her head firmly between his hands as if he could snap her neck with the slightest of moves. Theron's forces hovered around them in a circle, waiting for some indication as to what they should do. Theron could not risk losing his sole remaining heir.

"No. Mace!" William shouted across the water. Mace held Aria's life in his hands. In an instant William and I traveled to a stretch of sand some thirty yards away from where Mace held Aria captive.

"You tell us how this is going to end Theron," William said to him as the standoff ensued. "Clearly you have us outnumbered. But surely you would not want to lose the life of your granddaughter, for the life of this hybrid girl."

"The girl killed Maris," he growled.

"And Maris killed my parents." William responded unable to hide the pain in his voice. "Will the killing ever end? How many of your men have you already lost here tonight? For what reason? Revenge? Is there not some other way to end this with honor?"

"Honor? Your life was once spared for a treaty that you now refuse to *honor,*" Theron spat.

"I was a boy, how could I agree to a marriage contract that was made in my name. I never agreed to any of it."

Silas appeared onto what was left of the ledge that once housed the crow's nest and light. "I was wrong to make that treaty on his behalf. I only agreed to it in an attempt to have the boy's life spared, he cannot be held responsible for it now that he is an adult and capable of making his own decisions.

"Silas! Hello old friend. It has been many years, has it not?" His greeting to Silas was both gallant and insincere. And yet, through it I could sense the respect and fear he held for Silas.

"It has, and now you come to spill the blood to those you have entrusted to me."

"It appears that you have turned my own soldiers against me."

"I have done nothing of the sort. Even Aria can attest to that. They only fight to protect the lives of humans, and this girl qualifies as a life worth protecting."

"Her existence breaks our law."

"The one who created her is to blame, not this girl. He is the one who should be brought to justice."

"Bring him before me then. I will take *his* life and spare the life of this girl. Oh yes…you cannot do that can you, because no one will reveal his identity. I will not continue to risk the existence of this abomination."

"I say, how could we destroy something so unique? I have seen no one that parallels the strengths of this girl. She learns quickly and seems to pick up on the skills of those around her at an unparalleled pace. Why destroy something that could be of such benefit to our kind?" Silas said. I knew what he was doing. He was making a deal to save my life just as he had once done for William. He was appealing to Theron's lust for power, making me sound of value to him.

"I can see you may have a point. You are correct that too much blood has been shed tonight." He turned again to William. "You seem to harbor some fondness for this girl. I admit—she is quite intriguing. If I were to offer you the treaty once again, for you to marry my heir—my granddaughter, in exchange for this hybrid's life, would you agree?"

"And you would spare the girl's life."

"I would."

"I will agree to marry your granddaughter Theron. On a day no less than two years from today, if you assure me that Marguerite will come to no harm and she will remain in Silas' care indefinitely. She is also to be free to safely swim within the inlets and sea without harm."

"Agreed…but under one condition. This girl is to take the place of the one she destroyed in my Legion. She will spend three months with me each year, three months in training for the position she will ultimately take when I feel she is ready."

"We will not agree to that!" William spat out immediately.

"I agree to it." I replied. I was still in shock that the one person on this earth that I had ever loved had just agreed to marry someone else. I may as well be dead, but at least William would live. I would make whatever sacrifices I had to make at this point; it didn't matter. "Mace, let Aria go." As he released her, she turned to him with a look of both hurt and anger before retreating into the sea.

"It is agreed. William will marry my heir, and you will join my Legion." We both nodded our agreement to this new treaty, and with that acceptance a bolt of energy sprang from his hand and his crest was painfully etched on the inside of our wrist to signify the agreement. We both grimaced in pain. The mark was a pale tone that could only be seen as the shimmer of a fish scale if the light hit it just right. But this symbol marked us as Theron's, as his entire Legion was marked with the same crest.

The eye wall of the storm finally began to pass, and the hurricane's full force began to once again beat down on the shoreline.

"We have agreed to your treaty Theron. Will you now continue to destroy our coast?" Silas roared.

"Even I cannot undo a storm of this magnitude, but I will quickly push it inland. It should lose force when it reaches land. This will at least leave you with a coast that can be rebuilt. And let me remind you of the penalty for not honoring the agreements we have made here today."

"We honor our treaties, just as I know you will hold true to yours."

"Above all." He said gallantly. "Best wishes. You all might want to head indoors; it appears we are having a spell of bad weather." His words echoed as he once again glided back into the sea. We all stood there in silence for a moment as what remained of the army retreated behind him. The strength of the storm was upon us once again in full force. The crew immediately sought to cover the hole left from the destruction of the crow's nest. I wanted to help, but Silas quickly ushered me back inside.

I was relieved to find James secure and well in his bed, but my heart sank as I realized Caleb had not been seen since before the incident. I frantically began looking for him. Muffled cries came from down the hall and I realized that they were coming from a locked closet. I easily crushed the knob with my hand to find my brother locked inside.

"Oh my gosh! Caleb! What are you doing in here?" He instantly threw his arms around me.

"You're alive!" He gasped.

"Yes. We all are, if we can make it through the remainder of this storm."

"When we saw the beacon light through the dome, we all guessed what you were doing. Kirby and Tobie immediately ran to stop you; I wanted to go to, but William locked me away in here. Why the heck would he do that?"

"Because they would have killed you for sure…and because I made him promise me to keep you safe."

Everyone was once again pretty quiet as the hurricane continued throughout the morning hours. We had survived, but my heart had been shattered in the process. William was to marry Aria after all. I stared at him from across the room, but this time, he refused to make eye contact with me. The pain was almost unbearable, but at least in the silence, we no longer had to say all the things that neither of us had the heart to hear.

The final phase of the hurricane did not continue up the coast as projected but went inland as promised by Theron. Sadly it didn't lose much of its strength and caused massive destruction as it moved slowly across the state. I had survived. My family had survived. The person I was in love with had survived. My heart had not.

28

"Come away, O human child! To the waters and the wild with a faery, hand in hand, for the world's more full of weeping than you can understand."

W.B. Yeats

T he crew helped to transport James to the hospital as soon as the storm had passed enough that it was safe enough to risk travel. Parts of the garage at Knoxx Point had collapsed onto William's truck, and the entire road had been washed out, so the crew and I had to take James by boat across the inlet to Silas' house, and then take Silas' vehicle to the hospital. We all knew that the hospital would offer little cure for him, but he needed the nourishment an IV could provide. We came up with a halfway believable cover story, as we were sure his family was already frantically looking for him. We decided that the most likely story would be that he was accidently shocked by a downed power line during the storm. It seemed plausible enough.

I tried to find the Inlet Joy from across the waterway, but it was impossible to tell if it were still standing. I had to admit that the chances were slim, as it seemed as if most of the houses of the peninsula had been washed from their pilings and pushed back into the inlet or into each other and torn apart. The devastation was almost unbearable. It paralleled the devastation I felt inside. I had been unable to even look at William since the treaty. No words could undo the promises made; no tears could take back the inevitable. We had walked away with our lives, but not each other. I was bound to Theron's Legion and William to Aria.

The phone lines were down for most of the morning but the hospital was somehow able to get through to James' parents who quickly rushed to his bedside. Amy was with them and continuously fussed over him. I stayed until I could take no more of her. But as I went to leave, I was unsure of where to go. Where was my home now? It couldn't be with William; whatever we felt for each other had to be forgotten, as he was betrothed to another. *I would have to find a way to let him go.* My home couldn't be in Florence, as I was too much of a Sironian to ever try to leave the coast. And the Inlet Joy? Was it even still standing? Caleb seemed to read my thoughts. "We will get through this. Our home is together. Wherever we're together…that's our home."

"What are you, Sironian? You can read my thoughts now?" I asked staring at my little brother.

He laughed, "Gosh I hope not, I am hoping for a much cooler super ability than mindreading! Maybe eyes that shoot sonic beams or…." As if by magic a familiar car pulled into the hospital parking lot and four familiar faces were coming towards us. It was my family. I turned to Caleb.

"The hospital was able to get through for me, and I was able to tell them we were here."

"How did you make it here?" I gasped, surprised that my parents could make it through the downed trees and power lines that seemed to be everywhere.

"There isn't a storm big enough to keep me from my children!" My mother gasped as she put both Caleb and I in a giant bear hug. Lucy tugged at my damp jeans, as I scooped her into the embrace.

We drove as far as Sam's corner before the road was completely washed away. The National Guard had blocked off the entire area and was only allowing residents to enter. My mouth hung open as I viewed the hangout that James and I had once loved. Sam's Corner was twisted and torn almost to pieces. The games and pool tables were now completely destroyed. I reached down and pulled a red pool ball from out of the sand and with a tear stuffed it into my pocket. I had lost William, would I now lose James too?

My grandmother took my hand and with tears streaming down her face we began the walk to see what remained of the Inlet Joy. Collapsed power lines now adorned the path where the road once stood, a road that was now buried under four feet of sand. Houses rested on their sides ripped open, some so carefully displaced by the current that the plates and pictures still hung on the walls, and yet, virtually nothing was still intact. The tears ran down my grandmother's cheeks as we completed the remainder of the mile expecting the worse. The closer we came the more our hopes began to soar as the blue house appeared to stand in the distance. Its saving grace seemed to be the concrete pilings my grandfather had built beneath it.

Both the front and back steps had been lost, and the breakaway storage walls and down stairs shower were destroyed, but the main part of the house had withstood all that had been thrown at it. As if by miracle, all of the contents of the upstairs and my room remained safe and in place.

My mother tried to insist that my grandmother and I return to Florence with them, but my father knew that it wasn't an option, and so when we protested, he was able to convince my mother that the house was structurally sound enough for us to remain with the property. The National Guard did not agree, however, so we spent the next week in a nearby hotel, traveling to the house each day to begin repairs and cleanup. It would be a long time before the Inlet Joy would be officially restored, and an even longer time before the peninsula would get back on its feet again.

I checked on James at the hospital each day, and on the third day he began to regain consciousness. It was a tiny boost to my shattered heart; at least one piece of it would survive. "They said something about me getting shocked by a downed power line when we were leaving the prom?"

"Yeah. You're lucky to be alive you know. I said taking his hand in mine. What is the last thing you remember?"

"I remember we had a fight, and then we were kissing, and then...."

"Ok. Slow down Romeo! You really are dreaming now! You must have had too many volts to the brain." I said laughing.

"No kissing?" He smirked as he pulled away the oxygen tube from his face.

"Not by a long shot! You were pretty much ignoring me throughout the entire prom because you had to take pictures, and I was having a pretty rotten time. So I asked you if we could go, but the wind had picked up and knocked over a power line that you didn't see in the dark and accidently stepped on it. I thought it had killed you!"

"Gosh darlin'. I am sorry. So I was a pretty bad prom date?" I nodded and laughed. "And you didn't have a good time." He grimaced. I grinned.

"You have no idea." I smirked.

"Well, crap! I guess I'll have to make it up to you," he said trying to get out of the hospital bed.

"Alright you!" I said helping him back into the hospital bed. "There will be plenty of time for you to make it up to me—once you are well!"

"Plenty of time? He asked in his usually flirtatious manner.

"It may take forever actually!" I said with a smile.

****

It had been two weeks with no sign or word from William. I ached over the loss of him. I had given up trying *not* to think of him and tried to keep myself busy for the main part of the day. I spent most nights crying myself to sleep. My boat was destroyed in the storm, so inlet travel was out of the question, and the phone lines were down, so that was completely out. He was near, I could feel it, but I just couldn't get up the courage to drive to Knoxx Point. Why torture myself any further? Even if he felt as I did, the relationship was impossible. He would belong to someone else, and I knew him well enough that he would honor his word no matter what.

It was a warm bright spring day when like a mirage he pulled up to what was left of the dock, in a beautiful wooden boat very much like the one he owned. I could barely catch my breath at the sight of him as he was still more beautiful than I could imagine in my dreams. I stood frozen tightly gripping the shovel I had been using to scrape the sand off of the drive just moments before. He strode across the lot in silence. My heart had stopped altogether. Why had he come? In an instant he was close enough for me to smell the soft scent of his skin.

"Hello," he said looking into my eyes for the first time since we had made the treaty with Theron.

"Hello," I repeated, a bit unsure if any sound had even managed to escape my lips.

"I need to talk to you. It is very important." His eyes squinted against the bright sunlight.

"Alright," I muttered, not wanting to blink as I was afraid he would disappear.

"Do you mind if we go somewhere private?"

"Ok," I said, following next to him as he began walking back toward the inlet. The floating dock had been washed away by the storm, but parts of the pier remained. He helped me into a beautiful boat that was waiting for me.

"I made this for you."

"What?" I asked confused.

"This boat. I made it for you and was planning to give it to you before the storm hit."

"You made this for me?" I asked unable to hide the surprise in my voice.

"Yes. Do you mind if we take it out?"

"It's beautiful." I said my hands beginning to tremble, as I stepped into the hand crafted vessel.

He started down the canal at a pretty slow pace. The inlet was now littered with everything from washers and driers to an actual kitchen sink. I wondered how it could ever once again regain a fraction of what it once had been before the storm.

He watched me as he maneuvered the small boat through the debris-filled water. I couldn't help but watch him as well, studying the lines of his face and the shape of his hands with care, for I knew now that this moment may be the last time I ever get to see him.

He pulled up to the point and helped me out of the boat. Knoxx Point could just be seen over the canal.

"I see Knoxx Point is still standing."

"It is. Thanks to you. Henry and Sadie are immersed in repair work as we speak.

"And Olivia?"

"She is doing well. She asks about you a lot. She misses you." I smiled despite myself. "And I miss you," he said taking my hand in his, as his eyes bore into mine with an intensity I wasn't prepared for. I slowly pulled my hand from his. All of the tears that I had been storing up began to roll down my face uncontrollably. His eyes had haunted my restless sleep, and the feel of his skin against mine was all I could feel each time I closed my eyes.

"You can't do this to me," I pleaded. "You don't belong to me. You can never belong to me now. I can't do this William! I can't!" He gently pulled back from me, but only far enough to brush away my tears. He again pulled me tight to his chest. I needed to pull away from him, but I couldn't. I didn't want to. The smell of his skin made it impossible, as I only wanted to be closer to him.

"I have been staying away these past two weeks in an attempt to find the right words to say, but I've realized that there aren't any, so let me just begin with telling you 'Thank You' for your sacrifice. If you had not done what you did, none of us would have survived."

"We have all sacrificed," I responded through my tears. "Your sacrifice kept me alive. I only wish that the cost had not been so great." I buried my head in his chest. The smell of his skin still made me feel intoxicated, even through my misery. I remembered the scent of Caleb's skin when I said goodbye to him before leaving Florence; I would now make a memory of the smell of William's skin. I closed my eyes to try to remember every essence of him, but he tilted my chin towards him.

"But you see. I didn't have to sacrifice at all." He pulled me back only far enough to see his face. "I knew exactly what I was promising in that treaty. It was something that I have wanted for many months now." His words were like daggers to me. I thought it impossible to hurt more than I had over the past two weeks, but his words proved me wrong.

"If you knew you wanted Aria, then why let things continue on with me," I said trying to pull away. He didn't let me go.

"I don't mean Aria. I have never loved Aria—only you. There has never been anyone but you."

"I don't understand. The treaty?"

"If you remember, I specifically agreed to marry his granddaughter— his heir." My mind became confused as I tried to fully grasp his words. "His heir is you—it's *you*. Theron is *your* grandfather, and *you* are his closest heir, not Aria."

"Impossible!" I gasp, as the impact of his words struck me motionless.

"We have all suspected it for quite some time. I am surprised you haven't picked up on how Kirby is always calling you princess."

"It can' be true!" I protested.

"I assure you I speak the truth. I found him still weak, but at least somewhat alert. Why do you think I resented you so? I thought of you as the granddaughter of the man responsible for the death of my family. I wanted nothing to do with you. But when I was bound to you—as your protector, as I watched over you, and then as I got to know you, I found myself falling more and more in love with you each day."

"But I can't be Theron's granddaughter!"

"It was Theron who deceived your grandmother and left her to die; only his seed could have been strong enough to create life with a human. And Silas confirmed it when he came after me, after you challenged me. Aaron Theron, the one who was once Silas' best friend. He became jealous of Silas' love for your grandmother. He purposely kept them apart and made her think he wasn't returning, and then seduced her to steal the one thing he thought he couldn't have."

"You knew this when you made the treaty?"

"I did."

"To save my life?"

"I would have agreed to anything to spare your life, but I could only ever agree to spend my life with the person I love…and that is you." He reached into his pocket and slipped my missing necklace back around my neck. The small slivery shell fell once again against my heart where it belonged.

"How did you find this?" I gasped.

"It was no easy feat, I can assure you, even for a Sironian, but I had to find it before returning to you. Another reason for my absence these two weeks. I know now, that my world will never be complete, without you." I pulled him tight against me, weeping tears for a dream I never dared to imagine.

"But wait!" I said suddenly pulling away. "Theron will one day *have* to know the truth. He will also at some point come for me as I had promised to be part of his Legion—and Aria! How angry she will be if she learns I am Theron's heir and that you have actually agreed to marry me?" It all rushed at me at once and my head began to spin.

"I cannot tell you that your life from this point forward is going to be easy." He said as he brushed his lips gently against my forehead. "And I cannot tell you that you will not face unparalleled obstacles. But what I do promise you is that you will not have to face them alone. I'm here as long as you want me."

"That will be a very long time." I admitted as I opened my eyes to the whole new world that was suddenly before me.

Across the waterway a couple could be seen walking along the shore together near Knoxx Point. Sadie and Henry, I thought, but my eyes narrowed to see Silas walking along the shore next to my grandmother. I smiled, too overjoyed to speak. No, life was not going to be easy, and I knew our biggest challenges may be yet to come. I wouldn't go back to the girl I once was, even if I could. Whatever challenges came our way, William and I would face them together.

His fingers gently caressed my face as he tilted my chin towards him.

"Now hold still." He said pulling my face to his.

"Are you trying to kill me?" I asked. I wanted his lips against mine so badly that death may be worth it.

"You have faced death quite a few times here lately and lived to tell about it, I think my kiss should be pretty low on the list. When my lips meet yours, just draw me in as you did James, and with that, his lips pressed against mine, first softly then with an intensity that was more than I could have imagined. As his lips moved against mine, I saw the girl I had once been transformed into the creature I had now fully become. All previous insecurities had vanished, all doubts erased. I could not help but to draw his essence into me, as I knew he had stolen mine. He pulled away.

"How did you do that?" I asked, trying to draw him to me for more. He laughed.

"Just a theory. I will explain it to you later. We will have plenty of time for practice. There is something else I need to show you." He said slipping off his shoes, then bending to slip mine off as well."

"What is it?" I asked still mesmerized from his kiss.

"Well, you *are* a princess. I think it is about time I show you your kingdom."

And with that, he took my hand—and together we slipped under the cool dark water.

ACKNOWLEDGEMENTS

There truly aren't words to describe my gratitude for the support and sacrifice my family has made during the years it has taken me to complete this novel. Had I known how much you would have to share me with the Sironians, I would have never put those first words to page. This book is not just my accomplishment; it is yours as well.

Scott, for your insanity to take on all that I throw at you! Your countless hours of edits and creative inputs were invaluable! This book would have never reached completion without you! Thank you for believing in me!

My magical daughters, Madeline, Merissa, Michaela, and Mia. You are my inspiration, my joy, and my life. Never lose your childhood imagination. This big girl fairytale is for you!

My editor Rea Myers for her expertise and polishing, and to Shelley Schadowsky for preparing this work for the world of ebooks.

My Mother for believing in me, and for being the first and biggest fan of this book. My Father for your motivation when I was discouraged, and for raising a daughter who was free to follow her dreams.

This remarkable team of beta readers: Kevin Todd, Marney Boatwright, Mary Todd, Becki Poston, Scott Moise & Anna Todd whose careful eye and enthusiasm kept this work in motion.

Patricia Taylor for giving me one of her most prized possessions, her son…and for stepping up to help my girls through
life's challenges.

My supporters: Carolyn McIntyre, Lea Arnold, Margaret Baker, Sara Blumberg, Melanie and Rob Taylor. Your encouragement, love and willingness to tackle anything has been invaluable.

A special thanks to Kevin Todd, Jason Lee, and the Lee family, as well as the countless others who have inspired the characters
of this book

And for those whom I have lost—you live on in these pages.

My students for their daily inspiration. Never grow
too old to dream!

L. M. Montgomery, Jane Austen, Walt Whitman, Rupert Brooks and all of my childhood literary playmates…as well as the creative genius of the musicians serving as my inspiration during the writing process.

Jeremiah 29:11

ABOUT THE AUTHOR

Meredith's fondest childhood memories are of her summers along the South Carolina coast. Her love for story telling began at an early age, so it is no mystery that she combined her two loves when writing *Churning Waters*. She graduated from the College of Charleston where she studied Theatre and English.

When not writing, Meredith teaches Theatre and serves as a musical theatre vocal coach. During the summer, Meredith can still be found vacationing with her husband and four magical daughters along the waters of Murrells Inlet.

For more information about upcoming books in the series visit her website.

http://www.meredithttaylor.com